Ch

Conspiracy

The Aliens, The Agency, and the Dark Lensmen

by

Nathan Gregory

Published by
Nathan Gregory Author *dot* Com

Copyright

Publisher: Nathan Gregory
https://www.NathanGregoryAuthor.com
Kindle eBook ASIN: B00ZM3RTP4
Paperback Edition: January 12, 2022
KDP ISBN-13: 979-8835779338
Lulu Press ISBN: 978-1-387-87586-3
Lulu Press Product ID: 15vqvdm5

Table of Contents

Writer in the Plaza

> *We lay together in the afterglow, her hand still holding, caressing my manhood as my hand cupped her warm pubis, a lone finger gently tracing the outline of her lips. My other hand gently squeezed her breast as my tongue gently teased its mate's nipple, our bodies soaked in the afterglow of our passion. God, I loved this woman! If only she would...*

"Tripe!" I slammed the laptop shut. "Balderdash!" I muttered through clenched teeth. After traveling to two distant worlds, destroying a runaway Artificial Intelligence, saving humanity, and successfully turning the wild tale into a science fiction and fantasy novel, why, oh why am I writing such putrid twaddle?

Because, they say, sex sells! Because I can't push HER out of my mind! Because I lack the imagination to write a purely fictional story, I draw upon the demented late-night fantasies that drift through my tortured brain.

Maybe sex sells, as they say, although I doubt THIS drivel will sell. I can't write romance; ironic, as I undoubtedly shattered all known copulatory records in my time on Planet Oz. But sex is not romance, and as for the torrid, steamy excitement of the novels. Harrumph, I have never experienced it and don't believe it exists outside of the bodice-ripper fiction sub-genre.

Perhaps it exists for women on some level; I can't say. Someone buys those books. But, seduction fantasies notwithstanding, does anyone do this stuff for real?

A gorgeous morning had erupted upon the City by the Bay. The brief rain the day before cleared the air, washed the streets and the warm aftermath attracted the usual socks-with-sandal-wearing counterculture types. The city spawns them as naturally as a lawn sprouts dandelions after a rain shower and just as prolifically.

Like so many others, this beautiful day finds me ensconced at my favorite table in the plaza at 17th and Market, languidly sipping an Arabian Mocha-Java and working on my laptop.

Working; yes, though barely. I'm here as much to bask in the sunshine and indulge in a spot of folkscoping as I am for writing. My first book still sells nicely in the eBook store. I shake my head in disbelief at every royalty check, marveling at the poor souls who accept it as fiction. But, heck! I was there, and even I hardly believe it. If not for the money and the extraordinary results of the brutal training regimen, sigh, I could imagine it was all a dream.

The income from the book, though small, adds a welcome ego boost. Strictly speaking, I do not need the money. As a result of my off-world adventures, my bank account is flush, and my lifestyle remains modest. My author's paychecks are but a scorecard, I suppose. I then thought I could turn my hand to original fiction.

I found fabricating a grandiose adventure tale from whole cloth and convincingly telling it is much more complicated than merely describing an experience. The latter requires memory and a facile grasp of English; the former involves imagination.

I discovered I lack imagination.

So here I sit, idly playing at writing an erotic story as I watch the group gathering on the far side of the plaza. With any luck, someone will disrobe today. So far, no shirts have come off, although anything can happen here. Trust me, I know!

After a couple of hours playing at authorship, my Java drained and meaningful distractions absent; I'm about to pack up and head home. I have dinner plans with a lovely lady of recent acquaintance and could do with some polishing and scraping, perhaps a wee bit of manscaping. Some time with my beloved pets also. My bulldog Petchy is always happy to greet his human, and in the evening, my felines ensure I never lack companionship as they sit on my lap and purr. The tiny gray female I named Lolita and the enormous, brassy, orange creature responds to Teena.

As I close the laptop and toss my empty in the recycle bin, I spot a giant black SUV speeding toward the plaza. It rolls up to the sidewalk nearest my bistro table and parks beside the yellow curb in a manner that would earn a civilian a parking ticket. The official plates and red and blue lights ensure this vehicle won't receive a citation; not that it would matter if it did. Rank doth hath its privileges, and I've always found these guys pretty rank.

The last thing I want today is to play reindeer games with the Men in Black, though it seems as if my wants are irrelevant. So, sure enough, out steps Certified Agent Alex Marco, my old buddy, and personal MiB. Ostensibly his job involves terrorists and threats to America, yet since we met, he has made me his particular project; he wants to be friends.

Oh, Joy!

We have been dancing around for months, and I've done my best to encourage him to lose interest and find another citizen to annoy.

I suppose Alex had been a decent friend; once satisfied, I was an innocent. He'd even given me money from his own pocket when I was alone, injured, and naked. I wouldn't claim he was a welcome sight; he remains a friend, though we aren't in the category of drinking buddies. We do maintain a professional relationship. I have consulted with him on several cases involving computer forensics and network security. Still, I believe he smells something; perhaps some strange sixth sense draws him to my secrets. I would much prefer he left me alone.

The hilarity is that my secrets are anything but; my entire off-world life story has been out there for months in the ePub world. The whole gruesome tale has been available to anyone with a few bucks, already downloaded and read by thousands of people. It's not my fault the readers believe it to be a fantastical tale, mere Science Fiction. But, not content with the truth, Alex can't bear to leave me alone.

Wonder what my own personal MiB wants today? I turned toward him. "Hello, Alex."

"Hi Fitz, I thought I might find you here. I could use a little help. I have something which should be right up your alley."

"I'm heading home; I have a date this evening. I still have a couple of hours; how can I help you? Still tracking those terrorists?" A private joke. Alex and I had met when I was his prisoner. Not a state to which I yearn to return! Frankly, I have no wish to be under Alex's thumb, not under any circumstances.

He scares the bejesus out of me!

"Wanna take a ride?" I cocked an eyebrow. He amplified, "Something you should see, straight out of your book." That piqued my interest! What could he have encountered which might resemble anything in my tale? Climbing in with him, I had barely clicked the belt when he floored it, hurling the SUV up Market Street as if a raging T-Rex were on our heels.

Alex loves to drive aggressively fast, and his badge gives him ample opportunities to indulge. I'm a queasy passenger with him at the wheel. I pray the seatbelts and airbags will be sufficient on the day he blows it. I wondered how many points he gets for pedestrians.

Flipping on the lights as he floored it, his tires screamed in protest as he hung an illegal high-speed U-turn and slalomed into an immediate right onto Duboce, heading for the ramp to the 101. Once on the freeway, he took to the shoulder, lights, and siren pushing mere mortals aside, then accelerating fiercely, heading for the Bay Bridge. We were leaving the city and making haste.

Not that I don't trust Alex, but I seriously wondered where we were heading and why the blankety-blank hurry.

And I don't trust Alex.

We roared across the bridge, and I became lost in the East Bay hills. However, it wasn't long until he pulled into a hidden, gated complex with no signs, no markings. I hadn't known the Agency had a facility here, though, with Alex, nothing surprises me.

Alex passed over a striped Visitor badge and whisked me inside. He whispered, "Don't leave my sight and don't speak to anyone unless I ok it." He led me into the facility and past an impressive security station, waving his badge, stepping around the short line, and insulting the metal detector. Of course, security screening is for mere mortals; those who make the rules don't need to follow them. Nonetheless, I shook my head in disgust at the lax protocol. I idly wondered what other exceptions there might be.

We entered an office suite, trekked past a bank of cubicles, down a long hallway, and entered a tired-looking conference room. Alex pointed at a chair, and as I settled, wondering what dire events were in store, he picked up a phone and mumbled, "Come on in."

A man and a woman entered, dressed in the same uniform as Alex, looking so straight out of central casting that I struggled not to laugh; they didn't appear to possess a sense of humor. The sharp-looking, petite Asian woman exuded mystery and menace, absolutely rocking the black suit and Ray-Bans. The man was close to my height and build; we could have been brothers. I reminded myself that not every tall, broad-shouldered mesomorph was a product of the genetic engineering that hatched me.

Still, I wondered.

"Is this him?" the man asked.

Alex nodded. The man shook my hand, pronouncing it a pleasure to meet me, and gave his name as Matt. The woman, Jill, nodded a similar greeting from the doorway, adding she had read and enjoyed my book.

I thanked them, standing and offering Jill a ritual handshake. Then without ceremony, Matt added, "We want to show you something which came in last night; actually, early this morning."

Jill hadn't wholly entered the room and paused, holding the door ajar. She pointed, and we marched down the hall to the elevator.

My mind flashed for a half-second to a wild elevator ride I had experienced months before, though this elevator was rather ordinary. Since the building wasn't tall enough to warrant a lift, I surmised we'd be descending. We sluggishly dropped a couple of floors, the classical Hollywood high-speed descent into the bowels of a massive secret underground government facility is not in this story. Not yet anyway.

The doors opened upon a basement area encompassing an IT Server room with about a dozen equipment racks, multiple wiring closets for different wiring classes, and general storage. There was also a Security monitoring station, unmanned, and a modest but well-equipped workshop worthy of Q-branch. Several technicians clad in lab coats were busy in the shop, but otherwise, the place seemed unsupervised. I blanched at the open insecurity. Doors to the server room and the wiring closets stood wide-open, and no one was around. The security station lacked any evidence of security.

Unbelievable!

Want to take bets on my guessing their passwords? I'd bet half the gear still has the factory password.

Oh, the fun, if only I were a SPECTRE, WASP, THRUSH, or even a KAOS agent! I could run amok! Of course, a villain would face the security screening we had skipped. Hardly a deterrent.

If these people are as lax in their online security as they seem in their physical controls, they are due for a rude surprise. Sooner rather than later, I'd surmise. Should I offer Alex my security talents? That could be rather interesting, Fitz inside the belly of the beast! Would they recruit me as a D-Warrior? I didn't think Alex or his bosses would favorably view the idea, although I'd be terrific if they hired me; I have the talents and technical chops. Sadly, they trust me as much as I do them. The difference is that I am genuinely a trustworthy soul.

We trudged down a long corridor and approached a door labeled "Morgue." Alex looked at me, and I looked at him. Then, under his breath, he muttered something which sounded like "Cinch up your ...," his last couple of words lost to the creaking of the hinges and the whoosh of air as he opened the door. No one appeared to welcome us, yet the function of the place was evident. It looked like the set of a TV show — everything was clean, sterile, and professional-looking. I half-expected to see an elderly secret agent pontificating on some bit of esoterica.

Slapping the overhead light switch, Alex guided us to a long wall of refrigerated lockers. Jill took a handle, stared into my eyes, and solemnly asked, "Ready?" I nodded, swallowing, donning my best poker face, steeling myself. I feared they had found Teena's corpse. Had she indeed died, I wondered again, for the millionth time.

The door opened, the sheet-draped stainless-steel drawer slid open, and Jill studied my face as she drew down the sheet, uncovering the still form beneath.

The corpse was petite, delicate, female, and endowed with exquisite, sensual, 'Russian Blue' gray fur. A resident, or should I say, a former resident of 'Planet Oz' lay lifeless on the morgue drawer!

The Furry Corpse

"Fascinating," I whispered. I knew the agents were watching my face for signs of a revealing reaction. Steeling myself, I jammed on a stone-faced deadpan as I studied her, deciding if I knew who she had been. I nearly collapsed in relief once I saw she wasn't my Lolita, her mother, or any others with whom I'd become intimately acquainted.

Still, odds were, I had not only met this poor child but also probably had known her during my sojourn in her dinosaur-cursed land. Simple mathematics dictated the odds as my mission was nothing less than the salvation of their infertile society by giving them as many viable babies as my loins could inseminate. I'd spent my time with every potentially fertile female they could present. The limits of human memory remain inescapable.

I did not know her!

My companions faced me with questioning eyes. Matt just stared, arching one eyebrow in a questioning expression.

"Well?" Alex voiced.

"Rather coincidental, isn't it?" Jill added.

Woodenly exhibiting my best dumb facade, I shrugged.

After replacing the sheet and returning the sad, broken body to cold storage, Jill motioned toward the door. After ascending, we retraced our steps back to the elevator and re-entered the conference room. Settling into chairs around the table, my escorts again put on questioning faces.

What could I tell them? What did I dare admit?

My knees knocked in fear as, in desperate self-defense, I usurped the inquisition and began asking THEM questions. I started firing rapidly, barely letting them sneak a word in edgewise, interrupting their questions and responses to ask yet another. By acting stupid, dull-of-hearing, and just plain brassy, I got them to supply some answers while I gave up nothing. I hoped. Or not too much anyway.

What do I know about police tactics? I'm just dancing as fast as I can and hoping for the best. I'm glad I'm here as a consultant and not a suspect. I only hope I can keep it that way.

When they played the video available from the *Domain Awareness Center* plus the images confiscated from other cameras, including those of bystanders' cell phones, I learned the poor unfortunate had mysteriously appeared the evening before in a rough neighborhood in Oakland. No one had seen her arrive, no one had seen her exit a car or other vehicle, and local security cameras missed her arrival. She had just walked into the field of view of one camera yet had failed to appear on the neighboring lens a few feet away as if she had materialized from thin air between the two.

Since I knew what to watch for, I spotted the telltale flicker of the portal's event horizon faintly reflected in the glass of the storefronts yet refrained from calling attention to this tiny detail. Perhaps they had already noticed it. If they hadn't, I wouldn't be the one to enlighten them.

She had appeared without clothing, shoes, or possessions of any sort in a scary neighborhood. She stood frozen, dumbfounded until a group of street characters noticed her and moved in her direction. Although the horrible video was without audio accompaniment, the implied threat and intense fear reaction were obvious enough. The impossible (to her) environment, the buildings, cars, lights, and the mere fact it was nighttime, which would naturally have filled any resident of Planet Oz with intense blood-curdling fear, must have instilled absolute, total panic. She had screamed and run. Again, there was no audio, but I could hear her stark terror as I watched the scene.

She'd run as if a Velociraptor was at her heels. My heart reflected the horror, pounding in sympathy for the child. She was not only seen but photographed by several locals, not to mention the ever-present security cameras, both private and those connected to the Domain Awareness System. She ran from the perceived threat, bolting several blocks at a speed only an adrenaline-fueled fight-or-flight panic response could empower. Her run ended when she dodged into traffic and collided with a fast-moving vehicle, leaving her crumpled and broken on the pavement.

Someone called 911, but when the buggy arrived, she was dead. She might have survived the physical injuries from the collision had she received prompt medical attention. But, according to the M.E., she suffered an adrenaline-induced myocardial infarction caused by a stress-induced coronary artery spasm, doubtless triggered by the sustained, intense mortal fear induced by her circumstances. She had died of extreme fright!

The local police collected the corpse and what they believed were all the videos from various bystanders' cell phones and security cameras and endeavored to block the content from reaching the news media. But, of course, they almost certainly failed — urban bystanders are rarely so compliant.

I can't wait to see what turns up on YouTube.

I sobbed inwardly, though I dared not tip my emotions. Instead, I steeled an outward calm I did not feel.

"Is she human?" I asked quietly.

Jill responded, "Our M.E. says she is as human as you or me, just as you described the fur-people in your book. Fur-bearing humans without clothing."

I nodded acknowledgment. "How old do you think she is?" I asked. She appeared very young.

She responded, "Our M.E. says she was just beyond puberty, only recently commenced ovulation."

A terrible shame, as, among the fur-people, the loss of a fertile womb was a disaster. They have so few. Yet the victim's youth also suggested I likely did NOT share my Chromosomes with her, as she would have been too young then, although I may have met her as a prepubescent child. Who was she? Where had she come from? How had she come to be here, I wondered?

Collecting my wits, I decided that for the time being, to continue feigning ignorance was my best approach.

"A mystery, to be sure, but other than a superficial resemblance to the fictional people I described in my book, why would you bring her to my attention? Why involve me?" I asked.

The three of them stared at me like they thought I was stupid. Doing my best not to disabuse them of the idea, I stared back, face locked in a forced deadpan.

"You found inspiration for the description in your book somewhere. We were hoping you could tell us something. Anything at all."

I shrugged.

"So-called Cat-People are an age-old staple of fantasy fiction. There are endless such descriptions in literature and several movies, even multiple ones bearing the title 'Cat People.' So why would you consider mine significant?"

Jill chimed in, "You will think I'm crazy, but it's my fault. I read your book and found the world you described captivating. She seemed perfectly matched to your portrayal of the Fur-People, too close to ignore. When I saw her, I thought you might be the only person able to appreciate this."

Matt picked up the thread, "This isn't the first oddity that walked right out of your book. Six weeks ago, a group of five off-duty peninsula cops walking from the station to the nearby watering hole at the end of their shift, all sober and alert, yet each reported seeing a naked man walk spectacularly out of thin air right in front of them. They did a Candid-Camera double-take, stunned, caught off guard. After a few seconds, one yelled halt, but the man ignored them and kept walking."

He shrugged and let out a sigh before continuing. "Cops seriously hate it when a citizen ignores them. He vanished just as they moved to grab him, again right in front of them, literally inches from their grasp. This wasn't some midnight 'spirit sighting,' but rather a broad-daylight sighting by five sober, reliable witnesses. We have fielded such reports before, but that one was especially blatant and impossible to discount. We started looking at these events in light of your fantastical story. The incident seemed to fit your description of a Rapid Overlapping Transition of portals."

I gave a weak laugh. "I'm unsure which is more fantastical, the idea of sober off-duty cops or a spirit sighting in broad daylight. You brought me here because I wrote a fictional story you think sounded similar?"

I let out a low whistle. "Okay, guys, look, I won't tell anyone if you don't. I dunno whether you bought it on the street or raided the evidence locker but go easy on whatever it is; keep it on the down-low. If your boss catches a whiff of that stuff, he will undoubtedly raise an unholy fuss. He might even force you to share!"

Our airy persiflage continued in this semi-comical, almost nonsensical vein for perhaps half an hour or a trifle longer. Then, finally, with my frantic improvisational humor, I managed to deflect them from the questions banging loudly at the back of my cranium. Putting forth a false air of unconcern and bantering with these people was painful, though there's nothing I could do for that poor girl on the slab, and I didn't want to make them more curious than they already were. I'd been hoping they would chalk it up to the unexplained and leave it alone.

Or at least leave ME alone!

I realized they hadn't the first clue as to who the deceased girl had been or where she came from, and they had reached out to me solely because of my book. It was a long shot; one they didn't expect to pay off. Attributing extraterrestrial origins to the corpse was a reach too far in the bureaucratic mind, which was doubtless why she wound up here in the first place.

Had they never read my book, she would merely be another unexplained Jane Doe without my input. Unremarkable, that is, save for her exquisite fur. But, of course, that was something they might eventually explain using vague medical technobabble coined by a clueless second-year Med School student. But, painful though it may be, I hoped they chalked her up as an unexplained anomaly and filed it wherever they filed other strange and inexplicable cases.

I wanted them to forget her and me entirely!

The verbal jousting continued as I strove to learn what I might without enlightening them.

Finally, I interrupted the discussion, "Folks, I appreciate your cluing me in on this little X-Files adventure; truly, I do. I hope to write a sequel to my first book, and this is wonderful grist for the imagination. I hope you will keep me in the loop, more or less, as it unravels, although I have made plans for a date with a special lady this evening, and I need to head home soon. I need time to primp, and I'd rather not keep a hot date waiting."

Words cannot convey how relieved I felt when they acquiesced. After a round of handshakes and routine pleasantries, Alex again played chauffeur for the return to my home, this time somewhat sedately; for him. This was almost surprising in itself since Alex was the Big Boss and mucky-muck there. Actually, I don't really know what his role is. When we met months ago, he was a Certified Agent, but he had since been promoted; to what exalted level, I'm uncertain. Clearly, he has a reason to give me so much personal attention, which scares me.

Minus the lights and siren, the ride back had been relatively quiet, our only conversation inconsequential social banter. Then, as Alex pulled up to the curb at my house, he turned to me.

"You know Fitz; we met under rather mysterious circumstances, as portrayed in your book. The stories have circulated about how you just appeared in the plaza buck naked, injured, and in the company of two other similarly naked and injured people. Initial blood screening at the hospital suggested a familial relationship. They thought the older man was your father and the young girl was your sister. Nice touch, the way you incorporated those bits into your story, by the way. I tip my hat to your imagination on that one. Then we performed more advanced DNA testing and disproved the relationship, notwithstanding obvious similarities in coloring, body, and facial structure. That seemed odd at the time and seems odder every day whenever I wonder at how they screwed up those tests so thoroughly; I experience a buzzing sensation in my brain."

Alex was getting uncomfortably close to home, and the closer he got, the hotter it felt in the car. I wondered what he would say if I told him that younger sister was instead my great grandmother! I presume Alex missed that detail in the book. But, on the other hand, he probably never actually did more than skim it. Either that or he is playing dumb, hoping to get me to spill something.

Alex continued, "For a long time, I discounted the mess as a gargantuan bureaucratic clusterfuck. Until I read your book, that is. I'm not saying I believe the entire fantastic tale, the wormholes, the dinosaurs, and all the rest happened just as your story portrayed. You wrote an obvious science fiction/fantasy story, and I believe you wove it around actual real-world events. Still, it isn't a total flight of fancy.

"A few of the depictions were superficially fact-based; the way you incorporated your own experience from the plaza that day, for example, and the tale of our meeting. However, I believe that additional real-world facts remain buried in the tale, fictionalized events not shared as such; I believe there are more facts here than are in evidence — more than you're admitting."

I stared blankly at him. Then, after a moment, he continued.

"You know what triggers my curiosity? After this fur-bearing female humanoid appeared, I started thinking. So I went back to that first day in the hospital and attempted to pull hospital records to find out what the records revealed about where those other two people came from, the nature of their injuries, and what happened to them — any morsel they might contain. Care to guess what I found?"

I raised my eyebrows questioningly.

"Bupkis! That's what I found! No records whatsoever! It never happened! No DNA tests, no blood work, no accounting records, nothing! Yet I was there! There's no way anyone could have swept those records under the rug that way, no way they could simply have disappeared! Not without someone on the inside of their system intentionally scrubbing the records, and even that would not be easy, would require administrator access. I've been dealing with bureaucratic screw-ups all my life, and this isn't reasonable!"

I continued giving him my best stupid face. It's a natural talent.

Finally, after peering squarely at me for several seconds, he smiled, winked, and extended his hand. "Relax, pal, I'm not pursuing this in any official capacity, as a legal or a national security matter. There's no official investigation of anything here. I'm your friend, and the Government has no interest in this mystery. As far as I can tell, no one has broken any laws, and I consider you my friend and hope you consider me yours. I am here to help and support you. I hope one day you will confide in me, that's all. I believe there's one hell of a story behind this, not just one of travel to distant worlds but a rather strange tale taking place here on Earth. And one day, I hope to hear it."

I shrugged, took his hand in a firm shake, and in parting said, "Let me know what happens. I do want to write a sequel, and this little mystery of yours is great fodder. Take care, my friend," and with that climbed out of the car and entered the house.

Friends, yeah, a close one, as Don Corleone advised. Little did I know how close this friendship would become. I would later learn that Alex was shading the truth and hiding even more than I.

The Writer Unleashed

Slowly, steadily, woodenly, I entered the house, carefully holding onto the world with both hands lest I fall off. I walked mechanically into my room and closed the door. Rather like a slowly deflating bounce-house, I softly collapsed against the door, sliding downward as my self-control evaporated. I gave myself over to a round of galloping shudders. I sat on the floor inside the door, breathing slowly, deliberately, forcing my racing pulse to slow and calm, throttling down the adrenaline raging throughout my body. My canine pal came rushing to greet me and, sensing my distress, snuggled down beside me and laid his head on my thigh as if to say everything would be all right.

For several minutes I sat there scratching Petchy's ears as I spun in wild paranoia, replaying what had just happened. Then, purring, Teena and Lolita climbed into my lap as I sat lost, deep in thought, with my mind still trapped in Alex's basement.

How had that child managed to come through a portal? Was it just a terrible accident, or had it been intentional? Was she looking for me, hoping I would grant her a boon and gift her a son? My rickety position under the scrutiny of the MiBs seemed close to unraveling too!

Why on Earth had I written that confounded novel? A rather severe lapse in judgment, or so it seemed in hindsight. If not for that blasted book, they would never have connected me to the poor child.

The vision of her so cold and lifeless haunted me.

For the moment, they seemed to accept my tales as mere Science Fiction, yet for how long would that hold up if there were to be further incursions, further incidents?

Teena and Lolita purred contentedly, kneading my thighs and marking their human with scents from their cheeks. As caring as they seemed, I knew their double-teamed actions merely asked when I intended to prepare dinner.

Cats approach the world differently than dogs. Petchy was content to lean against my thigh and snuggle as I idly scratched his fur, letting his calm reassurance flow into my soul. He trusted dinner would come in its own time, so he was in no hurry. My girls were no doubt practically concerned lest poppa's emotional state impacts the day's essential matters, particularly dinner.

If something were happening to inspire the fur-people to brave the dangers of the portal in an attempt to reach me, wouldn't Petchy — the human one, I mean — or an agent of his organization have come? We hadn't explained the mechanics of portal travel to the locals, although we didn't try very hard to hide it either. Heck, even I haven't the faintest clue about using portals. I understand barely enough to recognize how dangerous it could be and know not to attempt it without a knowledgeable guide. The fur-people are extraordinarily intelligent. Stone-age society and brutal living conditions notwithstanding, we might have been far too careless.

I don't trust Alex or his friends for one second! Were they watching me now? My home bugged? A black SUV parked in the shadows somewhere outside? I rose, unlapping my girls as I went to peek out the windows. I looked around for surveillance signs, not that I could see much from my vantage point.

Glancing at the clock, I realized tempus was furiously fugiting. I didn't intend to blow off my planned date, so I needed to hustle. With a mighty effort, I pulled myself together and reasserted my self-control. I have no time for my anxieties, worries, and nerdy introspection, not with a lady waiting.

Meals and treats for my babies, a quick shower, shave, and a light dose of a scent guaranteed to drive women wild, and I was ready. Thanks to my genetic good fortune, I've never needed to work exceptionally hard to attract the opposite sex, except for one red-haired Amazon; yet again, I wonder if she might still be alive somewhere.

Heading out the door, I grabbed a little package I had picked up the day before as a gift for my date. Before I beat happy feet down the street, I did take one crucial precaution. No, not that one. If this first date were to go well, perhaps that would come later. No, not that one either, since I limit my use of pharmacology to my morning Arabian Mocha-Java.

This particular precaution was of a technological bent. I set my laptop up with a simple security program to watch over my apartment. If my home received visitors during my absence, I wanted a record.

I resolved the next day I'd pick up a few sophisticated high-tech surveillance tools of my own, but for now, my little laptop would serve to pinch-hit. I also set my ancient, retired droid to a similar duty, monitoring the front door. Crude but effective.

As I bounded down the street, I kept an eye out for suspicious vehicles, strangers lurking, or anything else which might tip off a clandestine presence surveilling my movements. After a few minutes of frenetic scrutiny, I relaxed somewhat and decided to project an air of unconcern; I began whistling. Despite my worries and distractions, I arrived just a couple of minutes behind schedule, comfortably within the margin of first date etiquette. I almost reached the agreed-upon meeting place when I realized I was still whistling; I was surprised to discover I was whistling 'Clementine'! I bit off the tune with a slight grimace and scanned for my date.

My makeshift surveillance gear hadn't yielded results of note, so I reset the toys. The following morning, I headed downtown. Careful to leave my phone at home lest someone track it, I took a circuitous route. First, walking to BART and taking a train toward the East Bay, only to hop off after a couple of stops to jump on Muni and backtrack until finally, I walked several blocks through side streets and alleys. I kept a sharp eye peeled for anything or anyone odd or suspicious. Although I seemed to be alone, I wasn't sure.

After several twists and turns, I convinced myself no one watched or followed my movements, and with a sudden quick run through an alley and a brief duck into the front, through and out the back door of a hole-in-the-wall "massage parlor," I approached my destination.

My goal was a tiny but discreet security establishment that caters to a niche market, a select clientele that values privacy and anonymity. I had used their toys in past consulting jobs and trusted them not to rat me out. They wouldn't cave to the first black suit who flashed a badge at them, although I had no illusions; if Alex decided he wanted to discover the nature of my purchases, he would. At least I trusted they would ensure he followed proper procedure, finding a sympathetic judge, showing just cause, and procuring a warrant. The process would slow him down, which would be the best I could expect.

Of course, I hoped that he hadn't noticed my destination and would never attempt to check up on my activities, or if he had been watching, had failed to follow my circuitous route.

Clandestine suppliers don't sell their wares at a discount. Even a long-time regular customer like myself pays the full freight when seeking the sort of discretion that was their stock-in-trade. I picked up a few toys, several high-resolution cameras, and a wireless signal sniffer. If Alex's people had bugged my home, I intended to catch them at it sometime relatively soon. These toys weren't cheap! I could have obtained them much less expensively online or even from a "big-box" toy store on the peninsula. In this case, I was paying a steep premium for discretion and anonymity and was glad enough to be able to do so. Nonetheless, I winced a bit at the bite. I'd never spent as much pocket money so quickly in my life!

Note to self: Better write another successful book, quick. You need the money.

Playing it safe, I'd raided my emergency stash and paid cash. My go-bag was lighter, but my peace of mind improved. I didn't want Alex checking my card transactions and finding the tracks of my new toys. I needed to replenish the go-bag; I was feeling a touch paranoid, I suppose.

Hours later, I was again home, new toys in hand. I examined the laptop and the droid for meaningful activity. Then, satisfied no one had invaded my inner sanctum in my absence, I shut down the equipment and began sweeping the place from top to bottom, inside and out, with the sniffer, seeking unidentified signals. An hour later, I concluded no one had invaded my home, and there were no improper or unwanted wireless devices.

More comfortable digging around inside the system software than drilling holes and hiding cameras, I fumbled around for a protracted time installing my toys. It took a few tries to tuck everything away discreetly and some touching-up with putty and paint, but I eventually completed the installation.

After a couple of false starts and some intense concentration, I finished the mechanical installation. Then I retreated into what was, for me, the more comfortable zone; setting up the software, double-checking the options, verifying the total blockage of unwanted access, and making sure I used the most robust encryption available. It wouldn't do to have Alex or his techs intercepting my signals, piggybacking on them, and using them against me. Just for good measure, I examined the droid and laptop for spyware that might work against my interests.

The absence of surveillance was troubling. Was Alex so inept he had not put me under surveillance or was he so extraordinarily competent that I could not spot his handiwork? That seemed an improbable feat. If his people were on my heels, I should have seen them. Could it be he had not concluded I was worth watching? Or am I paranoid in thinking I am worth watching?

With the task completed, there were tiny, hidden, virtually invisible cameras peering down around my windows, watching the hallway outside my front door, the outside doors, front and back, and monitoring the inside of my apartment. Motion triggers are set, everything programmed with arrangements to send event alerts and videos to my phone whenever I'd be out.

Role-playing as Alex, I cogitated on how I might attempt to break inside without tripping an alert. I considered the tools and techniques Alex and his coterie of techno-clowns might have at their disposal. I worried about my over-reliance on technology.

What would happen if there should be a power failure? Could they bypass my elaborate precautions by cutting the power? Yeah, I thought so.

Perhaps my time on Planet Oz had taught me a few lessons as I pondered ways to perform the equivalent of a technological solution without technology. What sorts of techniques might the stone-age people of Planet Oz employ in such a situation? What kind of stratagem doesn't depend on high-tech gear? What tactics would I utilize if my ever-present, friendly electrons weren't here?

After some thought, I procured a few toothpicks from the kitchen and positioned them on the tops of doors and in a few other strategic places. If an intruder opened a closet door or various cabinets, etc., they would disturb the toothpick. I did the same with a few tiny pieces of clear tape, positioning them such that if a prowler opened a strategic drawer, I would be able to spot the intrusion.

Take that, Men in Black!!

Last night's date had been pleasant, although my distractions and worries interfered, and I fear I fell short somewhat in the role of the attentive, sparkling dinner date which I otherwise strived to be. Nevertheless, I decided it was time I texted and thanked her for a wonderful time. I composed a polite, slightly sexy note to her and experienced a brief moment of anxiety when autocorrect insisted on amplifying my double entendre, inserting ribaldry I didn't intend. Fortunately, I was paying attention, changed the text, and reviewed it again before sending it. Whew! That was close.

When I completed composing and sending my message, I called the local florist as an afterthought. I might as well lay it on thick. Julie seemed a fun date and deserved a more attentive companion than I had given her on our first outing. I promised myself that I would do much better the second time if there were an encore.

With my traps all set and my romantic shortcomings acknowledged, I picked up my laptop and headed for the Plaza. I still had a couple of hours left in the day, and I had a story to write. I had conceived a short story that I bet the magazines would snap up. I don't lack so much for imagination now!

Interlude – Threshold of Worlds

Shameya sat cross-legged on the close-cropped grass, molding the soft earth, creating round depressions fitted perfectly to her form. For perhaps the 98th time, she repeated the self-admonition to bring a rug or even a blanket to her duty. No matter. The shifts were not arduous, and hers was the last one today. The sun drifts toward the horizon; danger will increase rapidly the closer the day's end. She must return to the castle safety, and the room she shares with her sisters, where she can wash herself of grass stains before the evening feast. It's not a hardship to sit on the grass.

It must soon be time for the Beasts, she thought. They prey ever earlier, and it's not safe out of doors. When she was a child, the creatures dared not appear while the sky still held light. Monsters are bolder now.

As she peered toward the Threshold, she wondered if she might be lucky enough to see the miracle that so few had witnessed. The phenomenon happened most when none see. She was confident she was looking in the right place, although she had never seen the aperture. She knew the tales of the portal opening and the Smooth Ones stepping into the world as People might step through a doorway. She hoped to see it for herself. She took every shift she was able. She was determined to be present when the *Smoothies* again visited.

Shameya remembered when the one called Fitz had spent an evening with a dozen of her sisters. Several now raised beautiful sons, but she was too young then. He treated her wonderfully, made her feel welcome, warm, and excited, yet though full of eagerness and desire, she was not ripe. She was heartbroken. Respectfully, he refused her; his blessing was only for those who were fertile. She could not blame him. She knew his boon was too precious to waste. But, though then denied, she was now ready, her body ripe, and she prayed he would return before she turned too quickly old and barren.

She wanted a beautiful son too.

However, it was not merely the desire for a child or a juvenile infatuation that prompted her focus and attention. While she wished to be the first to greet Fitz and hoped she too would receive his boon, her present vigil wasn't about fertility. Her vigil was, in fact, her contribution to the Project. Although she wanted to be present when the legendary ones again appeared, greeting Fitz or any other Smooth one wasn't her mission. Her mission was to monitor the Threshold and record anything she might preserve for the Mathematician. Information desired for her calculations — calculations which the Mathematician hoped would one day unlock the secrets of the Threshold.

She eavesdropped on many conversations among the Smoothies, listening as shamelessly as her sisters. She understood the portal would open according to its secret whims and not the desires of any person, smooth or furred. The Smoothies alone possess the knowledge of when it would open. Though they understood it, they could not themselves command it. The mystery remains theirs for now. However, the Mathematician sought to alter this, to learn the secret for the People. Shameya's duty was to monitor the portal as much as possible with her sisters to record and report anything that might add to the calculations.

The Threshold had long existed, a strange doorway between the familiar world and the mysterious Smoothie realm called Ashera. For countless generations, before Shameya, before her mother, before her grandmother, and even before HER mother, the Smooth ones had stepped into the world from beyond. They brought nothing with them, nothing one might carry, yet they conveyed knowledge. Sometimes their gifts included odd, valuable ways of doing things, and often ideas and philosophies. They are also full of stories and songs.

They brought other things too — the boon of babies. There once was a time when the People did not need the Smooth ones, a time when fertility came easy, and there were males enough for every castle. Her mother had once told her in her own grandmother's time, castles possessed as many as three or four fertile males. Males had proved fragile. Even with the best of care, many families now have none, and of those who do, many are no longer able to grant — those who can present a boon seldom sire infant males.

Her castle possessed a male, though he's aged and frail. It had been more than a decade since his last boon. But for Fitz, there would be no babies in this house. Some worried babies from his loins might be smooth, but the smoothies had promised that they would breed true with a proper pelt. Thanks to his boon, the family now had more than a dozen infants, all to become fertile Males when grown. The family was proud to possess so many fine Males in the offing. Nearby families with none at all will pay a hefty fee for the boon of such as these. The scarcity they would alleviate will make them and their family quite wealthy.

Learning the secrets of the Threshold was the goal. Shameya was but one member of the group giving the project attention. From morning until afternoon, she and her sisters take turns sitting in this spot, watching. She would happily do so through the night, except she did not wish to fill a Beast's belly!

Monsters prowl from dusk to dawn, only the thick stone walls keeping them at bay. Outside is certain death!

Mastering the Threshold was more than curiosity — it is a necessity. The Monsters had ceased confining themselves to the night! For untold generations, the People had a quiet detente with the beasts. They would walk and forage at night while the People hid behind thick stone walls. The creatures would sleep during the day; now, the beasts violate the truce!

Midday still seems safe enough. Watchers have spotted them nearly an hour before dusk and almost an hour after dawn. The People feared they were becoming bolder.

Those caught outside before dusk fell to their terrible hunger before this became recognized, and now the People spent much effort tracking the wakeful monstrosities. A sighting automatically topped the list of all the Criers, with much banging of the Crier's drum whenever a beast hunted in daylight. Thankfully sightings remain rare, though when a Monster appears near a castle, People who live there hide most of the day behind thick stone walls.

The Crier often intoned the warning:

Do not prowl the woods when the Beasts are up,
for thou are crunchy and good with ketchup.

Caught outside by a Beast, night, or day, was certain death. There's no defense. They are impervious to the swift-fired hunter's arrow. Only a Hero's bow might pierce such hide, yet no mortal such a bow may draw. The People fervently hope the Smoothies might kill such beasts or show how.

Thus, the reason Shameya sits in the meadow, making smooth depressions, staring at a spot in mid-air. The People desire to reach out, reach through the portal, and demand aid to kill the Monsters!

Focused on the purported location and musing over the dangers of the beasts, Shameya was startled on hearing something approach along the forest trail. She is a nervous, high-strung girl, given to panic at the slightest provocation. She considered bolting for a full two heartbeats, knowing full well if it was her worst nightmare approaching, she was already dead. A human couldn't outrun the creatures. Not even Fitz himself could approach their speed!

She rose to her feet, about to bolt in panic when a familiar voice called out. It was her sister Williya. Shameya calmed her racing pulse and turned to greet her sibling. Williya stepped into the clearing; baby cuddled in her arms, suckling at her breast.

"Hey Sis," she called out, "doncha think you should be getting behind stone? It's getting late."

"Aww, how's little Fitz today?" Shameya took the infant by the arm and made cooing noises. The child giggled and gurgled at his auntie and returned to his sustenance, greedy to finish his meal.

"I was about to head back. But it's not so late, and besides, the last Crier said no Beasts have been sighted near our castle."

"I don't care; you know how Mama worries. Besides, because the last sighting wasn't near doesn't mean the next one won't be! Those Crier reports are guesses anyway. Don't bet your life on them.

"Unless you want to run all the way, we must go now. Besides, I must carry little Fitz! He's heavy."

"Let me carry him if he's finished nursing!" Shameya turned away from the Threshold one last time and reached to take her nephew. As Williya reached to hand him over, she glanced at the portal. Her sharp breath intake caught her sister's attention, and Shameya released the child to his mother's arms as she turned toward the faint, shimmering haze.

Sing Clementine!

The next few days were fruitless, almost dull. My 'spidey-sense' began tingling in overload following the visit to the morgue, though, and I could not shut it up! I decided I preferred to risk taking a few precautions for naught than to remain unprepared. I restocked my "Go bag" — over-stocked it, in fact, and, as an afterthought, packed a second smaller bag with extra clothes and toiletries. I approached my friend Julie and asked if I could store a few items in her car.

"What is it?" she inquired. "Nothing important, and I would rather you didn't know. But, trust me; I promise you it is nothing illegal, immoral, or fattening on my word of honor. Just a little bit of precaution, just in case." She laughed at my cliché and, to my surprise, acquiesced. Ah, the fair sex, so trusting. Then I asked her for a spare key to her car. She found that somewhat less humorous yet still agreed reluctantly. But, of course, I didn't let her see the hat, scarf, masks, and sunglasses I later stashed under the front seat!

Later I gave her an envelope and told her not to open it unless something weird or unexpected happened. I promised she would know it when she saw it. Inside I placed a simple note with a brief, somewhat incomplete explanation, asking her to trust me and not to call the police no matter what. There was also a list of code words, with instructions to destroy the list as soon as she memorized it. I was trying to cover all possible bases. I couldn't believe she was so accepting of my strange behavior; for a moment, I was almost suspicious of why she was so agreeable. Does she genuinely find me attractive? Or does she have another motive?

Julie and I had three additional enjoyable dates, including a Saturday morning outing to the Redwoods and a pleasant hike in the forest. I reflected on how different the Northern California forest was from "Planet Oz." There are real dangers here, though nothing remotely comparable to a hungry Velociraptor. We carried a modest picnic lunch and headed for a stream with a tiny picturesque stream-side beach tucked into the forest. The gorgeous view and the wonders to see were not limited to trees. It was not for nothing that the trail-side sign named the secluded little beach 'Eden Beach,' and it was MUCH pleasanter than "Planet Oz!"

We arrived at the woods early as our time was limited. Julie's employer had insisted she work an evening shift, and she had to return much too soon on a Saturday. We hiked for more than an hour and then spent an hour at the stream-side beach watching other couples and enjoying our picnic lunch. The day was getting pleasant when we concluded our time had expired — a shame to be heading home so early on such a beautiful Saturday.

On the way home that afternoon, I put my droid on to replay the previous night's edition of a favorite late-night radio show to which I refuse to admit my addiction, a program featuring news and tall tales regarding fringe subjects from Cryptozoology to UFOs. Not that I'm a believer, but I find the stories fascinating.

The opening news segment featured a story that hit me in the gut! Someone reported a 'Bigfoot' sighting in Oakland a few nights ago! I blanched at the tale and struggled not to let my date notice how interested I was in the story. Then, the show took a commercial break and returned with a prominent cryptozoologist on the line to talk about the sightings.

Plural. As in more than one!

The news story chattered away, littering the tale with the usual hyperbole and fantastic claims. However, sifting through the exaggerated reportage for the meat within, I surmised there had been no less than three sightings of furry humanoids. I hurried back to the city as rapidly as practical, took my date home, put her vehicle away, and gave her a fond farewell before making a quick jog toward my house. When I arrived, I checked the show's website, and sure enough, there was a rough and jerky video of the poor girl I had seen in the morgue, running for all she was worth, scared into an utterly terrifying panic! Mercifully, the video didn't contain the ending and her sad death. Absent hostile observers, I freely shed tears that one of those gentle people would experience my world so distressfully. Somehow it seemed so unfair.

I had believed Alex's people had managed to quash the story, yet it was out now, and though we know the fate of the unfortunate child in the morgue, what of the others? They must have come through different portals; they had not been in Oakland. Where were they now? Are they still alive?

I agonized over what to do for a brief while, then the phone rang! Alex! "There's two more of them," I told him. "Yeah, I just found out. You want in on this?"

"Absolutely!" I responded forcefully!

Curtly, he said, "I'll be there in ten minutes! Be out front!"

I quickly hit the head, reset my traps, scooped up my droid and laptop, and bounded out the door, leaving a note for my house manager to care for my pets. I wasn't sure how long I'd be gone. I had barely reached the curb when Alex's black SUV screamed up. The door flew open, and I scrambled in. Tires wailed as we tore back down the street while I struggled to buckle up.

Settling into the leather, I realized more people than just Alex and I were in the car. Matt and Jill were with him; all three suited up with Kevlar vests and sidearms. They appeared solemn.

I joked, "Do I need a vest that says Writer on it?" That earned a dirty glance from Alex and Matt and a subdued, almost imperceptible laugh from Jill. Ah, the ladies, they always love me.

I couldn't guess where we were going, but we were sure in a hurry. Once on the freeway, Alex added his ear-splitting siren to the already flashing lights. Not getting the response he wanted, he moved to the left shoulder and pushed the pedal down, punctuating his siren with the horn. I could not read the dashboard display from my angle, though I could see the needle nailing itself into the red zone, and we were passing everything. Although not a sports car, this hunk of metal mounted some mighty muscle. We rocketed past everything, forcing other vehicles to move right and yield to Alex's siren and lights. Then, as the traffic thinned, he reclaimed the left lane.

Then he floored it!

After a while at reckless speed with no hint of a destination, I asked where we were going. "Fresno!" That seemed a long way to travel at Signal 9, but he was in the zone, and his vehicle was a powerful one, able to sustain three-digit speeds with ease on the straight and flat, and flat-out was what we were doing! Perhaps the official land speed record was not in imminent danger, but I hoped his tires carried at least a 'Z' speed rating.

I rechecked my seat belt, tightening it a notch.

We must have set a Guinness Record time down US Highway 99. But, then, two CHP SUVs, with lights and siren, also making heroic speeds, fell in with us, one in front, one behind, forming an escort. I'm not sure what they knew and weren't telling, but they were serious!

I asked a few questions and received grunts in response. Focused intently on driving, Alex had tuned out all distractions. I was in favor of not distracting him! However, I wondered why he hadn't grabbed a helicopter, not that I believe it could have beaten our time by much!

After a few moments, Matt elaborated, "We have a report from the Fresno County Local Law Enforcement that hunters had spotted two furry humanoid creatures and cornered them in Kings Canyon. We intend to arrive before the locals wind up shooting them or worse."

Alex chimed in, "Perhaps I should not have brought you along, Fitz, but I have a hunch you know more than you've admitted. I'm positively betting on it!"

I sat in silence, awed, and slightly terrified. Running 'Signal 9' at insane speeds, the massive vehicle covered the near two hundred and fifty miles in record time, the sun not quite having set as we pulled up to a congregation of local police units. Ordering "Stay in the car!" my companions jumped out and began talking to the local cop. Shouting and gesticulation punctuated their words, and moments later, we reloaded and roared off, flying down a dirt road. I presumed the two other vehicles stayed with the locals to question them for more details. However, Alex seemed to have a gut instinct and wasn't waiting for specifics.

A mile or so down the dirt road, police and a cluster of local civilians in hunter's garb grouped, facing a wooded canyon as the sun's crescent began dipping behind the hills. They had weapons aimed at the woods. As we pulled up, I didn't wait to be told to stay in the car again; I flew out almost before the car had stopped sliding in the dirt. Things were about to get interesting.

I decided that the time had come to bring the thunder as I ran at my nearly superhuman full speed into the congregation and bellowed, "Hold your fire!" I surprised myself with a force and tone of command unlike anything I had ever known. They stopped; shock and surprise marked their faces. "Talk to me! Where are they? What have you seen?"

One of the hunters raised his rifle and pointed toward the woods. So quickly he didn't see me coming, I reached over, jerked his gun from his hands, and, doing my best imitation of the comic book archetype, bent the barrel double!

THAT got attention! If they were awed before, they were doubly so now. It might have been a mistake.

It also got Alex's attention! The look on his face was priceless. Well, he had said he wanted to know my secrets; my cat was about to be well and truly out of the bag.

The hunter whose rifle I ruined glowered at me with a mixture of hatred, awe, respect, and fear! He didn't believe what I had just done. I could not blame him — I wouldn't have either, not so long ago. I almost didn't today; adrenaline is remarkable stuff.

After a stunned silence, they began talking. The quarry was last seen heading into the small canyon before us and was likely nearby. The creatures were probably watching us from behind the trees; there was nowhere they could go as the canyon was boxed in with steep walls. The county police had called for a helicopter with a searchlight to aid in the hunt, and it would arrive, no doubt, just as the last of the late evening summer sun's rays faded.

I ordered Alex to stay here in a tone to brook no discussion. I told him to grab the radio and cancel the helicopter. He balked for a moment, then, with a strange expression, picked up the microphone and did as I ordered. I told Matt and Jill to keep the locals in check. I would go alone into the woods!

Matt opened his mouth; I gave him an icy stare. Finally, I repeated, "I'm going into the woods; disarm these a**holes, as I don't want to be shot at when I come back out!" He seemed shocked at my aggressive tone and authoritarian manner, but he yielded after the briefest possible hesitation. I was surprised he gave in, as submissiveness is not in a cop's DNA. Presumably, he was still in shock from my strength demonstration; perhaps Alex still considered me a friend; in any case, they yielded to my orders. I hoped this did not come to be the terrible idea my 'spidey-sense' was screaming it was!

Seeing momentary submission in his eyes, I turned and launched for the woods at a pace intended to prevent further discussion; I could not continue to stand around and play dumb. I had a strong sense my friends were there and in trouble, and I was NOT going to allow them to be shot! The time for assertiveness had arrived, and a dramatic exhibition had convinced these people, including the cops, that I meant it. Once the shock wore off, I assumed there would be the Devil to pay.

As I started for the woods, Jill moved to accompany me. I motioned her back. She asserted in a low voice, "Sir, you may need help. Let me back you up." I didn't need help, and I wasn't inclined to waste time arguing. There wasn't much daylight left! So I ignored her and launched myself toward the woods at reckless speed.

Running into the woods, I started calling out in Language. Jill made a comic figure or would have under other circumstances as she tried to match my pace and discovered she could not even come close. I quickly ran away from her, though I knew she would soon follow. That gal may be petite, but Jill is not frail and is fiercely determined. Qualities I usually admire, but I feared she would complicate matters.

Out of sight of the Feds, I stopped and started singing 'Clementine' and, between the verses, calling out in Language. "I'm here; it's Fitz. I'm here, come dears." I sat on a large rock and continued singing and calling out to them. Jill came up, huffing and puffing, winded. I motioned for her to sit on the rock, too. "Sing Clementine!"

She hesitated, though she had claimed to have read my book. She should understand the song's significance, my signature among these people. Then, after a moment, she joined in. Not an unpleasant voice, either, under the conditions.

A half-hour elapsed. It was getting seriously dark when I heard a rustle in the underbrush. Then, in Language, a frightened voice called out, "Fitz, is that you?"

"Yes, it is I; who's there?" She stepped out into the open, looking frightened half to death. It was Stapleya with her daughter Wisceya. Jill produced a flashlight and shone it in their direction, which didn't help! Seeing Jill, they retreated. Jill moved as if to draw her sidearm; I placed my hand on her arm and called them, "It's OK, she's a friend and here to protect us." After a moment's hesitation, they ran to me in tears!

We hugged and nuzzled each other in the twilight for several minutes, the girls blubbering into my chest as they described their ordeal, being hunted and terrified to be out of doors at night. They had been out here two nights, had gone without food save a few berries they had found. I reassured them it was alright now, that I would protect them. Yet, even as I told them all this, I wondered how. Could I defend them? Which constituted the greater danger, the civilians, the local cops, or the feds who had brought me here? How might I fix this? How can I take them home?

Jill stood by, dumbfounded. I suppose reading a description in a book presented as fiction, even though there were strong hints otherwise, constituted inadequate preparation for meeting living, breathing alien-visaged humanoids in the flesh. My chattering away with them in a language she had never heard probably didn't calm things.

I introduced the girls to Jill, translating as needed. I was only mildly surprised when Stapleya responded with "Pleased to meet you, Jill" in quite passable English. I had long suspected she was holding back.

Picking our way through the brush toward the encampment where the others waited, I explained to the ladies that there was danger, and I would protect them. But, I emphasized that they must precisely do as I instructed them!

We reached the edge of the tree line, and I positioned the ladies behind a pair of large trees and ordered them to stay put until I called. I wanted to ensure that no one would overreact on seeing them. I didn't wish to provoke a panicked reaction, especially as these cops are heavily armed; I hoped to calm the waters beforehand. Trusting the ladies to stay put, I walked back toward the waiting cops. Unsure what to do, Jill waited for a few moments, then changed her mind and followed me, picking her way with her flashlight. I went over to Alex and told him to chase all the others away!

For a moment, he balked. He'd had time to think and wasn't sanguine with my 'take charge' manner; he expected to be the one in charge! He was the 'Authority,' not me! I lowered my voice conspiratorially lest the others overhear. "You wanted in on secrets? Get rid of those others! Let's contain this! Once they're gone, I will bring my friends out, introduce them, and we'll find out how they came here. And yes, they're the fur-people from the dinosaur world I described, and they are my friends! The mother is Lady Stapleya, who I named in my book as the head mother of the castle." I noted how Alex blanched at this, an odd reaction from him. That puzzled me; why would Stapleya's name be significant to him? I continued, "They're good, gentle, but frightened people. Now chase away those God damned circus freaks with the guns! Let's contain this before tales of alien sightings appear on late-night radio shows. Grab their damned cell phones and cameras and anything else that might have recorded this scene!"

Digesting what I had told him and seeing Jill walking up as she nodded and gave him a thumbs-up, Alex went over and talked to the county mountie and his civilian cohorts. After a spate of cursing and waving around his badge, he convinced them to leave. The one whose gun I bent was carrying it gingerly and giving me a strange look. I guess I couldn't blame him. I felt a tinge of guilt for ruining his weapon, but he shouldn't point it at my friends!

I suggested to Alex that it was a matter of time before pictures of the gun were on Facebook, Twitter, or other social media, although the guy himself seemed a bit old to be active in social media. Or was that just my agism showing? Perhaps Alex could use his badge to head it off. He nodded.

Once they began to leave, I asked Jill whether we had food in the car. She produced a couple of cereal bars, though nothing substantial. I told her to hold them ready and find water too. I told Matt to dismiss the other SUVs and agents. The situation was under control, and there was nothing of consequence. I suggested that he imply it was only a couple of kids playing a joke with costumes. Again hesitant to accept my authority, Matt glanced at Alex, who gave a little shrug and nodded. Matt picked up the microphone and did as I had asked.

A few minutes later, satisfied that the circus had gone, I called out to the girls in Language. They came walking out of the woods. I motioned them to come on as Matt stared slack-jawed. I introduced them to Matt and Alex, acting as translator to trade a few words. Alex seemed almost shy, ducking, and avoiding Stapleya's gaze.

I told Jill to pass them the food and water. My ladies were hungry! They needed more food than that, but the cereal bars would dull hunger's edge.

Matt still acted a bit freaked out, but Alex seemed to be taking the alien ladies in stride, scarcely acknowledging them. I told Alex I wanted to take them to my home. He balked at that; he wanted to take them to a holding center. We argued over it until I convinced him that I would explain all and translate for him and his people. They could talk to them as much as possible; they could interrogate them as much as they wanted, under my roof, in my home, and with my hospitality, but not in a government facility. He feared they might run; I countered that they were terrified of our world and would not leave my side!

He still resisted. He wanted them under his control; his instinct to be the one in authority was strong. Finally, I sighed, "Look, you read my book. You see the ladies from 'Planet Oz,' just as I described them in my writings. You saw me bend that gun barrel. I may not be from Krypton, but you understand what I wrote describing the genetic enhancements and training I received on another planet is genuine. Surely you can recognize that working with me and doing things my way is the best course. Trust me; this is my wheelhouse! You demanded I let you in. You told me you were my friend. Was that idle chatter, or were you serious?

"It's not a case of national security. These women are no threat to anyone or anything, no broken laws, just a series of unfortunate accidents. No criminals, no terrorists, nothing in the official purview of Homeland Security, no threats to the nation. Just a pair of lost, terrified women a long way from home. They want and need to return home. I'm the only one who can make that happen. So I will welcome them, shelter them and do all in my power to take them back to their home and I will explain everything I know, which isn't much beyond what I wrote in my book anyway. It's all the literal truth, even though you thought it fiction.

"Surely you recognize that now."

He calmed down while I was speechmaking and then grinned and laughed, responding, "Don't call me Shirley!"

I almost choked at his unexpected witticism, if you want to call it that. I groaned and rolled my eyes at him, at which he smirked as though he had silently passed gas in a crowded elevator. Yet, though still unwilling to trust him to have our interests at heart, I felt relieved. We climbed into the SUV; the off-world women wide-eyed with disbelief at the unimaginable conveyance, and started back toward the city.

I told Alex, "Stop at the first In-N-Out, I'm hungry, and these ladies are half-starved. We can all stand a few calories, and it's my treat." He nodded without answering.

Stapleya began describing their adventure. I translated for the others, and Alex drove along calmly, for him. The return trip was nothing compared to the outbound insane thrill ride. First, we hit Fresno and the burger joint. The girls had never seen anything like it — they discovered they like burgers. Well, I think highly of In-N-Out myself. They stayed in the back seat out of sight while going through the drive-thru, then appetites temporarily sated, we hit the road for home.

Language barrier notwithstanding, Matt and Jill soon accepted that despite wearing sensual fur instead of clothes and finding our technology overwhelming, these ladies were as human and as civilized as anyone, more so than most. Alex avoided talking and seemed unwilling to interact with the aliens. Instead, he drove in silence, at legal speed — or close to it — giving us time to become acquainted.

At Home with the Aliens

As we started toward home, I expanded on my initial introductions, elaborating on who was who and the role each played. First, I told the MiBs of Stapleya's position as the Castle Mother as featured in my book and that the other two, Wisceya and the poor unfortunate in the morgue, were her daughters. Next, I introduced the girls to Alex, Matt, and Jill and explained their role as cops, which I found difficult to frame in stone-age society concepts.

Jill, I felt, was almost on my side, or so I convinced myself, and Matt seemed to be somewhat willing to follow her lead. I didn't read either one of them as a threat, except insofar as they might follow another's lead. That potential other was Alex! Although he seemed calmly accepting outwardly, Alex constitutes an unknown, the alpha of their team, and he frightens me! Not in a physical sense; I outweigh him. Of course, I'm physically much stronger and faster; I'm not even particularly fearful of his weapon, trusting my ability to disarm or outrun him.

He has power and resources he can call on, the power and authority of the Government! I had no wish to find myself or my ladies detained, locked in a detention center against our will. Perhaps I'm paranoid. Or maybe not, as I feared that Alex wasn't coping smoothly with not being in control, with my newly revealed secrets, or the now undeniable fact that aliens indeed are among us.

Despite his outward calm, I felt he needed to be in control, the authoritarian, and I worried about what steps he might take to regain that status. For the moment, he seemingly had accepted my self-asserted authority in these matters, though I didn't expect that to endure; that calmness itself is frightening. I needed to court him to keep him nominally my friend. If he began to view me as also an alien, I might be in real trouble.

Stapleya greeted them in accented English. When I arrived on her home world, she spoke but few words of English, and those few thanks to Petchy's visits. He had not intended to teach her English. Nonetheless, she seemingly had picked up a smattering. When I arrived, she took responsibility for teaching me Language, and she improved her English skills while practicing with me. Far from fluent,

Stapleya knew the elementals of hello, please, thank you, etc. However, I now discovered she knew far more than I had suspected. I would later learn the full extent of her English mastery, as she had been keeping her skills hidden, the better to eavesdrop. I, of course, could translate freely, and with just a minor difficulty, we could all communicate.

Jill was the first one to overcome her shock, surprise, and xenophobia and begin earnestly trying to communicate, accepting them as people and not an odd sort of furry animal or Hollywood aliens bent on destruction, invasion, or eating our brains. Alex remained enigmatic. He spoke rarely and did not talk to Stapleya if he could avoid it. He almost hid from her gaze as though he had something to hide from her. His behavior worried me, but I would only come to understand it weeks later. Matt insisted on talking in the third person. He almost acted as if the women were not present, perhaps inanimate objects or pets. Nonetheless, their story came out piecemeal during our ride home.

Best intentions notwithstanding, we had been careless visitors to their world. Perhaps whoever thought up the fictional concept of the 'Prime Directive' might have been onto something.

When we had discussed matters of worlds and cosmology and threats to the galaxy, we had done so in English. Mostly. There were two flaws in our actions, though. First, while I was still working on my Language skills, we would at times hold our conversations in Language, or a pidgin combination of Language and English — mainly when we thought we were alone. We were careless of being overheard, even perhaps a little disdainful of the natives' grasp of the esoteric topics we were discussing.

Second, although we knew they had learned a few English words, we underestimated how much and how fast they had learned. I admire and seek to surround myself with intelligent people. Their raw intelligence is one of the many reasons I so love the fur people. Their scintillating intellect shines through even in the face of their often-startling ignorance of many things I take for granted. I must constantly remind myself that ignorance does not indicate a lack of intelligence.

It is too easy to discount the intelligence of people living a stone-age existence. So even though we knew they were intelligent, we underestimated them. Not just once, repeatedly, over and over again! The result had been that often when we thought we were in private conversation, we were not so much.

The fur-people had deduced a lot regarding the portals and how to spot them to a limited extent. In truth, they learned almost as much as I have, which was near zero despite traveling through them. But there may be a vast difference between zero and 'near to zero.' Profoundly terrified at the prospect of stepping through a portal, our friends should have remained safely at home, except they had a crisis on their hands and needed our aid.

A couple of the vermin infesting their planet had discovered the joys of daytime dining. Specifically, a Deinonychus, maybe a pair, as they tend to travel in pairs, had begun hunting in the daytime, early mornings, and late afternoons. The natives now believed that these creatures were responsible for the invasion of the Dark Castle. I had told that story and the gruesome deaths of its inhabitants.

Fortunately, the warning sounded after our terrifying visit to that grisly site. The fur-people took extraordinary precautions, including keeping the colossal stone castle doors closed and locked more than usual during daylight hours. As a result, no more castles had fallen to the vicious beasts. Nonetheless, a few citizens caught outside the castle walls became their victims. The people are now living in fear and desperate to exterminate these deadly beasts; unfortunately, they have no weapons powerful enough for the task.

Conventional bows and arrows, slings, and rocks are useless against these beasts. Perhaps my magnificent Hero's Bow, The Lady Seven, with her metal-tipped hardwood arrows, could muster enough force driven by my highly developed muscles to pierce that thick, leathery hide. Or perhaps one of her eight sisters, given that I had left her concealed near the portal to Planet 'K,' a considerable distance from Stapleya's castle. The energy to propel an arrow, no matter how elaborate and powerful the bow, ultimately comes from the archer's muscles. Not precisely the biceps, but instead, the large muscles of the upper back. Genetically enhanced muscles I spent endless hours developing.

The Lady Seven and her sisters were not merely weapons. Created as art, they were mighty, finely crafted weapons of heroic proportions designed to hang on the wall, not used in battle. Art is for display, admired for the artist's craftsmanship. The artist had created nine of these bows, nine identical, mythologically powerful weapons too large, too powerful for any mere human; until I came along! I was the only person on the planet, either planet, who could adequately draw The Lady Seven and drive an arrow fiercely enough to kill a Deinonychus, and I was terrified even to try!

It was risky, as a miss could all too easily be fatal! These Dinos are fast and tough! Even if my arrows penetrate its hide, it will not die quickly. The only guaranteed lethal target is the tiny, heavily armored brain! Miss that, and you're dead even if your first shot inflicted a nominally mortal wound on the beast, and any archer facing such a beast was unlikely to get off a second shot, even one as fast as me. It will keep coming until it falls from blood loss, and they are much too speedy to outrun. Still, the fur people's faith in my ability must be immense. The ladies decided they must try to reach me even if it meant risking their lives. They had no way to contact anyone not on their planet and thus resorted to the dangers of the portals to reach out and secure my help.

One of the younger daughters of the castle, Shameya by name, thought herself to have the best understanding of portals. When I heard her name, I remembered her. I shed a tear as I recognized her as the poor unfortunate in the morgue. I hadn't known her well, although once prodded, I remembered her. She had been too young for my boon when I visited. Had she come searching for me, not just because of the threat imposed by the day-walking Deinonychus but because — now mature and fertile — she had wanted a baby like her sisters?

Whatever her full motivations, by the simple expedient of sitting in the place where others had observed Teena appear and watching for weeks and weeks, she had learned how to spot the portal on its regular appearances. With no understanding of the hyper-dimensional physics underlying them, she naively assumed all openings led to the home of Petchy, Athena, and myself, not even understanding that we were from different planets. We were all 'Smoothies' to them; her people have a limited grasp of other worlds.

A group had taken turns, often two together, keeping watch. Finally, by sheer dumb luck and perseverance, Shameya and her sister Williya spotted an opening. Acting on impulse, Shameya had stepped through and wound up in Oakland that terrible, tragic night.

Williya had panicked at seeing her sister disappear into the portal and ran to her mother in tears. Stapleya and another sister, Wisceya, returned to the spot of the entrance and resumed the vigil. Again by sheer luck, they spotted an open portal several days later, and that portal too connected to Earth and not another random planet. They might have transited into more hostile environments, although it would be difficult to name one more hostile than Oakland had been for dear Shameya.

Stapleya, determined to rush to the rescue of her daughter, better equipped, she thought, by her limited English skills, to communicate with those on the other side, had stepped through the portal into a rural area east of Fresno. Spotted and hunted several times by the locals, they ran in panic. They spent a couple of terrifying nights out of doors in the forest, fully expecting to fall prey to some terrible predator. Reports of their sightings had made it to late-night talk radio, where I heard it. The local citizens hunting them had involved local law enforcement, reporting two fur-covered humanoids as a 'Bigfoot' sighting in the canyon. Given their diminutive stature, 'Big' could hardly apply to their feet or anything else. Nevertheless, facts seldom intrude on an exciting cryptozoological hunt! Jill had spotted that report, put two and two together, and she and Matt had called Alex, and he had called me.

We had collected the whole story on the ride home, and Matt and Alex grudgingly accepted my friends as human after all, though Alex barely spoke to them and would hardly look them in the face. I called them out, the two of them, and reminded them of their manners a few times until they came around. By the time we arrived at my home, the worst seemed over, or so I hoped. Though Alex didn't want to leave them with me, he could not find a legal reason to detain them. I suspect he felt afraid of me after seeing my strength demonstration. He wanted someone to stay with us, and Jill volunteered.

I reminded her that we would be staying in a one-room apartment. I emphasized that she was welcome into my home, crowded although my tiny man-cave may be, and explained she might not be comfortable. She insisted; I shrugged and told her okay, though I explained the tight quarters again. Finally, I explained that I only had one bed.

She shrugged and said she would manage. "I am a Warrior," she said. I raised an eyebrow but said nothing.

It was well past midnight when I got the three ladies into my apartment. Thankfully, my house manager had taken my pets; I trusted her to care for them as well as I would.

It was a good thing it was late; we didn't encounter the household's other residents. I did not want to explain why I had three female houseguests, two of whom were unclothed, fur-bearing aliens. It would no doubt be a challenging visit.

Beyond the immediate problem of keeping their alien presence quiet, the second critical agenda item was that I must contact Petchy, Teena — if she were even alive, I reminded myself — or some of their people for help. I'm not brave enough or ignorant enough to venture into a portal, even if I could find one, without a guide who knows the mappings. My poor dears had taken a horrific chance against terrible odds. It was sheer dumb luck that they made their way to me, and only one of them died.

Then we need to address the problem of killing a few Deinonychus without real weapons, with heartfelt apologies to *The Lady Seven* and her eight sisters.

Shopping for Clothes

As we started towards home, I expanded on my initial rudimentary introductions of the alien women and the MiBs, elaborating on who was who and the role each played. First, I told the MiBs of Stapleya's role as the Castle Mother as featured in my book and that the other two — Wisceya and the poor unfortunate in the morgue — were her daughters. Next, I introduced the girls to Alex, Matt, and Jill and explained their role as cops, which I found difficult to frame in stone-age society concepts.

Jill, I felt, was almost on my side, or so I convinced myself, and Matt seemed to be somewhat willing to follow her lead. I didn't read either one of them as a threat, except insofar as they might follow another's lead. That potential other was Alex! Although he seemed calmly accepting outwardly, Alex constitutes an unknown, the alpha of their team, and he frightens me! Not in a physical sense; I outweigh him. Of course, I'm physically much stronger and faster — I'm not even particularly fearful of his weapon, trusting my ability to disarm or outrun him.

He has power and resources he can call on, the power and authority of the Government! I had no wish to find myself or my ladies detained, locked in a detention center against our will. Perhaps I'm paranoid. Or maybe not, as I feared that Alex wasn't coping smoothly with not being in control — with my newly revealed secrets — or the now undeniable fact that aliens indeed are among us.

Despite his outward calm, I felt he needed to be in control, the authoritarian, and I worried what steps he might take to regain that status. For the moment, he seemingly had accepted my self-asserted authority in these matters, though I didn't expect that to endure — that calmness itself is frightening. I needed to court him to keep him nominally my friend. If he began to view me as also an alien, I might be in real trouble.

Stapleya greeted them in accented English. When I arrived on her home world, she spoke but few words of English and those few thanks to Petchy's visits. He had not intended to teach her English. Nonetheless, she seemingly had picked up a smattering. When I arrived, she took responsibility for teaching me Language, and she improved her English skills while practicing with me. Far from fluent, Stapleya knew the elementals of hello, please, thank you, etc. However, I now discovered she knew far more than I had suspected. I would later learn the full extent of her English mastery, as she had been keeping her skills hidden, the better to eavesdrop. I, of course, could translate freely, and with just a minor difficulty, we could all communicate.

Jill was the first one to overcome her shock, surprise, and xenophobia and begin earnestly trying to communicate, accepting them as people and not an odd sort of furry animal or Hollywood aliens bent on destruction, invasion, or eating our brains. Alex remained enigmatic. He spoke rarely and did not talk to Stapleya if he could avoid it. He almost hid from her gaze as though he had something to hide from her. His behavior worried me, but I would only come to understand it weeks later. Matt insisted on talking in the third person. He almost acted as if the women were not present, perhaps inanimate objects or pets. Nonetheless, their story came out piecemeal during our ride home.

Best intentions notwithstanding, we had been careless visitors to their world. Perhaps the person who thought up the fictional concept of the 'Prime Directive' might have been onto something.

When we had discussed matters of worlds and cosmology and threats to the galaxy, we had done so in English. Mostly. There were two flaws in our actions, though. First, while I was still working on my Language skills, we would at times hold our conversations in Language, or a pidgin combination of Language and English — mainly when we thought we were alone. We were careless of being overheard, even perhaps a little disdainful of the natives' grasp of the esoteric topics we were discussing.

Second, although we knew they had learned a few English words, we underestimated how much and how fast they had learned. I admire and seek to surround myself with intelligent people. Their raw intelligence is one of the many reasons I so love the fur people. Their scintillating intellect shines through even in the face of their often startling ignorance of many things I take for granted. I must constantly remind myself that ignorance did not indicate a lack of intelligence.

It is too easy to discount the intelligence of people living a stone-age existence. So even though we knew they were intelligent, we underestimated them. Not just once, repeatedly, over and over again! The result had been that often when we thought we were in private conversation, we were not so much.

The fur-people had deduced a lot regarding the portals and how to spot them to a limited extent. In truth, they learned almost as much as I have, which was near to zero despite traveling through them. But there may be a vast difference between zero and 'near to zero.' Profoundly terrified at the prospect of stepping through a portal, our friends should have remained safely at home, except they had a crisis on their hands and needed our aid.

A couple of the vermin infesting their planet had discovered the joys of daytime dining. Specifically, a Deinonychus, maybe a pair, as they tend to travel in pairs, had begun hunting in the daytime, early mornings, and late afternoons. The natives now believed that these creatures were, in fact, responsible for the invasion of the Dark Castle. I had told that story and the gruesome deaths of its inhabitants in my novel.

Fortunately, the warning sounded after our terrifying visit to that grisly site. The fur-people took extraordinary precautions, including keeping the colossal stone castle doors closed and locked more than usual during daylight hours. As a result, no more castles had fallen to the vicious beasts. Nonetheless, a few citizens caught outside the castle walls became their victims. The people are now living in fear and desperate to exterminate the deadly beasts — unfortunately, they have no weapons powerful enough for the task.

Conventional bows and arrows, slings, and rocks are useless against these beasts. Perhaps my magnificent Hero's Bow, The Lady Seven, with her metal-tipped hardwood arrows, could muster enough force driven by my highly developed muscles to pierce that thick, leathery hide. Or perhaps one of her eight sisters, given that I had left her concealed near the portal to Planet' K,' a considerable distance from Stapleya's castle. The energy to propel an arrow, no matter how elaborate and powerful the bow, ultimately comes from the archer's muscles. Not precisely the biceps, instead, the large muscles of the upper back. Genetically enhanced muscles that I had spent endless hours developing.

The Lady Seven and her sisters were not merely weapons. Created as art, they were mighty, finely crafted weapons of heroic proportions designed to hang on the wall, not used in battle. Art is for display, admired for the artist's craftsmanship. The artist had created nine of these bows, nine identical, mythologically powerful weapons too large, too powerful for any mere human — until I came along! I was the only person on the planet, either planet, who could adequately draw The Lady Seven and drive an arrow fiercely enough to kill a Deinonychus, and I was terrified even to try!

It was risky, as a miss could all too easily be fatal! These Dinos are fast and tough! Even if my arrows penetrate its hide, it will not die quickly. The only guaranteed lethal target is the tiny, heavily armored brain! Miss that, and you're dead even if your first shot inflicted a nominally mortal wound on the beast, and any archer facing such a beast was most unlikely to get off a second shot, even one as fast as me. It will keep coming until it falls from blood loss, and they are much too speedy to outrun. Still, the fur people's faith in my ability must be immense. The ladies decided they must try to reach me even if it meant risking their lives. They had no way to contact anyone not on their planet and thus resorted to the unknown dangers of the portals to reach out and secure help.

One of the younger daughters of the castle, Shameya by name, thought herself to have the best understanding of portals. When I heard her name, I remembered her. I shed a tear as I recognized her as the poor unfortunate in the morgue. I hadn't known her well, although once prodded, I remembered her. She had been too young for my boon when I visited. Had she come searching for me, not just because of the threat imposed by the day-walking Deinonychus but because — now mature and fertile — she had wanted a baby like her sisters?

Whatever her full motivations, by the simple expedient of sitting in the place where others had observed Teena appear and watching for weeks and weeks, she had learned how to spot the portal on its regular appearances. With no understanding of the hyper-dimensional physics underlying them, she naively assumed all openings led to the home of Petchy, Athena, and myself, not even understanding that we were from different planets. We were all 'Smoothies' to them; her people have a limited grasp of other worlds.

A group had taken turns, often two together, keeping watch. Finally, by sheer dumb luck and perseverance, Shameya and her sister Williya spotted an opening. Acting on impulse, Shameya had stepped through and wound up in Oakland that terrible, tragic night.

Williya had panicked at seeing her sister disappear into the portal and ran to her mother in tears. Stapleya and another sister, Wisceya, returned to the spot of the entrance and resumed the vigil. Again by sheer luck, they spotted an open portal several days later, and that portal too connected to Earth and not another random planet. They might have transited into more hostile environments, although it would be difficult to name one more hostile than Oakland had been for dear Shameya.

Stapleya determined to rush to the rescue of her daughter, better equipped, she thought, by her limited English skills, to communicate with those on the other side, had stepped through the portal into a rural area east of Fresno. Spotted and hunted several times by the locals, they ran in panic. They spent a couple of terrifying nights out of doors in the forest, fully expecting to fall prey to some terrible predator. Reports of their sightings had made it to late-night talk radio, where I heard it. The local citizens hunting them had involved local law enforcement, reporting two fur-covered humanoids as a 'Bigfoot' sighting in the canyon. Given their diminutive stature, 'Big' could hardly apply to their feet or anything else. Nevertheless, facts seldom intrude on an exciting cryptozoological hunt! Jill had spotted that report, put two and two together, and she and Matt had called Alex, and he had called me.

We had collected the whole story on the ride home, and Matt and Alex grudgingly accepted my friends as human after all, though Alex barely spoke to them and would hardly look them in the face. I called out the two of them and reminded them of their manners a few times until they came around. By the time we arrived at my home, the worst seemed over, or so I hoped. Though Alex didn't want to leave them with me, he could not find a legal reason to detain them. I suspect he felt afraid of me after seeing my strength demonstration. He wanted someone to stay with us, and Jill volunteered.

I reminded her that we would be staying in a one-room apartment. I emphasized that she is welcome into my home, crowded although my tiny man-cave may be, and explained she might not be comfortable. She insisted; I shrugged and told her okay, though I explained the tight quarters again. Finally, I explained that I only had one bed.

She shrugged and said she would manage. "I am a Warrior," she said. I raised an eyebrow but said nothing.

It was well past midnight when I got the three ladies into my apartment. Thankfully, my house manager had taken my pets; I trusted her to care for them as well as I would.

It was a good thing it was late; we didn't encounter the household's other residents. I did not want to explain why I had three female houseguests, two of whom were unclothed, fur-bearing aliens. It would no doubt be a challenging visit.

Beyond the immediate problem of keeping their alien presence quiet, the second critical agenda item was that I must contact Petchy, Teena — if she were even alive, I reminded myself — or some of their people for help. I'm not brave enough or ignorant enough to venture into a portal, even if I could find one, without a guide who knows the mappings. My poor dears had taken a horrific chance against terrible odds. It was sheer dumb luck that they made their way to me, and only one of them died.

Then we need to address the problem of killing a few Deinonychus without real weapons, heartfelt apologies to *The Lady Seven* and her eight sisters.

Rabbit Run!

Once the Agents departed, I surveyed our off-world visitors and decided that their appearance was acceptable. Their furry faces should not draw attention, given the immense variety of spectacular-looking characters found on our city streets. So we didn't bother with the masks. My city can sometimes be a bit of a zoo; my friends should not stand out.

I turned to Jill, "I need to find a way to leave a signal for Petchey or his people, and I'm most decidedly not allowing these ladies out of my sight. In your opinion, can they safely accompany us to the plaza?"

Jill eyed them and agreed they would not stand out in that eclectic crowd. I asked Stapleya if she were comfortable going out. I asked in English, then repeated in Language which she interrupted and answered in perfect English. "Yes, I would like to see the city." Her English is increasing exponentially. Wisceya nodded. "Yes, please, me too."

Satisfied, we set out for the plaza, Jill and I with the off-worlders. I know there are at least two portals in the plaza. I believed I knew what 'secret signs' denote the location and tell when they are active. I intended to put a mark that I hoped a traveler would recognize as a distress signal in hopes that a traveler might spot it.

Arriving in the plaza, I decided to treat my companions to my favorite Arabian Mocha-Java blend; I could stand one myself. I ordered the drinks, seated my little group at my regular spot, and watched with interest as my visitors tasted the hearty brew. At first, they made faces yet cautiously went back for a second taste after a moment. Although they found it unusual, they decided that they liked it. On the other hand, these people are meticulously polite and would have 'liked' motor oil rather than insult a host.

We sat there and casually people watched. Our visitors displayed a range of fascinating emotions as they took in the fantastic city scene. Unlike anything in their experience, this mundane plaza seemed exotic and foreign. A few passersby noticed our ladies yet didn't react beyond a double-take and stare. I kept a watchful eye, though there were no problems.

After several minutes of careful study, I spotted the marks I sought and chalked my distress symbol. I hoped to come back soon and find it crossed out, acknowledging a message received. Petch had explained how they use subtle chalk marks this way, although it seemed a long shot. Chalk on the sidewalk and the silly newspaper ad was all I had.

As I pondered my situation, I again realized just how little I knew of Petchey, Teena, and the organization they represented. Yet, it seemed evident that their organization was massive and had a presence on many different planets. How extensive and how many worlds, I have not the slightest clue! Contacting them, likewise, lies beyond my ken.

My ignorance, I realized, was stunning! I speculated whether the lack might be due to my lack of persistence or whether Petchy and Teena had intentionally thwarted my curiosity. I pondered our time on "Planet Oz" and remembered the times I had asked questions only to allow my attention to be redirected and whatever answers were pointedly vague. The more I considered, the more foolish I felt! A little knowledge could come in handy right now!

The counterargument was obvious, nonetheless, given my precarious position with the MiBs. If I were Petch and Teena, I would hope to keep me ignorant too! What I don't know, I cannot reveal. Or put it in a book! For the thousandth time, I regretted publishing that fantastic tale.

The question on the table now was a simple one, where should my loyalties lie?

We finished our jitter juice, and I guided the ladies toward the derelict building where I had applied for a job months ago. I had come here numerous times over the last several months in hopes of finding someone or some sign of life and had not seen anyone. Nonetheless, I figured we could spend a few minutes observing, just in case. I hoped that perhaps if a traveler came through and spotted our guests' furry faces, they might recognize our problem. I scrawled distress marks on the wall, too, just for good measure.

We parked our derrières across the street from the building and chatted a while as we watched the building. As I had often noted before, there was no sign of life, and no one came or went. I noticed a black SUV with government plates a short distance down the street. Whether they were watching us, watching the building, or merely evidence of my private brand of paranoia, I could not decide. I wished I could ask Jill about it, though I didn't ask her for two reasons. First, I didn't want to alarm the girls, and they understood entirely too much English now. Second, I was unsure where Jill's loyalties reside or, more accurately, doubted they were with us rather than the MiBs and didn't wish to make them aware that I had spotted them. I kept my own counsel in the matter.

Jill seemed to be nothing other than helpful and supportive, though I had no illusions where her loyalties would lie when forced to choose between my goals and supporting those of her employers. It was much too tempting to forget she's not my friend.

As I pondered the question, my phone slightly vibrated, calling attention to motion at home. I surreptitiously checked my phone, looking at the array of hidden security cameras I had installed. At first, all appeared copacetic until I rewound the video for closer examination, and reasons for concern became obvious. Several people were just at the edge of the camera's field of view, and I could not determine what they were doing. I teetered on the verge of panic, imagining all sorts of unsavory motives behind the image on my phone. Were they waiting there to jump us when on our return? However, I concealed my thoughts and concerns, acting as nonchalant as possible for Jill's benefit. I dared not permit her to warn them I had spotted them.

We watched the storefront for a while until I decided we may as well head back home. I was developing a strategy to avoid our welcoming committee. As we walked back past the shops around the plaza, I noticed an Ice Cream Shoppe and decided to treat the ladies.

My dears had no idea of a frozen treat. They had no concept of 'frozen' anything! With their home world's ambient heat and the absence of refrigeration technology, I doubted they even knew water could freeze.

Jill accepted a single scoop as my treat, and the others followed her lead. I watched as their eyes widened when they tasted chocolate ice cream. They ate it enthusiastically, and when they finished, I asked them if they wanted another. Both nodded eagerly! They had politely accepted my coffee, but this evoked honest enthusiasm. Though their travel to Earth had been a harrowing ordeal, they were warming to select aspects of my world.

Adjacent to the ice cream shop was a Pizza Emporium. Putting on my best masculine charms, I handed Jill a few bills and casually asked, "Jill, would you be a dear and buy us some pizza for lunch? I want to escort our guests home. Grab us some lunch, please and bring it on as soon as you can, and we will meet you there." I watched the indecision playing in her eyes, reluctant to leave us to our own devices, though she reluctantly agreed after a few moments of hesitation.

I guided the girls, and we started strolling toward the house as Jill disappeared into the Pizza Palace. We walked casually along for a few moments as I scanned in every direction, seeking signs of followers. I sneaked another peek at my phone and noticed Alex, gun in hand, just at the edge of my field of view. I'd been hesitating, but now he had congealed my decision! I suspected my girls had realized something was about to happen from my manner. I spoke to them in Language, explaining that we were in danger, that they needed to trust me and do as I say. I casually strolled as we approached my friend Julie's home. Her car was in front of the house. Perfect!

One last glance around, and I whipped out the key I had borrowed, pushed my charges into the car's rear seat, told them to lay low, jumped into the driver's seat, and started rolling! I would apologize later to Julie.

I hoped she would forgive me.

Before starting the car, I popped the back off my phone and removed the battery. I gave thanks for picking a phone that is easy to disable, as many have sealed-in, non-removable batteries. The only way to ensure they are dead is to destroy them. I wasn't ready, just yet, to bust my shiny new phone, although I certainly didn't want anyone tracking it.

We rolled down the city streets within seconds, trying to avoid the major thoroughfares. I know a bit about the city's surveillance capabilities, as I had provided consulting services to the network contractor. When the Domain Awareness System first came to the Bay Area, the first installation was in a neighboring city across the bay. The traffic cameras in my city were in the process of being upgraded and incorporated into the system. The system, developed in Manhattan, was gradually extended to other cities. Although the legacy system still managed most cameras, primary routes had the upgrades, a hodgepodge of analog and early digital systems with limited capabilities.

It helped that they didn't suspect what type of car I was driving—or so I believed. I'm hoping that Julie is not on the MiB radar screens. Either way, I didn't wish to make it easy. While rolling down the street, I donned the hat, scarf, and sunglasses. I hoped that this would fool a traffic camera if one happened to spot us. The best facial recognition systems would not be this easily fooled; I was counting on the fact that the city's legacy system was not the best! I sought to avoid the newer cameras.

The girls took my actions in stride. I gave them little explanation while concentrating on driving and watching for black SUVs. They seemed unconcerned, trusting implicitly in my judgment and abilities. We wasted time avoiding freeways and arteries; nonetheless, we quickly escaped the city proper. I figured by now they would have realized that we had rabbited and were searching for us. I turned on the News-talk radio in case there might be mention of anything that might affect us. My friends seemed surprised by the sound system but said nothing.

It took a long time to navigate our way down the peninsula to the south bay avoiding traffic corridors and cams. My destination was the home of a friend of mine, a fellow networking professional with the unlikely-sounding name of Philemon. Usually, he merely goes by Phil. His given name's origin is a mystery to me. Nevertheless, I must ask him about it sometime.

I knew Phil lived a bicoastal lifestyle, having a house in South Carolina, where he spent much of the year. I believed he was currently in his east coast home, but if he was home in the South Bay, I planned to throw myself on his mercy and beg his aid, maybe even force him, if necessary. On the other hand, if he wasn't home, I had a lock-pick set in my bag. I hope I didn't damage our friendship either way, but I desperately needed a safe house.

Finally, we arrived and pulled up in front of Phil's house. No car was in sight, and no one seemed home. I quickly picked the lock, ushered the ladies inside, and scouted the place. As suspected, he wasn't present, but his computer was! I'll come back to that in a few moments.

I disconnected the Internet and booted the computer. His machine was quite ancient, which worked in my favor, though it also meant it would require a while to boot up. That was okay, though, as I have a more urgent priority.

I checked the garage. No dice! Like most Californians, not having to cope with severe weather, the garage becomes a storeroom with cars left to sit outside. There was no way to bring it inside, and it could not remain in the driveway.

I parked the girls on the living room couch and suggested they relax until I came back. Then, I returned to the car and drove away. I assumed that the MiBs might have figured out that I had taken Julie's car and dared not risk leaving it in the driveway in front of our hideout. I racked my brain about how I might seem to abandon her vehicle without doing so; then, I had a brainstorm. I had noticed that Julie needed tires. In fact, I had worried about it on our recent outing to the redwoods. Then, I saw a tire store with a giant sale sign out front. It was near closing time; I parked and went inside.

I explained to the owner that the car belonged to my girlfriend, and I wanted to buy her a set of tires as a surprise present. I told him I intended to catch a rideshare to the airport for a quick overnight trip and that I would be back tomorrow afternoon. I told him I intended to catch a taxi to the airport for a quick overnight trip and that I would be back tomorrow afternoon, So I asked him to take the car, put a set of tires on it and hold it ready, and I would be back then to pick it up. I paid him cash in advance and took his receipt.

Undercover parking, security for the car, and hopefully, forgiveness from Julie for taking her car in one slick package!

Routing The Onion

I ran back to the house as rapidly as possible without attracting attention, a gentle lope considerably below my best pace. My friends were patiently waiting where I had parked them. Inwardly, I smiled when I saw they had removed their clothes. It seems they regard the clothes as a masquerade costume to facilitate their fitting into my world, a disguise to be worn in public and didn't feel the need in private. I do not disagree; I, too, prefer clothes-free comfort when in private or with like-minded friends.

With the vehicle taken care of, I returned to the computer. The ancient desktop lacked the latest software; however, with obsolete software comes a degree of simplicity. Newest isn't necessarily the best. I checked and quickly discovered my instincts were correct; Phil had a remote desktop system installed. If the machine had been on the network, he might have observed when it came online and realized an intruder had usurped his computer and house. That could have negative consequences, I fear!

I disabled the Remote Desktop and examined the machine for other software which might betray my presence. Once satisfied we were safe from detection, I reconnected the Internet. Okay! We were online!

My first site visit was to the newspaper to look for indications anyone had seen my advertisement. My ad appeared as I had placed it, and I scanned for anything which might be a response. Shazbot! I can't say I honestly expected otherwise, though a reply would have set my mind at ease.

Where are you, Petchy? Maybe later.

Next, it became tricky. I must check my email, and I dare not access it from a fixed location. If the MiBs are watching, I'm confident they are, that would lead them straight to us! They'd identify my IP address and, in turn, Phil's Internet account, and from that, it would require mere seconds to find us.

I needed obfuscation.

Fortunately, I know a thing or two about obfuscation on the Internet. If logging into my email was sure to trigger alarms back at MiB HQ, I could not stop it. However, I can minimize their chances of tracing the connection to this computer in this house. I can make their task tremendously challenging. Indeed, any savvy networker has one or two tricks up their sleeves. This 'savvy networker' invented a few of those tricks.

I'm a savvy network security professional! I have spent my professional life with tools and technologies with cryptic names, from BIOS to Barnfire, PassionatePolka to Stuxnet. So I know where the hidden bones of the network are and how to make them dance the Polka!

I'm also modest and self-deprecating.

In the 1990s, a mathematician and a couple of scientists with the US Naval Research Lab developed something they named "Onion Routing." Based on a multilayered approach to security and encryption superficially resembling the layers of an onion, they designed the concept to protect US Intelligence. In 1997 DARPA took over the project and continued developing the technology. The NSA rightly called it the "King of Internet Anonymity."

Originally known as "The Onion Router," it escaped the exclusive control of the US Government, is now known as TOR, and is used by anyone, hero and villain alike, who seeks privacy and anonymity on the Internet. It's also widely and loudly despised by those vociferously opposed to Internet privacy and anonymity.

Such as, ironically, the US Government!

I won't claim it's invulnerable, although I have never found a reliable way to crack it, and I'm reasonably skilled; I want to meet the hacker who can successfully penetrate it.

I installed the TOR browser and checked it over, blocking all known vulnerabilities. Then, set to appear as if my traffic were coming from Mexico, I logged into my email account. It wouldn't serve to stay on long, so rather than read the email online, I downloaded it all quickly and logged off. Though TOR is secure, I didn't intend to allow the MiBs time to play.

I checked the emails. Nothing helpful, nothing of consequence. Until the last one! I did not immediately recognize the sender, deleted it unread, followed moments later by a quick retrieval when I realized the sender might be Jill.

Plain and terse, the message merely read, "All a giant misunderstanding, please come home."

I considered the message for a while, pondering if there could be a hidden meaning I was missing. I crafted a reply and discarded it several times, finally just wrote, "Apologies. I hope you and the boys enjoyed the Pizza. We understood perfectly. Armed men lying in wait send a clear message."

Anonymously sending email is significantly easier than retrieving it. Moreover, email can originate from almost anywhere, especially if one knows a few insecure mail bots on the Internet. Accordingly, a few minutes later, a compromised computer in Kazakhstan disgorged a message to Jill with my answer.

I returned to the newspaper site and, again using TOR, posted a new ad replacing my previous one. If my off-world connections were to rescue us, I needed to reach them, and soon.

I posted the following:

Are you Petchy?

This is for you!

Things are too hot

Open a door, ASAP.

I had no clue whether I might expect rescue from that quarter, and I was running out of options rapidly! I rechecked the email and found a response from Jill. Just a phone number. No comment, no plea to call, only a phone number.

Now what?

Do I trust her? Was she on my side after all? Do I dare call her? If I call her, what could she possibly say to convince me she's my ally? What test of her loyalty would be worth anything?

I certainly needed a supporter on my side. As long as my friends are present on Earth, we're in danger. The only absolute safety lies off-planet, so I need assistance from Petch or his organization.

Still considering Jill's message and phone number, I debated for a long time whether to call. Though I thoroughly understand they would almost instantly trace a call from a regular telephone, I felt tempted. I knew a few tricks which should tilt the odds in my favor, ways to call that were much more difficult to trace, yet it's a risk I dared not assume. Without a clear path to resolution, I decided I could not risk it, although, to be fair, I felt torn. I believed I could trust Jill; at least my every instinct, my 'spidey-sense' as I often refer to my subtle instincts, believes in her. I'm deeply conflicted. I needed an ally, and my sensibilities tended in her favor, yet I couldn't test her motives or loyalties.

I pondered the conundrum. I needed an ally, unquestionably. But, on the other hand, if I trusted Jill and she betrayed us, it would be difficult to recover from the mistake — I have no wish to be confined, to be in Alex's clutches.

Finally, I logged back into the TOR network and placed a VoIP call. Respected 'experts' in the field will insist voice via a TOR connection is impossible. I said I knew a few tricks. Those 'experts' were not aware of the TORFone. Originating a call, apparently from Kansas, via a clandestine TOR – VoIP gateway, I dialed Jill's number.

Jill answered on the first ring.

"Is this line secure? Or are we being monitored?" Exasperation leaked into her voice, "No one's listening. Why did you run?"

I pondered the question a moment. Was it possible Jill honestly was unaware? Finally, I responded, "Alex and several armed men were around my apartment. I assumed they were lying in wait to grab us. I have no wish to be sequestered in a windowless room in a dank government facility basement, and neither do my friends. Alex betrayed us; I opted to run before they could close their trap. Would you expect to tell me that wasn't the case?"

"I won't claim it was not the case. But I will insist that I knew nothing of it if it was. Will you believe me?"

"I would prefer to believe you were unaware, yet how can I afford to trust you? What could you possibly say to suggest you're not just trying to help them find us?"

"Fitz, I won't lie; I do want to help them find you, not because I want to entrap or harm you, but because I want to make sure your fears are groundless and that you can come back home safely and remain free. I do not want my organization to threaten you or anyone. There is a terrible misunderstanding. We mean you no harm and want to help you. You have opened up a larger universe and remain our best hope to understand it. Harming you or your charges helps no one."

"What do you propose then, Jill?"

"Give me an hour to work on it. Will you call back in an hour and perhaps talk to Alex himself?"

"Okay, one hour." I hung up.

My hands shook as I ended the TOR session. I didn't THINK Alex's tech people could track that, I wasn't aware of any way to do so, and if I couldn't, it's a safe bet they can't either. Still, I worried!

Late afternoon was upon us, and my ladies had not yet eaten. I rummaged through our host's sparse larder and found a couple of cans of soup. Quick heat and stir, and lunch, of sorts, was served. It would tide us over for the moment, though we would need to search out a decent meal soon.

Shortly, I again fired up the TORFone and placed the promised call, and as before, Jill answered on the first ring.

"Status?" I asked. "Negative," came the response. "I'm sorry, Fitz, they want to bring the alien women in, place you and the ladies into protective custody for your protection. Alex fears for your safety and the Aliens. He wants to convince you to come in peaceably."

My rancor surged at her words! Fear and anger converged in a fierce determination to have nothing to do with their plans. Why can't these people leave us alone? Pushing a modicum of calm upstream against the current of my anger, I asked, "Is Alex there?" She responded, "Yes, he wants to speak with you." I replied, "Put him on."

I could hear her handing him the phone. "Fitz, buddy, where are you?" I ignored the question. "Alex, I thought you claimed to be my friend! No one has committed a crime, made no threats, yet you want to lock us up. Why?"

His voice turned dark and somber, "Fitz, there's more at stake than you know. There is much you don't know that I must tell you face to face. You must understand my position, there are more and bigger threats you don't know about, and I cannot let the aliens remain free. We don't understand everything happening and what these people are doing. So I need to protect you and them."

Protect us, my clavicle! He wants the girls, under his thumb, to be examined and treated like lab animals. So intolerable! I exploded, "You've seen too many 'B' movies! I understand these people much better than I do you, and I know who I can trust and who I can't. I'm disappointed at your betrayal. You could have had full access to them, to my knowledge, and, if you had been reasonable, full access to everything we know. I cannot let you take them into custody and treat them like lab specimens. I'm sorry, but that's how it must be. Goodbye, Alex." I hung up before he could respond.

Again, I found myself shaking, quaking with fear. The entire black-ops force of the US Government was out to capture us, and I had nowhere to run! My friends joined me on the couch, embracing and comforting me as I sat there for long minutes in silence.

We must leave the country, get off-planet even, yet I have no clue how. I needed assistance from Petchey or his associates. I knew Teena had been severely wounded, at a minimum, and quite probably had died. Petch had also received a few nasty wounds, although nothing had indicated his injuries were seriously life-threatening, to the best of my knowledge. Yet, somebody had absconded with them or their remains and cleaned up all records of their presence. That party must still be around, I desperately hoped, yet how could I contact them?

After a while, I decided to recheck my Guardian ad and download the mailbox again. Once again, TOR browsed safely to both sites. There was nothing noteworthy at the Guardian site, and other than the assorted spam, there were two emails of note. One merely contained a phone number. Jill, perhaps, trying to reach out yet again? I decided not to call it right away, tabling it for the moment.

The other email came from Julie. Strangely, she merely wished us a pleasant trip. I wondered what that meant; she had not used any of the code words I had given her. That by itself seemed to suggest she had heard nothing from Alex's people. Dare I hope they had not noticed my recent dates with her? Or at least discounted our relationship?

Had they connected Julie to me, was she in danger? Did I dare risk calling her? If I continue using the TORFone, they will figure out a way to trace it sooner or later. If she's not on their radar, it would be no harm to call her. But, if they're monitoring her, I would be giving them another bite at the apple. How many nibbles could I afford?

After further thought, I decided to risk an email. "Having a wonderful time, wish you were here. See you soon." The code phrase 'having a wonderful time' should tell her, essentially, not to talk to strangers and to trust me.

The mysterious phone number bothered me. Was Jill trying again? The number's different. Was she calling clandestinely from another phone to say she's on my side after all? Or might it be another agent or someone else seeking to support or capture us? It seemed unlikely, although I decided I must check it out.

I agonized over it for a while. I'm frightened to call again from here, even using the TORFone. I didn't believe they could trace it, but these people scare me, and I'm not inclined to take chances. I'm not the arrogant 'Dread Pirate,' I know many ways to penetrate anonymity. Staying untraced means less of how creative I can be at hiding and more of simply not giving them opportunities to trace my activities. There must be a thousand ways to accidentally tip one's hand, as the 'Silk Road Mastermind' learned to his chagrin.

While considering ways to obfuscate our location further, I remembered this community had a free community WIFI service. So, looking out the front window, I confirmed that indeed there was a WIFI antenna on the lamp post across the street. That should bring a slight amount of additional anonymity.

My host's older desktop, firmly anchored to a hardwired Ethernet cable and tied into an ancient DSL modem, has a fixed IP address. I needed WIFI to connect to the municipal network. This machine, antique though it may be, was of a vintage that should have WIFI built-in, and a quick check confirms the assumption. Unfortunately, Phil never configured it. The lack presented only a modest difficulty, though I needed to download a proper driver for it.

Twenty minutes later, I disconnected the Ethernet connection and connected to the civic WIFI signal. TORFone online, I placed the call, half-expecting Jill to answer. Instead, a male voice answered.

"Who is this?" I asked.

He replied, "Fitz, It's Matt!"

Fifth Column

"Why?" I asked.

"Fifth Column," came the reply. "Deep cover. Your situation warants extraordinary action. I didn't intend to reveal myself, but we need to get you off-world."

"Why should I believe I can trust you?" It made a certain sense Petchy's people would have somebody embedded within the organization. It also made sense Matt could be executing a ruse at the behest of Alex, hoping I might fall for it.

"I don't know. I have no credentials, nothing to support any claim." came the response. I stated, "I need a password, something only an operative of the 'Planet K' people could know or something about "Planet Oz" which only one who had been there could provide."

"I have never been to "Planet Oz" and have never met Petchy. I'm just a local low-level operative tasked with only being an observer here, serving as eyes and ears, gathering information. So I know almost nothing of the larger war. I got a great deal of that from your book."

"Then I see no way I can trust you. Can you send word to Petch? Or Teena?"

"Off-world communications is difficult and tricky. I sent an emergency message as soon as the first poor unfortunate girl came into our morgue. It may take several weeks yet before I can expect a response. Typically, briefings and serious communications occur face-to-face at quarterly intervals. Otherwise, I can only send blind messages via dead-drop."

"Can you provide us with access to a portal, somewhere safer than here?"

"Unfortunately, no. I'm not able to travel off-world. You must understand technological acumen is compartmentalized. No one permanently stationed on Earth may possess off-world skills which they might leak."

It made a particular sort of sense, I supposed. "Then what are you able to do for us?"

He answered, "I must be meticulous not to compromise my cover. So I cannot do anything except pass information and such limited support as I can and connect you with your extraction team when they arrive. My purpose in contacting you was to let you know you are not completely alone, but even so, you are in real danger. Are you secure for the moment?"

"We're secure for the moment," I admitted. "but cannot stay put long."

"Call this number tomorrow at the same time." and with that, he hung up. I quickly disconnected from the city WiFi signal and watched the street for a while for unusual traffic.

I pondered what I had learned. Assuming Matt wasn't just a puppet of Alex, he probably functioned as a classic deep cover operative of the sort one reads about in spy novels. Such operations are typical in covert circles, at least in fiction. Matt likely only had one communications channel, and that was probably via a form of 'dead-drop' whereby he never, in fact, met or spoke with anyone. It's highly doubtful he even knew the others in his cell or any other operative.

I am no expert at this level of spy-craft, but security was my profession, and I had read enough to understand the generalities. Just enough to lead me to fret about Matt's position.

The term "Fifth Column" comes from a Hemingway play and describes a group of covert supporters of a foreign invader. It all derives from the Spanish civil war in the 1930s. His use of this terminology gave me pause, as I had no wish to 'overthrow' anything, especially my government. Until Alex's xenophobia and now Matt's curious employment of this semantically loaded term, I had not thought of Petchy's people as invaders. I had just taken them at face value, as an advanced society fighting a war of survival against a terrible force. Why they had been secretive and not revealed their presence to Earth raised questions I had not considered in depth. I have not thought of them as invaders of any sort until this moment.

I hope Earth's society can openly join the broader community of humanity and spread throughout the galaxy. As I ruminated on these ideas, I told myself that the other worlds did not wish to invade or harm us. Or so I believed. I wasn't a traitor despite whatever Alex's xenophobic ideas might be. I'm certain. I think. Was it possible Matt is not what he claims? The use of a loaded term such as "*Fifth Column*" seems much more like something Alex would say than Petch or Teena.

Or perhaps Matt does represent an alien fifth column, which causes me to reconsider how I have thought of Petchy and his people.

Such fifth-column cells consist of a small number of people, typically three, with only the leader knowing the others. People at this level are generally referred to as '*assets*,' not agents, and are kept purposefully ignorant. I laughed silently at the thought that it could be barely possible both Matt and Jill were fellow fifth columnists in the same clandestine cell, each completely unaware of the other. Occasionally assets were husband and wife couples. Each watched the organization under scrutiny reported anything anomalous up the chain of command. They communicate with their handlers by various secret methods, dead-drops, and similar.

Often, the person who recruits the asset is the only person in the organization they ever meet. Should they become compromised, they risk no one else, as they know no one else! The only person they could betray was their handler, and they often had little knowledge about them. Even when situations call for them to meet and work with others, they rarely learn their actual identity, name, or other information about them. They're merely shadowy figures united in a common cause.

I had seen hints a clandestine organization existed when I'd been in the hospital after returning to Earth. The 'lawyer' who had visited my hospital room presumably was a local asset, not knowledgeable of the larger organization. He seemingly had a task of limited scope and possessed little information. I wondered how many such operatives were on Earth and what their real mission might be.

I wondered again about Jill and where her loyalties lay. I debated calling her once more, decided the risk outweighed any possible reward.

Reconnecting to my host's Internet and again using TOR, I rechecked email, finding nothing important. Time to go offline for the day and stop risking being traced.

Shutting down Phil's aging desktop, I turned my attention to my ladies. They had been taking in the day's events with wide-eyed wonder, not equipped to understand what was happening, but trusting me implicitly.

When I shut down the computer and pushed back from the desk, they came and put their arms around me, sensing that the day's stress and worries are now tabled, as we relaxed a little and rested ourselves. We cuddled and snuggled for a bit, basking in the moment's intimacy.

After a while, Stapleya broke our silence. "Alex is not our friend?" I pulled back slightly from her, "Maybe," I said, "or not." I shrugged. "I worry that dark suspicions might drive him, that he's insecure and retreats to a position of fear when he sees something he doesn't understand. He thinks we're a threat to his world and would lock us up, or worse, in panic."

"What of the others?" She wanted to know. "Are they also fearful?" I grimaced a bit and gave a slight shrug. "I believe Jill's a good person and might help us but wooing her away from long-established loyalties to the agency – and Alex – seems difficult. Matt said he is on our side and will help us, but I suspect it's an act that he's pretending, to draw us from hiding."

"Then we must not trust either of them," She stated matter-of-factly. "Where are Petchy and Teena, and why don't they help us?" She must have sensed my body language when she mentioned Teena. "Has something happened to them?"

I shook my head. "I don't know. Unfortunately, both Petchy and Teena sustained serious injuries. Teena was injured quite badly, Petch not as badly. I also sustained some wounds, though my injuries were relatively minor. I became separated from Petchy and Teena in the hospital. I don't know what happened to them, I've been trying to find out, yet thus far, I have failed."

Her face fell at this. I knew she and Petchy had long been close friends. I didn't wish to be the one to tell her he was dead, and though I would like to believe he's alive and healthy, I'm unable to offer positive reassurance.

"Petchy has visited my people since before my mother's birth, always welcomed and loved. Teena, we don't know as well, though she too we always welcomed and loved on her visits."

We hugged a few moments longer. I answered, "Petchy and Teena have many friends who worked with them and helped in the quest. I'm hoping to contact somebody who can help us. It will require time, and we must hide and stay safe. Although he doesn't know we are using it, the man who owns this house is a friend. We cannot stay here long.

"We need to eat, and my friend doesn't have much food. So I need to go and buy supplies. Are you comfortable staying here alone for a little while?"

They both nodded.

Donning clothes and grabbing my wallet, I headed out of the house and down the street, jogging to the small shopping center I had noted just over a mile away. I purchased a few essentials, including fresh meat. From my time on Planet Oz, I know the ladies would especially love bacon and sausage, so I bought an ample quantity, along with flour and other staples.

Unfortunately, I didn't have the appropriate government-mandated reusable fabric grocery bag to carry my purchases home. Therefore I must pay a penalty fee to purchase a couple of government-approved paper bags, a minor nit, one additional annoyance in my mind's ledger tallying life on my "Planet Oz" against that in California.

Leaving the store with my purchases, I chafed that the time required to prepare a meal from fresh staples made for an annoying delay. Then, I noticed a Pizza Palace immediately next door and remembered my unkept earlier promise of Pizza. So, on impulse, I executed a sharp right into the den of cheese and ordered a pair of large platters well-populated with bacon, sausage, and other assorted meats and trimmings. I paid for the purchase, gave the address, and asked that they deliver as soon as possible.

I had hoped that, with luck, the Pizza would arrive soon after I did, and I wasn't disappointed. The brisk walk home passed uneventfully, except that the government-sanctioned paper bag split as I stepped onto the porch, nearly dumping my groceries. Fortunately, I barely managed to hang onto the goods, thanks to a bit of help. I struggled to juggle everything, fighting a losing action, when another pair of hands came to my rescue.

Stapleya had been watching for my return. On seeing my struggles with the paper bag, she ran out onto the porch to assist. I handed her a few items, and then looking around to check whether potential observers were in sight, I quickly urged her back inside. I hoped that a distant observer might mistake her fur for clothing. I silently wondered whether being recognized as nude or outed as a fur-bearing human might be less traumatic.

Carrying the foodstuffs into the kitchen, I noted that the ladies had given Phil's messy kitchen an exquisitely thorough cleaning in my absence. I smiled and stifled a silent laugh as I imagined how some of my friends in the City by the Bay would react to this scene. Some would undoubtedly invoke *The Stepford Wives* as if the act of cleaning the space where one was about to prepare food is somehow being robotically submissive.

Anyone who might bring forth such a metaphor doesn't understand these people. The fur-people are tenaciously clean and fastidious, and I'm sure they would have reacted strongly to the idea of preparing food in a kitchen as mucky as this one had been. Equating cleanliness with robotic submissiveness is something that only a narrow, mind-numbed cultural outlook could even conceive. The fur-people are many things, but submissive is not one.

Prima facie evidence of spiritless servility or not, the sink and countertop and the table were sparkling, ready for food prep. I thanked them for their efforts with a slow, intimate hug and proceeded to put the meats and other goods away.

We had barely deposited the groceries in the kitchen when a car in the driveway signaled the arrival of cheesy delight. Motioning the ladies out of sight, I opened the door and received the bounty, giving the delivery driver a generous tip. She seemed to be trying to gaze past me into the house, although I was uncertain.

I began worrying anew. Too late, it occurred to my feeble thought process that I was once again a brainless boob! Worse, a triple-plated bumbler! Being so conveniently located, my friend Phil might be well-known at the Pizza Palace, and a delivery to his address when he's known to be out of town might not pass unnoticed. Kicking myself, I worried the delivery driver, not seeing Phil, might even now be calling the cops! What an idiot! We had no vehicle, no way to run, or anywhere to go!

I didn't share my worries with the ladies immediately, letting them relax and enjoy the Pizza. It was a tremendous hit! Troubles on my mind, I only ate three slices, and they devoured the rest! The risks aside, Pizza had been an inspired choice! They loved it!

I remained distraught, though at a loss as to what course of action I could pursue. I booted up Phil's ancient computer once again and checked my Guardian message drop and email. Nada! Not a hint of aid or even of pursuit. Zip, swabo, and nit!

A couple of hours passed, and nothing happened. I began to relax slightly. Nevertheless, I remained helplessly fearful, though beginning to believe we might skate by — perhaps I was paranoid for nothing. I had undoubtedly committed a boneheaded move, one which could have compromised us but so far, no damage. Nonetheless, I kept looking out the windows, watching for signs of black SUVs or anyone observing the house.

I could not judge how much support Alex could bring to bear in his manhunt. I believed he was acting rogue, tapping only the resources directly under his command. We were sunk if he could muster the full power of government behind his witch-hunt. I suspect crying 'Alien Invaders' wasn't likely to win him support from his superiors. If the total resources of the government were behind him, I believed he would have already captured us. The fact we were still free in the face of my continuing ineptitude argues Alex and a few of his people were the only ones looking for us.

I resolved to pick up Julie's car early tomorrow and get us moving anywhere. I was entirely unsure where to go. Who else do I know who I could impose on? So, I ensconced myself conveniently near the window, watching for signs of trouble and thinking, planning what to do next.

It was near midnight, and I was still contemplating our situation. Near midnight and I had no intention of sleeping. I was doing my damnedest to keep watch, trying to decide my next move. I was sitting in the dark, looking out the window for the slightest hint of government surveillance or movement for at least the ten-thousandth time, when a familiar beep-booo-beep sound echoed from the bedroom, which served as a computer den.

Damn! I had left the computer on and had forgotten all about Skype! I'd been so careful disabling the remote desktop and related software that might give away online my use of the computer and had ignored Skype. For the second time today, I was a total boob! Someone's calling Phil via Skype!

I ran into the bedroom, intending to shut the machine down immediately, and on seeing the name displayed on the incoming call dialog, my mouth fell open. A moment's hesitation, then I reversed course and answered the call.

"Hello Fitz, is that you?"

"Hello, P-Phil," I responded, with a lump in my throat.

Skyped!

"S-sorry to intrude on your h-home this way, but I'm in a terrible quandary!" I began, almost stuttering.

"Mi casa es su casa. Don't worry about it. I have been trying to find you for hours; I find you right under my nose! Couldn't have worked out better."

Befuddled and disconcerted, I enabled the camera as his was already on. From his reaction, I must have appeared as stunned and discombobulated as I was. His eyes widened momentarily, "Fitz, old buddy, you always did have an instinct for trouble without the good sense to run the other way." Then he leaned in close to the screen, "Relax," he said, lowering his voice conspiratorially, "I'm your rescue. They sent me to help you."

What did he mean by that? Matt had said he was the fifth column. Had he been lying? Can I trust Phil? I must have stood there for several seconds with a stupid expression on my face as I considered the possibilities. To the best of my knowledge, Phil had no connection to Alex's highly intimidating organization or my off-world adventures. As I slowly processed the data before me and concluded that trusting him was the more attractive option, I suppose Phil grew tired of watching the figurative wheels spinning in my head and intruded on my sluggish mental processing.

"Fitz!" he spoke loudly and firmly, "Pull it together; what's your situation?" Then, biting my lip sharply to draw my focus back to the physical world, I finally regained control. "As you can tell, I have invaded your home. I'm hiding from the government with the ladies from Planet Oz. I do not believe the government forces suspect our present location, though I suppose I foolishly tipped my hand at the Pizza Palace. Is that how you discovered our location?"

As I'd been speaking, Stapleya and Wisceya entered the room, momentarily awed by the visage of Phil on the computer screen. Then Stapleya exclaimed in recognition. In doing so, the girls stepped into range of the camera, giving Phil a view of their furry forms. He didn't bat an eye, shifted to Language effortlessly to greet them as friends!

Small Universe!

Unbeknownst to me, my friend of several decades had also been to "Planet Oz" and knew Language! And Stapleya knew HIM, although not by the name I knew. So I was puzzled momentarily by the subterfuge of an alternative name, my mind hanging up on that detail for a moment before I pushed it aside and moved forward.

It turned out he too had been one of Teena's heroes, her chosen talent for interplanetary machinations, though not for the quest I pursued, instead, another mission, which we did not then discuss. I was curious about that, but we had other more pressing matters. After his mission, he returned secretly to Earth and now functions as a member of the fifth column organization Matt had suggested existed! Except in Matt's case, it seemed a ruse on behalf of Alex, though Phil was well able to authenticate himself, not the least of which by knowing Language! And Stapleya vouched for him! Recommendations don't come stronger.

"Listen, Fitz, I would love to chat, but there's work ahead, let's use something a bit more secure. I doubt your pursuers would be monitoring MY Skype, but Skype isn't very secure in the best of times. So let's not use it again. Stay put in my house, maintain a low profile and check your email via TOR for instructions. Write down this key; you will need it to decrypt messages." He recited a string of numbers and letters to serve as a security key. I reciprocated, giving him my key. "We will employ steganography and public-key cryptography for all future communications. Disable Skype immediately! Check for Drafts! Good luck!"

With that, he signed off, and I immediately exited Skype! I opened the services control panel and disabled the underlying Skype service, and removed the application from the autostart folder. I bet I won't make that mistake again! While poking around in the system, I examined it for anything else I might have overlooked and then shut the computer down.

We had agreed to communicate further using email. We would, of course, use TOR to keep sending and receiving identities and locations secure, but that was not enough. I'm sure the MiBs are watching the email since Alex's people had used it — that they can read my messages is probable.

We had agreed to employ 'Public Key Cryptography' to ensure our messages remain private. Those who need to share secret messages have two complementary needs: encryption and authentication. You need to be able to encrypt your data so that only the intended recipient can read it, and you also need to authenticate that the claimed sender is, in fact, the author and that the message is intact.

These are two distinct yet complementary needs. So, unless you can ensure you're doing both correctly, your communications can be subject to a weakness known as the 'Man in the Middle Attack.' Such attackers place themselves between two parties and pretend to be the other to each party, all the while intercepting the secret communications freely.

In Public Key Cryptography, every participant has two keys. Their public key, which they reveal to the other party or even the general public, and their private key, kept secret, known only to the sender. You freely share the public key, hence the name, making it available to almost anyone in general usage. In our specific situation, we only share it with the other party. Nonetheless, it's still considered 'public' because multiple people know it, even if only the sender and receiver.

Confidential communications can be a complicated topic. Nonetheless, the general idea remains simple. One party writes a document and encrypts it with their private key. Anyone who has the author's public key can later decrypt it and confidently KNOW beyond doubt that it came from the claimed sender and is unaltered.

This dual-key approach accomplishes the authentication function and is perfectly fine as far as it goes. Alone, it does not keep anything secret since the public key used to decrypt the data is not itself a secret, presumably widely available. Anyone with access to the public key can use it freely and read the message. Authentication, certifying the person claimed authored something and that it's not altered, is a valuable service, even though the result is that anyone with the public key may read the data. You effectively have authentication without having trustworthy encryption.

On the other hand, if you intend ONLY ONE person to read it and no one else, encrypt it with THEIR Public Key. Now only their private key will decrypt it. The public key cannot decrypt it — it's a one-way process! Once encoded, it's locked until the intended recipient unlocks it. Your secret makes it to their eyes and only their eyes. That sounds wonderful, but how might they verify it indeed came from you? You have encryption without authentication. After all, everyone potentially has your Public Key, and without authentication, anyone could encrypt a file and claim it came from you.

The solution to that problem lies in a double-whammy using both keys. The sender encrypts the file with both the recipient's public key and the sender's private key, producing a file that only the intended recipient can read and that only the sender could have originated. Anyone else can neither authenticate nor decrypt it. Thus you have both authentication and encryption, reliable and secure.

That's the process we proposed to employ. The MiBs might still detect that we exchanged a message, though not its contents or the locations of its senders.

Even with public-key cryptography, each time we communicate presents an exposure, a risk of detection. Additionally, although the MiBs cannot read our message, they can still learn things from the simple fact of the exchange. Therefore, minimizing the opportunities for the MiBs to find us is still a serious concern.

Once I had signed off with Phil and de-Skypified the machine, I relaxed. I no longer worried that at any moment, a team of MiB thugs might be kicking down the door and hauling us off to prison. Not right away, anyway; we had a little breather. I still didn't know what Phil had in mind or how we might get away; at least we had safely contacted the fifth column if that's what they were. I still didn't buy the idea Petchy's people were looking to 'overthrow' anything on Earth. Phil's contact was welcome, but I remained cautious.

With the pressure off, the ladies and I retired for the evening. Snuggled with my furry friends and the weight of espionage temporarily lifted, I slept more peacefully than I had slept in several days, although interrupted several times most pleasantly. I thought again of Lolita, my son with her, and Teena. I am very much pleased to be here and now with my lusty furry friends, at peace, for the moment at least.

Breakfast

The summer sun rode high in the sky when we roused from our slumber. The day before had been demanding and stressful, and we had been late to retire. Nonetheless, it was not precisely late in the day when we awoke. We had too much in the works to be lollygagging!

The previous day had been long and stressful, and too many hours have elapsed since the last of those heavenly Pizza Palace slices disappeared. Consequently, we were once again famished.

Fortunately, I had just the magic incantation for that condition standing by, in the form of freshly procured comestibles and, thanks to the efforts of my companions, a sparkling clean cookery in which to perform my enchantment. But, of course, I love to cook, especially when I have an appreciative guest to please and the time to work my magic. So I took the liberty to indulge in a variation on my retro favorite, the classic southern-style biscuits, and gravy breakfast.

I conjured a batch of my infamous 'muddy creek' biscuit dough for my grand production, a variation on the traditional southern style biscuit recipe made with dark whole-grain flour instead of the traditional white variety. In addition, I flavored my dough with a touch of heavenly bacon drippings. Said critical flavor ingredient must be first derived from my warm-up act, skillfully frying a couple of pounds of old-fashioned smoke-cured bacon to a perfectly exquisite state of crispness. That's a bit of conjuration, as getting bacon appropriately crisped is an art form. I followed this bit of legerdemain by grilling up a pound of spicy sausage, the drippings of which magically transformed into a magnificent skillet of southern-style white gravy, rendered just a touch off-white by the whole-grain flour.

My hypothetical grandmother would doubtlessly have expressed her displeasure at the off-white character of my masterpiece. The cooks of her generation expected such foods to be flawlessly white. On the other hand, I prefer the heartier flavor and healthier constitution of whole grains. Fortunately, my guests had no such grandmother as I imagine and aren't inclined to be critical.

As the gravy coalesced under my flying fingers, a melodic ding echoed off the tiled kitchen surfaces and the plat de résistance; my magic biscuits arose fluffy and warm from the oven perfectly on cue.

So we indulged ourselves in a luxurious, leisurely breakfast feast, replete with perfectly crisped bacon, perfectly hard-boiled eggs, spicy-hot sausage, with not-so-white gravy and biscuits, savoring every morsel. After eating our fill, I wrapped leftover biscuits and sweet pork meats in foil for later, as a traditional 'Meat Biscuit;' handy when the day's exertions inevitably bring forth midday pangs.

On "Planet Oz," high-calorie meals of such a nature are standard and routine as their stone-age lifestyle is intensely physically demanding. Burning thousands of calories per day is the norm in that brutal world. Not so much here in my pampered, civilized society; I cannot often afford to indulge in such extravagance. My thrice-weekly addiction to intensive workouts at the local gym offsets the rare occasions when I do. Unfortunately, my friends and I have been far too sedentary the last few days; not a sustainable trend. Remarking on the topic while cleaning up and washing the dishes, I observed that we risked getting fat from continued meals of this nature. They are always ready with helpful solutions to any problem, no matter how intractable. They both chimed in and quickly suggested a few vigorous activities by which we should endeavor to burn a few calories.

An hour later, it was approaching noon when I once again turned my attention to our precarious situation. I felt immensely better for momentarily having our worries abated by Phil's promise of support, but we were still not without a rash of serious concerns.

Our most urgent priority was Julie's car. I must retrieve it, and I need to hide it, lest our pursuers find it. Leaving it at the tire store would not do. Sooner or later, it would likely come to the attention of the MiBs, and even if it didn't lead them directly to us, it risked involving Julie in our conspiracy. That was simply unacceptable! Besides, we might need wheels soon. I went into Phil's garage and surveyed the situation. Like so many living in the Bay Area, lacking genuinely harsh weather to encourage keeping cars sheltered, his garage had transformed into a de facto storage warehouse. There's just no room to add a vehicle.

The garage was adjacent to the house's third bedroom, which likewise has been consumed by clutter. Suppressing criticism of my friend's packrat nature, I examined the space to determine whether I might rearrange the mess enough to make space for the car. I decided it was barely possible, although it would require significant effort. But, of course, Phil was going to hate me for this!

The girls and I spent the next three hours picking, carrying, moving, and shoving. We would often execute a little touch and squeeze as we passed each other in our movements. One must enjoy one's work. Right? The vigorous work and equally energetic diversions helped justify our breakfast excesses and harmed nothing. After all, staying fit ranks high on the scale of life's necessities.

After our efforts, we had moved and rearranged enough of Phil's hodgepodge to be able, barely, to fit a single compact car into the two-car garage. It would do! The overflow filled the third bedroom, threatened to block the hall, and intruded into the master bedroom and living room. Yeah, Phil will not be pleased!

Mission accomplished, I dressed and headed to the tire store, making a brisk jog. I could, of course, run much faster and be at the store in mere minutes, but that would call unwanted attention to myself. So instead, I considered various ways I could further blend into the world around me and avoid attracting attention.

A city bus passed me, stopping at a bus stop along my route. For a moment, I considered taking the bus for a few blocks but decided against it. Too public, or so I feared.

A few blocks away from my intended destination, I noticed a taxicab in a parking lot. Its driver seems currently out of service, apparently taking his lunch break at a convenience store. It occurred to me that given my cover story of an overnight flight, arriving at the tire store in a taxi rather than walking from the nearby neighborhood was more consistent, less likely noticed or remembered. I was slowly learning to be much more careful with the details!

I approached the driver and asked if he wanted a fare. He paused while devouring his sandwich and stated that he was 'out of service' and wanted to eat his lunch, asking if I could wait a few minutes, and offered to call another cab if not. I pulled out a Franklin and asked if he would like to earn a quick yard off the books. He appeared conflicted for a moment. I pointed out that he was off-duty for another twenty minutes and thus not suspected of turning off his meter, and besides, I only wanted an anonymous ride a couple of blocks. Waving the currency before his face, I watched the conflict unfold as the wheels turned invisibly in his head.

I knew that he could lose his job if caught taking an off-the-books fare. But, on the other hand, the risk was minuscule, and he probably needed the money. So, moments later, the sandwich lay uneaten in the front seat, and I had engaged a taxi for the brief ride to the tire store. I made a point of having the driver make a virtual theatrical production of pulling up, blocking their roll-up doors for a moment as I fumbled with payment, etc., to complete the illusion of having just come from the airport. Most excellent!

The manager instantly met me as I entered the store, observing my arrival precisely as intended. He pulled out the fob to Julie's car and presented me with a form to sign. I scribbled a quick illegible doodle and thanked him, and headed outside to the vehicle. A quick visual once-over ensured all was well; I noted the much healthier-looking tread gracing the circumferences, then jumped into the car and drove away. I congratulated myself on successfully behaving much more clandestine today.

I had asked the ladies to watch for me and open the garage door quickly when I drove up. Sure enough, I had barely turned onto the block, not even reached the driveway when the door began to move. I pulled in, and the door immediately closed. Whew! I had the car safely hidden in Phil's garage and do not think anyone noticed. I hoped.

Rushing inside, I again hugged my ladies as I shed my street clothing. Adventure successfully concluded, I grabbed a handy 'Meat Biscuit' as a reward. So far, today had been a good day, and I was getting the hang of this secretive behavior, or so it seemed.

After a brief respite, I again fired up Phil's aging desktop and, taking every possible precaution, checked my email. At first glance, there was nothing from Phil. So I quickly downloaded the entire inbox, spam included and logged off.

Once I verified the computer was offline, I opened the downloaded email and examined the individual messages. When I realized there was nothing overtly from Phil, I recognized that he would likely not risk compromising his identity by sending me an email in his name. I chastised myself for even thinking he might have been that foolish. I felt silly for even looking for anything bearing his name. I seem to excessively indulge in self-flagellation as I flail away at playing hero.

I remembered his closing remarks, suggesting public-key cryptography and steganography. I had not immediately picked up on that! But, again, I'm an idiot! This adventure is taking its toll on my ego. I can only plead that I'm still a bit of a novice. Hiding from MiBs is a skill and, as such, requires practice.

Steganography is a technique of hiding data in plain sight. It takes many forms, but the most common type is to hide a message inside an image. A digital image contains tons of data; adding a bit more inside an image file should pass utterly unnoticed unless you know the dark arts of spycraft.

I started examining the messages I had downloaded for images. After a brief run-through, one stood out. At first glance, it was merely a typical spam message for a male enhancement product. Pointedly, it was precisely the type of message that my ISP's spam filters should have trapped, but it had made its way to my inbox nonetheless. Of course, that itself is not so unusual. Some vermin sneak through on occasion, despite the ISP's best efforts. What caught my eye, however, was the model in the ad. The sexy model selling me blue pills I do not need was Teena!

Well, not exactly. It was not an actual photo of Athena herself. But it was her in the essential particulars: the taut, muscular runner's build, the voluptuous mammalian curves, and the long red hair. I paused for just a moment and savored the image, wondering whether my lost beloved was alive.

This spam had to be the message I sought — it must have hidden data. I wasted a few moments inspecting the metadata first. The trivial bits were routine; resolution, encoding format, color palette, and other technical tidbits. Unfortunately, someone had scrubbed all metadata that might identify the actual source of the image. The metadata and the photo itself betrayed apparent signs of the photo editor, but beyond that, there was nothing to discover. No messages resided within the metadata.

I would have been surprised if there had been. Metadata isn't precisely what a techie would think of as hidden. It's visible to anyone who knows where to look. Steganography is much more subtle than that! Poking around on my friend's ancient computer, I discovered he had already installed some capable steganography tools, specifically an open-source tool well respected in secret circles. I had a passing familiarity with such software, but although my field is computers and security, my specialty is networking and data communications. Tradecraft-style secret messaging is a security subset beyond my competency and which I only possess peripheral knowledge. I know barely enough to recognize the tools and their purpose, yet I lack significant experience. So I was slightly surprised by the presence of this software. "What have you been up to, my old friend? What have you been doing to have such tools handy?"

When hiding a message inside an image using these sorts of tools, the first level of protection is a simple password. Without that, you're stuck, unable to confirm the message exists without the password.

I had no clue what the password might be.

I considered it for a few minutes and decided that the password to this file probably would be something we would both know but no one else would. So there were only a few possibilities, namely the cryptographic keys we had exchanged.

I examined the picture using the tool with Phil's public key as the password and immediately hit pay dirt. There was indeed a block of confidential information. It was not, however, readable. Instead, it appeared to be mere gibberish, which it would if encrypted.

I saved the gibberish to a file and, opening the public-key cryptographic tools, which also just happened to be on Phil's computer, applied his public key and my private key together. The cranky old desktop presented a spinning hourglass cursor for a moment and then disgorged a few lines of clear text. I was staring at a message from Phil!

Black SUVs

I felt pleased with our first attempt to communicate secretly. However, given the layers of obfuscation and the tools used, I highly doubted that Alex's organization could intercept it or decrypt it if they did. Moreover, I assume he is, for the moment, acting independently and on the down-low, not pursuing a formal investigation. Hence, he would hesitate to invoke the almost unlimited government resources of computing power and surveillance capabilities that his office could bring to bear. At least not without good cause.

The message wasn't long. It merely congratulated us on finding it and told us to stay put! I should wait two days before going online again, and then I should expect another message with instructions. I was to acknowledge receipt by placing the same fake spam message, minus the steganography insert, into the drafts folder of an email account. His note provided the login credentials for this dropbox. It seems the girls and I had some waiting to do.

It took a moment of thought, though I quickly recognized what he was suggesting here, brilliant in its simplicity and something I would never have thought of by myself. It's dangerous to send emails between my online account, known to the MiBs, and his account, which isn't known but would quickly be at risk once encrypted emails began to fly.

Often when spies monitor email or even postal mail, the actual content of the message is less significant than knowing who's talking to whom. But unfortunately, it is all too easy to track emails. So we won't send any messages anywhere!

Instead of emailing them across the network, we place them in an online hidden location where no one would think to look. Every email service provides an excellent dropbox as a standard practice. All that's needed is an online email mailbox unknown to the MiBs. Thus, we share a login to an account with which neither previously had any known association.

Instead of sending messages, one creates a draft message and places it in the drafts folder. Once the recipient has read it, he deletes the draft. The deletion serves as an acknowledgment to the sending party. If an answer is required, merely place it in the same folder. It is brilliant, straightforward, and difficult for our opponents to detect, as long as they don't know about the secret email account.

This precise method appeared in the news recently in a high-profile case where a high-level military officer, caught up in a clandestine love affair, sought to exchange love notes with his mistress via the drafts folder of an email account. Although, in his case, they didn't encrypt their secret messages, and law enforcement detected him logging into the hidden account via his military computer. Had they used encryption and otherwise taken precautions, I will leave it to the reader to imagine the effect on his scandal. I remembered reading of the case in the tech blogs, seeing him berated for making stupid mistakes, compromising what otherwise was a brilliant plan.

I quickly placed the fake spam email into the indicated drafts folder, shut down the computer, and as an extra precaution, unplugged the broadband modem too. I had already determined I would not be going online again using Phil's broadband connection. The municipal WIFI was just a bit more anonymous — one additional layer in our protection.

My charges and I sat snuggled together on the couch as I struggled to explain to them what was happening — not a simple task. Their minds are already quite boggled by automobiles and computers. Using analogies they could quickly grasp, defining our world's 'MiBs,' and surveillance-state paranoia required some effort. But, on the other hand, they had been incredibly patient, accepting my instructions — orders even — without hesitation, bewildered by the seemingly illogical actions I had taken. I knew they were burning with questions.

We often say that humans are tool-using animals, which is one major factor that separates us from animals. That's undoubtedly true, but I believe it over-simplifies a larger reality, and besides, some animals do use tools, after a fashion. I suggest that tool usage is, in fact, an outgrowth of our ability to spot analogies and relationships in the conditions we seek to influence. Hence, I believe it is more accurate to consider humans as analogy-using animals.

Intelligence in humans, as usually measured, may, instead, be a measure of one's store of analogies to draw upon, not the objective facts one retains. One's local store of facts, while not unimportant, is less significant than one's store of analogies from which to draw new inferences. Facts are the tenterhooks from which analogies hang, but the metaphors allow us to frame, extend, and create knowledge.

As I have often remarked, the fur-people are extremely intelligent, although their society is a simple one. While quite rich in analogies about their rugged and resourceful lifestyle, they lack the necessary parallels to cope with the complexities of my world. I struggled to construct analogies on which to hang the concepts I needed to convey. We worked on the task for several hours, and eventually, I hoped I had at least gotten the basics across. In my struggles to fit complex modern ideas into a series of stone-age metaphors, I learned as much about their society as they did of mine.

Steganography, surprisingly, was a familiar concept. The idea of hiding symbols and codes within an image was something they grasped almost instantly with little explanation. Stapleya pointed out examples of simple yet exquisite paintings on the walls of her castle, drawings, and carvings I had admired innumerable times. She assured me they were rife with hidden symbols and meanings readable by those who know what to look for.

Contrariwise, the concept of a government-sponsored organization such as my 'MiBs' looking over the shoulders of ordinary citizens as they went about their daily business, that analogy I could not find in their world. They barely could grasp the idea of massive government as we practiced it. Their minimalist, matriarchal system was much more sensible in their eyes. Mine too, I had come to realize.

Struggling as I might, I could not adequately explain what might motivate Alex to do what he does; the more I attempted, the less I understood the idea myself. So, in the end, I just assured them it was so and asked them to accept my word for it.

We covered a vast panoply of subjects, from our people's obsession with being clothed to our complete lack of personal weaponry, which to their minds meant archery equipment or at least blades and slings. I struggled to explain firearms and why mainly officials such as Alex and his people carried them and not all citizens. They repeatedly asked how an individual might protect themselves from predators and aggressors, questions for which I could never provide a satisfactory answer. Going about without sensible defense against threats both animal and human, depending entirely on others to come to one's aid in the face of a threat, seemed silly and irresponsible to them.

As we talked, I had intentionally seated myself to easily peer out through the slightly askew Venetian blinds over the large front window. I was sure we were secure in our hiding place, but I remained just nervous enough to want to keep an eye on any traffic that passed by. Our quiet residential street bore little traffic, almost all the residents going about their business.

Suddenly I stiffened with a sharp breath and focused intently on the scene outside. My burgeoning paranoia seemed justified when I spotted an all too familiar shiny black SUV cruising slowly down the quiet residential street!

The vehicle drove slowly as though the driver were looking for a specific address. I could not peer into the car to identify the driver from my limited vantage point, though I assumed it was Alex. I froze in fear, wondering what to do. How on Earth had they found us?

I realized they had not found us even as I asked the question. Not yet anyway, though indeed the MiB were uncomfortably close! I sat watching, holding my breath as they glided past the house in one direction and moments later passed by again, traveling the opposite direction. They were looking at homes and parked cars, it seemed. Thank goodness I had hidden Julie's car!

After two passes, the vehicle did not return. The direction of travel suggested they were moving to the next street over. I surmised that they were systematically sweeping the neighborhood, looking for hints of our hiding place.

Something had exposed us, but what? What did I miss? I was so careful, yet I had made a mistake somewhere along the way that had led them to our neighborhood. What could it be?

In the City, I had worried about the traffic cameras. The marriage of high-resolution cameras and routine, automated facial recognition software had virtually made it impossible for citizens to appear in public without machines tracking their movements. Fortunately, the sheer volume of data was daunting, and it took a motivated effort to make much use of such tracking. Usually, city governments don't have the resources. Alex's organization was another story, a crucial consideration on my walkabout a few days earlier when I had procured my surveillance gear. I had made a determined effort to evade tracking that day, seemingly successfully.

Biometric systems such as the Facial Recognition systems employed by the government are nowhere near as capable as the TV detective shows suggest. Identifying a person from a random security shot and automatically tracking them is difficult. Nonetheless, they're a genuine concern when one's on the lam. If the heat's hunting you seriously enough to throw human resources and computing power at the job, they can be effective!

I had chosen to come here to Phil's quiet residential suburb precisely because advanced tracking cameras were nonexistent here, so far. No doubt, the Domain Awareness System would eventually extend here, but not for several years. Or so I believed.

Every indication hinted that they had spotted me! So, probably, my jog to the tire store was my undoing — a camera tied into the government systems must have recognized my distinctive silhouette!

That they had not already kicked down our door indicated that they didn't have enough video to locate us effectively. Perhaps we were still relatively safe if the cameras had merely spotted me walking along the street.

What about my taxi ride? Was that recorded? Had they followed me to the tire store? Were they aware that I was using Julie's car?

As I pondered these questions, I noticed a city bus pass the house and stop to discharge a passenger. With shock, I realized that the bus had a surveillance camera! Such cameras exist mainly to deter crime, and although bus cameras are routine in the larger cities, I had not considered their potential presence here! Transit systems don't have cameras in every venue, focusing such technology where it had the potential to pay off by reducing crime. This quiet neighborhood would not seem a candidate. My clandestine skills are still at the novice level, at best!

I mentally kicked myself as I remembered being passed by a bus as I walked to the tire store. My self-confidence in my ability to avoid capture was on the wane.

The quality of security video can vary dramatically. Not many years ago, banks of VHS tape recorders captured fuzzy low-resolution images that were of severely limited usefulness. Suddenly the world went digital, and the quality of the images improved markedly. However, they still employed the original analog TV video format, albeit with cleaner, if low-resolution photos. When the Hi-Def revolution came along soon after, it wasn't long before state-of-the-art systems captured video at full HD quality, although many systems were slow to upgrade.

I suspected it's likely that when the City had upgraded its bus fleet with newer surveillance gear compatible with the Domain Awareness System, the older equipment became repurposed to lower crime-prone areas. With luck, Alex had a grainy, low-quality image that he could perhaps not even be confident of identification and only that from a few brief moments as the bus had passed. I sincerely hoped this was the case.

Even so, to have picked my image out of a deluge of surveillance images was impressive! I doubted automated facial recognition could have picked me out in such a low-resolution image with certainty unless the lighting was perfect. I surmised he had the agency's supercomputers search for pictures of anyone approximating my features and of my body type and pass them to a human for the final say. On the other hand, I'd been outdoors and in the sun, so even an old-fashioned analog video system had a good chance of grabbing a decent quality image!

I speculated long and hard about other possibilities, other rookie mistakes I might have made. I could identify various ways the spooks might have detected me if they had been looking in the right place at the right time, yet everything I could imagine would have led them directly to us. Had they caught us via that system, even the municipal WIFI would have had our block filled with black SUVs and a house-to-house search in progress. That wasn't the case.

No, they didn't know where we were. At best, the MiBs had only a rough approximation based on a single sighting several blocks away. Ergo, the bus camera must be the most likely source of the present anxiety.

I hoped they did not link me to the taxi driver or the tire store. If not, they probably didn't know I had Julie's car. Therefore, we can flee if we must, though waiting until they're no longer cruising the neighborhood seemed wise. If they had made that connection, our options were decidedly limited.

I explored Phil's garage clutter. I remembered seeing an old-fashioned radio in the junk. The rise of the Internet and streaming services had moved audiences away from classic AM radio, and plenty of terrific sets are now gathering dust in people's garages.

After a few minutes of digging around, I found what I sought — an aging Superadio III, a popular high-quality AM radio from the 1990s. Quality radios like this had cost quite a few more bucks than the garden variety cheap receivers widely available in the era. However, their quality design and excellent performance seemed worth the price. Moreover, they should last for decades.

I hoped it wasn't stored away with batteries in it, as they would by now no doubt have corroded and ruined it. Quickly popping the battery cover, I felt relieved to note it was empty and clean.

Batteries weren't necessary, as the radio also accepts household AC power. Dragging it out and plugging it in, it rewarded my efforts by instantly powering up and, with a twirl of the dial, tuned the local stations perfectly! It may be old, but it's a keeper! Quality in electronics, as in anything, always shows.

Who needs the Internet for communications!

I dialed around for a few moments, rejecting various music and sports programming formats before settling on the principal News-Talk station in the Bay Area. If there were news reports of an extensive organized search, I wanted to know about it!

Alex's activities would not be in the media, of course. His operations were more covert, and if he were hunting us, it would not be in the news, especially if he were hunting extraterrestrials! THAT, he would never admit! I had not, however, ruled out the idea that he might have leaked some fabricated story of a dangerous felon to engage the support of local law enforcement, and anything curious on their roster might well make the news.

It seemed improbable yet worth a listen. Besides, I felt bored with nowhere to go and nothing to do, especially as I dared not access the Internet! If nothing else, I could listen for the entertainment.

My friends had stared at the radio with a look of astonishment when I first turned it on, though they hadn't commented, seemingly accepting the wonder of a voice coming from a black box in stride. I chalked that up to their having heard the same station on Julie's car radio during our drive; they had not displayed overwhelming wonder at that time either. Finally, after listening for a few minutes, Stapleya voiced curiosity.

She asked where the Crier was. When she asked the question, it dawned on me that the announcer on the talk radio station represented a close analog of a character in her world. Instead of being baffled, Stapleya had understood perfectly the role and purpose of the voices. Pointedly, she had deduced this quicker and more clearly than I had, when I had encountered the "Planet Oz" equivalent.

Every castle I had visited had a person, often several people who fulfilled the duty, the role of the Crier. While it might seem trivial, it wasn't. The purpose of the Crier is to disseminate information crucial to daily life in the castle. During the day, a Crier walks a regular course passing various locations inside and outside the castle. In these places, groups of people labored; the Crier visits anywhere citizens might be working to keep the castle running smoothly. Thus, a Crier is a sort of walking, talking bulletin board. In addition to carrying general-purpose announcements, personal, even intimate messages travel via the Crier. Not that the Crier functions as a postal service. The messages were seldom if ever, written. Writing did not come easily in their world. A Crier needed an excellent memory and would naturally know every person in their domain.

The path of the Crier passed the gardens, the kitchens, workers in the fields, clusters of working people anywhere in the domain. Whenever the Crier came within earshot of groups of people busily engaged in their daily pursuits, the Crier banged a drum to call attention, recited the Language equivalent of 'Hear ye, hear ye' and announced the news of the moment.

I remember being surprised and curious the first couple of times I noticed the Crier making her rounds. Once I learned Language, I quickly anticipated and welcomed the daily interruption in our demanding training regimen and the news updates. It was traditional that workers took a short break in their project, paused and listened to the latest reports, and spent a few moments discussing the events with their fellows. The Crier might also carry messages to another location or even news. If the latest crop of Squash was ready, for example, the Crier might spread the word that Squash would be on the menu of that day's Evening Feast.

Criers at castles we visited on our journey had carried the news of our quest, our adventures. In addition, the Criers disseminated far and wide many of the messages we sent using the primitive communications tools of the fur-people. The system of Criers played a significant role in spreading the word of our mission, ensuring our welcome, and passing the news of our exploits. For example, after our experience at the Dark Castle, the tale of that adventure and the warnings to keep the stone doors closed quickly spread throughout the land. The Criers probably saved numerous lives, if I correctly understand the crisis the fur-people currently faced back home. I was continually astonished at how effective this simple process was in keeping the population in sync and informed regarding critical issues.

We discussed the similarities between the "Planet Oz" Criers and the news-talk programming on the radio and the importance of keeping an ear tuned for news that might impact us.

Soon my friends and I were nestled on the couch, snuggling, talking low, and keeping an ear to the Crier. While keeping ourselves informed, we were not entirely without interesting diversions to pass the time! My ladies do find pleasure in the simple things!

Praetorian Guard

Several hours passed with nothing alarming on the radio, and no new black SUVs cruised our street; at least I spotted none. I wondered whether they had abandoned the search or were still out there, hidden in anticipation of our eventual appearance.

I was chafing to do something! Pleasant though the company might be, sitting here in the dark, feeling powerless, helpless, and scared, waiting for the MiBs to pounce and burst in our door at any moment was unbearable! I wanted somehow to take the battle to them, to kick in THEIR door. But how? I WAS powerless in this situation. My only possible path to avoiding a detention cell was finding an off-world portal, and I needed to find one soon. If we stayed here, we were sure to be caught sooner or later, and if we tried to run, they would likely grab us sooner.

Long after midnight, I decided the pain of inaction exceeded my tolerance level. I resolved to discover if Alex's people were out there, stationed somewhere nearby, poised for action. I believed if I dressed in dark clothing and stayed away from the open streets, I might reconnoiter without much risk. I also thought even if I did encounter one or even two of the MiBs, I would not seem in danger of capture. I didn't believe they would shoot me, and I trusted my ability to outrun and outfight them if necessary. In my arrogant opinion, I was more than a match for whatever force they might employ shy of lethality, and they wanted the fur-people too much to risk killing me.

I explored Phil's closets and drawers, looking for suitable dark clothing. Finally, I found a heavy black motorcycle jacket and dark sweatpants. Excellent! The thick leather would provide a degree of armor against such non-lethal force as a taser, and the dark colors would render my silhouette less visible in the night. But, of course, the Agents might possess night vision and other technological toys; therefore, I still needed to be extremely careful. Even so, I judged it worth the risk! Perhaps I was foolish, though my need for action was intense.

After careful preparation, I hugged the girls, cautiously opened the back door, and crept out. Slinking past the garage, I peered in every direction, looking at parked vehicles, other homes, even dark shadows between houses. Almost anything was suspect, government plates more so, and a black SUV is a red alarm! I wondered whether Alex would employ his SUV fleet or bring something less stereotypical. I hoped he was still keeping this off the books and thus hesitant to bring in the extensive government resources he commanded.

I inspected several parked cars for occupants — no one in evidence, nothing suspicious. Next, I climbed the backyard fence and crossed the neighbor's yard to the neighboring street, examining every vehicle.

I repeated this process, stealthily crossing from street to street, examining vehicles for threatening presences: Nada, nothing, no threats. I made my way around several blocks, circumnavigating the neighborhood, at no point spotting indication of MiBs or anyone else. The bucolic suburban setting seemed almost obscenely quiet at this hour; a ghost town utterly devoid of human tenancy.

Once, I spotted a police car down the block, headed in my direction. I dove behind a hedge, flattening myself on the ground against the shrubbery. But unfortunately, I had not been quick enough! The cruiser stopped, and a brilliant spotlight shone out, illuminating the shrubs around the area where I hid. I held myself rigid, burying my face in the dirt and hoping my dark clothing masked my presence.

The car backed up and shone the light all around the area, yet it seemed they didn't spot my rigid form lying frozen against the ground. The light disappeared after several anxious moments, and the cruiser crept away. I lay in my place, motionless for a long, slow count to one thousand before I dared raise my head. I glanced around to confirm I was alone, scanning the streets carefully before resuming my walkabout.

I had covered a six-block radius from the house without finding a hint nor sign of MiB presence and was ready to conclude perhaps I was over-reacting to a false alarm. I had circled the area, heading for home-base, when I rounded a corner and spotted a beat-up older van oddly parked on the street, partially blocking an empty driveway. It had not been there earlier, I was sure. My eye latched onto it. Something felt 'off' about the way it was parked as if the driver had no regard for suburban parking etiquette. It did not belong there!

The van had government plates!

I retreated, though it was too late. The owner had not been staking out the neighborhood from inside the vehicle. Instead, she was sitting on the ground in the shrubbery much closer to me, some twenty feet from the van, which I had not realized until the brilliant beam of a tactical-grade flashlight hit me in the face!

Blinded, I turned from the light and was about to bolt, run away from the spot at the best speed I could manage with splotches dancing in front of my eyes, when a familiar voice called out, soft and low in the sleeping neighborhood.

"Wait, Fitz! I'm not going to chase you; there's no one here but me. I only want to talk." It was Jill!

I stopped. "Why?" I asked as I paused, still blinking.

"Because I recognize a bigger picture — I hope to open up our world to other worlds, to a universe of humanity previously unknown. Perhaps Alex sees threats, whereas I recognize opportunities."

I considered this. "Alex is overreacting," I responded, "and he has the power and ability to confine my friends and me without reason, and I believe given a chance, he will do precisely that. He already had Matt trying to deceive me into trusting him. Now you're here. How can I trust you?"

"You cannot," she stated. I raised my eyebrows at her flat, if honest, statement. She continued, "From where you stand, I and anyone from the organization are suspect. I can offer nothing beyond my word; I have no desire to see you and your friends confined or harmed."

She said, "I believe Alex has overlooked an opportunity the likes of which can only come once in a civilization and culture's lifespan, an opportunity to forge relationships unlike any other in humanity's history. I believe we have missed a tremendous opportunity, and I hope to salvage that prize if it's possible to do so and will go to any possible length to ensure it happens."

I remained standing during our conversation, ready to bolt on any alarm. Jill sat cross-legged in the shrubbery beside the walkway, displaying a disarming calm and tranquility, making no move to stand. I debated for a moment sitting beside her to facilitate our quiet conversation. I chose not to; I still feared a trap!

Disarming as Jill seemed, I didn't trust her. I remained wary, alert, ready to bolt. Even now, others might be closing a net around our location. I expected to run or fight at any instant. Also, I was still squinting and blinking, trying to regain my night vision.

"Take me with you!" Whoa! What was she saying? She had long since extinguished her light, and I doubted she could interpret my features, my stunned look of disbelief, in the low light cast by the nearby streetlight. Even so, she must have sensed my reaction.

"I want to travel with you when you leave the Earth. I intend to be humanity's ambassador to another civilization." Though I doubted she truly grasped what she was suggesting, she was earnest.

"What? How?" I stammered, "I kinda already did that myself, and you see where it has gotten me. People I thought were my friends pursued me, and I am now hunted and chased by my government! Why would you want that?"

She sighed and took a breath as if she were a professor launching into a long and tedious lecture. I steeled myself to endure her words without letting my attention to the neighborhood lapse.

"Alex and people like him play an essential role in fighting back against the violent, uncivilized, criminal forces invading society. They are not wrong to do so, not mistaken to pursue anything seen as a threat. You would understand if you knew how many terrible events his efforts and those of his peers have prevented. Yet undeterred by the actions of Alex and many others cut from the same cloth, the dark forces are winning. The threat is severe, and unless something changes dramatically, our civilization is doomed.

"Organized crime, drugs, weapons, human trafficking, and more are exploding in a manner and at a rate unlike anything seen in history, and we are powerless even to slow it down, not just in this country, but across the world. We are fighting with one hand tied, unable to gain a foothold or even define the enemy. Our world is overrun by those with no regard for life and culture, who enrich themselves preying on human weakness.

"We are locked in a binary, we kill them, or they end our worldview. Yet the more blood spilled, the worse it becomes. So we must find another approach!

"You have shown me a higher reality. Perhaps I have merely viewed too many Star Trek episodes and read too much Science Fiction. I see the organization as a Praetorian guard, valuable, indispensable, narrowly focused on guarding core institutions and infrastructure. There are barbarians at the borders of our civilization, where the Legions should be turning them back. Instead, our Legions are powerless to repel the hordes, almost inviting them in as they indulge in destructive, baser pleasures.

"Much as the Romans formed their Legions from the citizenry, massive in numbers, we must galvanize our citizenry to reject the dark temptations, to turn back the hordes. Alex has a narrow focus, the Agency is the tip of the spear, but society itself must oppose the descent into chaos.

"I hope to shape humanity's future as a member of a Galactic civilization. Humanity will change and grow once the reality of other worlds and other civilizations emerges. I believe, faced with a larger reality, humanity will become focused, energized, able to push back against evil. But, we must first show humanity a larger world or perish, overrun by darkness. I need your help; you hold the key to unlocking that larger reality."

Oh, wonderful! It was not enough that I saved all humanity; now she wants me to save all civilization too!

A Galactic Society

I stood and stared down at her for long moments! My brain spun, trying to wrap itself around the implications of her words. I was looking around for signs of a trap, of duplicity, yet, as near as I can tell, it's just Jill and me talking in low voices by the sidewalk of a quiet neighborhood street.

Casting common sense to the winds, I sat myself down beside her. Unable to imagine anything to say, I sat there quietly, contemplating this turn of events. Jill, I presume having spent her passion, sat quietly too.

Assuming her ideas had merit, that humanity's destiny lay with a galactic civilization, how might we accomplish it? Would people of Alex's mindset listen to her more readily than they would me? How might we establish diplomatic relationships between the President of the US and whoever's the leader of Petchy's society?

I am darned if I have a clue!

What of the blood-thirsty enemies of Western culture? Who might she consider our enemies beyond the obvious, and would they abandon their violent ways in the face of the reality of extraterrestrial life and civilization? Will Latin American drug cartels lose interest in selling drugs just because humanity contacts aliens? It seems a questionable proposition.

External alien threat as a unifying force wasn't exactly a novel idea. Countless movies and even US Presidents had treated the idea seriously. I recalled a long-ago speech given on the floor of the United Nations by a US President.

"Perhaps we need some outside universal threat to make us recognize this common bond. I occasionally think how quickly our differences worldwide would vanish if we faced an alien threat originating outside this world."

Would the enemies of today recognize Petchy, Teena, and their people as a reason to abandon their hateful ideology and pursue peaceful unity with their fellow Earthlings? Seemed doubtful. Call this fellow a skeptic on that for now.

Finally, I asked her, "Assuming I trust you, what is your proposal? If I discover a way off-world, you would find yourself as one additional woman in a female-dominated stone-age society if you came with us to Planet Oz. What valuable skills do you offer the fur-people?"

She seems surprised at this. I continued before she could interrupt. "I'm a desirable personage there due to simple biology. If I did not possess muscular biceps and functional male genitalia, they would not grant me the time of day. Pointedly, my computer and technological skills aren't in demand. My stone-age life skills are minimal at best; I'm a lousy hunter, a fair storyteller, and can contribute little to their lives. I find a personal Shangri la there mainly due to the simple fact that a vigorous, healthy penis is a rarity. How would you demonstrate value in their society?"

She held her hands out to her side in submission.

I rolled on, not giving her a chance to interrupt. "The fur-people of Planet Oz understand nothing of the larger galactic society, assuming it exists. I only saw the fur-people and two rather extraordinary humans who claimed to be from a planet other than Earth. The extant of a Galactic society isn't proven, not to my satisfaction. The most I can vouch for is one pair of self-proclaimed aliens.

"Further, even if such a society as hypothesized exists, I cannot promise they're interested in being joined by our brand of humanity. However, I see hints they already manifest a significant presence here on Earth and could reveal themselves at any time if they wished.

"That they have not done so argues that they're unwilling to do so anytime soon. Perhaps the hypothetical galactic society wishes nothing to do with our world beyond using our DNA and Earth as a breeding ground for their own genetically enhanced warriors. Maybe they're decimated after the war with Planet K, depleted to the point where they have no resources to spare us.

"What do you believe you can accomplish by going to Planet Oz?"

She shrugged. She raised her hands slightly in submission, grimacing as she did so.

"I'm not certain I can do anything," she answered. "All I say is that I need to attempt it. If I can talk to the right person and present my case, I might change a few minds. I may fail. I hope not. If I don't try, I cannot succeed. Take me along, and I will do all I can. I will present my case and my arguments to all who will listen. What happens after that is in the hands of greater powers. I need to try."

Another long silence as I digested her words.

"How is it you come to be here?" I asked her. "How did you come to search for us in this area?"

"We were searching for you using available video cameras. I spotted a form that seemed to be you a couple of blocks from here in a video from a passing bus."

Ha! I knew it!

"I pitched Alex if I came alone, I could approach you with less risk; if he put a large team in place, it would spook you to run again. He would not let me come alone, though he let me come as a member of a two-person team, myself and Matt, with two vehicles. We came here and spent a day sweeping the area near where I had spotted you, looking for a sign.

"Matt gave up and headed back to headquarters earlier this afternoon. I disobeyed the recall, sticking around longer. I will be in trouble if I fail to show up at my regular station tomorrow morning."

"If you knew I was in this area, why did he not put a massive team and conduct a massive door-to-door search? Such a low-profile, quiet approach seems uncharacteristic for Alex."

She responded, "I suppose he would, had he believed it was you. Unfortunately, the image was poor, and face recognition placed a bare 30% match probability. I convinced him it was only maybe you. I felt certain, though, I didn't need the computer. I wanted the chance to make contact myself!"

"Okay, you found me. What happens now?" I asked.

"I'm unsure. If you found a way off-world, I hope to travel with you. If you believe there will be a way off-world soon, I hope to hang close until it appears."

I pondered that for a moment. I was uncertain when or if Phil might be able to arrange for portal access. Even if he can, it might require weeks. The prospect of having Jill hanging around with us, hiding with us, and trusting her didn't seem attractive. If I let her see where our refuge was, she may betray us!

On the other hand, she could do that now! We were already exposed if she intended to betray us. She already, beyond doubt, knew we were in this area. If I let her return to Alex, it would be disastrous.

If I released her, we had to again rabbit to stay safe. If I brought her into our confidence, she might betray us.

Doubting she understood the "Planet Oz" society or the requirements to transit a portal, I asked her, "Are you comfortable nude? Do you believe you could be comfortable in a world without clothing? Have you thought through the implications? Have you ever experienced non-sexual, social nudity?"

She grimaced. "Indeed, I'm not particularly comfortable with nudity," she began.

As she spoke, I held up my hand. "It's much more than just the nudity. Their entire culture approaches sex and sexuality very differently than ours. Sex there is usually a group sport, often a spectator sport! They will invite you to share a bed, and everything implied, intimacy with people who are entirely free of body shame, uninhibited in ways that our society finds starkly unimaginable. I did mention this is a virtually all-female world, too, right?

"In my Science Fiction tale, I hardly touched the subject of their sexuality since I was writing for a general audience and considered it too extreme for even the uninhibited free-spirits of Earth. Moreover, in a society that never conceived a need for clothing, the concepts of personal modesty, shame, and coyness we take for granted are wholly and utterly foreign, almost incomprehensible to them.

"I don't know you well, though based on our limited time together, I see you as prudish in such matters, reluctant to embrace your sexuality, disdainful or fearful of open sexuality in others."

She opened her mouth to object, and I held up my hand to forestall her interruption. "Perhaps I'm misreading you, and if so, I apologize. However, I fear you would experience serious difficulties upon being thrust into their society." I motioned her to proceed as I had completed my thought.

"It's true," she began, "you've not entirely misread me. I grew up in a highly prudish family, common in Asian cultures. My father was American of Irish ancestry, yet had lived in Shanghai much of his adult life and became thoroughly inculcated in Asian ways. We considered ourselves modest rather than prudish; perhaps that's a distinction without a difference. For years, even after I became an adult, I lived in a cultural bubble that propagated and reinforced such myopia.

"It's only in the last few years I came to view a larger world and began to consider being relatively open to sexuality and sexual experimentation. Until recently, all I understood of sexuality came from reading romance novels. Non-sexual, social nudity remained absent from my worldview.

"When I first read your book, your description of the nude protests and the Urban Nudist subculture in the city grabbed my attention. I found myself, frankly, shocked. My initial reaction — one of 'Eww, who wants to see THAT!' — came straight from my upbringing, yet your writing was fascinating, raised questions in my mind and piqued my curiosity, induced me to research the topic. Finally, I understood just how extensive the nudist subculture is in the Bay Area. I became curious enough to promise myself a real nudist experience on my upcoming vacation.

"I had decided to travel somewhere distant, away from home, away from California for the experience. I understand the Bay Area is home to several world-class nudist resorts, yet I would die if I encountered somebody from work or other circles. So, I must travel where I can be anonymous, among strangers.

"Your Planet Oz, as you call it, fits my criteria of far from home better than Florida or even Europe. I may experience difficulties, though I'm eager to explore them.

"As for the uninhibited sexuality of the fur-people, I'm admittedly somewhat reserved, uncomfortable. I learned the nudist environment isn't, as a rule, one of open sexuality, and I steeled myself to experience that much, confident I would not face uncomfortable sexual pressures. I recognize I might encounter immense difficulties with that on Planet Oz. I only recently took a lover; sexuality's still novel and a little spooky. My lover is older and more experienced sexually and probably would be right at home there. I find the prospect of sharing a bed with a group of happy, horny, hedonistic libertines terrifying. Honestly, it scares the living crap out of me!

"It also excites me just a little. It seems weird but weird in a way I want to try. I'm inexperienced sexually and view much of this as unknown territory.

"Scared as I am, no matter how uncomfortable the libidinous lifestyle of our hosts might be, I'm committed to the higher mission, establishing trade and diplomatic traffic between Earth and other worlds. What's personal discomfort compared to that?"

I put my arm around her shoulders. She leaned into my shoulder and gave way to momentary sobbing as the tension of our confrontation evaporated. After a couple of seconds, she regained her composure and straightened up. I pulled out a handkerchief and cuddled her slightly; I wiped her eyes. As I dried her tears, I pondered the antiquated sexist stereotype playing out before my unbelieving eyes. It seemed like high camp comedy playing out in real life. Frankly, I doubted it was genuine! I became convinced she was playing me.

Were her tears indeed an expression of deep catharsis at having unburdened herself of the weight of her intentions, or is she merely using feminine wiles to play my emotions, to manipulate me? I had thought that Jill seemed too strong a person to succumb to the first and possessed too much integrity to resort to the second. I was unnerved, unsure what to think about this strange turn.

The moment of seeming vulnerability passed. In a whisper, I addressed her request head-on. "Jill, you've placed us in a deucedly awkward position. Without a doubt, you understand that we're sequestered nearby. If I permit your return to your employer, you could bring down a massive house-to-house manhunt and ensure our capture. I cannot tolerate the possibility that my friends and I might be illegally confined based on Alex's whims. I cannot allow that; I cannot permit your return to Alex's organization."

She interrupted, "Then take me with you!"

I held up my hand to cut her off. "The alternative's that I hold you hostage until I can find a way off-world if I can. That's undesirable too, as you could betray us at any time, contrive to signal our location to Alex. Even if you don't willfully cross us, if you fail to appear at your office on schedule tomorrow, they will come looking for you and blanket the area with a massive search.

"Either way, we're well and thoroughly fracked!"

"Please, Fitz," she interjected, "I knew you were nearby for almost 24 hours. I didn't call down a search. I contrived to come alone to talk and present my case. I'm on your side! You can trust I won't sell you out! I have my own goals and plans, and I need to go with you."

A Determined "Woman in Black"

I continued to stare at Jill in silence for several long moments as I contemplated our choices. The only safe option was to abduct her, restrain her, gather my friends and our few supplies, and pile us into Julie's car and rabbit again, releasing her when we're well-headed somewhere else. The flaw in that idea was that we had nowhere else. Running away demands someplace to run to, a destination, a haven that we lack.

The lack of an identified refuge made the "only safe choice" decidedly unsafe, looping us back to step one.

Jill interrupted my mental machinations with my path forward still undecided.

"Consider this, if you will not trust me to return to work for fear I will expose you, what if I call in and ask to use my vacation time?" I raised my eyebrow questioningly. She continued, "Fitz, you're right; they will come looking when report time comes without me. On the other hand, if I ask for a few days off, they will accept that. The office has been yelling at me for not taking my vacays anyway. I will say that I need a break. I will hint to Matt that I met a hookup in a bar and am starting a vacationship. You understand how their minds work. He and Alex will believe I'm taking a rutting break and not question it for a moment."

Hmm, an interesting turn of phrase that, I mused. Jill's selling me on the idea of how sexually naïve and repressed she is, yet in the next moment retreats to the gutter, using her sexuality conspiratorially? Does the fact I find this surprising mean I'm even more gullible than I thought? So it would seem. Jill seems to possess dimensions I had not suspected. If she puts forth this subterfuge on her employer, can I trust her not to lie similarly to MY face when it suits her? Doubtful!

Setting word to deed, Jill stepped over to the van, climbed inside, and closed the doors and windows. I climbed in beside her as she turned on the radio, low and tuned in a station with raucous music, picked up her cell phone, and dialed Matt. As the phone rang, Jill turned up the volume on the radio slightly. She fluidly adopted an inebriated voice and manner, giving the impression that she was in a bar or at a party.

"Hey Mattie," she slurs, "Will you tell Alex I won't be in the rest of the week? I'm taking a little twiddle time." As she slurs out the last, she gives a little drunken giggle and then drops her voice, half-covered the phone with her hand, and muttered, "stop that I'm on the phone," soft and low. Then, louder, she says, "Thanks, Mattie, you're a pal. See ya Monday." and hung up.

She made another call, now speaking mechanically, obviously talking to voicemail. Much the same routine, slightly less drunk sounding, a little more professional, she told the machine that she ran into a friend, and since HR had been after her to take time off, she intends to use a few of her vacation days since the scouting trip was a bust. She said to text her if a promising lead comes up, and she will cut her break short and come on in right away; in the absence of a tip, she was taking a few days hiatus.

Impressed with her acting skills, I also noted her proficiency with deception and willingness to use the slut-route and gutter slang to sell her story. Naïve little lotus-blossom my gluteus maximus! This petite Amerasian Mata Hari is dangerous!

Dangerous or not, she had thrust our course upon us. I now see no choice other than taking Jill to Phil's house and trusting we can find a connection off-world before everything comes unstuck. I was not confident about the prospect of taking Jill through a portal. Perhaps I can find an alternative when the time comes, though my direction's set for now. I wondered if I dared even sleep in her presence. Must my friends and I take turns guarding her? Must I tie her up, like some strange '50 shades' vignette? Wonder how she'd respond if I did?

I contemplated the next step when inspiration came; she had claimed to want a nudist experience. I was going to give her one! We shall find out how earnest she is!

First, I held out my hand, demanding she surrenders her phone. With a blank expression, she complied. Next, I asked if she had other phones, tablets, or gadgets, anything they could use to track us. She shook her head!

I looked at the phone, turned it off, and popped out its battery. I pocketed the now-dead device and turned to Jill with a determined glare in my eye. I asked, "Are you sure you want to do this?" She nodded. "Last chance to retreat," I warned. Seeing no response, I dropped the bombshell. "Then remove all your clothing, shoes, everything."

Her jaw dropped, she froze in place, a blank expression, morphing toward fear, crossed her visage. She seemed unsettled! I suppose she hadn't expected the nudist portion to begin so soon.

I elaborated. "If we step through a portal, you'll need to be nude at that point anyway. Plus, without clothing, you will prove you're hiding nothing from me, nothing that threatens our safety or can lead Alex to us. Also, the fur-girls and I are more comfortable nude. Having a group member clothed is distracting, and I will worry less about your running away, and besides, you need to acclimate to it anyway if you intend to travel to Planet Oz."

She stammered, "H-here, on a residential street in the open?" I shrugged. Perhaps there was slim justification for this; I wanted to test her resolve and put her off-stride.

"It's quiet, and no one's around. Middle of the night, everyone's asleep except us. I believe you can walk to our hiding place without being arrested. Hurry up, though, as the early risers will be about soon, and the paperboy could begin his route any moment."

As though reaching deep for a heretofore hidden courage reserve, she straightened herself, her expression of fear evaporated, and she shucked her clothes rapidly and without hesitation. I noted with surprise the small, well-concealed holster hiding a tiny but formidable weapon in her bra. I was impressed! I knew such garments existed, though this was the first time I had ever seen one. I was also glad I had insisted she disrobe. That she might have a weapon hidden there would never have occurred to my trusting persona. Note to self: 'You're *a dork! Don't be so trusting!'*

Unclothed, she stood coolly, calmly, making no effort to cover herself with her hands or other protective movements non-nudists instinctively make upon finding themselves naked in unfamiliar company. I sensed she wasn't as shy and repressed as she had pretended. How much of the last half-hour's conversation dare I believe?

I made a bundle of her clothing, handling her weapon with care as I unloaded and pocketed the bullets. I whispered, "That way," pointing across the street. Unbeknownst to Jill, I hoped, we had been standing directly across from our destination all the while. At least I believed she had not known how close she had parked to our lair! I realized I needed to second-guess everything with this incredible person. How did she come to park so closely? I marveled that I had not spotted her when looking out the front window, wondered when she had stationed herself there. My lack of faith drove my sudden decision to force nudity on her. It's not for nothing that we equate nudity with vulnerability.

I wanted her to feel vulnerable.

Insisting she be nude was my way of playing a psychological game, attempting to throw her off-stride and making her feel vulnerable. Also, it is an insignificant factor in the equation that she's a trim, athletic, spectacular-looking young woman. While I love the unfettered female form as much as anyone, the stakes are too high; I'm too paranoid and wary. I can't allow her pulchritude to distort my judgment. I have more significant worries on my mind, and she wasn't, at the moment, a woman, not in my mind.

Instead, she was a threat and a serious one that I found terrifying! Of course, once we're off-world, I will pay attention to her pulchritude. But, for the moment, she's merely another antagonist, one who is dangerous and whom I need to keep under tight rein, off-balance and confused.

Stapleya and Wisceya greeted us at the door. They had been at the window all along, monitoring our actions. I handed Stapleya the bundle of clothing, the gun, and the cell phone, suggesting she put them in a safe place, keeping the keys to the van for the moment. I explained our agreement to Stapleya and Wisceya briefly and in English.

I warned the ladies not to trust our guest and be wary of her using Language. We're not accepting her as a friend, not yet anyway. She must earn that.

Taking Jill's key fob, I crossed the street, climbed into her van, and drove it several blocks, parking it near, although not directly in front of a hole-in-the-wall dive bar. Then, locking the vehicle, I trotted back to the house, wondering whether removing the van helped our cause materially. If she had so nearly located us, could Alex be far behind with his fleet of black SUVs? I worried myself sick, close to retreating to my original idea and rabbiting, dropping Jill near her van on my way out of town.

A mental image of leaving her with only her keys, forced to drive back to the city nude, flitted briefly through my brain. Although the tactic might be helpful — might delay her a few moments in bringing Alex down upon our heads, I wouldn't do that to her or anyone. I live by higher standards than that in how I treat people, even those who I consider enemies or at least antagonists. However, I doubted she would grant her antagonist the same consideration if it suited her purpose. Still, the imagery evoked a slight smile as I momentarily entertained it while ruminating on my fears. I worried that she would soon betray us, and if I had somewhere tenable to run, I would bolt in a heartbeat! Perhaps I must anyway.

The three were sitting on the couch when I returned, Jill on the far left, the fur-girls close together on the right. I shucked my civilian costume and joined them, snuggling between Stapleya and Wisceya, luxuriating in their silken furry touch. Jill moved to a nearby chair rather than remain so close to Wisceya. Her loss. Their sensuous fur is so pleasurable, so erotic, that snuggling with the girls feels almost supernatural. Ignoring her discomfort, I invited Jill to expand on our earlier comments, to explain to the two off-worlders her vision of a mission to bind a Galactic society. I wondered whether the fur-people grasped the concept of a Galaxy, though they seemed to understand the gist of the idea. The more I spoke with them, the more I believed Stapleya had been sandbagging her English skills for years.

Although Stapleya and Wisceya had displayed remarkable progress with English, I played with the language gap, pretending to translate for them while adding my personal and private commentary to her tale. Jill's a cunning, highly trained agent of a shadowy, almost unaccountable government body, and I didn't wish Stapleya and Wisceya deceived by her. She's tricky, and I didn't even trust myself to resist her deceptions.

The Doctor

The sky tinged with a crimson herald of the coming dawn as I stifled a crocodile yawn. I'd been awake and active all night, and the sleep deficit was mounting. We had been talking, exploring our options, and making plans.

Jill stuck to her claim of seeking a higher goal, overruling her nominal loyalty to her employer. She insisted, my misgivings aside, that we could trust her. I remained unconvinced but opted not to rabbit just yet, my nervous, contrary inclination notwithstanding.

I prepared breakfast for the ladies, again focusing on pork products. As I did so, I observed Jill's body language. At first, she kept her distance and remained aloof. Then, food ready, I was relieved as she joined in on the repast and tucked away her fair share and a bit more besides. She commented that it had been many hours since she had eaten. She commented that she usually fasted when preoccupied with a mission, as she considered food and drink a distraction. I admired her resolve — I consider hunger a distraction.

Stapleya and Wisceya crowded into the tiny kitchen when it came time to clean up, opportunistically brushing against me and each other sensually. Their sensual fur is a delight to touch, even in the most casual, non-sexual context; it seduces one into contact, like a purring cat that draws one to pet and stroke it by some deep-seated instinct. The effect plays no small role in my imagination. Despite an otherwise complete absence of feline characteristics, it is easy to envision them as 'Cat-People.'

Their natural scent is delightful, too, and, with their sensual fur, evokes a pleasurable stirring. Pheromone-like, barely perceptible, they exude varying flavors with their mood, especially as their arousal waxes and wanes. Cinnamon and black licorice, pumpkin pie and lavender, and even pumpkin pie and cinnamon buns wax and wane, scarcely at the threshold of perception, faint, yet arousing. Indeed, males find them irresistible, as I can well attest, yet they also attract other females. These ladies exude sensuality; no one with a pulse is immune.

Jill held back at first rather than insert herself into the tight space and thereby avoided the quasi-intimate contact my fur-bearing friends revel in, seemingly reticent at the prospect of female-on-female contact. I wasn't surprised by this. I expected it, as despite my growing suspicions otherwise, I still believed she was fundamentally prudish and would be uncomfortable with their sexually charged faux flirting.

So I was more than a little surprised when the time came to clean up, notwithstanding the natural charms of the fur girls. But, prudish or not, Jill reversed course after a few moments of hesitation, pushed aside her inhibitions, launched herself into the middle of the workspace, and took charge of the sink and drainboard. Then, with speed, agility, and practiced skill, she dispatched the detritus, packing items that remained viable for the refrigerator and shoveling the waste down the disposal.

As we fetched and carried plates, pans, and utensils as needed, our tight quarters necessarily resulted in unintentional touching of my skin and that of the furbearers. However, the causal contact seemed not to vex Jill unduly. She didn't flinch or pull back and once put forth a tiny but blatant hip grind as if to engage in a bit of faux flirting of her own. I was bemused to note that she didn't withhold from touching the fur girls once she overcame her initial reluctance, seeming to revel in their sensual contact. As she became more comfortable doing so, her touches lingered on the furry visitors, taking every opportunity to extend connection beyond the minimum. She gradually overcame her shyness. Well, my fur-girls have that effect on people.

The complexities and contradictions of this new addition to our group puzzled me. Each time I believe I understand this woman, new facets emerge. It is safe to say that she had trashed my initial assessment of her as a prim, sexually inexperienced, and naïve young woman. That I considered her the timid 'lotus-blossom' type was a startling and alarming testament to my naïveté. I would make a poor secret agent! I'd best stick to computers and leave the people-hacking to others.

Computers are logical and consistent.

It was still morning when we finished our breakfast and cleaned up the mess, returning Phil's kitchen to pristine condition. It was not yet twenty-four hours since Phil's message told us to stay offline for two days. Nonetheless, I worried that these new developments, the addition of Jill to our group, were too significant not to pass the word along. After some thought, I decided to break our radio silence to send a message.

Once again, I fired up the aging desktop, letting the elderly, cranky machine boot in its sweet time as I ensured it didn't connect to the Internet. Presently, Phil's antique was ready to perform. I composed a message describing our situation, including Jill's intention to cross through a portal and somehow reach Petch and Teena's organization and present her case for disclosure. I emphasized that I didn't trust her but felt I had no choice other than to bring her along as her presence was a ticking time bomb, waiting for Alex to deduce she was with us and not merely taking some time off. I surmised we had about another twenty-four hours, perhaps a bit more, before we needed to be elsewhere, one way or another. Preferably off-world.

The fur-girls had shown little curiosity about my computer activities. As they had no concept of such devices, I supposed they regarded them as magic beyond their ken and ignored the technological marvels. I often pondered how the brain secures new knowledge by the tenterhooks of that already known by creating analogies to connect the new idea just encountered to an existing idea well understood.

When the Studebaker boys began building automobiles in 1902, they came into the new field with broad and deep experience in building wagons. That their first auto resembled a wagon is no coincidence. Nothing revolutionary is created or learned in a vacuum. Likewise, with zero grounding in the principles of computers, learning anything of significance would be difficult, no matter how intelligent an individual might be.

This time, I noted, was somewhat different. In our conversations over recent hours, I told them a little about computers and how my field of expertise lay in their use and application. I elaborated a bit on their extraordinary benefits. I wondered at the time if this might be a mistake. It was evident that I had illuminated their curiosity and given them a few basics on which to build. They watched with wide eyes, now paying rapt attention, letting no action escape their gaze. I wondered how much they could comprehend, but I know they're brilliant. I didn't imagine they would return to "Planet Oz" and immediately begin building computers. Their homeworld lacks the necessary infrastructure. Still, I worried about the implications and unintended consequences of everything they learned while on Earth.

I tried to shield my computer activities from Jill. I didn't wish to give away the tools and methodologies of my contacts with Phil. I wished I had the power to keep his identity secret, but his name is on the property records for the house. Armed with the address, anyone may readily find the owner. If Jill reported her experiences, I assumed that tying Phil into our adventures was a given. Without intending to, I had endangered my friend by bringing Jill in. This realization troubled me to no small degree.

I encrypted the message, for better or worse, explaining in rough terms to the fur-girls what I was doing as I went along. But, of course, I did so using Language not to enlighten Jill. Then I inserted it steganographically into the same fake spam image as before, setting Phil's public key as the password. When complete, I turned on the WIFI, connected to the municipal wireless network, and placed the fake spam into the drafts folder of the dead-drop email address.

I considered checking my email or sending an email to Julie. They are certainly monitoring my email, and I must assume that they had connected Julie to me. Too much risk, I decided. I can still use the list of codewords if I send her a message. I desperately hoped she remained unknown to the MiBs and her safety was not at risk.

I shut down the WIFI and then the computer. Then, returning to my position on the couch, I turned up the volume on the news-talk station and again settled where I might keep a convenient eye on the street.

We passed the next few hours in peaceful quiet. The long night and lack of sleep were telling. I napped briefly, and sometime later, I realized Jill had become the meat in a furry sandwich, snuggled between Stapleya and Wisceya in a cozy repose as all three slept soundly. The tableau before my eyes was somewhat suggestive, and I wondered whether I missed a spot of fun while myself dozing. Not to worry, as I'm sure my furry companions will not neglect me, although I once again found myself in awe of the beautiful petite Asian and wondered at how I had so misjudged her. I can see that my skills at assessing people need work.

I may have undergone a tremendous transformation, from computer jock to super athletic hero archetype and super inseminator. I may have spent months living in the known universe's bawdiest and randiest female-dominated society. Yet, I remain naïve and am continually surprised by the broad panoply of human sexuality. For all my experience at the physicality, I remain a bit of a dork when connecting with people emotionally. Once an introvert, always an introvert, I surmised.

I took a fresh look through the curtained window to compare the quiet repose indoors with that mirrored tranquility on the outside streets. It was a peaceful afternoon in suburbia. I continued watching the outdoor scene as I considered my options. I was again seriously considering rabbiting, taking the three girls in Julie's car, and heading, somewhere. Anywhere. The MiBs were too close to finding us, and if I stayed put, they surely would.

Countering the nervous impulse to run was the need to stay in touch with Phil. His venerable desktop computer was too bulky and impractical to take on the road. But, frustratingly, I owned an almost new, high-performance ultra-portable, sitting on my desk at home, locked down with a steel security cable. If the MiBs hadn't already confiscated it and attempted to break into it, that is. I wondered, if so, how they were faring against my encrypted folders. I want to think they found my particular flavor of encryption to be challenging.

I may be a poor judge of humans, but I unabashedly admit I know somewhat more than most about computer security. I locked away several folders on my laptop to ensure they were proof against decryption. My goal was merely to store financial and other sensitive data. The irony is that there is nothing much of interest to the MiBs in them, but of course, they would not know that. I laughed at them, spinning their wheels futilely, trying to crack my encrypted files.

Admittedly they command almost unlimited resources. It MIGHT be possible. It would, however, take them some significant effort unless I miss my guess — which they would not be spending on me, I hoped. I would have liked to be there if and when they might open my files and find my pathetic attempt at an erotic novel and my banking records. There isn't even porn on it. After living among the fur-people, who needs porn? If I had anticipated the need sooner, I might have provided them with an enticing collection as a distraction.

My premium ultra-portable was out of reach, but many stores sell inexpensive computers. Taking Phil's ancient desktop on a road trip was impractical, but I might buy something more portable. It didn't need to be an expensive, premium machine like my beauty at home. A more generic laptop would serve nicely.

How to safely procure such a machine was the question. After my blunder with the bus line's surveillance camera, I was somewhat reluctant to walk into a computer store and buy a new machine. I would pay cash, do so anonymously, and even give a fake name, but one security video could expose me, risking our all despite my best efforts. Moreover, I doubted we could weather a second sighting.

I could send Jill to purchase one, but the risks inherent in that option are best left unstated. Perhaps that is the one option riskier than my doing so, and the fur-girls could not do so either, for numerous reasons. I needed a portable computer but could not fathom a practical way to procure one. Perhaps once we're on the road and well out of the area, we can risk stopping in a rural big-box store and buying a machine. That was also less than ideal as I would need some hours with an Internet connection to set it up with the encryption and steganography tools I needed. I should be taking advantage of the quiet time here and now. I was frustrated and worried that I could not.

Still considering taking a powder, I began wondering where we should go. Getting outside of the surveillance state of the Bay Area, heading to somewhere rural, somewhere the tendrils of the Domain Awareness Center didn't extend, seemed obvious. I wondered how many years would elapse before no place would remain remote enough to hide from AI-assisted surveillance. Petch was right when he said we were busily building the same sort of systems that had escaped their control. The death spiral was visible to my newly opened eyes. Unquestionably, we are on a path toward universal surveillance, impossible to hide from anywhere on the planet. The confluence of inexpensive yet powerful computers and inexpensive, readily available high-resolution cameras makes it inevitable.

I found myself longing for the innocent world of Planet Oz. Still, one must wonder if it were not for the best. I recognize abuses happen. Abuses of power are currently happening to my ladies and me. Alex's determination to capture us even though neither my ladies nor I have committed any crime is an abuse of his station. Our mere existence frustrates his sense of authority and power. Is this not a necessary cost to pay for safety and security under most normal circumstances? What if a brutal terrorist were on the lam, as we are? Would we not want the authorities to have the power, all the technological tools, to prevent loss of life?

Or is this a self-fulfilling condition? Does the surveillance state use the threat of the occasional brutal, violent thug to justify their existence? Is it reasonable to subject the average citizen to such massive surveillance to apprehend the occasional dangerous scofflaw? Do these tools appreciably improve the odds of capturing the real criminals? Or are they toys, diversions, a technological substitute for honest policing skills that too many in authority lack or are too lazy to acquire?

These thoughts and more were bouncing around my noggin as I sat on the couch, half-sleeping, half watching the girls sleep, and half watching the neighborhood. Then, suddenly, my attention was piqued as a car pulled into Phil's driveway! The bright red two-seater sports car stood out, out of place parked in Phil's suburban driveway, a beacon to anyone who might be watching. I stood and carefully gazed out the window to see who might appear.

An impeccably dressed and meticulously coiffed middle-aged lady of African ancestry stepped out of the car. She straightened herself and walked resolutely towards the front door. I moved to the door to open it for her before she could ring the bell and startle the still sleeping ladies.

I opened the door and said, "Hello, Dr. Rawls, won't you come in?" She startled momentarily, then smiled. After a momentary hesitation, she accepted my invitation and stepped through the doorway into the house, undeterred by the fur and skin visible within. Her eyes flit briefly here or there, then, after the briefest of hesitations, she relaxed and became totally at ease with our nudity.

"I must say I'm surprised you are here, Dr. Rawls," I commented.

"I rather supposed you would be," she responded, "I hadn't expected to reveal myself, but circumstances forced my hand. We need to put our friends in the government off your trail and take these poor unfortunate women to safety, back to their home."

At the sound of our voices, the ladies awakened. The visitors from Planet Oz jumped up and enthusiastically greeted our visitor. Surprisingly, I noted she answered them in hesitant Language, uttering a few routine pleasantries before shifting back to English. Fluency eluded her, though she knew more about them than she had previously admitted. And I told her to 'do her homework!' Funny!

Momentarily embarrassed, Jill shirked briefly before visibly steeling herself to greet the newcomer. The older, impeccably dressed academic was undoubtedly off-putting to the unclothed agent. I had wanted Jill off-balance and vulnerable, and it seems I succeeded. She was unsettled for a few moments, shifting her hands and arms strategically before reasserting self-control. I smiled inwardly at her discomfiture. However, it didn't last long; she acclimated to the new dynamic and calmed quickly.

After a moment spent acknowledging the fur girls, I again addressed the Doctor. "I take it from the simple fact that you are here; that you're another fifth column operative looking out for the extrinsic interests?"

She frowned. "I don't like to describe it in such politically charged terms. Earth has been under the eye of the former inhabitants of your 'Planet K' for centuries, possibly millennia. I'm unsure when they first came. Various other worlders and their descendants live secretly on Earth. They were often a guiding force, championing ideas and ideals, subtly shaping our society. Their contribution to our modern world is immense.

"There is no us versus them dynamic at play. The aliens are us, and we are they. They came here in significant numbers long before their world became inhospitable. Then, when the machines destroyed their planet, the migration surged, and they came here in multitudes as refugees.

"These strange immigrants make up a tiny yet significant percentage of Earth's inhabitants. Moreover, many younger descendants born to the original aliens do not even suspect their extraterrestrial roots.

"They are, in an amusing sense, illegal aliens and often intermarry with native Earthers, spreading their genetic heritage deeply into our indigenous population. We cannot guess how many generations are involved, but many generations of Earth-born people have descended from ancestors who came here long ago.

"Many of our brightest minds perhaps were of extraterrestrial origins, spending their time and energy shaping our society positively."

"I see," I said. I had often imagined such possibilities as I had lain awake listening to late-night radio shows that discussed possible UFO visitors and a believed 'government cover-up.' Could there be, I wondered, something solid underlying all the midnight talk of UFOs and the 'Disclosure Project' meme?

I continued, "So, a significant percentage of our outstanding geniuses came from other worlds; aliens were some of our most exceptional minds? Was Da Vinci born on Planet K? Tesla, or Edison? Or Locke? Jefferson? Spinoza, Bayle, Smith, Voltaire, Newton? So, just how much of our culture and technology comes from Planet K?"

She shook her head. "I do not assert any of those named were aliens, or perhaps they all were, I cannot say. I don't know when the extraterrestrials first came; I'm sure they were here a long time ago, and their immigration escalated, beginning well over a hundred years ago. I believe a few of them played significant roles in our history, even though I can't document specifics. Just because we have aliens helping our native geniuses does not mean our people lack ability. However, the sudden, exceptional acceleration of the pace of progress in the last century presents a strong argument for outside assistance.

"I'm sure much of the last century's scientific advancement has directly resulted from their presence. Edison, for example, probably was not an extraterrestrial. However, I would bet one or more of those who worked under him were subtly guiding him along his path of experimentation and discovery.

"On the other hand, Edison's arch-nemesis Tesla worked alone and seemed to be autistic, exhibited symptoms consistent with Asperger's Syndrome, deeply introverted, and possessed a stellar, universe-class mind. Whether he was an extraterrestrial or just an extraordinary homegrown genius is unknown. But, although there is no proof, I would not dispute a hypothesis of alien origins of the man and can point to factors suggesting precisely that conclusion. It is a shame he left no progeny of whom we could test their DNA."

I motioned to a chair for my guest and then seated myself, eager to continue this fascinating conversation. "You're not helping much. I'm eager to learn more about them and their presence here. That they manifest a presence is undeniable. Even with my service in the war with the Singularity, they kept me almost completely in the dark. Can you suggest any idea why?"

She shook her head. "Truly, I do not understand much. I believe, just as in your case, their Earth-born children suspect nothing of extraterrestrial origins, having assimilated into Earth's society. I appreciate your example is extraordinary, as they were intentionally breeding warriors for a specific cause, yet even outside that narrow focus, the ascertainment still holds. Their elders appear to play their cards close to the vest and conceal plenty of secrets.

"Most of what I believe is conjecture. For example, in every case I'm aware of, the individual possesses high intelligence, and there is often a link to Aspergers or even full-on Autism. However, those as severe as Tesla seem uncommon. There is usually a link between intelligence and eccentricity, and a degree of Asperger's is frequently in play. His teachers thought Einstein retarded early in his life, although the story he failed math is an urban legend.

"Even high intelligence is an untrustworthy marker. These people often hide their aptitude, living, and functioning as under-achievers in their day-to-day life, keeping their intellect under wraps. Often they disguise themselves as assistants to exceptional Earthly luminaries, as in the Edison conjecture.

"We native humans produce genius-level underachievers as well, so one must be careful jumping to conclusions considering the highly intelligent. Nonetheless, a true genius often may not necessarily descend from Planet K's extraterrestrial immigration. Yet, linkage of an average or mediocre mind to an extraterrestrial source is unlikely, at least in my experience. Possibly only their top-notch, highly-intelligent members escaped the cataclysm and spread their chromosomes.

"Another hypothesis worth exploring is the connection of the alien genes to blood types, which is why I asked to draw your blood when we first met." I started to interrupt; she held up a hand to forestall. "Do not worry, the samples I took didn't make their way into the hands of the Men in Black or other Government organization. They were for my private research, and I encrypted the test results, anonymized them into my data compilation, and destroyed the actual blood samples. So no one can view those results except as an anonymous data point in a private study."

I relaxed and withdrew my original question, only to interject a new question. "Has your study of blood types produced insights?"

She nodded in response. "Thus far, I find consistency in correlating the lack of Rh proteins with alien ancestry. Rh Protein originated in the Rhesus monkeys or at least a primate ancestor and may reflect a genetic heritage from humanity's common origin with other primates. It does appear as if only humans with Earth native blood possess the Rh protein. Approximately 15% of whites, about 3% of Africans, and roughly 1% of Asians are absent the protein. Thus, an average of around 7% of Earth's humans lack the Rh protein in their blood.

"My working hypothesis is that humans of pure alien blood do not reflect the odd genetic intersection with the Rhesus ancestor, thus lack this protein. Thus far, the data supports the contention. Thus, up to as much as 7% of Earth's humanity potentially descends from alien origins. The actual figure is probably lower, as we do not positively know all Earth humans possess the protein, only that every known extraterrestrial descendant tested has lacked it. There are too few trustworthy data points.

"Another unproven conjecture is African chromosomes originated solely on Earth. No one ever said so in precise words, yet one observes what one observes."

The implied bias of her last statement hung in the air for a moment as I struggled with the temptation. After a moment, I decided to let that one slide. I needed to brainstorm some fresh ideas on that radical thought. It didn't seem possible the only 'pure earth' chromosomes came out of Africa, did it? Isn't her conjecture ignoring the 3% of Africans who lack the protein? Or are they merely Earth-native humans naturally lacking the protein, suggesting the remaining might be of extraterrestrial heritage? And what of those pesky Asians? Aren't they even more closely tied to the Earth than Africans based on the blood profile theory? It all seems like BS to me. I tabled the questions for later thought, but I wasn't buying it, not yet anyway. Her hypothesis was insufficient by my lights.

I grabbed the floor, still digesting the implications. "So, we are in a clash of cultures, where a highly advanced culture has deeply infiltrated our own and subverted our native culture. They do not respect any 'Prime Directive,' in fact, appear to be intentionally molding our culture towards their uncertain ends?"

She laughed — the first time I had heard her do so. "Well put, though, be careful of your use of 'we and they' since from where I sit, you are the one bearing alien chromosomes, and I'm seemingly the one that is of Earth."

That stopped me in my tracks!

As I mulled the thought over, I thought I heard our Amerasian companion emit a faint chuckle beneath her breath at my takedown. The fur-girls were staring in open-mouthed wonder as though they were struggling to make sense of our words.

"Touche," I responded after a moment. "I suppose a disinterested third party might doubt my loyalties. But, on the other hand, from my standpoint, Earth has always been my only home, and although willing to be a mercenary to fight their battle for reward, I never considered them 'my people' in any meaningful sense. So I suppose my chromosomes and my nurture are at odds.

"Honestly, isn't that likely to be the case for many? Even though descended from off-worlders, are they not prone to believe themselves solely from the Earth?"

She shrugged. "The possibilities are endless, and we cannot afford the time to unravel the complexities of Interstellar society. So instead, we must decide what to do about your troubles with the Men in Black and take these lovely ladies home."

"About that, I cannot help but wonder, given the larger picture you painted, if Alex and his organization are not after us for larger reasons than Alex's ego disguised as possible Homeland Security issues. Might the extraterrestrial society and the possibility of government involvement, a possible cover-up, and the pressure for disclosure factor in his obsession with us?"

"Definitely!" She responded, "I can't say how much Alex knows of the extraterrestrial presence. It seems clear he had not been 'read-in' on the story at all, or else you would not now be free.

"Nonetheless, his organization seems at the forefront of the fight to keep the presence hidden and preserve the status quo, although perhaps only the upper levels are aware of the full picture. That is why he swooped in and took possession of the body of that unfortunate girl who died in Oakland. He was not there to solve the mystery of her origins or her death. He was there to cover up the fact it happened at all. He was not well informed; he was merely following directives from his superiors and had not planned to apprehend you until his superiors learned of your connection. I believe orders came down, and he switched tactics from monitoring and waiting to containment, meaning he received orders to bring you and the girls in and confine you. I'm amazed you escaped."

I nodded in agreement. "In light of the picture you painted, I am a bit surprised at our fortune; we were indeed lucky, although we are not free yet and remain in danger of being entrapped."

I pointed at Jill. "That one found us and now wishes to join us — puzzling in light of her involvement with Alex's Men in Black. I'm not sure how much I trust her yet. Perhaps our conversation will affect her plans and goals.

"You paint a fascinating picture. According to you, alien influences guided and molded Earth's civilization for a long time, possibly centuries, and our government, at some level, understands this and is complacent with the cover-up. Why?

"Are the alien influences limited to the people from 'Planet K' or are there other groups?"

She nodded before responding to my question. "I believe so, although I lack definitive proof. I'm certain there is at least one other group. Where they originate and what their motivations might be, remains unclear. Whereas the 'Planet K' contingent seems content to influence our society and politics gently, the other presence I believe exists seems wholly inimical, bent on exploitation, domination, and even enslavement. Assuming I'm correct and they do exist and the actions and events I attribute to another, different extraterrestrial influences are, in fact, that and not just plain, ordinary, human cussedness. If they do exist, they are a minuscule few. I do not wish to veer off on a tangent discussing my theories; there are more pressing matters."

"I agree; we need to define our next step. I fear we cannot stay here much longer." Something was tingling in the back of my brain as I digested her words. I glanced at Jill, noting her reaction. She seemed attentive.

I asked Dr. Rawls, "What is your role in helping us, and how do you come to find us here? Do you know my friend who has assisted? You rejected my characterization of a fifth column, yet your actions seem to fit the definition. What do we do next?"

She smiled at my barrage of questions, shaking her head and sighing as if trying to decide where to start.

"As Hemingway coined the term and described the world he was writing about, the "Fifth Column" was a group of traitors within an organization aimed at assisting an external force in overthrowing said organization. I suppose I bristle at the term "Fifth Column" as we are certainly not traitors and are not looking to overthrow anything. Quite the opposite!

"I would coin another term, a *Sixth Column*, to describe our activities and interests. We are loyalists to humanity first and Earth humans, not infiltrating the defending organization but rather the attacking organization or its fifth column. The relationship between Earth and the people from 'Planet K' is a kinship of stability, coexistence, and mutual benefit. We claim our role is acting in the interests of Earth to maintain that balance. Humanity lacks the tools, the science, to repel the invaders. I and my sixth column cohorts are instead working to maintain the status quo until we develop those tools. Currently, Earth would lose a head-on conflict, so we avoid one. There is at present no conflict, and we wish to ensure that remains unchanged; we intend to protect and care for the interests of humanity.

"We are in favor of and pushing for what you called the 'Disclosure Project.' Our goal is to bring the alien presence on Earth from the shadows into public view. But unfortunately, there are those on both sides opposed to disclosure and who believe humanity cannot accept the whole truth of our role in galactic society.

"If we are in opposition to anyone, something I would debate, we are in opposition to forces that would seek to disrupt this peaceful coexistence. In the immediate sense, your friend Alex and his 'Men in Black' represent those forces who would take our alien friends into his custody for reasons that are not clear, though perhaps quite unsavory. It is all a complex swirl of 'Disclosure' versus continued secrecy, Alien versus Earthly agendas and more, too complicated to unravel."

I mulled her words for a moment. "I like your invention of the term sixth column. That puts a different face on the questions before us."

"Yes, as I stated earlier," she interrupted, "There is truly no 'Us versus Them' conflict. These people have shaped our society for hundreds of years, and as near as I can determine, their influence has been overwhelmingly positive. With the demise of their world as a habitable sphere, they are now as much Earth people, in addition to being fully human, as we are. There is no conflict, only assimilation, as they assimilate into our world, just as every immigrant group to arrive in America has assimilated and changed America. Much the same process is happening to the entire planet Earth."

I resumed, "In light of the "Sixth Column" perspective, what is your organization's role, and how do you and I and my friend Phil all fit in?"

"I do not know your friend Phil, not personally; we are a clandestine organization and operate in a covert cell structure so that no one understands the full extent of the organization." I nodded, acknowledging that I understood; she continued, "I spent years, much of my life, establishing my credentials as an expert in my field, available for consulting whenever something of an 'X-Files' nature occurs. So meeting our friends here was quite a surprise." She nodded toward Stapleya and Wisceya. "Of course, I knew of their existence. I visited their planet, once, briefly, although not to Stapleya's home castle. It's surprising how your nickname of their world as "Planet Oz" has taken hold; all our members use the name. Perhaps they never told you that Nekomata is the proper name for the planet."

She took me by surprise. I nodded, as indeed, I had not heard that name before.

"Your book is required reading throughout our organization. It's interesting; in fact, the size of the organization is secret, though I suspect the sales figures for your book represent a close proxy for the true size of the organization. I bet you can make a closer guesstimate of the expanse of the group than anyone!"

Really! The tens of thousands of books I sold mainly went to members of a clandestine Sixth Column organization? That's a bunch of books! That's a big organization! Required reading? I'm flattered! If I had known I held a captive market, I would've charged more. Much more! Once again, I wondered if writing that damned book had been a wise decision.

New Team Members

Our conversation had momentarily stalled, and I took advantage of the lull to meditate on the implications of all I had heard. Then, suddenly, a thought surfaced.

"Something you said puzzles me, Dr. Rawls." She tilted her head and lifted her eyebrows questioningly. I continued, "You said that the Sixth Column group, though not aligned with the 'Planet K' aliens, at some level infiltrated their organization. Yet you said you had been to Planet Oz, and clearly, you know some Language. How do you reconcile that? You must have had alien support for those; how else could you navigate the portals? That would seem to align you with off-world interests more than you suggest. You implied that the Sixth Column is unknown to both sides; is that not the case?"

She responded with a wry smile. "It is true; we are not entirely unknown to both sides. The Sixth Column, as an organization, remains hidden as an entity. Some aliens know that sympathetic individuals exist and have interacted with various members solely as individuals. We consult with and support some of their projects. As a result, some have been invited off-world on rare occasions. The same is true of the government operatives as well. Therefore, we operate clandestinely, using a cold-war-style cell structure to mask our organization and members. I maintain more than one persona in my covert life.

"Alex's people know my involvement as a NASA Scientist who is available to their organization in 'X-Files' style cases; they know nothing of the Sixth Column or my involvement therein. I think. The Aliens know nothing of Dr. Rawls, at least insofar as I'm aware, and remain unaware of my carefully cultivated scientist's personality. Dr. Rawls is at least two cells removed from anyone interacting with them. Should events become complicated, only a small number are at risk from either direction. On the other hand..."

Sensing she was rambling, I interrupted, "How do you propose to transport us off-world?"

She was startled, as though unprepared for such an obvious question. I immediately followed with another. "If the Aliens know nothing of your existence, much less your involvement in the Sixth Column, how did you travel to Planet Oz?"

Again, a fleeting yet even more apparent 'deer-in-the-headlights' instant. I became troubled; this woman had presented a compelling story, one I wished to believe, though one with a couple of holes I could drive Alex's monstrous, black SUV through, and she was entirely unprepared to answer the obvious questions. That triggered alarm bells in my skull and set my 'spidey-sense' to jangling.

The wide-eyed expression disappeared as she struggled to regain her momentum.

"I'm not, not personally. My role is to protect you from being captured by the government forces who would imprison you. Once I'm confident you can remain free, I will pass the two girls along to another who can take them home."

We had survived and remained free until now due to my sense of paranoia and my tingly senses. I trust my instinct more than I do anyone.

I shook my head. "I do not believe that will be acceptable. I'm not inclined to allow these ladies out of my sight until I can escort them safely to their home myself. Entrusting their welfare to an unknown party requires faith, in you, in your organization, and that faith is something I do not currently possess. There are numerous slippery players in this convoluted game, and I do not understand their motives, not those of anyone besides myself. I cannot hand them off to you or anyone.

"I'm sorry, Dr. Rawls, I need to take a few special precautions; I need some time to consider several claims you have made and verify whatever I can. I worry that I cannot trust you just at this moment. If proven wrong, I will humbly apologize and beg your forgiveness later. Until that later arrives, I must ask you to submit to some indignities.

"First, I must ensure you are not carrying any electronic devices; I cannot risk anyone tracing you here. Hand over your cell phone, please."

She shook her head. "I anticipated the risk of being tracked; I didn't bring any electronics. Not on my person, not in my car. You can trust me, Fitz; I will conform to whatever steps you think necessary to set your mind at ease."

I smiled at her. "Thank you for understanding. When Jill found us, I forced her to strip to ensure she had no tracking devices or weapons, knock her off-balance, and make it difficult to escape. Although uncomfortable at first, she has adapted. I noted that she seemed uncomfortable for a few moments when you first arrived, which I had chalked up to an initial discomfort at being nude with any stranger. Perhaps that is the case, or there is a deeper reason underlying that discomfort." I narrowed my eyes and gazed penetratingly at them, "Is it possible that you and Jill are collaborating?"

It was Jill's turn to act surprised. Dr. Rawls avoided my gaze and responded with a stony-faced expression that did not betray surprise at my accusation. Jill's visage, on the other hand, spoke volumes. But unfortunately, those volumes were in a language I do not read. I knew something odd was up, yet had no clue what!

"Confiscating Jill's clothing is not for prurient or arbitrary reasons. On the contrary, joining us in clothes-free mode adds to our comfort as we prefer to be nude. Still, far more importantly, it adds materially to our security, an alternative to physical restraint lest she might attempt to escape — I judged her unlikely to bolt bare-skinned down a public street." Then, looking her squarely in the eyes, I lowered the boom, adding, "I must now ask the same of you."

Without a word, Dr. Rawls stood and shucked her clothing rapidly, almost as though eager to do so. I was shocked at how quickly she gave in on that score, yet if she had been to Planet Oz as claimed, which I doubted given her previous statements, casual nudity should not concern her. It didn't, to my shocked surprise.

My 'spidey-sense' still jangled at her furtive glances at Jill. I began to suspect that my wild jab had hit home. Were Jill and Dr. Rawls collaborators? Are they members of a sixth column organization as described, or are they working for another party altogether, and if that is the case, what is their motivation? The possibility of a second alien presence nagged at the back of my mind.

As I took her possessions, she laughed. "Now that we are naked together, I suppose you should drop the formality and call me Estelle. Somehow it seems strange for a man I'm naked with to address me by my title."

At least she can find humor in an otherwise awkward situation. So I laughed with her on that. "Estelle, as I say, if I'm wrong, I will humbly apologize. At the moment, however, I find the present circumstances and the wildly moving pieces of this conspiracy terrifying, and I'm unsure how to proceed; I need time to think and verify what I can. Then, I must decide our next move."

I asked Stapleya and Wisceya to stay with our guests and watch them while I went online. I played it a bit coy with Estelle and Jill; I had not let either of them observe my methodology and wanted to ensure it stayed that way. They, of course, knew I'd been communicating with another person, and I'm sure they surmised it might be the owner of this house. I had carelessly let his name slip, though, given the ready availability of property records, I'm sure that is a minor nit. Nonetheless, I intend to play my cards as close to my smoothly manscaped chest as possible.

While the ancient, tired computer cranked itself awake, I sat deep in thought, trying to identify all the players in our conspiracy and organize them in my mind. Phil himself seems to be a member of a genuine fifth column, allied with Petchy's organization. He had been to Planet Oz, knows Language fluently, and Stapleya and Wisceya vouched for him. So, let's designate Phil and whoever is behind him, the fifth column.

As I considered what I honestly knew of my friend, it occurred to me that his possible connection with or knowledge of Petchy and Teena is unclear. He had name-dropped and claimed to be one of Teena's heroes, yet I had no independent confirmation. What had he stated that could not have come from my book? That he knew Language and knew the girls proved he had visited Planet Oz, it didn't show he was allied with Petchy and Teena. I need to question Stapleya and Wisceya more closely; perhaps they can shed light on my puzzlement.

If Phil represents the fifth column, Petchy and Teena must represent the Alien forces, the 'four columns' in this thin-stretched Spanish War analogy.

Estelle and, if I believe it, the majority of the buyers of my book are the "Sixth Column" of loyalists, stretching Hemingway's terminology. Yet it is an imperfect analogy. Who are they loyal to? Only those Earth humans carrying the Rhesus protein?

That might suggest they are NOT loyal to me. All Earth humans in general? Maybe or maybe not. Estelle had tipped her hand slightly with that comment regarding African origins, yet precisely what did she reveal? I can't see a connection between an Afro-centric worldview and the conspiracy swirling around us.

Then there are my dear friends from Planet Oz, unconnected to anyone's columns. They are innocent non-combatants trapped within the field of battle. Maybe we can extend our wordplay and call them munchkins? That seems silly. I wish I could leave all of this behind and be a munchkin myself right now — not likely to happen.

Finally, the darkly hinted, unsubstantiated alternative alien influence with a claimed taste for exploitation, enslavement, and domination. Are these the players we need to concern ourselves with at this time? How does Estelle know they exist? I need a name for them, a handle to tag them with should they appear. I will think on that one for a while, as there isn't a tremendous urgency.

There are one or maybe two more players to catalog. My thought process considering these additional players became interrupted when I realized the computer had settled down and awaited my attention.

I went online and checked the drafts folder. A different message replaced the fake E.D. Pill Spam I had placed there earlier, indeed a reply. I downloaded it and took the computer offline, leaving it running, ready to jump back online at a moment's notice.

A message from Phil awaited. The curt response stated that he thought Jill's motives were questionable and not to trust her. However, he claimed he would investigate and check for another message soon. He also asked if there were new developments.

I composed a new message for him, adding the latest info concerning Estelle and a few of my thoughts about the sixth column analogy. Then, I deleted some of my prose, deciding I wanted to talk to Stapleya and Wisceya regarding Phil's visit to their world before sharing my thoughts.

I proofread my text several times, hesitating on almost every phrase. I was developing a severe case of nervous paranoia, worrying about trusting whom, approaching the conclusion that I was a mere leaf on the wind, caught between multiple swirling tornadoes, between warring factions, each looking for the upper hand. No one is on my side, and which contingent is actively after us and which will find it within their self-interest to assist us is a puzzle I cannot resolve without more data.

All I wished to do was escape to Planet Oz — the Interstellar War can go on without me!

Finally, I decided I had told Phil just enough. I encrypted the message and re-deposited it in our online dropbox. Now I must wait for Phil to revisit our dead drop and respond. I wondered how long that might be.

While waiting for a response from Phil, I decided I wanted to start making preparations to rabbit. I still had no destination in mind. I only knew that an unacceptable number of people knew where we were. I need to be ready to run on a whim, and I suspect I might have that whim quite soon.

Without saying anything to the ladies, I went to the garage and started loading Julie's car with stuff that might be useful. Food, some items of clothing I stole from Phil's closets, and other stuff. My go-bags with my cash and other supplies were already in the car.

I returned to the living room where the four ladies were waiting. In Language, I addressed Stapleya and Wisceya, observing Estelle for signs of understanding. I believed she only knew a few words and did not speak Language fluently. I asked Stapleya to come into the bedroom a moment. Once we were out of earshot of the others, whispering, I asked her what she could tell me regarding Phil. Had he come to Planet Oz with Petchy and Teena? She acknowledged he had. How long had he stayed? Were they friendly? Had Petchy or Teena discussed him notably?

She thought a few moments, "I'm not sure, Fitz. Yes, there had been some difficulty, though they did not tell us anything. Petchy got angry, and Petchy never gets angry. He used a word in English I had never heard until today, and I'm still not certain what it means; I'm sure it is not good." Now, this pricked my ears! "What's the word, beloved one?" I asked. She responded, "The word Estelle used today describing what you called fifth columnists. Traitor."

"You are right, my dear lady; it is not good. A traitor betrays the trust of their family or society. As if a friend in your trusted inner circle were to move to another castle and provide them some information that could harm you."

She recoiled in horror. "I presumed it was something similar. Our world is so much simpler than yours. No one would do that; I would kill them and serve their carcass at Evening Feast if they did!"

Now it's my turn to recoil! Stapleya and Wisceya and the wonderful fur-people of Planet Oz, cannibals? I had no idea that could be a possibility!

Seeing my shocked expression, she laughed. "It is only a joke! An extreme expression of outrage, taken from a scary story told to children." I relaxed a bit after a few seconds; now, I had a new nightmare to obsess over. I had never seen a cemetery on Planet Oz.

A Strained Analog

After several moments spent spinning in horror within the confines of my skull, I decided to table the question of corpse disposition on Planet Oz for now. I have enough worries regarding corpses, in particular, avoiding becoming one here on Earth. If Stapleya had been making a joke, her sense of humor was decidedly macabre, and I can't afford to fall down that rabbit hole right now.

I jerked myself back to our more pressing issue. Stapleya's comment on Phil's apparent relationship to Petchy, the usage of the word 'Traitor' was troubling! Could I trust her statement at face value? Random words overheard in a poorly understood language could lead to boundless misunderstandings. Four Columns, Fifth Columns, Sixth Columns, MiBs, Alien Invaders, Alien Immigrants! It's all too confusing; I realized I was on the verge of losing my way entirely in a maelstrom of dissonant forces.

I prodded Stapleya a bit further on her memory of a conversation overheard long ago and poorly understood, translated via the lens of memory. However, she could add nothing new to the account. If Petchy and Teena had considered Phil a traitor to their cause, I must become wary of him. However, I must also acknowledge that I could imagine several possible circumstances where, in the heat of a disagreement, such words might be used and yet not wholly impugn the individual's trustworthiness.

The problem is, I must trust someone. My core mission, to return Stapleya and Wisceya to their home planet, was beyond my physical capability. I don't possess the tools to access a portal. In the end, only Petchy, Teena, or someone within their organization can do so.

Phil had represented himself as of their organization. However, his relationship isn't directly in the alien organization, not in the Four Columns of our increasingly strained analogy, instead, in an allied fifth column. Assuming he had not turned traitor to the larger organization, can he even assist us in the first place? It seems unlikely Phil can help navigate a portal. The best I can hope for is that he might connect us to someone from Petchy's people, the Four Columns, who can.

Estelle's Sixth Column seems useless. Perhaps she can assist with supplies or shelter, or maybe she could keep us out of the clutches of Alex or his Governmental bosses, assuming I decide I can trust her, but fundamentally, she seems of little help.

I sent Stapleya back to the living room to supervise our guests and asked Wisceya to come in. I questioned her regarding Phil's visit to her world. Still, she was then too young and had known too little of English to add much, other than a vague reinforcement of the perception that Petchy and Teena had been upset with Phil before he departed Planet Oz.

I sent Wisceya back to the living room and just sat for a while, considering our options. Then, finally, I realized that trusting anyone other than Petchy or Teena, if she still lives, was problematic. If I understood more about Phil's organization, perhaps I could trust him, but for the moment, the unknowns were overwhelming, and the risks were ill-defined.

I concluded that we must rabbit and soon. I just had a few logistical details to settle, and once decided, we must hit the road. But, first, I must check our dropbox. I hope for a response to my last message. I must also attempt once more to reach Petchy.

Back online, I noted my response was gone from the drafts folder, but no new message. Phil was probably decoding my message at this moment. I went to the online Guardian paper website to check my previous ad placement. Something had happened! My ad was gone, replaced by a response.

Well, that is interesting! Baffling but interesting! But what does it mean? Is it indeed a message from Petch? Or merely someone who read my book and decided to play? Worse, perhaps Alex's MiBs are playing games.

Who is Greeley? Who is Mr. Charles?

Pondering this new mystery, I opted to take a chance on checking my email. Since I planned to leave this address soon, I decided the risk was minimal. While using every precaution and misdirection I could muster, I popped in and downloaded my inbox and dumped it into a local file. I was not about to sit online and read the messages one at a time. I jumped in and out quickly, giving our nemesis minimal time to spot my activity.

Download complete, I popped back over to the dropbox and discovered a new message had just appeared. I grabbed it and took the computer offline once again. I pulled out the tools and decoded Phil's message. He reiterated his prior precaution and told us to stay put. I wasn't feeling particularly trusting.

I left the computer running and returned to the living room, where the ladies were sitting and chatting amicably. I seated myself between the fur-girls and joined the conversation. After a moment's pleasantries, I addressed our erstwhile sixth columnist.

"Estelle, I wonder if you can clarify something. How did you find us, how did you know to come here? I suspect you intended for us to believe that Phil had sent you, but I now know that's not true." Of course, I was exaggerating, but I harbored a strong suspicion, especially in light of Phil's recent message. Before she could answer, I continued, "Either you found your way here by some trick or betrayal I overlooked, or else I can only assume you and Jill are collaborators, and you were watching when I brought her in here. It's time to come clean."

She smiled wryly and nodded acquiescence. "I'm sorry, Fitz, I never intended to deceive you. Old habits die hard, I suppose. Spending years in undercover work, keeping secrets, and revealing the minimum necessary becomes second nature. I wasn't attempting to deceive, merely keeping my cards close to my, um, vest." She gave an almost imperceptible laugh and a faint movement, lifting her attributes minutely to emphasize the absence of the aforesaid theoretical garment. I sensed Estelle had a ribald sense of humor similar to my own or the fur-girls. We might get along well, given half a chance.

"Yes, Jill and I are indeed cohorts in the Sixth Column organization I described. Jill had tracked your presence here, to this neighborhood, while throwing Matt off the trail. When he tired of chasing your wild goose and returned to home base, she stayed behind, claiming an intention to rest and eat dinner before heading home. Instead, she texted that she was certain you three holed up in this block, and she planned to make contact somehow. In our last conversation, she seemed confident she had narrowed your location down to one of two streets. I scrambled to come to her aid when she missed the subsequent check-in. As I prepared to leave the City and drive this way, I received an odd phone call from her, realizing she had made contact. She managed to provide enough information to guide me close to you, although I still wasn't certain which house you were occupying."

"So that call to 'Matt,' huh?" She nodded, admitting the deception. "How did you discover which house to come to?"

She smiled faintly, "I didn't, exactly, when she had parked and staked herself out, she had placed indicative chalk marks on the curb. I merely drove around the neighborhood until I spotted her telltale, by which I was sure I was near. When the letter carrier navigated her rounds, I discounted houses receiving mail, as I assumed you commandeered an empty house. After driving around and observing the neighborhood for a while, I picked out the one house nearby that seemed unoccupied, no car in the driveway, no evidence that anyone lived there. It helped that you were almost directly across from where she had placed her marks."

I smiled at how simple it seemed. That's always how it goes — even elaborate legerdemain becomes simple once the trick's exposed. There's a reason a magician never reveals his secret.

"So Jill's your plant inside Alex's organization?"

She nodded. "That's how I arrange to be called in as a consultant on interesting cases with an X-Files flavor."

"I also bet that's why Alex brought me in when poor Shameya appeared."

Jill nodded in agreement, joining our conversation. "Recall I mentioned when we first met, I had read your book and suggested calling you in. That's the literal truth, if incomplete."

"I wish you had just explained all of this, in an honest, open fashion, from the beginning. But, unfortunately, your dissembling and deceit raised all sorts of alarms, and even now, I find difficulty in trusting you.

"I do not wish to be involved in politics or Exopolitics — columns — four, five or six — or MiB xenophobia. Wheels within wheels, webs of intrigue, I've had enough. All I want is to take my friends," I pointed at the fur-girls, "to their home and be left alone. If they let me, I would love to adopt Stapleya's castle as my home and live there with Lolita and raise our son — this conspiracy has all become too much. I don't want to play."

Stapleya and Wisceya both smiled at this, nodding at me. I returned their smile, gave Wisceya a conspiratorial wink, and continued. "I don't believe I can trust you. Can you offer me a valid reason to do so? Can you truly help send them home safely, or are you just another player looking to further an agenda I profoundly don't care about?"

Jill and Estelle eyed each other strangely; the fur-girls were staring wide-eyed at the three of us, trying to figure out this strange conflict. So was I.

After several seconds of uncomfortable silence, Jill cleared her throat and began, "Fitz, I'm sorry, it seems that we got off on the wrong foot, and we both have two wrong feet. We've stumbled at every turn. Much of that's my fault. I must shoulder the blame for numerous missteps. I tried to walk a narrow line and mostly failed.

"You're right; we're not directly able to assist your friends to travel back to their home. The sixth column organization, I mean. We have a much bigger cause than merely our own possible, personal self-interest. Our precise cause is, as we had claimed, protecting the human race and, consistent with what I stated before, protecting civilization. Dr. Rawls had mentioned another alien culture. But, again, we had played our cards a little too close to our breasts. The threat is not theoretical, is not in question, although the proof's thin and circumstantial. Evil forces are at work."

Jill glanced at Estelle as if uncertain whether or how to proceed. Finally, Estelle picked up the narrative. "Petchy and his people fought a decades-long war to the death against the Singularity. We don't understand the particulars; we have no connection with them. However, we have other plants similar to Jill, embedded as friends, neighbors, and coworkers, close to known operatives of Petchy's organization. What did you call them? The Four Columns? We'll utilize that term for shorthand.

"The Four Columns vanished! Approximately the time or perhaps slightly before the time you were engaging against the machines on Planet K, every known Four Columns operative disappeared from Earth. We are clueless as to where they went! Perhaps they are here under new identities, or maybe they went elsewhere. I presumed their absence was an artifact of the all-out, go-for-broke assault on Planet K.

"A few humans of alien blood, descendants of Four Column families who almost certainly know nothing of their origins, remain on Earth. We monitor them, although they can tell us zilch. They're as mystified and puzzled by their friends and family's disappearance as we."

Jill took up the gavel again, interjecting, "I'm serious about accompanying you through the portal, desperately hoping I could reach the Four Columns people if anything remains of their society. We need their support if they're able to provide aid at all. The threat is exceptionally grave.

"Alex and his superiors and the organization behind them are fighting the same threat, from a different perspective, with a profound lack of reliable information. They don't wish to lock you and the fur-people up as much as to figure out where you fit in a puzzle they fail to grasp. Our Sixth Column organization works with them, embedded in their ranks via numerous others, such as I. They aren't aware we exist as an organization; we work independently and guide them where possible through plants such as myself and academic consultants such as Estelle."

Estelle picked up the conversation. "We nurtured my Dr. Estelle Rawls, MD, Ph.D. persona as an academic 'egghead,' expert in exobiology and unconnected to any political factions, independently called in by organizations in all branches of government whenever anything that might seem to be of an X-Files nature appears. She's one of their essential resources."

Jill again picked up the baton. "She presents herself as a lone scientific consultant to the world, though she has several layers of support behind the scenes via the Sixth Column connections. In addition, there are additional scientist types on-call to provide corroborating analysis.

"It's critical to understand that the Sixth Column doesn't exist, not to anyone else. We're extraordinarily secretive and allow no one on either side to learn about our organization! We operate as individuals when interacting with other organizations, never admitting to more extensive organization involvement. For example, Estelle's Dr. Rawls persona is widely known as an academic consultant on-call for various needs, yet no one she deals with knows of the Sixth Column or her actual mission and expertise.

"Our power comes from secrecy! You're the only person outside of the organization to learn it exists. But, as I will explain at another time, numerous actual members remain ignorant. They aren't aware that what they're involved in is a clandestine organization. We're indeed so secretive that not even all of our members understand the nature of the organization!"

Estelle jumped in when she paused, "We need your assistance and will aid and protect you, however possible. We need to contact the Four Columns to recruit their aid, or our entire civilization is surely doomed!"

A Hard Drive

Jill and Estelle sat somewhat close together on the couch during our discussion. As the conversation became animated, I sensed a bit of chemistry between them as they had bounced back and forth, advancing the narrative. I started paying attention to their body language first subconsciously; then, my frontal lobe began to engage.

While on Planet Oz, one lesson I learned was that sexual desires will always find an outlet. That connecting these two took this long, I must plead the various distractions on my mind, not to mention the pressure of running for my life.

When I had first brought Estelle into where Jill waited, I had sensed a certain level of discomfort in Jill's demeanor. Still believing in Jill's basic prudery, I had chalked it up to basic nudiphobia, to being placed in a room with a clothed stranger while forced to be naked, especially if that stranger was somewhat older and another race. Add the complication of being a coworker or work acquaintance, and there appears ample reason for her discomfort. She had expressed a grave fear of that exact situation. Although a few are natural exhibitionists and would not object, most people would find it acutely uncomfortable. At least I certainly would! That's how I initially read her reaction. I thought that being forced to be nude in front of someone different in age and race, an acquaintance or coworker had disconcerted Jill.

Now I began to realize that was not the case at all. I'm not sure my own life experience can explain Jill's reaction. Perhaps it might be akin to having a spouse unexpectedly present one's clandestine lover, provoking shock and discomfort while attempting to mask the guilt in one's eyes. At least that's the closest analogy I can suggest.

Regardless of the precise emotional origins of Jill's initial discomfiture, it became clear that Jill and Estelle knew each other well indeed and not only from work-related associations.

Illumination came when, moments after Estelle had pronounced the impending doom of our civilization, she had leaned back and placed her arm around Jill in a comforting, loverly embrace.

Unquestionably, they were not the strangers I had thought, not even the mere co-conspirators I had since come to accept. They were indeed much closer.

Once again, human sexuality manages to surprise, even shock Fitz, the Great Inseminator. So hilarious! Or it would be if I had time for hilarity. How can I be so experienced in a field yet wholly inept? So ignorant?

I suppose experience isn't everything.

"We need your assistance," Estelle repeated, "We are desperate to contact Petchy's organization; we need help from his people. Not just to return your friends to Planet Oz, but also to learn what they can tell us of the greater threat, help us obtain weapons, tools, and aid in the coming battle. We must repel these invaders, and we lack the first clue how and don't even understand their origins."

I sat snuggled between my furry friends, arms around them much as the couple across from us were embracing. I studied Estelle and Jill for a moment in quiet contemplation. Lovers, unquestionably. They were dedicated to their cause, undoubtedly. But is the threat Estelle is talking about real? Unknown. Can Petchy's people help? Unknown.

I responded, "I may have a hint of how to proceed. I received a message from Petchy." The couple straightened; Estelle's face lit up. I raised my hand to forestall her question, "Possibly, I should say. It is cryptic, and I'm unsure of the meaning, and I can't be certain it is even from Petch. Many people read my book and might send something like this as a prank. It might even have come from Alex."

They looked puzzled. "What's the message?" Estelle asked. "I'm uncertain. The first line says, "Greeley Wrote it Backwards!" but that's meaningless. So who is Greeley, and what did he write?"

Estelle's eyebrows arched, Jill's pulled together in puzzlement! Estelle's momentary astonishment gave way to a half-spit-take and a brief spate of outright giggles. Then, Jill's puzzlement shifted to amazement. Estelle sobered after a moment. "You young people lack education these days! Greeley is almost certainly Horace Greeley, longtime editor of the New York Tribune. He created that grand newspaper in 1841 and topped the masthead for decades. He died in the 1870s; the paper lasted until the 1900s before it failed, absorbed by another paper. In its day, the Tribune was the greatest newspaper in the country."

Now, I suppose it was my turn to appear astonished. "Okay, how is a man who has been dead 150 years relevant to our problems of the moment?"

"For one, he was a genius who had all the hallmarks of Asperger's. His blood type is unknown though I would bet he lacked the Rh protein marker. Whether those aspects of Mr. Greeley's existence are relevant or not is unclear; more importantly, he is significant due to something he wrote, his catchphrase!"

I sat there, open-mouthed. Then, after a pause for effect, Estelle continued, "His famous catchphrase 'Go West Young Man' urged Civil War-era pioneers westward to settle the country."

I jumped up, "If Greeley Wrote it Backwards, the message suggests that Petchy's telling us to go East!"

"So it would seem," Estelle agreed.

"The rest of the message says Heed Mr. Charles, any clue regarding that?"

Estelle was pensive for a moment. "There isn't a black person or Jazz fan alive on this continent who doesn't hold a special, profound respect for the late jazz and pop artist, Ray Charles. Some suggested he was more significant to the American pop music culture than Elvis Presley."

"Okay, and what sage advice did he give that we should heed?"

Estelle glared at me in amused frustration, "Fitz, you're a smart fellow, you're masculine and strong, magnificently bronzed and beautifully built, but you don't know twiddle outside of computers! Ray Charles had a tremendous hit with a song that hit the charts in 1961, won a Grammy award, made the list of "The 500 Greatest Songs of All Time," and became forever associated with his name. I cannot believe even a young fellow your age doesn't know "Hit the Road, Jack!" You should've Googled and saved yourself embarrassment!"

Perhaps. I do feel stupid, though, in my defense, both Mr. Greeley's academic tenure and Mr. Charles' classic hit occurred long before my birth. Somehow, pointing that out didn't seem likely to win any points today. I must suck it up and take it like a man.

Petchy's telling us to hit the road and head East; I guessed that made sense, as much sense as anything had the last few days. He seems to imply urgency, too, so what should I do? Take the fur-girls and Julie's car and head out? We could be rolling within roughly 15 minutes! Do I take Estelle and Jill with us? Let them loose or tie them up and leave them here? Where should we go? East isn't very specific.

I asked, "Where should we go if we leave here?" Estelle shrugged. "Greeley lived in New York much of his life. Charles lived in a variety of places. Nothing in his song suggests a destination."

I opined, "Petchy would not send us to a major city like New York. Any place with centralized surveillance would be problematic anyway, with the MiBs looking for us.

"No, if we run somewhere, it has to be someplace with little surveillance and where Alex's people are less likely to look for us."

Jill suggested, "Why not head East, drive for a day and stop and check again for a message? Perhaps Petchy will provide additional directions."

"You would intend to accompany us?" I asked. They both nodded. "I debated what to do with you two. I can't be hauling around prisoners, and I do not want to turn you loose if you are not on our side. So, I'm relieved you have chosen to join us. The only question is whether you will swear to be full, trusted members of the group and not betray us. I need your sworn assurance you are honestly joining us and will support our mission. Do I have that?"

Both women stood and solemnly swore allegiance to us and our cause, promising to do everything possible to see the fur-girls safely home. I studied their faces carefully and consulted my 'spidey-sense.' I decided they meant it. Perhaps it is psychologically unsound, but I believe that duplicity does not come naturally while nude. Or possibly that's just my hope.

I figuratively pulled out my earlier note to myself, contemplating whether I was once again foolishly trusting. After a moment of self-examination, I accepted both women as trusted members of our venture. Then, I asked, "How are we to accomplish this logistically? Estelle's car's a two-seater, useless to us. The car I borrowed from Julie has enough seats, barely. Taking multiple vehicles would seem to be problematical."

Jill pitched in, "My van?"

I shook my head. "It's a government vehicle. They're aware of it and will be looking for it once they figure out you're missing. It probably has a tracker?"

She shook her head, then responded, "It's not an official vehicle, just an older utility vehicle occasionally used for undercover work. They probably don't realize I took it; I grabbed it at the last minute without authorization. I didn't wish to ride with Matt."

I cocked an eyebrow at that. Was there some reason Jill rejected riding with Matt? I filed that query with my earlier note to myself for later reference.

"Isn't Matt aware you took the van?" She slumped in acknowledgment. After a second's thought, she brightened. "Perhaps that works in our favor." I leaned forward in interest.

She continued, "The problem with getting out of the Bay Area is the few routes over the mountains. They can catch us too quickly. So instead, we lay a false trail. We drive two vehicles and leave via different roads. I drive my van up I-5 and leave a distinct trail by buying fuel with my credit card. They will spot my false trail and concentrate in that direction.

"I will veer east and somewhere around Fernley, NV. I will abandon the vehicle and meet up with you at the intersection of the Lincoln Highway and the Reno Highway. That's not far from Fernley. I'm confident I can hitchhike a ride, and even if I walk a few miles, I can handle it. Although I can't run the way you can, I'm fit and able; a few miles hoofing it isn't a hardship. I am a Warrior.

"They might track the vehicle to Fernley, but they might not if I hide the van well. Even if they do, by the time they figure out our deception, we will have rendezvoused and left them far behind."

Retiring to the computer bedroom with Jill, we studied the maps online. She was right. If she bought gas somewhere around Williams, off I-5 with a credit card, they would believe she headed North, assuming she's with us. She can cut across through Yuba City, pick up I-80, and head East. Once the MiBs note her absence, they will search for her and, by extension, us along Interstate 5 and points North.

Meanwhile, the rest of us will head out through Oakdale, pick up highway 395 and turn onto the Lincoln highway at Carson City. It seemed as if the strategy might work. Those looking for us should not search in our direction until long after we had escaped, if at all.

I gave Jill and Estelle their clothes and other items and told her where I had left her van. She and Estelle went to find the vehicle and send Jill on her way.

While they were doing that, I sadly decided I must destroy Phil's computer. I was not fond of the prospect; it's a capable machine, although tired and cranky. However, I could not risk that the MiB computer forensics techs might find anything useful. I almost shut the computer down when I remembered the downloaded emails.

I found a spare thumb drive forgotten in the back of a drawer. Copying the emails to the thumb drive for later reading, I stuffed it into my bag. Again, I was about to shut down when I realized I should leave Petchy a message acknowledging his instructions. I went to the Guardian web page and posted a Personal:

Are You Petchy? Mr. Charles is wise.

With that last action, I shut down the machine for the last time. So long, old friend, you've served me well.

It's unnecessary to destroy the physical machine, though I needed to wipe the disk drive beyond any hope of recovery. Perhaps Phil will put a newer drive in it and rebuild it. He might even be grateful for the upgrade once he forgives me. A modern Solid State Drive should do wonders for the old machine's performance.

Estelle returned as I finished removing the disk drive. I prepared to destroy it, though instead of taking the time at this moment, I instead tossed it into the car along with the other stuff I had purloined. The fur-girls had dressed in the meanwhile, and I grabbed my clothes and did likewise.

Estelle and I swapped the cars around, putting Estelle's bright red, flashy two-seater in Phil's garage, out of sight. We didn't believe anyone would come looking for her car here. Nonetheless, we decided to play it safe. If things go as planned, she will return and reclaim the roadster in a few days.

I scribbled a note for Phil in case he should show up, and the three ladies and I jumped in Julie's car and motored away. I was glad now that I had put quality tires on her car. We had some driving ahead.

The Amnesiac Incognito

While organizing to hit the road, Estelle called 'Shotgun' and claimed the front passenger's position; purely whimsy, of course, as Stapleya and Wisceya were oblivious to the colloquialism and had no clue as to the meaning of shotgun, in either the everyday slang or as a weapon. They would naturally prefer to sit together in the back anyway. Rather petite beside Estelle, it's only natural that they defer and grant her the roomier front seat.

The middle of the night saw us pulling out of Phil's driveway. The late hour should work in our favor. We could travel out of the area, over the Sierra Nevada range, and reach the Silver State before most of California's citizens awakened. Six hours of industrious traveling should put the significant woes recently associated with the slightly tarnished Golden State behind us.

We hit Carson City just after dawn, and I began to relax somewhat. Unless Alex pulled out all the stops for a full-scale dragnet, we were relatively safe now. A quick stop for nature's necessities and fuel, both for our bodies and the car, and we were soon rolling again, though not before Stapleya and Wisceya voiced an unfavorable opinion of the toilet facilities of the Instant Stop. Estelle did not dissent. I wondered why our society so consistently neglects public toilets. For an instant, I reflected on how different Planet Oz seemed in this regard. In my months living with the fur-people, I never encountered a dirty toilet anywhere — theirs is a fastidious society.

An hour later, we reached the Lahontan State Park and decided to stop for a break and a brief rest. We were well ahead of schedule, early for our planned rendezvous with Jill.

After the tortuously long drive, the interlude was welcome. The intersection of the Lincoln Highway and the road that connects Fallon and Fernley, our original rendezvous point, is not far away. We were quite a bit early, or so we believed, as Jill had more miles than we to drive. She had a thirty-minute head start on us, but we still had the advantage. We had plenty of time to walk around and stretch our legs.

I worried that merely stopping and waiting along the side of the road at the target intersection might attract attention. Spending an hour visiting the park seems an innocuous way to equalize our schedules without attracting attention. I worried that the fur-girls might draw unwanted stares, so we kept our distance from others, and they wore their masks. Fortunately, early on a weekday, there were few tourists present. We lacked the time for an exhaustive tour but spent an hour walking around the lakeshore. The spectacular scenery impressed the girls, and the Lahontan Dam left them in awe. However, our time was limited, and we soon resumed our trek.

After the brief diversion at the park, we again hit the road and arrived at the appointed juncture still too soon. Jill was nowhere in sight, but I hadn't expected her to be. We were still ahead of schedule.

Not wanting to park and wait, I turned the car north and drove leisurely toward Fernley. We motored into town and reached the local Walmart Supercenter without spotting our party. I searched out a shaded parking spot near the rear of the lot and kept a sharp eye on the passing traffic.

It became too warm to sit in the car as the day warmed up. The fur-girls were not distressed by the heat, as their home-world is much warmer. I, too, remain acclimated to warmth, although back on Earth for months. Poor Estelle, on the other hand, suffered as the temperature climbed.

Time passed, and I was becoming concerned at Jill's tardiness. Although not severely overdue yet, I had expected her by now. So, I decided to wait a few minutes longer before heading back down the road looking for her.

While sitting in the car, I realized we had an opportunity to buy a computer. I was reluctant to do so in person, even though this store was quite remote. They would hardly carry the latest and best premium high-performance machines. Fortunately, our modest needs do not require premium hardware.

I asked Estelle if she could make the purchase, as going shopping would give her relief from the rising heat without risking the store's surveillance flagging my too recognizable silhouette. Even though the Domain Awareness System's net does not extend this far from the urban centers, my height and build are distinctive, and the risk of someone spotting me remains worrisome.

A professional-looking middle-aged black lady buying a discount computer raises not an eyebrow, whereas a hulking giant draws eyes no matter what. I tend to be self-conscious about my size, feelings not assuaged by being in the company of tiny women. Next to my fur-girls or even Jill, I'm a giant. I'm much less self-conscious when paired with a more 'full-sized' woman like Estelle or my girlfriend Julie, even though she's shorter than Estelle.

My friends reassure me I'm not the cartoon caricature I sometimes imagine, though being on the lam has disadvantages for one with a distinctive silhouette. Regardless, pairing my frame with petite ladies such as my friends from Planet Oz ensures attracting attention. Moreover, I suspect the alien's fur-covered faces pass unnoticed in my shadow.

Estelle jumped at the opportunity, undoubtedly eager to reach the store's air-conditioning. I gave her cash, as we presumed using her plastic would not be wise, even though no one hunted her as far as we knew. I explained the hardware needed, a simple generic economy machine. She left us, walking briskly toward the storefront, eager for the more comfortably cool air.

She remained in the store a long time, and I teetered on the ragged edge of worry as the time progressed. My anxiety level slowly climbed until she reappeared. Indeed, she had gone shopping, buying numerous items in addition to her primary mission, including a case of bottled water, fruit bars, and other assorted food items.

The little machine Estelle purchased proved excellent for our needs. She also had the foresight to buy a mobile charger and a couple of inexpensive thumb drives. This woman is as intelligent as her doctorate implies. I scrutinized the machine, made sure it booted and operated as it should, plugged it in to charge while driving, and stashed it under the seat.

We decided to motor back down the highway in hopes of connecting with Jill. She should be in the area now, even after all possible delays, and we started to worry we had missed her. The day was getting quite warm, and if she was walking in the desert heat, she was facing some severe dehydration risk. It is, of course, much hotter on Planet Oz, though dehydration is a lesser concern due to the tropical climate and the frequent rains. This climate is different, much dryer, and an unprotected human without ample water cannot long survive. I appreciated Estelle's foresight to buy water; we might well need it!

We were circling the parking lot preparing to depart when I spotted a familiar van pulling into the back of the lot where the store employees would park. At first uncertain, I watched with interest as the vehicle parked in a rear corner, and Jill climbed out. Once again, my subtle instincts served us well, my 'spidey-sense' drawing us here. I do love it when a plan comes together.

I glanced around the store roof for surveillance cameras. Walmart is known for having a decent level of surveillance, although, as far as I know, not connected to any intelligent law-enforcement systems such as the Domain Awareness System. I could see no cameras covering this remote rear corner of the lot.

I drove over to where she gathered a few items from the back of the van, angling the car so her vehicle would block the view from the store rooftop in case I missed a camera. As she turned to lock and leave it, she was startled to see us. "Need a ride, miss?" I asked with a grin as I pulled alongside her van. She broke into a broad smile, although I think she was looking at Estelle.

After hugs all around, Jill climbed in the back seat and snuggled between the off-worlders. Of course, everyone loves to snuggle with Stapleya and Wisceya.

Once again, we hit the road — our pursuers should be looking for us elsewhere, and we had supplies, comestibles, and other necessary equipment. Jill had taken the opportunity to withdraw additional cash since she intentionally left a misdirecting trail. I carried a significant stash of funds, but that would soon run out if we stayed on the road long and paid cash for everything. Nevertheless, every dollar helped, and her contribution to the cause was welcome.

We headed east on the Lincoln Highway since staying off of the Interstate seemed wise, and we needed to distance ourselves from Jill's purloined government-issue van. We spent several hours making time out of Nevada and into Utah. Then, jumping off Highway 50, we headed toward Fillmore, finding a seedy mom-and-pop motel not associated with chains. Fortunately, our only absolute requirement beyond the essential amenities, a decent WIFI connection, is ubiquitous these days.

The motel we settled in seemed straight out of the 1960s and only accepted cash. That was a desirable feature since I didn't wish to risk flashing plastic. Unfortunately, the chains insist on a credit card even if you're paying cash, and merely verifying the card without charging anything would still set off alarms. Money doesn't need verification.

The WIFI seemed sluggish. Otherwise, the rooms were cheap and acceptable. Jill and Estelle opted to share a room to no one's surprise, and the off-worlders and I took another. We were not averse to sharing one room, though, at these favorable prices, they preferred a separate room.

After our long cross-country trip following nights with little sleep, I decided we needed downtime. Further, I needed to configure the computer and pursue my online detective work. So, we reserved our rooms for two nights and paid in advance.

The off-worlders donned their masks, I checked us in without letting the motel proprietor see their furry faces, and we settled into our adjoining rooms. It was still daylight, but we all were tired; a nap seemed in order.

I relaxed for the first time in days and slept long and deeply. The girls and I did rouse for gentle night music a couple of times, although we were more interested in sleep than passion. Snuggling with my furry ladies is always heavenly — what I wouldn't give right now to be back on Planet Oz with my Lolita. I wondered about Jill and Estelle, but they were not on our minds.

Though still dark, I arose and began working on the computer. Shortly, the girls became interested and settled in by my side, following my activity, asking questions, and, it would seem, gaining a rapid, if superficial induction into the mysteries of the digital realm. Of course, no matter how smart, no one can jump from the stone age into the digital world and become an expert overnight. Nonetheless, I marveled at how quickly they picked up the basics. I never answered the same question twice, and from their questions, they grasped far more than they missed. I find myself again in awe of their sheer intellect, especially their memory. For example, I gave them the barest superficial overview of the powers of two math and how it relates to computers, and they grasped it instantly.

The first task was to render the computer serviceable. The factory OS, of course, demanded to download all the latest manufacturer's updates. Of course, I didn't wish that since I was not about to use the manufacturer's software — none of it. Certainly, consumer-grade OS software and integrated telemetry are worse than useless when seeking online stealth. So I skipped steps and hit 'later' repeatedly until I could finally launch a browser. Once I had a browser, I downloaded the latest image of a security toolset and operating system known in the trade as 'TAILS' for *The Amnesic Incognito Live System*. A dubious acronym, though the software is stable and robust.

The motel's WIFI preferred moving at nearly the speed of growing grass, and I weathered many false starts due to driver issues with the hardware. Nonethcless, several hours later, I had the system running with the TOR Browser, TORFone, and other tools. Setting up a virgin system from scratch to be a secure and untraceable system is not trivial, but this is my field. In the middle of this, a soft knock came at the door.

Wisceya answered the door. Jill entered bearing breakfast, including, notably, coffee. Perfect timing! Caffeine withdrawal was becoming a real tragedy here. Admittedly, the diner's java was far from my preferred Arabian Mocha-Java, but it would do. Fortunately, I am not addicted to coffee; I merely require the elixir of life.

Moments later, Estelle joined us, also bearing food. We took a break and ate breakfast. Surprisingly, Jill and Estelle shed their clothes and joined us in bare-skin comfort. I no longer forced them to be nude for security reasons, but as I and the fur-girls were Skyclad, they opted to join us. Despite her original protests, Jill seemed to have found her comfort zone. Nonetheless, I noticed she stayed closer to the other women, especially Estelle. Our rooms shared a doorway between them, and we promptly opened it, converting our adjoining rooms into a mini-suite.

The motel showed its age, but the rooms were large and decent. Perhaps we will stay here for a few days while making our plans. I toyed with the idea of going to Roswell, figuring our companion's alienesque appearance would blend in there. However, until we could contact someone who could show us to a portal, all we could do was to stay low, out of sight, and not stay in one place too long. My 'spidey-sense' was quiet now; I trusted we were relatively secure here.

When I started teaching the girls about computers, I hadn't expected them to grasp much and was surprised. I had not intended to share my methods, my secrets. My computer security skills are my stock in trade and how I earn my living. I also worried that I risked enabling those hunting us to anticipate my moves by giving away my secrets.

I found myself showing Estelle and Jill some of my close-held security tricks. They seemed interested. As educated, computer-savvy people, they are not ignorant. However, they lack my systems-level expertise. After agonizing a bit, I consented to the idea of their learning too. I hoped it was not a mistake; I had already decided to trust them. I did not, however, share my passwords and security tokens. Some things need to stay private. Furthermore, I was not allowing anyone online without my direct and immediate supervision.

Once the installation was complete and the machine seemed trustworthy and secure, I went online. My first action was to check the dead drop I'd been using to communicate with Phil.

The drafts folder was a disappointment; it was empty. Phil had retrieved my previous message but left no reply. I assembled another brief text and placed it in the folder, telling him I thought I had run out of time and that I rabbited and went into hiding. I didn't say where or allude to Jill's or Estelle's involvement. I let him think I had merely taken the Planet Oz residents and run. I did apologize profusely for taking over his house and told him I would check the dropbox daily or as near as I could manage.

I was mulling over the possible reasons for Phil's radio silence. Had the MiBs somehow caught him? Had he departed his home on the East Coast and headed to California? I expected he would have left a message.

As I considered the possibilities, I remembered the batch of emails I had earlier downloaded. They sat unread on the thumb drive I purloined from Phil's desk drawer. Although I did not expect to find anything worthwhile in them, I decided to check.

As expected, they consisted of worthless, annoying spam. All save one, a message from Julie! Short and simple, all it said was to call her! I was uncertain whether I should; I did not wish to drag her deeper into this mess than she already had been.

The Faux Venetian

Calling Julie had not been in my plans. I'd avoided contacting her to protect her; I didn't wish to put her on the radar of the MiBs if she wasn't already. Still, I felt I owed her; I had technically stolen her car. Notwithstanding that, even though I might argue that I had her permission after a fashion, she would have destroyed any hope of avoiding the Men in Black if she lost faith and reported it. So we are at her mercy.

I considered it for a while, eventually deciding I must call her. If they aren't already surveilling her, it won't matter, or else if they are, they shouldn't be able to trace the TORFone anyway. Calculated risk.

I set up the clandestine telephony software and placed the call. Julie answered on the first ring.

"Don't say my name," I interjected before she could say anything. "They're likely listening. You're probably under surveillance. I've caused you trouble, for which I deeply apologize."

She responded, "No one's listening, no one's watching. I'm not on Alex's radar, and I'm aware you're helping the ladies from Planet Oz."

"What? How?" I sputtered.

"Petchy sent me to keep an eye on you."

I almost fell out of my chair! How did Julie learn of Petchy and Planet Oz? I hadn't even known she had read my book. We hadn't been together long, and I had not raised my adventure story with her. It's not something people believe easily, so I don't talk about it with just anyone. "Hi, my name is Fitz, and I wrote a book about an all-female planet where the women don't wear clothes. But it's not fiction cause it all actually happened." Yeah, I don't say that.

Had she been in touch with Petch since we hit the road? How would she meet Petchy? Is every single person around me involved in a grand conspiracy? If I put this in a book, readers would revolt!

Stunned, I sat in silence for a moment. Then, with forced calm, I asked, "Have you talked to uh... Did anyone contact you? No! Wait, don't answer. Not a word! I can't trust this connection's safe. I'm sure my end is secure, but I can not trust yours is secure."

"It is, I'm certain."

"Sorry, I'm not. Listen carefully. Stay out of this mess; you don't need the trouble. You don't want to be involved! Whatever you do, stay away from Alex. If they connected me to you, they are watching you. They might arrest you, to pressure you for our whereabouts, or merely to intimidate me. So run! Get out of town and don't tell anyone where you are going.

"You have been working hard, putting in long hours, need a vacation, and have saved up plenty of vacation days on the books. You said that your boss was on your case to take time off. Venice is beautiful this time of year. You should see the Grand Canal while you're young and can afford it. Go away until this blows over. Be careful! I will see you when I'm able."

With that, I terminated the call and shut down the TORFone! I hoped she paid attention to my words.

Four pairs of eyes were staring wide-eyed when I glanced up from the computer. Doubtless, they thought I was harsh on an innocent.

Grumpily I said, "We need to prepare our strategy, and we check out in the morning. We must be on the road early; we have a long drive."

Estelle asked, "Where are we going? Did you decide on a plan?"

I addressed all four of the ladies. "Things have changed, and I need to make plans. I will explain it all as soon as I can. But, for now, relax and rest. Take in the local scenery. I trust no one is hunting us here; be careful and be ready to roll in the morning."

I busied myself with the computer, and after watching for a few minutes, Estelle and Jill decided to go for a walk and check out the pool. Stapleya and Wisceya debated what to do and, after a brief discussion, asked the other two if they could join in, at least for the walk. They discussed the topic with the Earth women and decided swimming in the pool might not be wise, as they might attract unwanted attention.

This last caution turned out to be almost unwarranted. We were the solitary guests at the run-down little motel. Not even staff seemed to be around except for one white-haired senior citizen at the reception desk, who appeared unwilling to stir.

None of us had bathing suits. We discussed the possibility of discretely skinny-dipping, but Utah is not California, and even though no one is around, strangers could appear without warning. The ladies chose to relax clothed, first at poolside for a while, and later they strolled around the premises, taking in the scenery. Finally, they ventured a short distance into the nearby desert. The off-worlders were unfamiliar with desert, fascinated at the plants and creatures so well adapted to the harsh environment. I don't know that there are no deserts on Planet Oz, only that I've never seen one, and neither have Stapleya and Wisceya.

While the ladies relaxed, I busied myself on the net, studying maps and preparing for tomorrow's plans, plans I was not yet ready to share.

Sometime later, they returned and announced they were hungry. Well, I was too, now that you mention it. The motel's breakfast bar was rolled up and put away for the day, and unfortunately, the immediate area is not well-served with fine dining establishments. I must complain to the management. Don't they expect guests to eat again after breakfast? Although there were no restaurants near us, a quick web search led us to Larry's Drive-in, less than two miles away. It seemed the perfect place where we might find decent food at a low price and be in and out quickly. A quick vote, and we piled into the car.

We considered walking. None of us were getting much exercise of late, and I had missed my workouts. So a nice brisk two-mile walk would be welcome.

Two miles is nothing to me. Wisceya had the ease and athleticism of youth, with no hesitation at even a vigorous two-mile run. Jill, likewise, is fit, able, and very athletic. Stapleya, although bearing the weight of her years and less energetic than her daughter, nevertheless, would be undaunted by the prospect of a brisk two-mile walk. Estelle, however, as the senior member of our band, or so I then believed, is not an athlete. Although she is spry and in terrific shape, she finds a couple of miles far more challenging and would slow the rest of us considerably. So we opted to drive rather than hoof it — a shame; I could have used the exercise.

Another reason for driving was we thought we might use the drive-thru; the fur-girls could stay in the car out of sight. However, it turned out that the eatery was nearly empty this time of day, and after a moment's debate, we decided to don our masks and risk it. Five people crammed into a car trying to manage fast-food meals can be frustrating and messy. Sitting upright at a table is more practical.

I hope masks develop staying power as fashion accessories. In this age of near-universal surveillance and computer-enabled facial recognition, masks bolster one's illusion of personal privacy.

We worried for nothing. From the lack of attention, one must assume that this tiny rural-American restaurant regularly served other-worldly, fur-bearing tourists. But, of course, the masks helped us keep a low profile, and I seated the girls facing the wall. My 'spidey-sense' remained quiet, and I felt relaxed and unworried. It's a shame we must leave this delightful little burg so soon. It is idyllic and peaceable, but we have a mission, and we'd best knuckle down to it.

Larry's Drive-in did not disappoint. The fare was inexpensive, and the staff paid our eclectic appearance little heed. The off-worlders loved these burgers almost as much as In-N-Out's. I love a good hamburger myself; the humble hamburger receives a bad rap from the nutritional nannies.

After our meal, I again floated the idea of a vigorous walk, and Jill and the aliens agreed. Not surprisingly, Estelle dissented. I handed her the keys, saying we would meet her in the rooms.

She opted to nurse a leisurely root beer, so we set out, taking advantage of the head start. We were not running, nothing so vigorous immediately after taking on a load of burgers (I ate six!), but we did walk briskly and took time to study the community along the way. We'd traversed nearly two-thirds of the distance when a short beep sounded as Estelle passed us. Waving, we stepped up our pace and arrived at the rooms shortly after she pulled in. After our meal and a modest walk, we all agreed a siesta was the next priority. Estelle and Jill repaired to their room, and my fur-girls and I cuddled on our bed.

I doubt any of us slept. I'm not one to sleep during the daytime, but we did find some relaxing activities in the afternoon calm.

Later, I went online and made the rounds of the Guardian site and the clandestine email dropbox. Nothing new at either location. I puzzled over Phil's sudden silence but hadn't expected anything from Petchy. I'm not sure how faithfully I trust that message was, in fact, from Petchy. Readers of my book all know of that mechanism; thus, I cannot confidently trust it.

The ladies joined me, and as the tawdry old motel still displayed an absence of occupants, we decided to take some sun by the pool before the orb vanished below the horizon.

Nudity is not welcomed here and we carried no bathing attire. However, we concluded our casual clothes were acceptable poolside wear. We worshipped another glorious sunset before returning to our rooms in the gathering dusk. The aliens now understand there are no predators here; nonetheless, my ladies are uncomfortable in the nocturnal out of doors; too many lifetimes of conditioning. We returned to the rooms and prepared to retire for the evening. Finally, I decided to brief the ladies on my plans.

"We must head for Las Vegas. That's about a four hour drive. If we roll out early, we should encounter no problem getting there by noon."

Estelle glanced at Jill, then stepped closer. "Why Las Vegas, Fitz? I thought we were avoiding major cities where they might spot us."

"We are. That is, I am, and our friends from Planet Oz are. Unfortunately, we are all too distinctive and actively being hunted. On the other hand, you, my dear, are merely taking your girlfriend on a short holiday to Las Vegas! If you are spotted, that's your cover story."

They looked at each other quizzically. The fur-girls were looking at all three of us with curiosity. Finally, after a moment of silence, Jill asked, "Aren't you going to explain, Fitz? We do not understand."

"I'm sorry, ladies, I do not mean to be secretive. I'm worried and inclined to keep things under my hat, perhaps more than I should. Indeed, the hope is that we are going to meet someone. The girls and I will keep a low profile stay out of sight. You and Jill will try to connect with our party."

Jill bristled, "You mean Julie, don't you? That stuff about telling her to go to Venice was misdirection; you told her to meet us at the Venetian, isn't that right? Why? Don't you trust us?"

I smiled sheepishly. "I'm sorry, my friends. It's not a lack of trust in you. On the contrary, I decided to trust you as soon as we started this trip. It's just that the deeper I delve into this insane conspiracy, the deeper the confusion and frustration.

"I only recently met Julie and didn't start dating her until roughly the time when poor Shameya died. Our first official date was the evening of the day I viewed her body in the morgue.

“I thought that Alex and his people were unaware of Julie, unaware we were dating.” At this, I arched an eyebrow at Jill.

She nodded, “I remember that day we met, you mentioned you had a date, but we didn’t notice or attach any significance to it. You are right; I, at least, didn’t know you were dating anyone. But, on the other hand, I was in the dark about much under Alex’s purview. I’ve only worked with Alex for a few months. Matt came on board only a couple of weeks ago. Alex is not one to share.”

I nodded to her and continued, “We only went on four actual dates. When I began to sense events might derail, I asked for her help but didn’t tell her what was up. I stored supplies and cash in her car and asked her for a spare set of keys. I was surprised, but she gave them to me without complaint. I gave her an envelope with a letter apologizing, telling her almost nothing of what was going on, just that I was in trouble and promised to tell all when I returned. I sealed the envelope and asked her to open it only if something happened. I also included a collection of code phrases, with instructions if she heard me use any expressions on the list, whether personally or by proxy.

“Julie left an email saying to call her. I assumed it was just ordinary worry and almost didn’t call. But when I did, she claimed Petchy sent her.”

I spread my arms and shrugged. “We encountered several false or suspicious claims to speak for Petchy. Matt tried it, and Phil had some connection, although I have since developed serious suspicions about his loyalties. You two also misled and deceived me.”

They both frowned and nodded; I continued, “Can you blame me for being worried? When this lady-friend that I was certain was entirely ignorant of my off-world experiences and unconnected to the conspiracy suddenly claims to have been sent by Petchy, I almost came unstuck, and my paranoia kicked into high gear. I did not intend to exclude you. I would have excluded myself if I could!”

I dropped my head, saying, “Yes, we’re meeting Julie, I hope, at the Rialto Bridge at the Venetian. She will be looking for me, but I’m scared to show myself. I hope I can describe her well enough that you two can spot her. Do you think we have a chance of pulling this off?”

A Close Shave

With the intense pressure of the last few days relaxed, we retired early and slept blissfully. We awoke the next morning rested and refreshed, ready for whatever the day might bring.

Stapleya and Wisceya were eager to experience the wonders of Las Vegas. Estelle and Jill had told them enough to pique their curiosity, although the fur-girls insisted it was impossible and refused to believe their tales. I'm sure our entire planet seems impossible to them. So why should they balk at one more impossibility? I had believed many impossible things while on their planet, sometimes as many as six before breakfast.

We rolled out of the motel parking lot well before dawn and drove along Interstate 15 without stopping except to refuel or attend to nature's necessities. Although we had eschewed Interstate highways in the previous day's travels, the lack of roads in desert country left us little choice. Vast areas belong to the tribal sovereign nations, and many are not open to tourists. Moreover, permit requirements and low population density mean few accessible roads. Besides, we had no cause to suspect Alex would be looking for us here.

Passing through the St. George area, Estelle remarked on the nuclear contamination of that area from the atomic bomb testing and the significant proliferation of cancer in the people living here during the following decades. I could tell this was an emotional issue for her. So naturally, our extraterrestrial visitors became curious about those events, which led us into a lengthy discussion of warfare on Earth and the horrors it had brought and the worries and politics of nuclear power. This unsavory topic clouded our conversation for miles upon miles as we lamented the missed potential, the waste, and the suffering brought forth by the nuclear genie.

Awed and depressed by the ugly history of warfare on Earth, the fur-people lamented the inability of their smooth-skinned cousins to get along. Viewed in the light of awareness of other worlds, we debated the influence of extraterrestrials on these events — who was working to calm things versus who might be trying to instigate war? Who were the fifth and sixth columns, and what were the Alien influences?

We reached the Las Vegas metropolitan area without incident. Before leaving our hotel, we had located online another seedy dive of a motel nearby, convenient to Vegas, one where we could establish ourselves. We stopped at our intended base of operations and let Estelle check us into our rooms since caution dictated the alien women and I must keep a low profile.

Shortly, accommodations secured, we resumed our trek toward the city. We stopped on the outskirts of town, refueled the car, and grabbed snacks. Then, on a sudden inspiration, I asked Estelle to purchase a prepaid phone from a small storefront in the strip mall. She did so, and I activated it, memorizing the number as I did so.

Safe telephone communications are a challenge when government forces are hunting you. Five nations, Australia, Canada, New Zealand, the United Kingdom, and the United States, have collaborated since the 1960s to create a massive signals monitoring network that spans much of the world. This five-nation collective is known as The Five Eyes. The network system, colloquially known as ECHELON, has a science-fiction-level of unbelievably powerful and extensive surveillance capacity, capable of intercepting almost any phone call worldwide. It uses sophisticated computer AI-powered voice recognition technologies and simultaneously monitors untold millions, if not billions, of phone calls. The average citizen has no idea of the extent to which this system eavesdrops on their everyday communications. If ECHELON is looking for you and you place a telephone call anywhere in the world, it will likely find you. My awareness of ECHELON is why I have stayed off the regular telephone system. ECHELON might recognize my voice and send Alex and his swarm of black SUVs in my direction.

We're not sure Alex has engaged ECHELON in his search for us. It seems, in fact, rather unlikely he had escalated his efforts to that level. However, we do not think we can afford the chance.

I purchased the burner for emergencies only; I did not intend to use it initially.

Even if Alex had not employed ECHELON, he still likely had a flag on Julie's phone and will tag any call she makes or receives. Any number that she calls, or calls her, will receive their scrutiny. They will quickly know her location. One call and they will know she is in Vegas, though to be fair, we assume they are already aware of her travels.

Refueled, refreshed, and with a new clandestine spy widget in hand, we entered the mouth of the beast, driving into the city proper, and arrived at the front entrance to the Venetian. Jill and Estelle had agreed they would attempt to find Julie and approach her. But unfortunately, the rest of us cannot afford the public exposure, and we cannot sit for hours in the car in the desert heat.

The girls and I returned to the motel to wait. We have no communication tools other than the TORFone and Estelle's burner. Calling Julie's phone with either was a risk, although the onion-cloaked computer-based TORFone was marginally safer. Since we assume the MiBs monitor Julie's phone, calling her with the burner would immediately compromise it. If they didn't already know she was in Vegas, calling her by any means was sure to alert them.

Given the risks, we must treat the burner as a one-shot tool. Once a call occurs between the burner and Julie's cell, security protocol demands the phone's immediate destruction. On the other hand, calls between the computer and the burner are comparatively safe, as long as we are cautious what we say and disguise our voices against ECHELON voice recognition.

The plan called for Jill and Estelle, armed with my description of Julie, to take up positions at different locations with a view of the bridge and contact her when she appears. We expected her about noon, but they would keep watch for several hours. We were to call the burner using the computer once an hour. As long as they have not contacted Julie, the burner remains turned off, and our calls will go unanswered. If she does not appear today, we will try again tomorrow and the next day. Perhaps the day after too, although we cannot stay too long. We will decide day-by-day whether to invest another day in the attempt.

When they connect with Julie, Jill will answer on our next call. I will not be on the call since my voice has a higher risk of recognition. Instead, Stapleya will ask for 'Maria.' Her voice is unknown to ECHELON. Jill is to say we have a wrong number and hang up.

We agreed upon three possible phrases, and which one she uses will designate a different meeting point. 'You have a Wrong Number' means to pick them up where we had dropped them off; a simple, curt 'Wrong Number' designates a pickup/drop-off point a block away from the bridge location, and 'No one here by that name' means to meet in front of another hotel some distance away. In the worst-case scenario — the phone turned on but unanswered, answered with a simple 'Hello' or answered by anyone other than Jill — means disaster. This response invokes a 'Run for the Hills' panic attack mentality, regardless of what Estelle or anyone else who answers says!

Direct telephone contact is a last-ditch method if Julie does not appear. We will call Julie from the burner, perhaps a public phone, or possibly the TORFone if we cannot connect with her otherwise, but that is something we prefer to avoid.

Jill and Estelle jumped out of the car at the Venetian and headed inside to practice their spycraft. Stapleya, Wisceya, and I headed back to our motel. We had hours to pass, but I must pay close attention and place my hourly calls timely and on the minute.

Traffic was heavier than expected, and it took longer to return to the hotel than I had planned. We had ample time, but by the time we settled in the room and had the computer online and ready, it was already time for our first call. There had been zero minutes to spare. At the appointed instant, I entered the number and hit dial.

It went immediately to the voicemail robot, which dutifully reported the subscriber had not set up a voice mailbox. As expected, they had not yet contacted Julie. We were, after all, early.

Connecting with Julie on our first day might seem optimistic. Traveling to Las Vegas from the Bay Area is quick and easy. It is only about an hour and a half by air. Transportation at each end of the trip takes longer than the flight. A 9 AM flight would land about ten-thirty, making reaching the Venetian by noon doable, if slightly challenging. Assuming one could book a 9 AM flight and no delays. Noon or even later flights would be correspondingly later in the day.

We must further worry whether Julie is under surveillance — Jill's training in the MiB organization will be an asset. Even if Julie is at the bridge at noon, they will not approach her immediately. Instead, they would hide and watch, looking to determine whether anyone was watching Julie. It might take a couple of hours to ensure she is not under surveillance.

We didn't expect to contact Julie right away. We hoped to connect with her today; tomorrow was almost more reasonable. Jill's training would be most beneficial.

After placing the first call, I decided to shower, shave and freshen up. I often wear a beard, occasionally for months at a time. While on Planet Oz, I had developed an impressive masculine thatch. Nonetheless, I prefer to go clean-shaven as it's more professional-looking, so I have convinced myself.

I'd been letting my beard grow the last few days in hopes of disguising myself slightly. Not that a bit of chin fur would conceal my silhouette, but I will take every aid available. It was now long enough to style it and sculpt it out of the worst of the scruffy stages, crafting a more civilized appearance. So I broke out my shaving kit, scraped and trimmed the coarse bristles, and performed a bit of manscaping. My furry friends watched the process in fascination but without comment. Upon finishing, I asked their opinion, and they pronounced approval.

With my grooming complete, the time for our second call was at hand. This call was the first point when I genuinely expected the ladies might have contacted Julie. However, the call again went straight to the virgin voice mailbox — still no action.

I decided we needed food, so with the appointed call completed, I dressed and left the girls alone while I headed down to the vending machines. Nothing there seemed appealing, so I walked across the street and visited a corner convenience store. A few minutes later, I headed back to the hotel carrying two bags and a carton of beverages.

I returned to the room uneventfully. My friends and I quietly passed the remaining portion of the hour, and I again placed the next call on schedule. Still, the robot mailbox attendant responded with the canned response.

Another hour passed; this time, the phone rang through. Stapleya stepped up to the computer to ask for Maria as planned. Jill answered on the third ring and responded, 'Sorry, there is no one here by that name,' presumably indicating I should pick them up at the second rendezvous location.

I was a little surprised, as it suggested there was a complication. Also, I worried that Jill had deviated from the script, if only slightly.

I assumed it was an indication of stress. My hackles raised, but my 'spidey-sense' remained calm.

With Julie in tow, we didn't have enough seats in the car. So Stapleya and Wisceya must wait here while I pick the three of them up. We had planned for this possibility; I instructed the ladies to sit tight, stay indoors and not open the door to anyone. Depending on traffic, I expected to return within about an hour to as much as ninety minutes or so. Cautioning them to be careful, I hugged them and left them alone.

I rushed through the afternoon traffic and arrived at the meeting with only minor delay. Jill and Estelle waited calmly at the passenger pickup point, but Julie was not with them. Unfortunately, our cabalistic communications contrivance wasn't flexible enough to convey every possible nuance. Nonetheless, all had worked satisfactorily.

The pair climbed aboard, and I soon learned the details. Julie had appeared as expected, but Jill had spotted another observer and refused to proceed with contact. After a couple of hours of surveillance, Estelle had managed to pass a note to Julie explaining she was under supervision, and we aborted contact. We will try again tomorrow at noon at the Luxor monorail station.

I questioned the ladies about who was watching Julie. Jill was confident the watcher was not from Alex's organization. She described the watcher as a woman not skilled in spycraft. They had no clue who she was. Jill had, however, purchased an inexpensive camera in one of the stores and took several covert pictures of the watcher while ostensibly playing tourist. Unfortunately, the no-frills camera was so cheap it had no display. Therefore, we must wait until we connect it to the computer before examining the photos. It didn't seem a high priority, though, as it seemed unlikely we could identify her.

After passing Julie the note, they had continued to watch her. However, Julie had been savvy enough not to read the message right away, and when she finally did so, she was not obvious about it. So it was doubtful the watcher realized what had happened.

After a while, Julie left the bridge area, and the watcher followed her. Jill and Estelle spent considerable time ensuring no one followed them and cautiously had decided to switch to the backup location instead of reconnecting where we had dropped them off.

The woman watching Julie was inexperienced in the art of spycraft. That didn't mean she or whoever sent her was less dangerous, but it did imply they were less likely to be with Alex's people. I was inexperienced in such skills myself. It is not my professional field, though I would prefer to think I would have been more covert than the woman Jill described. Maybe not, as muscular giants tend not to pass unnoticed. It is Jill's professional field, and she knows her craft thoroughly, so I should stop second-guessing her.

Jill had only spotted the one operative, but that didn't mean there weren't more. The one unskilled operative she had spotted may have been there as a misdirection to draw attention away from other players. Jill insisted this was not the case, and if there had been others, she would have seen them.

The ladies reported on their efforts during the ride to the hotel, and shortly we arrived back at our room. I knocked on the door, and Stapleya opened the door. I was halfway into the room, following Estelle and Jill, when both of the ladies stopped in their tracks with a massive double-take and released a startled exclamation. A soft "What the..." escaped my lips as I abruptly bumped into Jill's backside.

I thought disaster had befallen the fur-girls in our absence for a moment. In a way, I suppose, though not a disaster, exactly, but certainly something unexpected. Jill, Estelle, and I tried hard to keep a straight face and not laugh out loud at the scene greeting us.

After a double-take and a moment of recovery, I reached out and put my arms around my fur-girls. They had reacted badly to our surprise, and Wisceya seemed almost on the verge of tears. After a few moments, we all began to chuckle.

Stapleya and Wisceya had decided to shave, and the effect was startling. Although they retained their bodily fur, they had coiffed their heads into an edgy, G.I. Jane buzz-cut, and their faces, from the neck up, were as bare and fresh-faced as any Earth native! Although initially jarred, I agreed that they looked beautiful.

"What did you gals do?" I asked, still struggling to suppress giggles.

"We did not want to hide our faces behind masks," blubbered Wisceya. Then, more calmly and minus the blubbers, her mother added, "We thought we might pass for smoothies if we shaved, and people would not stare at us. We want to see this fantastic place and not just while hiding inside the car."

I comforted them with a massive bear hug as Jill and Estelle stood by, trying not to laugh. "I'm so sorry, my dears; I had no idea how much this bothered you. We worry about protecting you from those who might cause harm or wish to confine you, people like Alex."

"It's not Alex; people stare at us. They see us as strange, a freak or an animal." I walked them to the bed, and we sat. Jill and Estelle grabbed chairs and sat near us. I sensed we were entering a minefield; did we wish to delve into the complexities of human prejudice and bias? Here we sit, three earth-humans of diverse racial backgrounds, consoling fur-bearing (or should I say formerly furred?) humans from another world who are fearful of stares, of prejudice and bias, afraid to show their natural faces!

Human prejudice is not a topic we could sufficiently tackle in one conversation or even a hundred. How can we explain the history of racial strife on Earth to aliens who seem uniform in appearance and coloring in their world? Shucks, they're even almost all the same sex! A more homogenous society would seem impossible. Yet, Stapleya's people are hardly class-free. The elite, such as Wisceya and my Lolita, do not work the fields, and field hands rarely reach the castle's upper floors. The fact that elites and commoners share the fortress is unavoidable, as nighttime outside the fortress walls is decidedly lethal.

Further, different castles occupy different societal levels due to their inherent wealth differences. Stapleya is a marvelous leader and astute manager of her castle's resources, and as a result, her people are much higher on the social scale. That, along with her age. Fur ages more smoothly than skin. Despite her apparent vigor and lust for life, seeing her face without her natural fur, I realized she is positively ancient. Good genes, I guess, but whatever the cause, she has weathered very well indeed.

Estelle interrupted my introverted musings and diverted me from a classic engineer's nerd wreck. I was focusing on the wrong aspect of our problem, the engineering challenges of the human condition, when I should have been considering the tactical issue at hand. She took their hands in hers. "My dears, if there's anywhere in the known universe where an unusual or uncommon countenance is acceptable, even unremarkable, Las Vegas is it! No one here would give your appearance a second glance. You hardly stand out between the fantastically costumed characters from the shows and just plain exotic and eccentric people drawn to the city. If shaving helps you feel comfortable, that's wonderful, and we will help in any way we can. Here in Las Vegas, though, no one will care. Painted bodies and exotic costumes are commonplace here."

I echoed my agreement and hugged them, relieved I had not launched into a dissertation on the foibles of human nature. I silently resolved that, if possible, we must allow the off-worlders a special night out to experience Las Vegas fully. Upon their return to Planet Oz, I imagined the cultural contamination when they tell of their exotic Earthly experiences. After a few moments, I put it from my mind, resolving to focus on the here and now, the nuts and bolts of returning them to their home. Such esoteric concerns can wait; I don't have the time to be a nerd today.

Turning to Jill, I asked for the camera, and after a moment's fiddling with the hardware, cables, and software, I had the camera connected to the computer. Unfortunately, the connection initially proved troublesome because TAILS is a specialized technological platform and poorly suited for mundane consumer apps. However, after installing a couple of drivers, the link came to life.

The first pictures were from a distance, and the low resolution of the cheap camera made it impossible to zoom in enough. All I could judge about the woman was her unusual height. Slowly, I paged through the images, carefully looking at the suspicious woman and studying her face. She seemed so familiar!

Jill had taken many photos from different angles, different vantage points over the hours they had staked her out, yet all were frustrating and unhelpful. It is not as if a spy can walk up to the target and say, "Smile."

Invariably they will turn their head, move in the wrong direction, or a passerby will walk in front of the subject at the perfect instant, ruining the shot. Getting a clear headshot of someone in a crowd without their knowledge is difficult, especially with a cheap, low resolution, point-and-shoot.

Despite the difficulty, Jill did take a few clear photos of the woman she thought was Julie, and I was able to confirm she was indeed our target. Julie sat quietly at a cafe table near the bridge, acrostically reading a paperback book. My book! I wonder where she got it? Typically, actual paperbacks are becoming rare in today's eBook-dominated world — she didn't display a tablet or smartphone.

Jill is nothing if not persistent, and she is a skilled and trained agent. Her persistence paid off. Finally, luck and skill combined to deliver a decent snapshot of the inept intruder. Two pictures, in fact, one full-on headshot and another showing her from the waist up.

She seemed so familiar! Plain-looking and tall, I should easily remember such a person. I know her, I'm sure! I might not recall the circumstance, yet I'm confident I know her.

Jill insisted no one resembling her had ever been in any group around Alex's team, not an agent, support person, or consultant. The woman could not be from Alex. Even if a recent recruit, the training requires months. If recruited before the discovery of Shameya's body, she would not yet qualify for fieldwork.

Further, she is so unskilled, so untrained; no spymaster would dare use her. If she is not there on behalf of Alex, why is she there?

Might Petchy have sent her? Somehow that thought resonated in the back of my head. Petchy! My 'spidey-sense' tingled at his name. I had seen her somewhere, somehow in connection with Petchy! My subconscious seems to be putting it together, though not yet communicating with my conscious.

Perhaps I need head-stooge Moe to whack me on the back of the head a time or two, like an old Three Stooges skit. I grinned to myself at the image. For a second, I considered cracking a joke by asking Jill or Estelle to make like Moe, but I knew they would disapprove, never mind the cultural gap the fur-girls presented. Stooge humor never works with the distaff crew, another of the infinite mysteries of the female mind. They tolerate us nerds without understanding, much as we do of them — an unbridgeable gap.

If Julie is working with Petchy, might this strange person be with Julie? A friend? A relative? A sister? Perhaps. I suppose there is a slight familial resemblance — possibly she was not spying on her; instead, she was merely hanging back so as not to spook us, to facilitate the contact? I guess that held an oddly logical sense; it might explain her ineptness. So, perhaps Julie brought a friend with her to Vegas. Had she asked her to hang back, and we had been too clever by half, thinking she was tracking Julie?

Still mulling the pictures, I let it go for the moment, suggesting that we should freshen up, dress, and head somewhere pleasant to eat. Our friends had made considerable effort to appear in public without stares, and we must take advantage of it before their fur regrows. My 'spidey-sense' is quiet. At the moment, I'm not feeling particularly fearful. If we maintain a low profile, we can indulge ourselves. I think.

Anticipating a night out for our off-world guests, I tried to imagine what would please them. I considered the incredible buffet served every evening at the nearby hotel and compared it in my memory to the traditional Evening Feast of Planet Oz and decided that even though the similarities are superficial, they should love it. They would delight in the varieties of food, and the dramatic, live-action cooking stations would enthrall them.

The theater nearby was hosting a magnificent circus show, always a delight. However, I feared the off-worlders might find the experience overwhelming. So I discussed the idea with Jill and Estelle. Together we explained the possibility to our alien friends and emphasized how vast the cultural gap is and how frightening the show might be to them.

I impressed them that if we elect to go to the show, it might overwhelm their senses. They took me seriously, abandoning English, and chattered at each other vigorously in Language. Even though I understand Language fluently, their lively conversation caused me to struggle to follow. Their fear and anticipation did come across clearly, though, and after a few moments, they solemnly agreed that they wanted to go, regardless. Although a bit frightened by the prospect, they determined to experience our world to the fullest and promised they would endure anything as long as I was there to hold their hands. They trusted me to protect them.

I was fearful of the prospect, not only of taking the off-worlders to such a show and risking scaring them to death, as poor Shameya had so sadly (and literally) experienced, but also of risking the sighting of my distinctive form in public. I considered the idea, and in defiance of my fears, my 'spidey-sense' remained quiet. I guess we are a go for a night on the town, my nervous misgivings notwithstanding. I decided to table the idea. I was uncomfortable enough with the prospect of dinner at the buffet; adding a show to our exposure seemed to be pushing our luck, taunting whatever evil spirits might be around. I was uncomfortable with the prospect, but my subtle sense remained calm. I debated how much I was willing to trust my instincts.

Jill was confident Alex had not surveilled them at the Venetian and felt Alex and his team knew nothing of Julie's involvement. There was no indication whatever that they might be looking for us here. Nearly a week had passed since we had rabbited, and Jill felt certain that Alex thought we had left Earth and was no longer looking for us. I was not so confident, but I conceded that there had been no signs of pursuit.

We five discussed the risks for over an hour. Stapleya and Wisceya insisted they wanted to see Las Vegas up close and personal; it was so fantastic they were willing to take any risk. Jill was adamant that the jeopardy was nonexistent, and Estelle seemed in agreement. They both firmly insisted that I was needlessly paranoid. Although I found the idea scary, my 'spidey-sense' remained calm, and I could not find a footing for objection.

I surrendered and agreed that we would, at minimum, dine at the buffet, and if everything remained calm, we would consider the possibility of a show.

Surrender, however, was not without a strategy. I would consent to dine in public only if we do not appear together as a group. We would also disguise ourselves with hats and other accessories to minimize our appearances on surveillance cameras. After careful planning and discussion, we agreed that Estelle and I would dine as a couple. She is a big woman and not the enormous contrast next to my bulk that the tiny fur-girls and petite half-Chinese gal provide.

Jill and the off-worlders would dine as a group since, freshly shaven, they no longer appear particularly alien. Notwithstanding Vegas' wildly diverse costumed and painted characters, the razor sculpting gave them more confidence. We were to stay within view of each other but not signal or communicate with each other. If the MiBs spot me, we hope the girls can escape while I provide a distraction. If need be, I will make a huge scene to draw attention so they can. Jill is to employ her covert skills and training, our beacon continually looking for danger.

I warned them of the overwhelming surveillance of this place. If the MiBs or anyone else wanted to monitor us, they might easily do so from the security station, or indeed, any remote location.

We arranged an elaborate system of signals by which we might surreptitiously communicate. For example, if my subtle sense began jangling to signal danger, I would place my cap on backward. Turning my collar up means they should quietly withdraw and return to the hotel. The addition of sunglasses meant 'run for the hills.' Various other casual clothing arrangements likewise carried hidden meanings. We established several escape plans, including provisions for Jill and the fur-girls to split up and each make their way to our hotel alone, this idea being the least preferred. The ultimate bug-out tactic had Jill taking the aliens and directly and hastily heading for Kingman, AZ, by any means possible, hitchhiking, stealing a car, or whatever they could manage.

After reviewing our plans and contingencies several times and tweaking our wardrobe to thwart surveillance, we were ready to take a chance on the buffet line.

Estelle and I dropped Jill and the fur-girls approximately a block from the restaurant that they may walk in alone. Then Estelle and I parked and walked to the buffet. We were to go in first; the others would catch up to us and fall into line behind us.

Our strategy seemed to work well; we kept each other in sight but didn't acknowledge each other. Wisceya kept looking in my direction and smiling, despite my warnings and cautions. I was nervous but didn't sense any particular danger. I hoped this did not turn out to be a colossal mistake. The girl had failed to grasp the concept fully; I suppose the novel experience overwhelmed her. Finally, Jill leaned in and whispered something, and she dropped her eyes and didn't look at me again.

We were about halfway through our meal when I felt a twinge from my subtle sense. Not a full-on alarm, more of "Hey, look at that" as if to call my attention to something. I'd been continuously scanning the crowd, and my subconscious told me I had missed something. So I rechecked the multitude. Finally, after several minutes of anxiety, I spotted the cause of my disquiet. The strange woman shadowing Julie sat a few tables away, her back toward us. Seeing her so close and in real life, I noted what a big gal she is, much taller and heftier than Estelle.

Although I donned my baseball cap with the bill pointing backward, I wasn't immediately alarmed. Instead, I kept an eye on the woman. She seemed to be dining alone, was facing away from us, and not paying attention to the crowd. She seemed oblivious, focused only on her plate.

I continued watching the stranger, and after a few moments, Jill signaled acknowledgment of my backward-facing cap, and I saw her looking around. She soon spotted the strange woman and discreetly shifted her chair to allow a direct field of view. I noted she was scanning the crowd for any additional cause for concern.

We continued eating, watching the stranger and the crowd. The fur-girls, overwhelmed by their surroundings, didn't notice my cap and remained blissfully unaware of my anxiety. Perhaps five minutes had elapsed in this strange juxtaposition, and I was considering pulling the plug on our outing when Julie pulled up a chair and sat down.

"Hello Fitz," she cooed in my ear. I nearly jumped three feet, and the color drained from my face. Focused on the stranger, I had allowed Julie to stroll right up to my table undetected. So much for subtle senses and subconscious warnings! I nearly had a coronary.

Thunderstruck, I struggled even to mumble. "Wha? Ho? Hu?" I said as I dropped the packets between my syllables.

She sensed my shock and thought it was comical. "Relax," she said, snickering. She grinned, barely suppressing laughter. "You're safe here; no one's looking for you. Alex thinks you have left Earth. Without support, he cannot command the resources to hunt you anyway. When you eluded his grasp last Sunday, Alex tried to find you for a few days but folded and abandoned the search. So you see, there was no criminal or terrorist event he could tie to you to justify a sustained effort. He obviously couldn't go about crying 'alien invasion' to raise support."

As I was recovering from the shock my girlfriend had inflicted, Estelle reached out, took Julie's hand, and introduced herself. After exchanging pleasantries, Julie asked, "Estelle, would you please step over there and ask my sister to join us?" Estelle stood to do so, and Julie placed her hand on my arm, "Relax, Fitz, trust me, I'm here to help. Where are the ladies from Planet Oz?"

I was still in a fog, debating whether to bash, bolt, bug out, or what? I took several deep breaths and stared deep into Julie's eyes. Two heartbeats. I monitored her respiration. Four heartbeats. I studied her and found only trust and support. Six heartbeats. I relaxed and signaled Jill to join us.

Being together in a group evoked a state of jittery nervousness. Nonetheless, the seven of us settled at a large table, finishing our meal while discussing Aliens, Men in Black, and other delights. No one paid us the slightest attention, and my 'spidey-sense' was not raising the slightest alarm. On the contrary, I gradually accepted that no one chased us.

Julie's sister joined the group, and Julie introduced her as Darla. She avoided my direct gaze after the introduction, seemed shy perhaps, or possibly my frame intimidated her. That seems unlikely.

Darla is no petite babe herself, not only towering over the fur-girls and Jill but inches taller than her sister Julie too. She was taller than Estelle; She towered over everyone at our table except me. And I knew her! I was confident that I did but could not remember from where despite struggling to recall. That was unsettling. I can sometimes be face-blind, but I excel at recognizing people by their build, especially women, double-especially tall, gawky, plain-looking women.

Careful to keep our voices low, we analyzed the events leading to our meeting until after we finished our ice cream and the fur-girls had taken seconds on the dessert. Then, finally, I asked Julie, "Shouldn't we move somewhere less public?"

She nodded. "Darla and I took a suite in the hotel. Let's adjourn to our rooms for more private discussion."

However, the alien ladies shook their heads in unison. "Can we please have more ice cream before we go?" I think they like it.

Presently, we headed into the hotel. Although I was not, at present, nagged by my subtle senses, my mundane paranoia was still at work. I did all I could to minimize whatever appearances we might make on the ubiquitous security cameras using masks and hats and keeping heads down, avoiding looking at any visible cameras.

Shortly, we settled in upstairs, safe from public view and could relax. The fur-girls instantly doffed their clothes, oblivious that no one else joined them. They innately grow natural fur clothing and only recently began to adopt Earth-style duds and then only in public. It seemed natural for them, although they did look a bit odd, faces bare and covered in fur from the neck down. I suppose they assumed all Earthlings went nude in private. That had been their limited experience with our hedonistic little traveling party until now. The rest of us were more restrained in the new dynamic with Julie and Darla present, although I had not yet identified the cause of my reluctance. I chalked it up to Darla's presence since she was a stranger.

Julie explained her role in the mysterious events of the last week. Petchy or his people — the group we earlier nicknamed The Four Columns — recruited Darla and Julie. As she began to explain, two more brain cells suddenly clicked in. I remember where we met! I stood, leaned in, placing my palms flat, looking her straight in the eyes, studying her face. Yes, I met Darla the day Petch recruited me!

She was the trans-woman I had met that day! Small world.

I interrupted Julie's story to confront Darla. "We met that day at the interview, didn't we?" I pointedly left out mention of specifics; it is up to her to reveal, or not, that part of herself.

Darla's eyes reflected a momentary disquietude, which dissipated to be replaced by resignation. Nodding acknowledgment, she explained they had not selected her the day of the interview, but later someone connected her to a company called TaskWalk. She signed on to do routine minor jobs for pay — micro-jobs for micro-pay. After a while, someone claiming to be 'Special Services' contacted her, asked numerous personal questions, then asked if she would like to accept specific 'special' jobs at a higher pay scale. She agreed. "They swore me to secrecy and installed a separate app for the Special Services jobs."

She discovered the 'special' jobs were often mysterious if innocent-seeming tasks and they paid significantly better than regular assignments.

She said, "Regular TaskWalk jobs continued to be available, but I liked the money that came with the 'special' jobs. Those tasks arrived from someone identified as Arisia, and I would perform whatever task Arisia requested. Although most were simple, I never spoke to anyone after that first day. At times weeks might pass between assignments; other times, they would keep me busy. The payments from Arisia arrived regularly, a weekly retainer, even in the absence of duties, plus a fee for each task. If I had expenses, reimbursement appeared with the payment, even if it was only pocket change for parking."

The jobs could be mundane, such as meeting a client and driving them, Uber-like, to another location or perhaps delivering a package. In any case, most were innocent-seeming activities of a mundane nature. None of the tasks appeared illegal, though occasionally, the job involved her cyber skills, and she worried they might indeed be illicit. She anguished over the risk of being caught.

She said, "The tasks took a sharp turn into the weird zone when the person I was to meet popped up naked; that startled me. The job was to meet them and provide them with clothing, but no one warned me that I was to provide clothing because they wouldn't be wearing any. So I began keeping spare clothes in the car, just in case. Sometimes I transported a client, fully nude, from one location to another, apparently without the slightest regard for the absence of clothing. Other times I collected the client fully clothed and drove them to a site, only to have them abandon all their possessions in my car, step out, and walk away fully nude, twice in broad daylight on a busy city street!"

Until she learned of portal travel, these strange encounters baffled her, but she was happy to accept the generous payments. Many of the jobs were trivial, but the workload increased, sometimes bringing several tasks per day. She asked Julie for help on a few occasions. Shortly, the mysterious Arisia approached Julie. Arisa recruited and added Julie to the Special Services group, and she began taking occasional freelance jobs in her name and accepting payments into her bank account. It was a welcome part-time addition to her day job.

Anyone might make an equally valid guess at how many operatives for the mysterious Arisia there might be, though there were many more than these two. The structure of the operations seemed designed to scale massively. The model, though secretive, is identical to the model used by various ride-sharing services and uses similar mobile apps to assign and track tasks. Most jobs require anywhere from ten minutes to a few hours at most. When a job is available, multiple contractors receive an alert via text, and upon accepting the task, instructions follow, with payment on completion. Simple, covert, and anonymous, all you need is a car and phone!

Some didn't even require a car. One of the jobs tasked to Julie was to monitor the Guardian website daily for advertisements containing a variety of specific keywords and to text Arisia if anything matching appeared.

One day, Julie accepted a task that involved monitoring a man and sending periodic reports of his activities. Nothing personally invasive, she promised, just health and welfare type reports.

Arisia had asked her to spy on me!

Unexpectedly, I spotted her when she appeared at the same cafe as me on multiple occasions. I had no thought that she was stalking me; I merely assumed it was a coincidence and started chatting her up, soon asking her for a date. She took the initiative, concluded that one way to fulfill her task was to become my girlfriend!

She could monitor my activities and pass along her reports without stalking me. Unknowingly, I had converted a stalker into a girlfriend! I was stunned by the revelation.

She said, "I was curious about this person they paid me to stalk. The Internet makes stalking easy. I learned you were an author, so I bought your book and read it. But, of course, I thought it was only fiction until I started seeing your appeals for help via personals in the Guardian. Those must have pricked the right ears because they assigned me to find and contact you."

Once she had maneuvered herself into my life, Julie was subsequently 'read in,' made marginally aware of the larger picture, and tasked with finding and helping us. Other Arisian operatives worked to quash Alex's interest in us.

The MiBs were not pursuing us. Our fears of pursuit to Utah and Nevada were baseless. We could have relaxed and enjoyed the road trip instead of worrying and looking over our shoulders. Jill and Matt's investigation of my bus-cam sighting was the last gasp of their dying effort to find us, and when Matt returned and reported failure, the hunt terminated. Alex is probably chafing at the frustration, seething in impotence, but for all practical purposes, the case is dead.

Of course, I wondered what Alex would do if I quietly reappeared at my home, minus the fur-girls. With no Aliens in tow, would he attempt to detain me? That might be harder to do than Alex expects. Would he try to be my friend again, or would he even have the balls to approach me after recent events? I decided he would; Alex does not lack for moxie.

As far as the MiBs knew, Jill was on vacation, quietly taking a few long overdue vacation days between assignments. Darla intervened to augment Jill's original message to Alex, protecting her cover. She could return to her regular job at any time.

Everything seemed neatly tied up. I wondered who the mysterious Arisia could be; they appeared to wield immense power. The name sounded familiar. I suspected that Arisia was not a single person; instead, a generalized group name.

They are likely the ones we previously dubbed 'The Four Columns,' those we had talked about as from 'Planet K' and nominally the good guys — or so I chose to believe until evidence contradicts.

Julie insisted Arisia was Petchy, or at least his organization. I hoped so but hesitated to accept the hypothesis just yet.

We were all sitting around the table in Julie and Darla's suite, and the conversation momentarily lapsed. Then, noodling all we had just learned about the players in our conspiracy, I decided it might help to diagram what we knew logically.

I asked Julie if she had something I could draw on. She not only had paper; she had a presentation easel and tablet, plus several colored markers. She had anticipated my engineer's mindset and tendency to draw diagrams.

I began attempting to diagram what we knew. I drew a vague circle and wrote 'Arisia' in the middle. Above the name, I wrote 'Petchy' and 'Teena.'

Below 'Arisia,' I wrote 'Four Columns' and 'Planet K.' Lecturing, I said, "These are all collaborators or merely multiple names for one entity. Perhaps 'Arisia' is the organization's name of which Petch and Teena are members. 'Planet K' we believe is their origin world and the home of the singularity."

The group studied the diagram for a moment, and Julie nodded. Darla injected, "Perhaps Arisia is their current home world, post-Planet K." I considered the idea and nodded. "Maybe."

I drew lines projecting below the circle, labeled them "Fifth Column," and added labels for 'Julie' and 'Darla.' We studied the image for a few minutes. Then I added another circle and wrote 'Earth' on it. Then below, in smaller text, I wrote 'Alex' and 'MiB' beside it. I studied the diagram a moment and then drew lines from a mirror image of Julie and Darla, wrote 'Jill' and 'Estelle,' and labeled them Sixth Column. Finally, I wrote 'Disclosure' in parenthesis under the label. I also added 'Secrecy' in parenthesis under Alex and his MiBs.

Between the two primary circles, I drew another, smaller ring and labeled this one "Planet Oz" and drew lines from it and labeled them Stapleya and Wisceya. Finally, I drew a dotted line connecting all three circles and tagged it 'Fitz.'

We studied the diagram for a while, and then Estelle picked up the marker, added a fourth circle, and placed a question mark in it. "There is another set of players, poorly understood and profoundly evil. We believe they are terrible villains but know little about them beyond the trail of death and destruction left in their wake, and even that is impossible to prove. They are ghosts, sensed but unseen."

We sat in silence for a while, contemplating the diagram. Perhaps it helped frame the questions, but it provided no new answers. Julie's laptop was sitting at my elbow, displaying the latest Google Doodle. I lounged in the chair, daydreaming, mulling the image we had drawn; without conscious motivation, I typed 'Arisia' into the search box. Several hits popped up for comic book references; superhero characters named Arisia. But, nothing rang bells for me.

I added 'Planet,' and Google displayed a fresh set of responses. The second hit led to a Science Fiction Convention. I glanced at the description of the convention and, with sudden inspiration, added 'Mentor' to the search. I studied the hits and then walked back to the easel, picked up the marker and crossed out the question mark, and wrote 'Eddore' in its place. The ladies looked at me quizzically.

We didn't know more about the players, though we named the villains. Someone was being cute with classic Science Fiction Space Opera nomenclature. Arisia is, Google revealed, a significant fictional name in the genre. I had read the Lensmen stories once, years ago. A wonderful, if dated, classic. As my memory retrieved the long-forgotten tales, I began to see similarities in our experiences. On either side of Earth, I added labels' Mentor' and 'Boskone.' Is Petchy' Mentor'? Then who or what is 'Boskone'?

Naming a problem is not the same as solving it, though it can help order the thought processes. I shrugged and laid the marker down, pacing back and forth in front of the easel.

None of my companions had read the Lensman novels; classic Space Opera seldom appeals to the distaff side, much like Stooge humor.

I fell into my 'lecture mode' as I explained my insight to the others. "There is a classic Science Fiction series known as 'Lensmen.' The first stories appeared in January 1934, and they continued in various forms into the 21st Century. They were once runner-up for the best all-time series, barely losing out to Asimov's Foundation Trilogy. Someone's a fan of the Lensmen, Arisia being the homeworld of the 'Moulders of Civilization' as the author originally put it, with Eddore being the home of their formidable adversary. I suggest other groups from the Lensmen books might be analogous to other players in our conspiracy."

Estelle asked, "How does that help us?"

I picked up the marker again, waving it around to emphasize my words, drawing lines and arrows on the sheet to illustrate. "I doubt it does, in any material way, but it does at least inspire us. Names serve as a handle but, beyond that, are useless. Calling Eddore 'Spaghetti' would mean as much. I do wonder at the thought process behind the selection of Arisia as the name for Julie and Darla's employer."

They all looked at me as though expecting me to explain further. So I went on, "The Lensmen tale is a classic, larger than life science-fiction tale of good vs. evil. Pointedly, "Doc" Smith invented the form of Science Fiction we call 'Space Opera' with melodramatic, risk-taking space adventures and chivalric romance. In the Lensmen universe, 'Arisia' is the homeworld of the forces for good. It remains unproven to my satisfaction which side this 'Arisia' is on."

Laying down my marker, I resumed my seat beside the computer and continued, "I also wonder who the Lensmen are in this game? Who is Mentor? Are Petchy and Teena Lensmen? Or are they Mentor? Are Julie and Darla Lensmen? Am I a Lensman? Are we? How are we to save civilization if there are no Lensmen?"

Boskone is Real

I mulled the diagram I had drawn — Four planets, Arisia, Eddore, Earth, and Planet Oz, each with groups of loyalists attached to it. If the Lensmen analogy runs true, three of these groups align themselves on the side of Civilization, against Eddore, and possible unknowns aligned with them. Where do I fit? Am I a Free Agent supporting Civilization? A 'Gray Lensman' in the parlance of Doc Smith? That seems a reach.

This conjecture is fascinating, though we must not lose sight of the mission. Stapleya, Wisceya, and I didn't come to Las Vegas to fight Eddore on the side of Civilization or even to attend a Vegas show, although that begins to seem an excellent idea. Instead, we came here to contact Petchy (Arisia?), locate a portal, and traverse it to Planet Oz, and once there, kill the vermin that prompted my friends to come to Earth in the first place. Of course, once my charges are home and safe, I will take up the Lensman's load if I must, but all this fifth column, sixth column, Arisia, and Eddore daydreaming is pointless.

"I presume you notified Arisia you have us in tow," I asked Julie.

She nodded. "We're awaiting instructions."

Estelle chimed in, "It seems as if every known agent of the four columns, which may or may not be the same as Arisia, disappeared from Earth about when Fitz battled the AI on Planet K. That occurred soon after Arisia recruited you, right?"

Julie nodded. "Yes. They recruited Darla months before me, but Arisia's recruits increased in that timeframe; what are you suggesting?"

Jill picked it up, saying, "We believe that Arisia withdrew their agents from Earth after the battle. They curtailed portal travel and left their remaining interests on Earth in the hands of Earth people recruited as assets, innocent laborers unaware of the off-world involvement, on a job-by-job basis as freelance contractors, such as yourselves. Whoever's managing this task assignment remains unknown, though. Petchy, Teena, and their known associates, all those tied to the Planet K battle, seemingly departed Earth."

Estelle resumed, "This has been a mystery for us. We thought perhaps they were licking their wounds after the battle. However, we know that both Petchy and Teena were wounded, and, unfortunately, we're not certain Teena survived; in fact, we doubt she did."

My heart crumbled anew.

Oblivious to my pain, she continued, "We believe they threw every resource they could muster into that battle. We suspect their losses were tremendous. They retreated to Arisia and blocked the portals, limiting contact with Earth and perhaps other planets too.

"One theory suggests possibly the other player, the entity you dubbed Eddore, might be the reason for their withdrawal. Perhaps they closed the portals to prevent attacks from Eddore. Maybe Arisia, in a weakened condition, has blocked the portals to restrain Eddore while they recover."

Still contemplating the Lensmen analogy and the diagram I had drawn, I drew lines from the circle labeled Eddore and added Ploor, the Eich, and Helmuth. Then, under Eddore, I wrote 'Gharlane' and 'All-Highest.' Below this configuration, I tagged the anti-civilization forces 'Boskone.' As I was doing so, Estelle grabbed the computer.

The issue of the blocked portals nagged at me too. How did these women manage to come through if Petchy and company had retreated and blocked the doorways? Or had they blocked portals to worlds that were potential threats and ignored harmless backwater places such as Planet Oz, thinking no danger could come from that quarter? Or had someone managed to override their blockade and open the portals?

I pushed aside my diagram and turned to Estelle. "This concept of 'Boskone' makes for a fascinating villain to counterbalance our vision of Arisia. But, I fear we've wandered off into the weeds and lost sight of the boundary between knowledge and speculation. Putting aside our beautiful chart and speculations, I worry we're making too much stew from one anemic oyster."

Estelle looked up from the computer and interjected, "Boskone's real, I'm certain. What I have been observing and tracking matches the chart and the summation of the Lensmen stories I just read online."

I held up my hand. "Maybe, but at best, you offer statistics, analysis, and intuition, by your admission and few supportable facts. Is that not correct?"

She nodded, dropping her head slightly, acknowledging a lack of reliable data.

"Perhaps you're correct, and we shall attempt to determine that, but it's also true that confirmation bias could have misled you. Humans are pattern-matching creatures, and we often discern patterns where none exist. Conspiracies arise all too easily in the human mind. We must be careful not to jump to conclusions."

I went on, "We're certain Petchy and Teena, along with their associates we have dubbed 'The Four Columns,' disappeared, why remains in the realm of speculation. In their stead, we see a mysterious entity known as Arisia hiring freelance agents to carry out various tasks, seemingly allied with the interests of The Four Columns and which may constitute a "Fifth Column" working for the Alien presence. Again, however, that connection draws heavily on speculation."

Stapleya said, "Then we do not know that Arisia has any connection to Petchy and Teena." Julie and Darla nodded in agreement.

I went on. "Alex and his organization represent Earthly government forces who seem to possess an awareness of the Alien presence on Earth and desire to control it. They want to keep it hidden. There is a rather large and secretive organization we called a "Sixth Column" of Earth loyalists, also aware of the Aliens and opposed to continuing the secrecy and desirous of bringing the Alien presence into public view."

Estelle and Jill nodded. Jill said, "If Alex is aware of an alien presence, he has given me no indication of it. So while some may know of such a presence, that knowledge must be constrained to the top tiers of the Agency."

I glanced at Julie, "You're certain that Alex and his people aren't actively searching for us? That's at least partly due to the intervention of the Fifth Column, specifically efforts directed by Arisia?"

She nodded.

My summation completed; I focused my gaze on the women. "Who then is in a position to help my friends and I return to Planet Oz and who is actively working to oppose our doing so?"

Julie and Darla looked at each other. After some hesitation, Julie responded, "I believe Arisia is the only party who can direct you to a portal and guide you to Planet Oz. I'm uncertain of the motives of the

Sixth Column." She nodded at Estelle and Jill. "We know they desire full disclosure. I'm uncertain how aggressively they might pursue that intent."

Estelle stood and moved closer, "Fitz, I promised you can trust me, and I swear I will live up to my commitment. Yes, we seek disclosure. However, we're not whistleblowers. We want it willingly negotiated between the aliens and our government. Jill and I have devoted ourselves, our lives, to that goal. Turning you and the ladies into victims, placing them on public display, or anything of such perverse nature is completely counter our intent. I will do everything within my power to return these women to their home planet.

"Our goal is to travel through a portal to Arisia or whatever they call their present home and meet with their government and present our case for disclosure."

Julie chimed in, "Our next move depends on Arisia. They know we are here and seek transportation to Planet Oz. They almost always respond instantly, it has been hours, and they didn't even acknowledge the report. I'm starting to worry. Perhaps it's time to send them a status query."

Darla nodded and pulled out her phone, pecking away at the screen for several seconds before putting it away. No immediate response was forthcoming.

As I realized the lateness of the hour, I suggested we ring Room Service for a pot of coffee. My companions agreed eagerly. We continued rehashing the situation as we waited, but we had pretty well exhausted our topic.

Soon coffee appeared, and we each settled in with a cup, contemplating the conspiratorial picture we had painted. We bounced some more ideas around and replowed ground we had already furrowed, but, unfortunately, there seemed nothing we could add, and we were getting tired.

Finally, there was a buzz from Darla's phone, and a terse message merely said: "K," leaving us as much in the dark as ever.

With that, I stood and stretched and suggested we should retire. Arisia will appear when they are ready; no sense worrying about it. With a few back and forth exchanges, Julie and Darla suggested we abandon our distant motel room and join them in their suite. They had taken a suite for that purpose and had beds to accommodate us all. I wondered who was footing the bill for this, assumed Arisia was but put the question aside for the moment.

Discussion ensued, and Estelle and Jill elected to stay. My charges and I opted to go back to our room for this evening since all of our toiletries and stuff were there but agreed we would gather our things and return tomorrow, and unless Arisia had other plans, we would join them in the suite.

Minutes later, Stapleya, Wisceya, and I headed back towards our dingy roost in Julie's car. I could not quite pinpoint why, but I felt a vague discomfort. Not in the sense of my 'spidey-sense' jangling away to warn of a catastrophe, just a low-level unease I could not name. I convinced myself I was worrying for nothing, that my mind was merely balking at the sudden, apparent lack of worries.

We reached our hotel and settled in for the night. My ladies and I were at peace and uninhibited, with the room to ourselves.

The morning sun rode high in the sky when my ladies and I grudgingly awakened. We assumed our friends likewise were sleeping in, thus felt no urgency as the girls and I arose and went for a leisurely mid-morning breakfast. Returning to our room more than an hour later, we attended to various needs and began gathering our supplies. With a final connection to the motel's WIFI, I rechecked the email drafts folder and noticed that the message I had placed two days ago remained undisturbed. Phil seems completely AWOL. My vague unease became a tiny bit less vague.

Where the heck was Phil, anyway?

I decided to hold my counsel, not wishing to worry my ladies. There was nothing to do until I knew something definite, something worth worrying about. So, I shut down the computer while the gals gathered the last of our supplies, then I checked us out of the room by the simple expedient of tossing the keys on the desk and closing the door.

We drove into town and parked in the hotel's garage. I felt a sudden, familiar nervous tingle. On 'spidey-sense' fueled inspiration, I asked Stapleya to step into the lobby and use a house phone to call Julie's suite and confirm all is clear. She returned minutes later, looking slightly anxious. "They did not answer the phone," she said. I began to worry in earnest.

Departing the garage, I drove aimlessly, fraught with uncertainty. Finally, I decided to risk calling Darla's number using the burner phone. No answer! Security protocol demanded I discard the now compromised burner, but I decided to bend my rules just enough to place a second call. I dialed Julie's number, and a strange voice answered, "Who is this?" My 'spidey-sense' screamed, "COP!!!"

I popped the back cover off and was about to yank the battery when I changed my mind and decided to bend my rules just a bit further and hope they did not break. I called the hotel front desk and asked for Julie's suite. "The guest has checked out," the operator responded.

I cursed under my breath as I yanked the battery from the phone and, accelerating the car, headed for Arizona! I have no clue what happened, I had thought we were safe, but clearly, something came unstuck. Whatever fate befell the women was undoubtedly after us! We're on our own and must run as far away from Las Vegas as we can, as fast as possible. Upon reaching open desert scrub, I hurled the burner phone into the desert sand as fiercely as possible, as far away from the road as possible. I can throw a cheap hunk of plastic a long distance. We stayed on the surface streets until forced onto the freeway by a lack of alternatives. After struggling to keep off the highway as much as possible, we reached Boulder City and crossed into Arizona.

I nervously scanned for black SUVs, low-flying planes, any possible threat I could imagine, yet all seemed quiet, peaceful. How narrowly had we escaped technology's noose this time? Finally, reaching Kingman, I merged onto Interstate 40 and relaxed.

We briefly hopped off the freeway outside Kingman to grab some burgers and hit the restroom. I noted a newly installed Charging Station that seemed to not yet be in service. EVs are becoming popular for good reasons, but they are less than ideal for road trips.

I idly contemplated the challenge of waiting for a charge while running for our lives. It would burn precious time we could not afford, and the transaction would be easily traceable. No anonymous cash payment was possible in the charging network. Running from government-backed pursuers would not be possible in an EV utopia. For a moment, I felt the closing walls of our modern world. The same technology from which I earn a living imposes an ever-tightening noose. One day soon, escape will be impossible. Is this what happened on Planet Oz?

Dismissing the mounting paranoia, I filled our tank, and we resumed our frenzied flight. If we had made it this far, I felt confident we had escaped their grasp — whoever 'they' were!

Sixteen hours after exiting the hotel garage in a full-on panic, the sun had long set. Albuquerque lay far behind us as we rolled down Highway 285, a bit under two hours away from the UFO capital of the planet, if not the entire galaxy, Roswell, NM. There was no particular reason I had picked Roswell other than seeking somewhere we could lay low and not attract attention. I could not name any single factor responsible for selecting that destination.

Sometime after 3 AM and far from Civilization, I pulled the car off the highway and parked on a rural side road. The girls were asleep in the back seat and did not stir. I scanned our surroundings listened intently; after hearing nothing other than the sounds of the night, I concluded we were alone except for the occasional truck passing on the highway behind us. I reclined the driver's seat and closed my eyes. I didn't wish to enter Roswell before dawn, and I needed at least a few minutes' sleep. I hoped to nap for about two hours before proceeding.

Sleep did not easily come, worried as I was, but I did rest, after a fashion. My brain spun itself into a paranoid whirlwind, attempting to process the latest events. What happened to Julie and Darla? What had happened to Phil? Are Estelle and Jill with Julie and Darla, or had their shadowy "Sixth Column" force intervened? Are they alive captured? Or had something seriously tragic happened? Are they being tortured somewhere, pressured to reveal our location? Did Alex renew his pursuit? Why hadn't my 'spidey-sense' given a decent warning? This last unnerved me. I had primarily stayed ahead of our pursuers by my subtle psychic sense, and it seems to have nearly failed this time! Somehow, that frightened me worse than the prospect of being captured by Alex.

I doubted this was Alex's doing; it was too subtle for him. He's more of the hit it with a hammer sort; black SUVs would have been surrounding the hotel if this had been his handiwork. Had someone been surveilling Julie's suite? Who knew we were there other than Arisia? Had my girls and I just barely escaped whatever befell them merely because I decided to return to our 'secret' motel? It seems so.

Dawn began to glow faintly in the east when I roused. My ladies awoke when I stirred, and we sat quietly, contemplating the glowing sky and our surroundings. Then, after a few minutes of quiet regard, I stepped from the car, walked to the road's shoulder, and unburdened myself. My ladies snickered slightly but chose to embrace my idea and joined me in their ladylike fashion.

Relieved, we strolled around the area near the car for several minutes, stretching our stiffened joints, admiring the landscape, and worshipping the spectacular desert dawn. Dawn in the desert is like nowhere else, uniquely worthy of worship. Later, having hoisted the sun aloft, we returned to the car, and I soon had us moving again, rolling toward Roswell.

I was looking for a cheap place to crash, and a few hours later, I spotted a seedy dive on the outskirts of town, so disreputable-looking it didn't even display a name on the giant rusty 'Motel' sign out front. Just the one word, 'Motel,' precisely the sort of place that would accept cash and not insist we prove our identities. We checked into a room and proceeded to go to sleep, even though it was still early morning. The stress of running for our lives had left us spent.

We slept a few hours before I arose and placed the computer online. Phil had left no response in the drafts folder dropbox; my previous message was still sitting untouched. I risked checking my emails using TOR, though nothing there offered a helpful hint. Finally, puzzled by the turn of events, I coaxed a computer in France to send an email to Julie's ID. It merely stated, "Sorry I missed you," followed by several question marks.

With that, I'm fresh out of moves!

Murder at the Bellagio

It had been many hours since our last meal, the fast-food burgers in Kingman scarcely counted. Unsure of our next move, I floated the idea of breakfast for lunch, to which my ladies were agreeable. Bacon, eggs, sausage, toast, pancakes, and plenty of coffee, and the world seems less bleak, although I'm still at a loss. The mysterious disappearance of our allies was beyond troubling! I compared the vanishing in Vegas to how Phil had gone silent and didn't care to pursue where that thinking pointed.

With nothing else to do, we languished at the decrepit desert diner, enjoying the ambiance, almost fearful of leaving, as though we felt safer surrounded by garish neon.

We debated our quandary. Phil, our original "Fifth Column" contact, now unaccountably radio silent, though whether due to his own choice or events forced upon him, I cannot guess. Although I had developed worries, nothing showed him as anything other than on our side. Everything seems suspicious while in the throes of paranoia.

The mysterious Arisia had recruited Darla and later Julie and sent Julie to me. Julie and Darla both seem firmly on our side. I'm less confident of Arisia, although sending Julie my way — to become my girlfriend — definitely placed a checkmark in the plus column. Nevertheless, though our dates numbered only four, a warm attachment enveloped us.

Along with their secretive "Sixth Column" pals, Jill and Estelle seemed sincere about being on my side. So although I still held nervous reservations, I had no reason to distrust them.

I utterly believed Alex was after us, though Julie insisted he had stopped looking. She firmly believed the Fifth Column had neutralized Alex.

It wasn't clear who might be behind whatever happened at the hotel or even their goals. Had the villains Estelle mentioned, the mysterious, unproven evildoers we dubbed Eddore, been behind that?

Round and round the circle went, daring us to wrest logic and sensibility from our troubles, seeking a sensible pattern in the string of events. But, with no new information, we were merely stirring the same tired, stale stew of bland ingredients. I wracked my brain for anyone, friend, or even mere acquaintance I could appeal to, but I knew no one I could approach. No one I dared approach!

Finally, we departed the restaurant to take a leisurely walk around town before turning back toward our seedy, depressing motel. We strolled toward downtown Roswell, enjoying the desert climate. Although warm, hot even, by Earthly standards, acclimation to Planet Oz inoculated us against distress. We were as comfortable as we could be under the circumstances. Of course, we'd all rather be nude, but this isn't Planet Oz. We agreed that not needing to hide from predatory beasts made for a happy trade-off.

Wisceya spotted a collection of colorfully costumed kids and parents. Then, as we approached the city's downtown area, we saw more costumes and soon came upon a colorful parade featuring imaginative 'aliens,' 'spacecraft,' and more.

I realized the annual UFO Festival was in full sway and showed the girls the posters and explained the origins and history of the festival. I pointed out with all the colorful 'aliens' in town, they could stop shaving, and they would fit right in, might even enter the "Alien Costume" contest, and perhaps win a prize as the most authentic aliens. They laughed at my suggestion, though they knew I was teasing. Despite the hassle, they felt more comfortable, better able to fit in with a more Earthly appearance, and drawing attention by joining a contest ran counter to our present predicament.

We passed the International UFO Museum and, on a whim, opted to partake in the Museum tour. The glimpse into the myths and mythologies of the UFO true believers fascinated the ladies. Although I am fascinated by the topic and a big fan of late-night radio shows that feature such fare, I remain firmly agnostic. There are indeed fascinating tales and disturbing purported 'facts,' though I harbor skepticism of the integrity of many players.

Quite a few of them present every appearance of a raving loon. Though there are mountains of claimed evidence, I have difficulty finding data that passes my 'smell test,' by which I mean data I consider as rising to reasonable scientific standards of proof. Perhaps my requirements are too stringent, yet as is often said, extraordinary claims demand extraordinary evidence. Perhaps my understanding of the word 'extraordinary' is flawed.

I do not consider UFOs proven; I find them fascinating for the potential insight into the human psyche as much as any purported alien conspiracy.

As for the thesis of Aliens among us, I defer the question.

We left the museum and made our way around the city for a time, the day wound down, and dusk approached. After being on the road all night, we had arrived at our motel, slept the morning away, and breakfasted in the afternoon. Of course, our biological clocks were skewed, but a restful night's sleep should restore our natural circadian rhythm.

Feeling rudderless and powerless, we returned to the motel and, after again checking mailboxes and message drops, retired for the evening, hoping tomorrow might bring enlightenment or at least new options.

Rising with the sun the following morning, we again breakfasted leisurely, although we didn't languish rehashing our speculations anew. We had exhausted every possible logic trail with nothing left to add.

After breakfast, we again strolled around the city for a brief while before returning to our hotel. On the sidewalk in front, I saw a newspaper rack with a new edition of the Roswell Daily Record. The garish headline situated above a stock photo of a familiar facade had ensnared my eye.

"**Murder at the Bellagio**"

For an eyeblink, I thought it was a promo for an Agatha Christie play; then, I recognized the editor had played word games with grave news, tweaking the headline to catch the eye at the expense of accuracy. Tragedy had indeed struck in Las Vegas!

Recovering from my momentary stupor, I purchased a paper and skimmed the story. Then, distressed, I ushered the girls into our room, sat down, and read the story aloud to them.

"Five bodies were found Sunday morning in a luxury suite at a prestigious Las Vegas hotel. Authorities have not released details or identities of the victims. However, all indications are that a person or persons unknown brazenly attacked a vacationing government agent. Five people are dead, two of the assailants, and three of the victims of the assault. Police are seeking the two assailants who escaped. One survivor of the deadly attack was in surgery at last

report. Police seek, for questioning in connection with the incident, a man spotted in the company of two women, seen leaving the suite before the assault. Their connection to the victims is unknown, although not considered suspects."

A picture of me with Estelle, my visage unrecognizable thanks to my paranoid fear of surveillance cameras, alongside another frame showing the aliens in the company of Jill and Darla accompanied the article. Considering the money they spent on surveillance, I thought it surprising that the hotel didn't have a more helpful picture of us. I suppose paranoia pays off.

Stapleya and Wisceya reacted to the story with shock and horror. Finally, as I finished reading the story, I broke down and collapsed on the bed, no longer maintaining a stoic facade as I gave vent to my grief.

Three of my friends were dead! A fourth was seriously injured and in surgery. Had they died because we left? Would I have been able to fight off the assailants and save my friends had we stayed, or would they have just killed me before I could engage them? A warrior and capable fighter I may be, even unarmed. I trained with a variety of weapons but never firearms. Speed, strength, and fighting skills are of limited usefulness against a gun. We refer to handguns as equalizers for a reason. If we had stayed, would we merely have died too? I prefer to believe my fighting abilities might have made the difference, yet am I kidding myself? Was that fierce attack intended to take me out? Did I escape by sheer dumb luck? Or did the villains instead target the fur-girls?

As near as I could determine, an unknown party had attacked the suite with deadly intent. However, it would seem they met unexpected resistance, as one of their victims fought back!

I could imagine Jill making a subtle motion to tuck her shirt and suddenly producing the compact firearm from her bra holster. It appears she took out two of them. Good girl! They killed three of the women, apparently, and one survived. Despite her size and male musculature, Darla was not a warrior and would not have stood a chance in a fight. I have no doubt Jill was the survivor! Julie and Estelle didn't even have appreciable muscles. No, Jill alone was armed and a trained fighter. She is the only one who would have stood a chance.

Stapleya and Wisceya tearfully tried to comfort me, or more correctly, we all sought to console each other. Minutes passed as we grappled with the enormity of the tragedy.

As I regained a modicum of composure, I reread the story and went online, searching for other reports. Though all were low-key and contained less information, I found only a few additional mentions. So, either some force effectively quashed the story, or five murders in a prestigious hotel is an unremarkable event.

Were the authorities suppressing the story, or were the hotel managers behind the silence? I could imagine reasons for either scenario yet didn't wish to believe either interpretation.

Closing the laptop, I sat silently in stunned disbelief for over an hour. I could divine no path forward — we were at the end of our rope, hiding, running out of resources, under attack by unknown assailants, and with nowhere left to turn. I had never felt so helpless in my life.

Fruitlessly, I once again made the rounds of communications portals. The drafts folder dead drop remained unchanged. I had several emails, though none seemed meaningful. I even checked the spam folder for a possible message hidden via steganography. Nothing. I almost disconnected before I remembered the Guardian and the semi-public communications fostered there. I logged on and skimmed the personals.

I almost missed it.

The tagline was in small print, not the large bold always used before; instead of the classic 'Are You a Boob?' it reads, '**Don't be a Boob!**' followed with a phone number.

I wrote down the phone number and disconnected the computer. I mulled the possibilities. Was this Petchy or Arisia attempting to reach out to us in a low-key way? Someone else who had read my book or otherwise knew the gambit having some fun? Eddore trying again to pick up our trail and complete the job? Or someone or something entirely unconnected to our little adventure, pursuing their own business, unaware of the similarities of their code words to ours?

I had no clue!

I considered calling the number, although I admit I'm frightened. The TORFone should keep us safe and obfuscate our location. Emphasis on the should! Deep Web tools and techniques are imperfectly secure when someone with real mojo looks. They captured the mastermind of Silk Road despite his use of TOR and the Deep Web! Did I consider myself more competent than he? Did I dare take the chance?

I decided to wait before calling. I wanted to think, and I needed to form some strategies. If I nibbled at this bait, I wanted to ensure I could avoid the hook it indeed must conceal.

Our dingy motel room, sad and depressing as it may be, is our last haven on Earth. I dare not risk exposing it. The same is true of our presence in Roswell. I didn't wish to give up as much as the state, much less the city. I needed a greater misdirect. Looking at a map, I recognize how close we are to Texas and Mexico. El Paso's roughly 200 miles away. If I could redirect my connectivity so that it appears to originate in El Paso, anyone tracing our call should find themselves spinning their wheels.

One of the weakest links in Internet security is the ubiquitous WIFI router. Many different companies manufacture numerous brands. Most of them operate using insecure, poorly designed, closed-source control software. There are endless variations, and often security is lacking and not improved by clueless owners who don't bother to make the slightest effort to secure them. All I need to do is find an unsecured router in or around El Paso that I can bend to my will.

The Internet is extraordinarily complex, offering access to a vast array of real and virtual resources. Information of nearly any sort and access to illicit sellers of goods, legal, illegal, and gray areas not defined. Illegal drugs, porn, and more drive Internet commerce. Much of the Internet is listed in the massive hierarchical distributed database known as the Domain Name System or DNS. DNS is the entity responsible for translating a URL such as http://www.google.com into the system of numbers necessary to address computers on the network. Search Engines scan these computers and index their contents, making them accessible for ordinary human beings who do not memorize lists of numbers.

However, not all Internet-connected computers are listed in the DNS, hidden by merely not appearing in any indexes. These obscure systems are accessible only if you know where to look. Instead, an ad hoc arrangement of unofficial and obfuscated indexes lists these off-book resources. Many of them are innocent pages and data the owners merely wish to keep private or sometimes are paywalled, requiring a subscription to access. This system has been variously called the hidden web, the invisible web, the Dark Net, Dark Web, or increasingly, The Deep Web, which has become the standard moniker for unindexed, hidden web resources. At the same time, we reserve the term The Dark Web for those hidden places where illegal activities flourish.

Some use the term Dark Net to reference the Deep Web, but that's incorrect, as the name Darknet has a different meaning. A Darknet is clandestine in nature. A true Darknet is a hidden network where the computers connect only to trusted peers and not the Internet itself. The user must first tie into the Darknet somehow to access those services. A Darknet is also known as a F2F (Friend to friend) network. Not every Darknet is necessarily engaged in nefarious activity, but those engaging in illicit activities often use Darknets. Sometimes Deep Web systems and services are built upon Darknet resources, accessed via special gateways requiring unique tokens or other mechanisms to access.

The Dark Web underbelly of the Internet offers multitudinous resources for those knowing where to search. Unfortunately, illicit information is one of the most freely traded commodities in the hidden corners of the web. Anything an enterprising hacker might need — Rainbow tables of cracked passwords, lists of compromised routers, compromised identity information — is freely available on the web. Digging around, I soon had a list of a dozen candidates.

I tried the first two from my list and discovered they're now solidly locked down. Perhaps the owners had become wise and had taken steps. The owner of the third one, however, remained blissfully ignorant. So I logged into the router and gained full administrative access with modest effort.

I set myself up with an encrypted Virtual Private Network connection to the remote WIFI router, making my connection more secure.

I checked the log and noted the router was not in use; no one was viewing Netflix or any other activity. I had a green field to play in.

Poorly locked-down WIFI routers are a crucial resource for secretive illicit activities — or desperate White Hats trying to stay alive and free.

A bit of twiddling, and I put the router in 'Client Mode' whereby instead of providing access to the Internet for computers, tablets, and phones, it instead behaved as if it were a computer, a tablet, or even a phone. Every piece of hardware on the network has a physical hardware address — known as the Media Access Control (MAC) address — that identifies the class of hardware and the manufacturer. Initially, these were supposed to be unique and unalterable. Even so, the truth is, in many cases, reprogramming it to make one type of hardware pretend to be any other is easy. So I changed the router's MAC address to add yet another level of obfuscation, making my remote router pretend to be a brand-name laptop. Anyone sniffing the WIFI signals would assume it was merely a laptop operating from a nearby cafe table.

Then, while scanning for open WIFI signals, I discovered a free, available hotspot belonging to a local coffee shop! A few keystrokes and my remote 'laptop' became a client on the public access point, clandestine, anonymous, and difficult to trace.

Even if the villains traced my call to the shop's router, they would 'discover' my easily identified laptop with its distinctive, fictional MAC address nearby. "Nearby," in this case, means over 200 miles away! So, finally, I'm ready for the call.

I hesitated a moment. Was calling this number wise? Who might answer, I wondered? I quickly ran down the list of possibilities in my mind. Might it be Petchy? I hoped for Teena! Setting my jaw firmly, I launched the TORFone and dialed the phone number. A man answered on the third ring.

"Hello, Fitz!" answered the familiar male voice. "Hello, Alex," I responded.

Matching Bookends

"RUN!" screamed my hindbrain. "It's the MiBs!" shouted my midbrain. "It's the FEDS! Black SUVs will be at our door in minutes!" screamed my forebrain. My cerebral cortex just wailed incoherently as panic signals flashed throughout my body. I swallowed hard and pushed down the adrenaline surge, held my breathing steady, slow, and forced myself to remain calm, grateful that I went to such unreasonable extremes to obfuscate my call. Though I'm not sure whom I expected, Alex's voice provoked chattering fear.

As I struggled to regain control of my hyperarousal reflex, Alex wasted no time getting to the point. "Listen, Fitz; you need to understand what happened in Las Vegas. Jill survived; she's okay. She's out of surgery now and will recover. I debriefed her, some, and I intend to continue tomorrow after she has rested and when she's stronger."

A sound of grinding came from my teeth.

Alex continued, "That attack went beyond vicious. The assailants displayed no motive and no intent or purpose beyond killing the occupants of that room. They had no idea who they were or why they needed to kill them, it was murder for pay, pure and simple. Fortunately, Jill carried a weapon and could defend herself. Four assailants attacked. She killed two outright, with clean headshots inside the room. The other two bolted and ran after the exchange of gunfire, though she wounded both of them. The local police caught them later."

Anger overwhelmed my fear and steeled my voice as I finally responded, "Thank goodness she survived; according to the news, sadly, the other three did not. I'm glad she tagged those two, and the police captured them. Do the police know anything, have any clues, leads, or suspicions of who sent them?"

"I'm sorry, Fitz; yes, the others died outright in the initial attack before Jill could draw her weapon and return fire. The assassins barged in and opened fire without warning. Jill happened to be the farthest from the door and had a bare moment to react to the attack; otherwise, she would be dead. She nearly died of her wounds. If hotel security hadn't arrived when they did..." His voice trailed off.

"Who were they? Why?" I stammered.

"They were locals, recruited anonymously, though I believe connected to known activists. Judging by the texts our techs recovered, they had little idea what the mission entailed other than entering the suite and killing all inside. These were retrograde jihadis. It wasn't a terror-suicide event; the assassins had not intended to die. An unknown party hired them anonymously via text, and we're trying to trace the source. Their mission was to kill you and the alien women. Fitz, please, I beg you, come in, let my people protect you; these people are bad medicine, and they seriously want you dead."

I brushed aside his plea as I harbor no wish to be in Alex's grasp. "How do you know they recruited them via text? Why do you believe their primary intent was to kill the girls from Planet Oz and me? Is there any clue why?"

"One of them foolishly kept his phone on his person instead of ditching it. As a result, Forensics discovered a custom app designed for secret communications. It revealed a message trail instructing him about the attack and providing details. Fortunately, the man not only stupidly brought his incriminating phone to the attack, but he also left the custom app running and unlocked. As a result, our techs were quickly able to retrieve the messages.

"Nothing suggested why; the messages revealed no motives; the contract merely required they storm the suite and kill the occupants. They expected seven people, including one man who they warned could be highly dangerous and whom they were to kill first and foremost. That was YOU, buddy. They had no expectation anyone might be armed. They underestimated our warrior; that became their undoing. If they had known Jill was armed and a highly trained deadly fighter, I doubt they would attack so brazenly."

I momentarily considered his comments, "The Planet Oz ladies and I opted not to stay at the hotel suite with the others. I had already paid for a room elsewhere, and we opted to stay there instead, favoring our privacy. Julie had insisted we all should stay with her and her sister in their suite. So the girls and I planned to join them starting on Sunday. We arrived Sunday morning and couldn't raise Julie or anyone, became nervous and bolted. We tried a couple of times to make contact, and when that failed, we assumed they were compromised and ran, ducking and hiding, not realizing what happened until I spotted a newspaper this morning.

"If not for the chance decision to stay in our original room, we all would have been present. Julie claimed Petchy's people had contacted her and were arranging portal access to Planet Oz."

"Fitz, listen, Jill has explained much I didn't understand, the conspiracy, the alien worlds, and the rest of the wild tale. Two weeks ago, I would have laughed at this tale as ridiculous. However, Jill has drawn a rather interesting chart of the suspected players, which she attributed to you. Please, Fitz. Turn yourself in, and I can protect you from these people."

I didn't answer for a moment, mulling over the nightmarish vision of the massacre in the hotel suite. First, Phil had reached out to us and then had unaccountably gone silent, and now my friends brazenly attacked in a luxury suite of a five-star tourist hotel. Someone's after us. Even if I trusted Alex, can he indeed protect us? Or is his organization compromised, too?

"Alex, another friend who helped us, has gone silent; I worry about his safety." I gave Alex Phil's contact information. I worried putting my friend on the radar of the MiBs might be a mistake, yet despite my troubles and suspicions, I worried about him. So, in the light of the hotel massacre, I decided it was the right move.

Alex took the information, muffled the phone, and muttered something at another person in the room with him. "Okay, Fitz, we'll check on him. Listen, I understand I spooked you last week, and Jill has explained how fearful you are of my organization. I suppose I can sympathize. I had intended to bring you and the women into protective custody. I wasn't arresting you; I only sought to protect you as I feared a threat. That's a generation ago, given what has happened. I have a better understanding and now believe the threat I merely suspected then is, in fact, genuine and far more serious than I ever imagined. I beg you; please trust I am your friend and believe we're the white hats here; I want to help you."

Another moment of silence as I cogitated. "Thanks for the reassurance, Alex; please don't take it personally if I say I don't quite trust you yet. I have reservations, certainly, but I also worry there may be a mole in your organization. I believe we're safer at the moment if no one knows our location, although we're running out of resources. Will you lend us support without trying to capture us?"

"Fitz, I am your friend, whether or not you believe that. I will help in any way I can. What do you need?" I mulled that over for a moment. "Alex, I need money, cash to stay on the road and stay hidden, and I need a safe way to contact Petchy or someone who can guide us to a portal. I don't know what Jill has told you; I thought we had reached Petchy's organization before the massacre. But, unfortunately, something came unstuck, accidentally or purposefully, we became exposed to inimical forces, I have no idea who or how."

"Fitz, I will send you money, although I would rather have you safe here where I can protect you. Just tell me how. I promise not to try to capture you. Instead, I will try to persuade you to come in freely. I've seen what you can do, and I don't want anyone hurt, you least of all. I need you under my protection, my security, but I want you here willingly."

Then Alex lowered his voice in a conspiratorial tone. "Listen, buddy; I know more about this than I've admitted. I well knew the Nekomata a long time ago; it's just that I couldn't admit it. I have secrets too. Also, now I'm aware of the secret contacts with the mysterious Arisia and how that party hired your deceased girlfriend and her trans sister. The texts on the gunman's phone came from a similarly mysterious entity, using the name Gharlane. Finally, your observation of someone's fascination with the fiction of 'Doc' Smith seems spot on, and I consider that a lead worth pursuing. I instituted a crosscheck of names and terminology from Smith's work against past cases. Whether that leads to Petchy, I have no clue."

My brain was spinning. What are the Nekomata? I'll worry about that later; I needed to develop a strategy to obtain money without exposing myself. That will require time. I told Alex, "I will call this number tomorrow at this time, and we will talk further. I have money in my bank account, although I'm fearful of tapping it. Hopefully, we can come up with a safe strategy. Talk in 24 hours." With that, I terminated the TORFone.

I monitored the remote router for suspicious activity. Then, after a half-hour of quiet, I downloaded the router's logs for later study, cleared the remote log file, deleted my tracks, and restored the system to its standard configuration. I hoped I could again utilize it tomorrow and wondered if I dared to use the same portal twice. Perhaps I should develop another access port.

I began thinking about creating a Virtual Private Network of subverted routers, providing more opportunities to obfuscate my sessions. Alex had given me much to consider, and I suspect Gharlane possesses mad tech chops. So, I not only need to fear the MiBs, but Gharlane's after us too! Who, or what the F**K is Gharlane? And the Nekomata? Is that Gharlane's organization? I wished I had asked him, but reluctant to betray weakness to an adversary, I kept my ignorance to myself. Despite his friendly overtures, I still do not trust Alex.

Was going it alone wise? Would my friends be safer in Alex's custody? It didn't seem right. Of course, I trust my skills and instincts more than I trust Alex, but am I foolish?

I sat in silence, attempting to rein in a herd of free flowing, soaring ideas that seemed to know no bounds and which seemed able to escape my every snare.

Retrograde Jihadis, Alex had called the shooters. What does that even mean? Is there an implication of a connection to the turmoil so much in the world news? Probably not, as if that were the case, instead of "Gharlane," the mysterious employer might have used a name like Muhammad or even Allah or something similar. Contrariwise, I presume they merely served as the convenient muscle; freelance contractors recruited for a job. I can't fathom why Allah might wish us dead, although clearly, somebody does.

I find it alarming that Gharlane used precisely the exact mechanism as Arisa to communicate with his freelancers and the same techniques. Might there be a connection? How similar are the apps each used? Are they foes, friends, or the same entity? The last made sense, as Arisia is the only one outside we seven who knew our location.

Of course, other players may have been following us. Julie and Darla were in active contact with Arisia and likely tracked. Estelle and Jill communicated with the mysterious sixth column, although I don't believe they maintained contact after joining us; I observed them closely. Still, our foe could have been following them, watching from afar. So, although confident no one followed me, I can't conclusively rule it out either.

Hours had elapsed since our breakfast, and my ladies felt closed in, housebound and neglected. Watching as I sit and fume over our predicament isn't enjoyable for them, and no one is in the mood for the sorts of activities with which we might otherwise occupy a lazy afternoon.

Rousing myself from my black mood, I suggested mounting a quest for Alien Pizza. The girls broke into smiles and agreed. Within moments, attired for a stroll, we aimed our sneakers along Main Street with no specific destination or direction in mind.

Unsurprisingly, mere blocks later, giant green alien characters adorned the windows of an establishment promoting 'Alien Pizza' as predicted. My hypothesis of nearby cheese was vindicated.

My ladies love Pizza; I strongly suspect the introduction of Pizza to Planet Oz may be the first cross-cultural contamination resulting from their visit to Earth. If only I could find a way to return them home before Gharlane finds us.

Walking and talking with my friends, I began to relax. But, of course, an influx of cheesy comestible generally improves my mood. The sun rode low as my ladies and I left the emporium and sauntered aimlessly, taking in the sights.

Wisceya quipped, "If we started a company that sold sex toys to aliens, could we name it SpaceXXX?"

Stapleya and I responded with a groan. Stapleya then asked, "Why do aliens refuse to visit Earth?"

"I dunno. Why?"

"They checked the ratings. Only one star."

"What do aliens serve Pizza on?'

"Flying Saucers."

With their improved English skills, Wisceya and Stapleya never seemed to tire of cracking jokes and puns based on the paradox of a city devoted to the idea of aliens, fictional or not, depending on your beliefs, unwittingly hosting a pair of honest-to-goodness extraterrestrials. Their gray fur made them 'grays' for puns, quips, and humor. The ladies enjoyed their paradoxical situation among the alien-obsessed locals immensely, making any reach, no matter how ridiculous to make a joke or pun. They were reveling in the spirit of Roswell.

Our discussion turned semi-serious as the girls expressed wonder at the fantasia surrounding us. The mixture of American Southwestern culture, Alien fantasy mythologies, and historical events — whether or not those involved actual aliens — combined to create a colorful and riotous fantasy land, replete with alien-themed restaurants and parking spots reserved for UFOs and even 'alien-head' shaped lamp posts.

The off-worlders understood and skylarked in the wackiness. They see that it's all in jest and a means to differentiate the community from the mundane and attract tourist dollars. So, they harbored no illusions that aliens trod Roswell's streets. At least not before they arrived. My friends found endless amusement that authentic, gray aliens walked Roswell's streets incognito.

The supposed UFO crash which started it all might be another matter. Although that something happened seems indisputable, what happened remains a question of faith.

Faith — the magic word that occludes so much! We found ourselves venturing into the philosophical weeds while seeking a vantage point to worship the sunset.

Stapleya stated, "We hear you speak of science, and now you speak of faith. Both seem to mean knowledge someone gives you. We don't understand the difference."

The fur-people seem remarkably free of the superstitious tripe that taints Earthly cultures, all the more remarkable given their primitive lifestyle. Though they lack almost everything I associate with science, they are not quick to venture into the supernatural realm to explain the unknown. I had poked at this before in conversations with the fur-people. Unfortunately, I had not received answers that made much sense.

We worshiped the sunset while debating the questions of faith and belief. Despite a lifetime of conditioning by the nocturnal horrors of their home, my ladies have adapted to Earthly nights. They face Roswell's night without fear, at least while in my presence.

The fur-people seem uncommonly willing to accept the unknown, that the answer doesn't exist, and feel little need to imagine fantastic and supernatural explanations for every mystery. Instead, they can marvel at the unexplained and accept it as is.

Religion as we practice it doesn't exist on Planet Oz, possibly because living gods walk among them. I credit the 'smoothies' that regularly visit with much of what makes their society function as it does. Alien visitors bring answers, ideas, and philosophies. The fur people have tales and parables, stories from ancient history, and mythologies from ancient times. Yet, their focus stays on the daily battle for existence on an exceedingly hostile planet. They lack time and motivation for the dualism between spirit and body asserted in Western cultures. Reality fills their day. The fur-people never appreciated the sunset or sunrise of their world because gory death walked the land during those hours.

Nerd that I am, I pontificated how my world had created twin ideologies, matching bookends bracketing humanity's quest for knowledge. Science and religion — proclaimed opposites, juxtaposed as though entirely different — yet sharing profound similarities. Both depend on followers' faith, brutally demand adherence to a system of beliefs, enforce consensus among adherents, and viciously attack the heretic who dares question the approved orthodoxy.

I explained, "A man climbs a mountain, spends forty days and forty nights, then presents stone tablets etched with words, proclaims them the Word of God, and commands all worship, praise, and obey. Such is religious faith."

Wisceya nodded, "Yes, he has revealed knowledge. However, those who accept his word that it came from God did not and cannot themselves speak with God. Instead, they accept his words on faith, trusting in his truthfulness."

"Exactly," I said, nodding. "Another enters a lab, spends forty days and forty nights, then presents a paper printed with words, proclaims them the Word of Science, and insists all worship, praise, and obey. Such is Science. Okay, I plead poetic license, though my point is nonetheless crucial. The similarities between religion and science often outweigh the differences."

Both nodded. "Also revealed knowledge, taken on faith in the truthfulness of the bearer."

I expanded, "Religion offers 'Revealed knowledge,' insists the adherent trust it. Untainted by man's flaws, it comes from divine sources, and we are to have 'faith' in the leadership and 'belief' in unknowable and inexplicable supernatural forces.

"Science also has its 'Revealed knowledge,' although science doesn't ask us for faith in unknowable supernatural forces. It instead asks for confidence in the competence and honesty of fellow human beings — at best, a risky proposition."

Stapleya said, "In both cases, we accept the words of someone and trust that she is honest and trustworthy."

I nodded, "Yes. Further, questioning religious orthodoxy will provoke mortal trouble, yet challenging science's 'revealed knowledge' scarcely differs."

Stapleya asked, "How is that? Are not scientific findings not provable by others?"

I said, "Precisely. Religion proclaims the origins of knowledge as divine and unknowable. Science ostensibly claims the opposite and declares the processes and methodologies are freely published and available for inspection, which no doubt seems a significant difference. Indeed, this is a profound difference. Yet if one accepts the challenge, studies the data deeply, and formulates a different conclusion than the accepted orthodoxy, anyone foolish enough to say so aloud will be ostracized, attacked, and destroyed. The viciousness with which the faithful defend scientific orthodoxy equals all save the most militant of religions, though incidences of scientists beheading opponents remain rare.

"The collection of methodologies colloquially referred to as 'The Scientific Method,' especially the technique known as the double-blind study, is, quite possibly, humanity's most outstanding single intellectual achievement. These are the hallmarks of rational thought."

The girls looked puzzled. Wisceya asked, "Is this not a contradiction?"

I nodded. "The problem is science doesn't always work as claimed. There is the ideal, the goal, and opposite those, we have human failings. Many humans are incompetent, often startlingly so, and many more are duplicitous, bending facts to their preconceptions for a purpose."

Wisceya asked, "That's what you mean by confirmation bias?"

I nodded. "Yes, partly, but it's worse than that. There is an unlimited supply of frauds, hucksters, charlatans, and predators in the realm of religion — unfortunately, the field of science fares scarcely better. Scientific cons are not rare."

Stapleya said, "Sometimes people don't want the truth. They want reassurance that what they believe is the truth."

I said, "Yes when one takes knowledge 'on faith' because 'it is Science,' invariably such faith leads to betrayal. Those who believe religion and science are different, that science is fact-based, and theology is faith-based, ignore fundamental realities of the human soul."

Wisceya added, "Dishonest people exploit others' beliefs for profit, but even honest, sincere people can fool themselves into perpetrating a fraud."

I nodded. "It is true; science emphasizes evidence, empiricism, and reasoned thought. Unfortunately, however, scientists may fake evidence, accidentally or intentionally. Our senses can fool us, and reasoned thought can all too easily carry us away into the weeds of confirmation bias. The principle of confirmation bias allows the most honest and most rigorous researcher to unwittingly ignore contravening evidence. Unfortunately, our capacity to fool ourselves is endless.

"Yes, science is often wrong, more often wrong than right, simply because science is an iterative process. Invariably, theories are proved wrong, falsified in scientific jargon, reformed to seem more nearly correct, falsified, improved, and falsified again until they can no longer be debunked.

"Even after many iterations and following generations of scientists unable to falsify the last theory, fresh eyes at any moment might discover a new facet that suddenly disproves the 'well proven' science. The history of science is replete with discarded theories, failed hypotheses, and scientists who saw their life's work demolished by a single newly discovered fact. It is no mystery why scientists can viciously defend their beliefs.

Stapleya asked, "So, you're saying that once we believe an idea, we tend only to see things that support it?"

"There is tremendous inertia, wherein the heretic who offers a fresh insight invariably finds themselves attacked, often with a stark viciousness which scientists pretend exists only in the religious sphere. Much as any religious heretic, those who would challenge an established orthodoxy are in for a mortal fight. Max Planck, the originator of quantum theories, said, '*...truth never triumphs, its opponents simply die off. Science advances one funeral at a time.*'

"Frauds and charlatans abound in the scientific fields as frequently as any religion. Again, purists will point to the 'Peer review' process as the mechanism for keeping them out, yet human failings taint the idealized process.

"Those who would deify the holy 'Peer review' process have not examined the enormous body of scandal permeating the institution. As with high political office, peer review is often for sale to the highest bidder.

"However, in defiance of claims to the contrary, religion does not, cannot offer truth, does not arise from supernatural sources. Supernatural is a null word. Faith, again like science, originates from the mind of man. Religion begets a false sense of understanding and a fatalistic acceptance of things not understood.

"Flaws notwithstanding, science offers something religion does not and never can. Science provides a pathway to knowledge; it is the one true path to understanding. Science, however, does not ensure we walk the path; it only places it before us.

"The fundamental difference between science and religion is the path placed before us — the promise of eventual truth versus unending supernatural blather."

I could see understanding dawning in their eyes. Stapleya said, "Without guidance, humans invent fanciful explanations for things we don't understand. I suppose our smoothie visitors often provide needed guidance. The scientific approach attempts to place rational guardrails around the limitations of knowledge and constrain the invented explanations to that which fits within those guardrails. But isn't this also a form of confirmation bias?"

I nodded. "Exactly. The same human characteristic that often causes scientific failure can also exclude supernatural fancies. Bias is neither good nor bad in itself — it just is. We cannot eliminate it; we must learn to recognize it and balance it carefully.

"Based on the proposed ideas, theories are supported when they deliver successful predictions of future behavior. They are falsified when those predictions fail. A falsified theory must go back to the drawing board, be recast in light of the failure, and emerge anew, reformulated, and tested again.

"Science also begets engineering. Scientific theories illuminate the path while engineering walks it. For example, consider the theories of thermodynamics. Formulating hypotheses, falsifying them, and crafting them again; iteratively until they held, gave us the knowledge and the understanding to harness the power of steam. Poorly guided by inadequate theories, early experiments resulted in many exploded boilers. Each failure resulted in refinement and improvements until boilers no longer exploded. Once those theories held firm, engineering gave us locomotives plying the rails.

"Today, we speak of the Laws of Thermodynamics — when theory begets engineering, theories become laws, and new truths form.

"Religion never built an engine!

"Science that has not beget engineering, not fostered the creation of functional hardware, and not yielded accurate predictions of complex behaviors remains only a theory, always ripe for disproof, no matter how numerous or how prestigious the scientists. A theory only deserves serious consideration when it stands the test of successfully predicting complex behaviors. Treat any scientific claim as provisional, and suspect if it has not met this standard.

"Falsification always awaits. Be wary of placing faith in a theory that has not yet rendered engineering; it will undoubtedly prove incorrect."

As I concluded my nerdy lecture on science versus religion, foreplay to an audience acquainted with neither, I recognized that the sun had long set and remembered there were more pleasant activities close friends might engage in together. So I figuratively doffed my scientist's smock and my engineer's cap and, without further discussion, took my ladies by the hand, and we strolled toward our sad, dingy motel.

Tomorrow is another day.

Meanwhile in El Paso

Sunrise in the desert is a softly quiet affair. The sky slowly lightens, illuminating high pastel clouds, starkly outlined in the still, crystal air. Early risers, loath to break the pin-drop silence, move languidly in the gathering dawn. The sun delicately reaches over the horizon, morning rays fiercely painting the landscape in sharp, brilliant colors, chasing away the remnants of the night.

Dawn in the desert is breathtaking!

My ladies and I never tire of the spectacular desert beauty, solemnly worshiping the sun's rising and setting equally. So, once the dawn was well broken, we headed to the diner for a sumptuous breakfast, then took an early morning stroll before returning to our room for some friendly relaxation before I settled down to work.

Arriving at the motel, I spotted The Roswell Daily Record. I purchased the dead-tree edition, commenting that I'm a devoted believer in the fourth estate, although I prefer retrieving my news online. My friends had not yet embraced written English, yet they too had come to appreciate the media from observing my habits. The ladies are fluent in English now, and it is easy to forget how foreign the language is to them.

When I used the term, 'The Fourth Estate,' Stapleya questioned the term's meaning. I explained that the Fourth Estate derives from the medieval social order, which defined the Clergy, the Nobility, and the Commoners as the estates of the realm."

"Before the invention of printing, the Clergy and Nobility controlled the dissemination of information, each fighting to control the masses. With printing, literacy grew, as did access to printing presses until there arose a free and independent media not beholden to either of those forces, ostensibly serving the Commoners. However, literacy among the Commoners remained uncommon."

Stapleya asked, "So, the media was only for the Nobility, then?"

I recognized that living in an essentially feudal society, she inherently understood Nobility. The Clergy, not so much, as they don't have that state in her realm, as discussed last night. I answered, "And the Clergy. With the invention of the printing press, the first use was to print the Holy Bible. But independent media soon followed, and the media crowned itself the 'Fourth Estate.' But literacy among the commoners grew, and the media ultimately targeted the masses.

"Some define the term's origin differently, naming the three estates as represented by the structure of British Parliament, Lords Spiritual, Lords Temporal, and Commons. I'm unsure that constitutes a difference, as the British parliamentary system also derives from the 'Estates of the Realm.' Regardless, the free and independent press became the fourth estate of the realm.

Wisceya asked, "Then what is the fifth estate?"

"A fifth estate is a variation now acknowledged or at least proclaimed by some — as an alternative media differentiated by trumpeting their bias, proudly flaunting a lack of impartiality. The term 'Fifth Estate' predates our Internet technologies by several decades, as it originated in the underground printed newspapers of the 1960s. The traditional news media," I pointed to the Daily Record, "claim to report the news without political leanings, although they continuously fail at being unbiased. Meanwhile, the fifth Estate newcomers are not so high-minded.

"As long as there have been media, individual organs have been admittedly biased, supporting a specific party or philosophy. Partisan interests are free to publish as they please to try and persuade others of the correctness of their views. In the age of the Internet, the ease of creating media has improved significantly, the barriers to publication greatly diminished. A variety of alternative information sources have appeared."

Stapleya chimed in. "So, the Fourth Estate presents itself as mainstream, uses traditional technologies," She pointed at the paper, "and tries to sell its views as unbiased. Is that correct?"

I nodded. "I dispute that the traditional 'Fourth Estate' media is unbiased or even less biased than others. Or that the so-called 'Fifth Estate' differs meaningfully other than using Internet technologies for distribution. Instead, I suggest the fourth estate engage in a game of deception, pretending a lack of bias and resorting to manipulations to persuade audiences. I suspect that finding an unbiased source is impossible, regardless of the field or topic. The best one can hope for is to discern an organ's bias and compensate as much as possible. At least the fifth estate sources are honest about their bias."

Wisceya asked, "But you usually read the mainstream newspapers online. Doesn't that contradict how you said the technology distinguishes them?"

I smiled and put my arm around her. I said, "Precisely. They are more alike than different and looking at it as a technological divide misses the point. They have converged technologically; there is scarcely any difference now. I prefer a source that is open and honest about their slant. I can read an opinion piece, then read a treatment of the same events from a competitor, compare and contrast the views and come to my own conclusions. Regardless of my preferences, many authorities name the independent, admittedly biased alternative media the 'Fifth Estate' to distinguish them from the so-called legitimate press."

Both women shrugged at that and left me to get to work. I think I was beginning to bore them. But I guess that's the price they must pay for hanging out with a nerd.

I sat before the computer collecting my thoughts and looking at the news before getting down to work. A quick scan of noteworthy sites of the fourth and fifth estates had become my morning ritual, much as it once was common to read the morning paper.

I concluded that my ploy of pretending to work at this moment was fooling no one, least of all, me. After a few minutes, I picked up the Daily Record and spread it open upon our bed, scanning the headlines and picking a few choice stories to read aloud to my friends. I noticed Stapleya following my reading with interest, and I aided her by pointing to various words, pronouncing them, and sounding out the letters. I noted to myself that if they stay on Earth much longer, these ladies will soon be reading English as well as they now speak it.

After a half-hour or so of dissecting the newspaper, I turned to the computer again and began working. I had decided to examine the logs from yesterday's router session just out of curiosity. Not that I believed anyone could have tracked our call, but still, I wanted to take a closer look.

I became curious when I recognized approximately two minutes before our session ended, there came a massive spike in WIFI Firewall events which continued from that point forward until I shut down the

WIFI radio itself a few minutes later. Was someone trying to break through my firewall? So it appeared, although apparently, they failed.

If so, that implied someone had spotted and traced my TORFone session, which I found incredible. Someone had identified our origination point and was trying to gain remote access to what appeared, to the casual Internet user, to be my laptop sitting at a cafe in El Paso!

Several minutes later, I was still examining the logs in hopes of learning more when Stapleya interrupted my mental fog to ask me about a story whose pictures she was looking at in the Daily Record. Her grasp of written English may be slight, but certain words stood out enough to get her attention. Those words included 'Gunman,' 'gun,' and 'El Paso.' When she voiced those words, my blood ran cold!

I grabbed the paper, hyperventilating as I read the story for myself! I had to read it twice to grasp it, then re-read it aloud to the ladies. Yesterday afternoon, a gunman opened fire on customers sitting at a coffee shop in downtown El Paso. No one at the coffee shop received any severe injury, although one man did receive a minor wound as a bullet grazed his arm, and his companions, his wife, and daughter received scratches and bruises as they dove for cover. The gunman himself was dead, killed by a quick-reacting off-duty police officer who was present.

I checked the timestamp; the shooting occurred less than five minutes after we had ended our TORFone session. I rechecked the address. Yep, it was the coffee shop whose free WIFI I had used!

The newspaper account provided little data. So I went online and searched for additional information. I found several renditions of the tale, including one with a picture of the three who had received slight injuries. The man was sitting in the back of the paramedic buggy, arm bandaged, his wife and daughter at his side. The online story indicated that they were tourists visiting the city and had stopped in the coffee shop to take advantage of the free WIFI to search online for their next tourist destination.

He was a big guy, a tall, broad-shouldered mesomorph, dwarfing his female companions. They project a somewhat similar silhouette to the fur-girls and me!

Whoever was behind this, Gharlane presumably, possesses mad skills and powerful, amoral resources.

The conclusion that someone had traced our TORFone session to the Coffee shop WIFI and dispatched an assassin to look for a muscular guy in the company of two petite females using a laptop nearby was inescapable. Someone had once again attempted to kill us!

My paranoia and seemingly ridiculous over-the-top misdirection efforts had saved us. Had I originated our TORFone session directly, that assassin might have been at our door.

Now I'm officially terrified to use TORFone again. I wondered if I dared use TOR to send and receive emails. We must risk it, I concluded; I must contact Alex.

Undeterred by the failure with TORFone, I concluded that TOR is still secure; it must be. The break almost certainly occurred when Gharlane spotted the same Guardian advertisement I responded to and somehow commandeered the resources to monitor Alex's phone and recognized the incoming TORFone call; how he did that, I offer no clue. That is beyond my pay grade; I would have bet it was impossible. It also implied that Alex's organization was compromised, at least partly.

Alex needed a burner phone we could use that Gharlane could not know about and monitor. A secure burner phone.

I used TOR to arrange an email to Alex from a computer in El Paso. We might as well maintain the illusion that we are there, for the present. I composed a brief text describing what happened, added links to the online news story, and sent it. I took care to jump on and off the network as quickly as possible. Perhaps Alex can find something the locals missed.

I also suggested he procure a burner smartphone and install the Android app "RedPhone," an ostensibly secure open-source phone app. I provided instructions to send the phone number in an encrypted message using my public key. I strongly emphasized that he must do this personally and not give the phone number to ANYONE, not even his assistant. I still feared a mole in his office. I also suggested installing TORFone and Public Key encryption software on his laptop. I wasn't sure Alex would understand the technobabble, but he had some excellent techs who could explain it.

I was mixing technologies in a convoluted manner. TORFone itself cannot call regular phones or cell phones. Regular phones, designated POTS in the telecom jargon, the acronym for 'Plain Old Telephone Service' or PSTN, for 'Public Switched Telephone Network,' are ancient technology. Although modern incarnations embrace significant digital enhancements, they remain founded on an antiquated structure. Cellular services employ an altogether different technology; VoIP phones use still another, as do TORFone and RedPhone, which are also different.

Placing calls between these disparate technologies requires a technological gateway to close the gap. Cellular to POTS is universal; every carrier interconnects these networks. VoIP to POTS is likewise commonplacc. TORFone and RedPhone are fringe services on the shadowy edge of the telephony world. Gateways for these aren't ubiquitous. They do exist, few and rare. Unaided, TORFone cannot call POTS phones or cell phones, nor can RedPhone, and these two cannot interconnect. The need for gateways is a weak point in these security scenarios. A pure TORFone to TORFone call is difficult to trace, as is a RedPhone to RedPhone call. Once you hit a public portal, security decreases dramatically.

I must assume that Gharlane spotted the advertisement in the Guardian and waited for my call to Alex. He doubtless monitored the POTS network for Alex's number to call the clandestine TORFone gateway I used. Tracing the TOR session from the gateway to the Coffee shop WIFI was a feat of legerdemain that baffled this cybernaut; I can only assume that knowing one endpoint, he could trace the session router by router through the Internet. That's not easy and requires Government law enforcement style access to the network. It may well mean that Gharlane has operatives inside Alex's office. If not for the assassin, I would suspect Alex himself of having this trace performed, as he has the resources. Pointedly, he is almost the only person I know of who does.

It then occurred to my muddled brain that the likely scenario was that Alex himself or his technicians performed the trace to my El Paso point of presence. Gharlane then somehow retrieved the info from his mole in Alex's office and sent his assassin looking for us at the identified location.

That was a chilling thought! The slightly warm and fuzzy feeling I'd been developing for Alex evaporated, and I swung back to my default position of a deep fear of the man and his organization.

After further thought, I decided to risk another email to Alex. I explained my theory and told him to email my regular email address but encrypt the message using my public key. I also told him to send his Public Key for future private communications. If he had a mole and didn't know it, he needed to recognize that fact and root him out.

As scared as I remain of Alex, I doubt he sent an assassin to kill us. He might have sent a team to capture us. Perhaps he did; I would have no way to know. Not, however, an assassin, or so I prefer to believe. That's extreme even for the Men in Black. So I decided that the only safe method to talk to Alex was a RedPhone to RedPhone call. Even that was only secure if he didn't let the mole discover he was doing so.

Or perhaps a TORFone to TORFone call. Either would work, but no gateways, no PSTN.

I had done all I could to address our situation for the moment. I consulted the local merchants briefly, then suggested to my friends that a walk and a fresh infusion of Alien Pizza might be in order. They enthusiastically agreed, and once again, we guided our shoe leather along Main Street.

Almost an hour later, we emerged from the house of out-of-this-world Pizza to stroll the boulevard once again, enjoying Roswell's wackiness. We walked a relatively long distance from our motel, not a problem, and we needed the exercise. Unfortunately, we had been eating entirely too well! Before leaving our room, I identified three stores on the web. We headed to the first on that list; I needed to buy a new toy.

Maintaining our illusion of an El Paso presence while using a RedPhone requires a plug-in WIFI interface for my laptop. The laptop's WIFI links us to the motel's service, on which I then run an encrypted VPN tunnel between the computer and our remote router in El Paso. So if the RedPhone must appear in El Paso, it must somehow tap into that tunnel. I considered putting a VPN tunnel directly on the phone, but I wanted to use more robust encryption than the phone supports, and I didn't have the resources to address that. Plus, the laptop provides a better firewall. That means the computer must support two WIFI ports, with the second pretending to be a hotspot to the phone. Simple enough, if I can find a suitable device.

I had identified three possible stores that might carry what I needed. I intended to walk in, pay cash, buying it anonymously.

Fortunately, the second store we visited had it, and an hour later, I was back at the motel configuring my RedPhone.

I pulled out my old phone and removed the SIM Card, as I didn't want it to pop up on the Cellular network and betray our location. Then I reinstalled the battery, booted it up, and connected to my private network via WIFI. Magic occurs! With my phone now appearing as though it resides in El Paso, I installed the RedPhone app and set it up. It took two more hours and a great deal of futzing around with setup, authentication, etc. Still, eventually, we had RedPhone capability with a convincing illusion that the RedPhone was in El Paso.

I wanted to use RedPhone with Alex for a couple of reasons. First, we still had TORFone as a fallback option if it became compromised. But second, knowing Alex, I knew he would be more comfortable talking on a 'real' phone. VoIP on the computer was not in his comfort zone. You might say he is a tad 'old school.'

With everything set up and functional, I rechecked my email and discovered an encrypted email from Alex, complete with his RedPhone phone number and his public encryption key.

Encounter in Mesquite

I stared at the phone number for several seconds, forcing my breathing to remain slow and calm, resisting the urge to hyperventilate as my panic response surged. Finally, after several moments of enforced calm, I launched the RedPhone app.

Alex answered on the first ring. "I guess it works," I said with a slight laugh.

He acknowledged, "Yes, we use RedPhone ourselves in the Agency; it's quite a decent app."

I noted the voice quality seemed improved over the TORFone, although it's still crappy, made worse, no doubt, by our El Paso misdirect. "Did you learn anything about my friend Phil?"

"Fitz, I'm sorry to report, yes. I sent the local Police to conduct a welfare check, and they found his body, by all evidence the victim of a home invasion."

I'm not surprised. "That's one heck of a coincidence, given the events in Las Vegas and the Coffee Shop attack."

"I agree," Alex responded. "I wish you'd let us protect you."

"Before discussing that, answer this. Were your techs tracing my VoIP call? Did your trace lead Gharlane to my point of presence via the mole?"

"Yes, our techs found your location right before the call ended. No one in my office knew except the techs, Matt, and myself. I'm sure there's no mole in our office."

"The mole may not be a human operative. Perhaps Gharlane bugged your office or tapped a phone or messaging app. Or your Tech might be the mole. Are your people tracing this call?"

"I vouch for my people, and our techs sweep our offices for bugs on a routine basis. Fitz, I'm certain we have no mole, I believe you're paranoid, and no, we're not tracing this call. I gave my word not to attempt to apprehend your sorry behind. Listen, pal, I understand your distrust, and I accept that. However, I want you to surrender voluntarily. My sole intent is to protect you and the Aliens."

"They say if in truth they're out to get you, then you're not paranoid. But unfortunately, it seems clear that someone's after us, and I can suggest no other exposure allowing Gharlane to find this coffee shop." I almost revealed the coffee shop misdirect gambit, bit my tongue at the last instant. Let him think we're nearby if he hasn't already figured it out. I still don't trust him, present circumstances notwithstanding.

"Fitz, please come in and let us protect you." I shook my head in disbelief. Alex is still singing his 'Let Me Protect You' tune despite overwhelming evidence his organization is tainted.

"Alex, you almost convince me, although as long as I suspect your organization's leaking information, I cannot risk it. I'm certain we're safer if no one, you included, knows our location. You had offered to lend us cash. That still a possibility?"

"Just say where to deliver it. I will send an agent to meet you."

I deliberated a moment before accepting. "Okay, how's the coffee shop where the shooting occurred? Send one agent alone and unarmed. Give your word, no tricks. When can your man be here?" I used 'here' rather than 'there,' we might as well maintain the illusion.

"I promise, on my word. I will send one agent, alone and unarmed; no effort to capture you. Noon tomorrow, okay?"

"That's satisfactory. Noon on the dot! Tell your man to ask the cashier for Fitz." With that, I dropped the connection.

I harbor no intention of meeting Alex's agent at said coffee shop. But, although he gave his word, I'm not taking chances. We're much nearer the coffee shop than Alex; I intend to be there long before his agent and long gone.

I ushered the girls into the car and hit the road as fast as possible — a quick stop for supplies and rolling again. Finally, almost four hours after hanging up with Alex, we arrived at the coffee shop just before closing. I had cut it razor close!

On entering, I asked for the manager, who turned out to be the only employee present, the owner in fact and in the process of closing for the day. I asked who would be on the register tomorrow at noon, and he replied that he would be.

Explaining I needed his assistance and would pay him for his trouble. I told him I was assembling an elaborate game ending with a bachelor party.

I said I needed him to play a role in our game, to pass the following clues in the hunt. He agreed.

I explained someone would show up at noon and ask for Fitz. I wanted him to hand the person an envelope—nothing else. I promised him a Franklin if he delivered the letter. Easy sell!

I prepared two envelopes with notes, sealed them, wrote 'From Fitz' on the front, underlining 'Fitz' on one but not the other, and handed them to him. Waving a $100 bill under his nose, I explained again; my party would show up asking for Fitz. His job was to hand the person one of the two envelopes. He should tell the person nothing, preferably not even speaking to him. He agreed for the second time, and I again impressed him with the importance that he could ruin our game if he didn't follow my instructions.

I expanded, explaining that if the person called for the envelope early, much before noon, he should hand them the first envelope, the one with the underline, and destroy the second without letting the person discover there had been a second envelope.

At fifteen minutes before noon, he must destroy the first envelope and hand the second to our player when he appeared. In neither case must the player realize there had been a second envelope. He must hide the envelopes out of sight until my player asked for Fitz. The envelope with the underline if he is earlier than 11:45 AM, the one without, after. Without fail, secretly destroy the other.

I gave him the bill and darkly hinted I would be back for it if he didn't follow my instructions perfectly. Given my size and physique, he inferred that my disappointment could be unpleasant. I may have subtly helped him form that impression by my manner. Nevertheless, he promised he would do as I asked.

The second note instructed the recipient to drive north on Highway 85 to Mesquite, park in front of the water treatment plant, and wait until contacted. The first note directed them to the airport Marriott. I believed if Alex planned to ambush us, his agent would appear early. If they were playing it straight, they would be on time. If they don't show in Mesquite as expected, I would assume they're instead at the Marriott, and I would have reason to believe Alex tried to deceive us. I hoped the coffee shop manager didn't screw it up.

Leaving the shop, I drove toward Mesquite, found another cheap, rundown hotel, and rented us a room. I considered not getting a room; instead, sleeping in the car near our rendezvous. I discarded the idea, deciding the comfort of my ladies outweighed my single-minded focus on the mission. Worried that agents might descend en mass on our rendezvous, I didn't intend to permit them to arrive unexpectedly early. Hence the airport misdirect. Yeah, I'm paranoid, and I have a right to be!

My ladies and I retired early and had a pleasant night, as with these ladies, it would seem impossible to do otherwise. They're excellent companions, and not only that they approach physicality with eagerness and enthusiasm, but they're also just delightful companions, full of laughter, wordplay, jokes, and raunchy fun. They are simply a pleasure to be around, even ignoring the intimate diversions. Not that one would ever wish to ignore those.

Rising early, before dawn, we again indulged in the morning ritual sun worship, followed by a hearty roadside diner breakfast. Nonetheless, the morning was still young when I herded us toward the intended rendezvous. Hours of boredom lay ahead, though boredom is relative and not unpleasant when in the company of my fur-girls. If Alex's agent followed instructions, he should arrive at the water treatment plant approximately 30 minutes past noon. If something went awry, I hoped I could spot trouble from a safe distance and run before they could spring a trap. I accepted that I might be kidding myself, though.

I parked over a mile away from the plant and positioned the car in an optimal position to oversee the area from a distance without drawing undue attention. I wished I had binoculars.

Time crawled. We watched the local traffic come and go; all seemed quiet and ordinary in this desert community. Finally, noon arrived, so far, so good. The clock is ticking now. Twelve-fifteen, twelve-twenty, all remained peaceful. Then, at twelve twenty-five, a speeding car appeared from the south. I spotted the light bar as it approached. Obviously, a cop car was approaching rapidly, although not running signal 9, no lights, no siren; it still spooked me. I nearly abandoned our post and rabbited; this wasn't according to my plans.

I suppressed the rising panic and held my ground. The police car stopped in front of the water treatment plant, and a form climbed out. After observing the form move a moment, I decided it must be a male. They spoke a moment, shook hands, and the cop car turned around and sped away, heading back in the direction of El Paso. Not quite what I expected, I guess I assumed our quarry would rent a car. I reflected and decided that a MiB appealing to a local LEO for transport might not be unusual, though I hadn't expected it. It added a complication, as the day is rather hot. Abandoning an agent in the desert was not my intent. But, I speculated, had he expected to stay with us? That troubled me.

The man stood calmly on the sidewalk in front of the water plant. He carried an ordinary sports bag. Too distant to recognize, I could tell he's a big fellow. I had hoped they would send a smaller person, even a female. A small man I can intimidate and females I can charm. A man of my stature is more likely to challenge me, and although I'm sure I can easily overpower anyone, I have no wish to fight. I may technically be a highly trained warrior, but I'm not a fighter. A conundrum, I'm sure, difficult to explain.

I let him wait a few minutes as I scanned the sky for signs of a helicopter, drone, or other aircraft, and I studied the road for unusual traffic. I chewed my nails! After a while, I decided he must be alone as promised. It's now, or never, I told myself. Hesitating for another moment, I suppressed my fears, started the car, and drove forward. As we approached, I recognized Matt. I couldn't decide whether I considered that good or bad, yet all seemed copacetic. I pulled alongside him and invited Matt to get in the car.

I greeted Matt, we shook hands, and the girls welcomed him with their usual unbounded enthusiasm. He handed over the bag, and I glanced at its contents — several packs of $100 bills, as promised. I thanked Matt profusely and inquired whether trackers or dye packs were in it. He shook his head and swore the cash was clean, safe.

I thanked him again and promised to pay Alex back once this was over. I had taken responsibility for helping my friends and merely asked for a loan since tapping my funds is presently risky. I passed the bag to the ladies and turned the car toward El Paso.

I had previously given the ladies detailed instructions. First, they removed the cash from the bag and scrutinized it, broke apart the bundles, and wrapped the money in aluminum foil, just in case there should be a tracking device within, although they reported finding nothing suspicious. Finally, with the cash foil-wrapped, they examined the bag and tossed it out the window, lest there be a tracker within its fabric, undetected.

They reported their progress in Language, so Matt would not understand. Once satisfied that Alex had not booby-trapped the cash, my dire suspicions aside, I told Matt to thank Alex for trusting us and providing clean money.

"I assume you've not arranged for return transportation?" He shook his head in reply. "Would you like us to drop you somewhere specific? Somewhere near El Paso?"

He paused a moment, shrugged, and then responded, "Fitz, I came here alone and unarmed, not even a phone. I want to be more than your courier. I want to join you, to help you. You won't come in and let us protect you; let me join you and help however I can."

Holy Deja Vu! Is he trotting out Jill's save civilization pitch too?

"Hmm. Thanks for the offer. You might check with Jill how joining us worked out for her. Estelle and the others might serve as a warning too. Even my friend Phil. People who help us don't seem to find it a rewarding experience. Unfortunately, I can't permit it simply for your safety."

His shoulders slumped in submission. I hoped he would leave it at that. I had no wish to explain that I didn't trust him any more than Alex. I assumed he would infer those reservations. Voicing them seemed pointless.

We rode in silence for a few moments, after which he tackled the subject anew. "I joined law enforcement with an open mind, knowing the job could at times be risky. But, yes, there unquestionably seems to be danger dogging your tracks.

"Jill joined your group; I believe she succeeded in helping and that you came to trust her. Unfortunately, she's off-duty due to injury, though we still believe you need our help. Jill convinced you to let her in. She could have betrayed your trust yet did not. Please let me take her place. You need me."

He is persuasive; I grant him that.

I asked, "Jill deceived me, or so I now suspect. She had me believing she had taken a vacation and was working alone, without the sanction of her employers. Am I correct in now believing this was merely a ruse?"

He grimaced with a slight shrug. There ought to be a word for that gesture. Shrimaced? Grugged? Or maybe not. "I don't know for sure. We all believed she had taken a vacation. Perhaps Alex knew otherwise; perhaps not, I'm uncertain. The first I knew of her working undercover came when I learned of her hospitalization and that her injuries occurred while undercover. If it matters, ask Alex. I thought she was vacationing with her girlfriend."

I raised an eyebrow. So Jill's co-workers knew of her relationship with Estelle? I had assumed she kept her personal affairs, well, personal. Matt noted my quizzical expression as he added, "Jill kept her private life low-key and didn't advertise her relationships. I don't believe she has often found satisfaction in her personal life, particularly in sexual liaisons. I'm not sure she understands her own needs, not comfortable with sexuality. She's focused on work, doesn't date within the office, and is extraordinarily private.

"Jill as a sexual person is not an image that resonates with those who know her professionally. I believe some suspect she prefers girls, though I doubt anyone else knows definitely. I once asked her for a date, and she confided she wasn't interested in men, asked me not to say anything, and I didn't, not that anyone cares about such things these days. However, when I visited her in the hospital, I saw how she reacted to Estelle's death and drew a conclusion I have not mentioned to anyone before now."

"I'm sure she appreciates your discretion," I responded, without amplifying or confirming his assumptions. I'm uninterested in adding to whatever gossip is circulating about Jill's private life.

"There is another concern, one that worries me." I continued, "From my perspective, Alex has a spy in his office. The attack happened within moments of his techs tracing my TORFone origin to the coffee shop WIFI. Alex seems blind to that possibility and declares it impossible that his office is the source of that leak. You're a possible candidate for that leak. What do you say to that?"

He seemed shocked, surprised. I could almost see the wheels spinning in his head as he processed the idea. Then, finally, he spoke, "I'm surprised beyond belief, tempted to side with Alex. I believed it impossible a traitor could be among us. Yet that is a lot of coincidence. I am Alex's number one and would ..."

His discussion broke off as our vehicle suddenly departed the roadway! Another car suddenly appeared, seemingly from nowhere, and tried to ram us. Fortunately, the driver underestimated my reflexes. As a result, I was able to dodge the oncoming blow. Instead of broadsiding us squarely, he almost missed us entirely, barely clipping our bumper as I spun the car off the road.

Fortunately, desert roadways tend to have broad, smooth, sandy berms alongside the paved road. As a result, I managed to leave the pavement in a somewhat controlled fashion, spin-out, recover, regain control and return to the tarmac without disaster. Unfortunately, our assailant was not so lucky. He hit the shoulder way too fast and lost control, rolling over, landing on the passenger side, driver's door in the air.

I slammed the brakes and brought us to a halt. Then, I launched from the car at my full speed, charging the offending vehicle several hundred feet away and on its side. As I approached the wreck, I spotted a glint of sunlight on metal and dove to the ground as gunfire erupted from the upended driver's door.

If I was moving fast before, the adrenaline surge kicked in. Now I moved as if a deinonychus were at my heels. I grabbed rocks from the ground and, madly dodging the swinging gun barrel, charged the vehicle, returning fire by throwing my rocks. When I throw, it means something! Even ordinary stones become deadly when powered by my throwing arm. My second missile caught the firearm squarely, knocking the weapon from the hand holding it and, unless I missed my guess, shattering bones and smashing the gun. I suspect that hand might never again grasp anything, much less a firearm.

I reached the vehicle. I hit the underside like a football player attacking a tackling dummy, rolled the car onto its roof, and then ripped open the smashed door, bodily yanking the assailant from the car.

The Mole Unmasked

Shouldering the unconscious assailant, I ran at speed toward our vehicle. Matt and the girls were out of the car, Matt staring in rank disbelief! I had tipped my hand before in the canyon, bending a rifle barrel and running into the woods. This time I escalated his suspension of disbelief several levels as he saw me take on our assailant with nothing other than my bare hands and a few rocks against an armed gunsel.

I think he was impressed.

I unceremoniously dropped my limp burden on the ground, checked to ensure he was unarmed, and turned to confront Matt. As I walked up to him, I gauged rising fear in his eyes as I leaned forward to place my face within inches of his.

Matt's a big guy. I'm bigger! He wasn't accustomed to confrontation since people naturally defer to him, between his bulk and the badge and weapon he usually carries. I have greater size, his badge is meaningless now, and he's presently unarmed. Adrenaline-fueled hot blood surged through my veins. Being shot at is stimulating; trust me on that. I made sure Matt understood just how stimulated I was.

Leaning in, I lowered my voice barely above a whisper and growled slowly, with as much menace in my voice as I could project. "Matt, who knew you were coming to meet us? Who knew where we were?"

Matt shrank from my intense, overwhelming presence, swallowed, shuddered, and slowly, visibly struggling, reasserted his composure. "No one. No one except myself and the local cop I asked to assist. On my word, Fitz, they didn't learn it from me! It could not have been anything beyond the coffee shop if something had leaked. Unless he followed us from the coffee shop, I have no clue how he could come here. I didn't tip them off, on my word, and he would have killed me too had he succeeded."

Our captive moaned, and we turned our attention to him. He was cradling his shattered arm and awakening to intense pain. I stood over him and glared into his face as he climbed toward consciousness.

"Who sent you?" I growled. He closed his eyes, holding his injured arm. I slapped him, grabbed his uninjured arm, and twisted slightly. "You want a matched set? Who sent you?"

Terror gripped him; he uttered one word and voided his bladder. The word was "Gharlane."

I checked his pocket for a phone. I checked the various apps installed. He had tons of them; nothing stood out at first glance. I opened the phone dialer and dialed 911, reported a single-vehicle accident, asked for an ambulance and wrecker.

Hanging up from the call, I turned again to our captive. "How does Gharlane contact you?" Silence. I took hold of his uninjured arm again and began to twist, just a little. "The App, Bleep. A direct encrypted line to Gharlane."

I turned to the phone, found the app, and immediately hit a password prompt. "What's the password?" Again, silence! How many times must I remind this idiot? I reached for his uninjured arm again; he pulled back. "They'll kill me!" he whined. I leaned over him. "What do you think I will do? The buggy will be here soon; it's your call whether they haul away a corpse or a captive." He melted. "Genghis Khan, the password's Genghis Khan." I laughed inwardly at the trivial password, yet I admitted I might not have guessed it quickly, though now I began to recognize a pattern. In Doc Smith's fiction, Genghis Khan had been Gharlane in disguise. Someone does love the Lensmen.

I entered the password, and the app opened. A few pokes revealed a message trail, instructing our captive to wait for my appearance at the coffee shop, follow until I joined the ladies, and kill the three of us, though how he should accomplish that wasn't specified. I glanced at the figure promised to him for our deaths and let out a low whistle. We were worth serious money, dead. The sender signed as Gharlane. Unfortunately, there wasn't much detail, and no clue how Gharlane knew I might be at the coffee shop.

Indications were that our captive had been in the coffee shop when Matt asked the cashier for Fitz. Matt didn't remember him. Matt's supposed to be a trained agent; I'd have expected him to note who was hanging out at a drop. Who knows? In either case, he had followed Matt to Mesquite. He had spotted us together with the girls and, desperate to carry out his instructions, had rammed us, expecting to gun us down while disoriented by the wreck. Gharlane had not, it seems, warned him of my capabilities beyond mentioning that I was dangerous.

I'm also lucky!

I nodded to the women, and they began to administer first aid, splinting his damaged arm. He will require surgery and therapy or be forever known as 'Lefty.' I hoped Gharlane's employees get decent medical insurance. Unfortunately, we couldn't do much for him; our first-aid kit was minimal. The ambulance should be here soon, however. I studied the messages intently until we began to hear sirens. Nothing implicated Matt in the events. I apologized to him for my brusque, accusatory manner. I decided that if he's the leak, he's unknowing. He might be an unwitting pawn, but he's not an enemy.

I suggested he may wish to flash his badge, take our friend into custody and start his people investigating this. I indicated that diverting scrutiny away from myself and the girls would be helpful.

I examined the app our attackers were using for covert communications. Rudimentary, I decided, even poorly designed. I could write a much more sophisticated one. I noted several weaknesses in the design. Gharlane is not half the badass he would have us believe, though he is a step or two ahead of us at the moment. I studied the message trail with Gharlane again, looking for clues, finishing with it as the ambulance appeared, followed moments later by the wrecker.

Matt took control of the situation; I told him we would be in touch later and surrendered the attacker's phone to Matt for forensic analysis by his techs. I examined the wrecked vehicle for clues, finding nothing significant, allowed the wrecker to haul it away. Matt promised his forensics people would study it thoroughly.

While this activity was ongoing, the local police wrote up the traffic report. Matt's badge again came in handy as he deflected the attention away from the girls and me and onto our attacker. The man, he claimed, had fallen asleep and run off the road, narrowly missing us. I wondered how he would explain taking the man into custody as a terrorist threat or the man's wounds or various other inconsistencies. Not my worry, I admitted, although the extensive, almost unaccountable power Alex and his people could wield when they wished bothered me.

Matt and the police left in due course, trailing the ambulance carrying our villain. We departed, careful not to let anyone notice the direction we headed as we cut across Highway 54 to pick up the route back to Roswell. As far as Matt and Alex know, we're hanging out near El Paso, and I see no reason to disabuse them of the idea.

Our harrowing experience behind us, we spent the next few hours driving toward the UFO Capital, stopping at Alamogordo for junk food. Unfortunately, there are no In-N-Out restaurants in this area, though my ladies agreed Sonic qualified as an alternative. Further, they found the drive-in kiosks and curb service fascinating. I noticed their interest and pondered what sort of cultural cross-contamination I was introducing. Planet Oz may never recover from the tales and ideas these ladies bring home. Prime Directive! Ha! Long ago, too late for that, I mused.

Nerves calmed, bellies sated, and wallet flush, we arrived back at our sad little motel home base without further incident, found our room again available, and settled in — we were just in time for evening worship.

Desert sunsets are fantastic!

My sleep seemed unsettled. I found myself worrying, reimagining the day's events, trying to find sense in all the details I'd observed. Who's Gharlane? Why is he trying to kill us? These and a hundred other questions tickled my noggin. Even the ladies seemed subdued. These events were too up-close and personal for even their nominally jovial nature — this wasn't an attack on a distant hotel room or unknown coffee shop. This violence had been close and personal and had nearly succeeded.

Morning found us again facing the rising sun, coffee in hand, somberly contemplating our next steps.

We didn't exactly have any.

We're hiding in a run-down desert motel, our only contact, a shadowy government agency I find myself constitutionally unable to trust. An agency proved to be vulnerable to our enemies—hiding, powerless, against an unknown foe seeking to kill us, with no idea why.

Even our usual Alien-motif'd diner's breakfast failed to restore our buoyant spirits fully. So after breakfast, the ladies and I strolled the city for a while. They gradually began cracking their usual alien jokes and sexually suggestive innuendos and humor, evidence of returning cheer. Although we had already taken in most of the city's Alien-themed attractions, including a couple of visits to the UFO Museum, today Stapleya noticed the Alien Zone, which we had missed before.

We spent a while there. By the time the girls and I had toured much of the facility, our good humor had reasserted itself. The horrific events of the previous day forcibly diminished to the level of merely unsettling.

Finally, returning to our room, I decided the time to contact Alex had arrived. I was anxious to learn whether he would still insist there could be no leak in his organization. I'm also anxious to know whether the MiB techs had uncovered anything useful regarding our enemy.

Setting up my WIFI redirect and verifying my digital presence once again gave the illusion of originating from El Paso; I enabled the RedPhone app and dialed Alex's number.

Alex answered quickly, and I skipped past the routine pleasantries, getting immediately to the core questions.

"I assume Matt fully briefed you on the breach yesterday. Have you uncovered the source of the leak?"

"We have been in full lockdown since yesterday afternoon. We're scrutinizing all personnel. I remain confident that there is no mole or bug in this agency, yet yesterday's events argue otherwise. So we're ripping the organization apart to find the facts."

"I'm sorry, Alex. You believe in your organization and people, yet Gharlane found us. When Matt picked up that envelope yesterday, he and I, along with the girls, were the only ones who knew we would be there. Less than an hour later, Gharlane attacked us. I can't imagine any way he could have found us other than via Matt, directly or indirectly. Only people in your organization knew Matt was to look for us there. I assume our attacker followed Matt from the coffee shop, yet the follower had to know to find him there! Who else knew?"

"I knew, a couple of my technicians knew, and Matt knew. No one else! Amend that! The techs knew we were connecting in El Paso. They didn't know where. Only Matt and I knew of the coffee shop rendezvous. We suspect that the treatment plant location could have leaked via the local Sheriff's office. Matt requested support from the locals, including transportation to the rendezvous point. Local rural cops still use Narrow Band FM police radio technology, which is trivial to listen to via a scanner. Our best guess is that's how your attacker knew where Matt went."

That set me back on my haunches! Radio! Amazing! So low tech! For over sixty years, public service and law enforcement have used the same classic, open, unencrypted communications tech. Listening in via scanner was a pastime for radio enthusiasts for decades. That VHF FM technology spanned the era from vacuum tubes and mechanical vibrator power supplies in the 1940s until sophisticated silicon electronics took over beginning in the 1970s, even until the 21st Century when sophisticated, encrypted digital trunking radios obsoleted F.M.

I had not considered that remote rural areas might still use technically obsolete radios, which might be a risk. Still...

"Our attacker may have used a scanner to track Matt to locate us in the desert. Unfortunately, that didn't lead Gharlane to El Paso or the coffee shop. Who knew where Matt was going?"

"Only Matt and I," Alex responded. "Who made his airline reservations?" I asked.

"I'll find out and search for other possible leaks. Trust me; I will get to the bottom of this."

Changing the topic slightly, I left Alex to chase his mole as I charged off on another tangent. "Did you learn anything from our attacker? What about his phone? Did your lab people uncover anything from the app used to communicate with Gharlane?"

I heard Alex sigh, and I knew something else had gone awry. "Fitz, something happened to the attacker. Unfortunately, he died on the way to the hospital."

"WHAT!!" I exploded. "His injuries were nowhere near life-threatening. So how did he die?"

"The Medical Examiner expedited his examination for us, at my request. His report says that a bone splinter from the shattered arm entered a vein, made its way into the brachiocephalic vein, and thence into the right atrium and penetrated the atrium wall. This splinter resulted in catastrophic heart damage. Unfortunately, it occurred during transport to the hospital, and he had deceased by the time he arrived. I'm sorry, Fitz. It seems he died from the injuries you inflicted."

I did not reply immediately; I sat quietly for several seconds. Had I killed that man? Or did Gharlane get to him? If the latter, how? Is the M.E. honest or an agent of Gharlane?

"I'm unsure what to say; he was alive and in excellent shape, minus the broken arm when I last saw him. He was shooting at me, trying to kill me. I didn't use lethal force, and that was purely in self-defense.

"How can we be sure he died of the injuries and wasn't a loose-end cleaned up by Gharlane?

"What of his phone? Did we learn anything there?"

Alex answered the last first, "I do not have a report yet on his phone; I gave it to my best computer forensic scientist. I think you met him, Dr. Holm. He is dissecting it to compare with the similar devices from other incidents."

"Yes, I believe I met him. His given name is Nels. Dr. Nels Holm, if I recall. Doesn't he possess a Ph.D. from Berkeley?"

As I asked the question, an alarm went off in my head. My 'spidey-sense' suddenly went into full alert, 'whooping' at me so loudly I could not think. Alex said something about Dr. Holm's qualifications, but I wasn't listening. My brain spun wildly.

Suddenly my thoughts congealed, and I interrupted Alex to ask a question. "Does Dr. Holm have a middle name? What is it?"

"I'm not certain, Fitz; let me check. I seem to remember only a middle initial, 'B,' yes here it is on his card, Nels B. Holm, Ph.D., Why do you ask?"

"You don't have his full middle name?"

"I'm sure H.R. has it; why? What's the significance?"

"Alex, this whole conspiracy, this mystery constantly employs names and character references to Doc Smith's Lensmen stories. So whoever is behind this is wrapped up in the Lensmen, though why I haven't a clue."

"Yes, I got that, though your point is escaping me."

"Alex, hold onto your hat. Nels Bergenholm, Ph.D. is a prominent character in the Lensmen."

Stunned silence from the line for three heartbeats! Alex blurted, "Call back later!" and disconnected.

Did we spot our mole?

A Terrified Bolt

I sat quietly for several minutes, digesting the revelation and the complications that logically followed. If Dr. Holm's the mole, is he also Gharlane? Or just another evil acolyte following instructions received via clandestine messaging? Will Alex be able to unmask him and unravel the conspiracy?

Tons of questions, zero answers. Alex and I had de facto established a regular time for our daily call. Tomorrow is soon enough to find out the fate of Dr. Holm. Unfortunately, Alex can't call me. My ploy of pretending to be in El Paso, not to mention that I'm hiding from some rather evil people, means I cannot leave my RedPhone online. Further, additional complications ensue since my phone isn't on the cellular network, as I removed its SIM card. For security and simplicity, my phone stays off, untraceable, only calling out using WIFI, VPN tunnels, and RedPhone — not receiving calls or messages.

I decided a little celebration was in order; finding the mole feels like a victory. So I asked my ladies for their suggestion, whether they preferred Alien Pizza as a celebratory snack or something else.

"Something else," Wisceya announced, stifling a slight snigger. "Chocolate Ice Cream!"

They didn't need to give me the hard sell! So, suiting up, we once more shuffled our shoes along Main Street.

While dressing, I observed, "Nudists aren't people who take their clothes off. Instead, they put them on when appropriate, whereas others remove theirs only when necessary."

Stapleya thought I was quite the wit. Wisceya only half-agreed with her mother.

The ice cream parlor meant a hearty walk down Main Street, excellent exercise, given the calories we were about to consume. Since we've been on the run, I have been too long absent from my gym sessions and eating altogether too often and well. Even with our long walks around the city, I fear for my fitness, despite the contribution of various other pleasant exercises. Staying on the run much longer requires finding somewhere private where I can let loose and tune-up. Unfortunately, muscles demand laborious work to maintain. At least yesterday's action provided a light workout.

We arrived at the Ice Cream Emporium in scant minutes. Although my fitness weighed on my mind, I refused to allow caloric concerns to dampen my mood. The girls seemed in total agreement, each willing to attempt their weight in frozen delight.

Cool confection dispatched; our footsteps traced an alternate return path. Along the way to our room, a hot debate ensued concerning whether Alien Pizza might head our menu later today or perhaps something a touch upscale might be in order, recognizing the day's success and our newly flush wallet.

Many eateries, high class, low class, and no class, reside within the range of shanks' mare. The debate recessed as our room drew into sight. Our party opted to return to the motel room and explore whether there might be an entertaining way to expend a few of those excess confectionery calories before focusing on the thorny issue of the evening meal.

Life is momentarily pleasant.

Somewhat later, I admitted my 'spidey' twinge surrounding the fate of Dr. Holm had become more than I could continue to ignore. I don't claim my subtle sense has a supernatural origin; I'm confident it emanates from my subconscious processing data faster and deeper than my conscious self can handle. Whatever it may be, it has saved my bacon often, and I have come to trust it, mostly. So, against my prior reservations, I decided to break our de facto schedule and call Alex now.

Resetting and double-checking my obfuscations and precautions, I again launched the RedPhone and placed the call. Alex didn't answer right away. Not entirely surprising, he had little reason to have the phone in hand, not expecting I might call at this time. He picked up on the fifth ring.

"Did you catch him?" I didn't waste words on pleasantries.

"He's our man, must be; while we were talking, he left the building and vanished! He abandoned everything, including his phone. It's locked and encrypted; our techs are on it. He had blue-jacked the RedPhone; he had every chance since he originally set it up. He has been my most trusted senior tech, and he was also my friend! He betrayed me!"

Darn his complacency; that was why I had explicitly told him not to trust ANYONE with the RedPhone setup. He had allowed the mole to set it up for him! Alex was still speaking, "He had been eavesdropping on every call! That's how your attacker knew of the rendezvous at the coffee shop. We don't know whether he was the sole mastermind or just another hired contractor, although until more info emerges, I'm betting he was the mastermind or at least one of them."

"How did he penetrate your organization, and how long had he remained hidden there?"

"He was a trusted employee, underwent regular deep background checks, entrenched here for years. I can't explain the breach. When I find him, I will ask him. If we can unlock his phone, we may find some answers there."

"Phones aren't that difficult to break into unless the user installs a strong password, and that becomes such a pain to unlock fifty times per day that no one bothers. So, what's the nature of the lock screen?"

"The phone presents a keypad, so it's probably a six to eight-digit number. We're looking for likely combinations such as birthdate and numeric information of that type. We have tried all the usual, obvious numbers people tend to use, with no luck. So we may resort to physically invasive approaches, maybe disassemble the phone and dig into the hardware if we can't guess lucky soon."

"Did you try anything Lensman-related? I would start with 'ARISIA' and 'EDDORE' as typed on a keypad. '274742' and '333673' respectively. If those don't work, I suggest trying names from the Lensmen. Mentor, Gharlane, Boskone, Ploor, and similar. If none of those work, go buy a stack of Lensmen books and start trying every name therein."

"Excellent idea." He muffled the phone, and I could hear him shouting. "Okay, I clued the techs. That may do it. I will let you know as soon as we try it."

"Was he working on anything on his computer that may provide any clues?" My 'spidey-sense' tickled as I asked that.

"My investigator went over it thoroughly; everything in-process connected to an active case, save one. Fortunately, he had departed so rapidly that he left several folders open and several tasks in progress.

The only one we could not tie to a known agency case was a seemingly innocuous IP trace. So we're unsure what he was looking for."

My 'spidey-sense' started clanging, a fire bell announcing a five-alarm conflagration in my brain. "Alex, that might be significant. Precisely what address was he tracing."

"According to my tech, he was tracing an encrypted VPN tunnel originating at the El Paso AT&T Cloud and connecting into Cable ONE in New Mexico. Unfortunately, other than one end in El Paso, it doesn't have anything in common with ..."

I tuned out his words as my blood ran cold! Gharlane nearly found us! He figured out our router subversion.

"Alex!" I interrupted, "Gotta run! I will call later!" and abruptly terminated the call.

Slamming the lid on the laptop and disconnecting chargers, wires, and connections, I shouted at the ladies to grab clothes and start throwing our junk in the car. We're rolling in two minutes!

I didn't bother checking out. I'd paid cash for our room and owed nothing. I had prepaid for tonight, but we weren't staying! Even if I had thought they would return my money, I wasn't sticking around for a refund. We have money; we lack time!

It might have been slightly longer than two minutes, though not much. Then, bolting from the room, I tossed the key onto the desk and, hitting the street moving quickly, turned onto 2nd street and headed west on State Highway 70, fudging the legal limit as much as I dared.

So long, Roswell, you've been good to us. I may settle here one day if the stars align in that manner. I enjoyed my time here but staying longer would be decidedly hazardous.

An hour later, we passed through a wide spot in the road named Hondo and veered north onto the 'Billy the Kid' trail. Another hour and we were north of the White Sands Missile Range. We picked up US 60 outside of Socorro and continued our westward run without stopping or slowing down until we departed New Mexico.

My tensely wound nerves calmed as our car approached the Grand Canyon State, nearly six hours after our mad exodus from Roswell. We stopped in Apache County, AZ, just in time to worship the sunset in the mountains. After relaxing and breathing the crisp Arizona mountain air, I felt relatively calm again.

Always prepared to depart, I had picked a destination to head toward and studied the routes days before. I had planned and reviewed three, with the option to choose one at departure. I can't say why I headed this way, although the beauty of the Grand Canyon State is enticing.

After our brief respite worshiping the sunset, we rolled on into Edgar, AZ, and found a cheap, anonymous motel with an attached restaurant. Not quite the Ritz, merely a place we can rest and regroup. No terrible rush now; we can stay here a day or three as we wish or continue further west, though there's little haste. We could improve our travel time by heading North and picking up Interstate 40, although I still preferred to avoid the major routes. US 60 suits our needs nicely for now, even if it is slower and winds sedately through the mountains. I'm rather enjoying the trip, as near as circumstances permit.

It had been hours since our overly-generous indulgence of ice cream. Calorically dense though it may be, our bodies, not accustomed to fasting, clamor for renewed sustenance. We checked into the Joy-El hotel. No one would rate this place five stars, but it beats sleeping in the car. Possibly three stars on a good day, though the rooms are clean, relatively inexpensive, with WIFI included. Once settled into the motel, we adjourned to the adjacent restaurant.

Much like the motel, the Jewel Restaurant aspired to a score of nearly adequate. Possibly our growing appetites enhanced the ambiance, although three stars would be generous. We dined sumptuously, and by the time our meal concluded, the night had firmly settled upon us. I was pleased that my ladies showed no trace of their deeply ingrained fear of the nighttime hours. The time of day and the depressing nature of the neighborhood argued against an extended after-dinner stroll. Not all predators are dinosaurs.

We settled into our room and retired for the night. I debated setting up the RedPhone and updating Alex, but the hour's late, and it would require too much time to set up the extensive level of security I intended. I dare not revisit my previously commandeered routers to mask our connection; I must assume they're now known to Gharlane.

Finding and subverting a fresh collection to my needs requires time. Tomorrow's soon enough. I could, of course, forego the added layers of deception and trust the RedPhone directly on the motel's WIFI. It intends to be clandestine, yet my paranoia has served us well, and I'm not confident that Nels is the only acolyte of Gharlane who might be looking for our dainty digital footprints. My clandestine mesh of subverted routers may seem overkill, but I'm not prepared to relax yet.

Despite the excitement, we slept pleasantly and awoke early. The Jewel Restaurant indulged us with a decent enough breakfast, and afterward, I made myself busy setting up a virgin, clandestine subterfuge for our router connection. I spent nearly three hours scouting out a few compromised routers and setting up my clandestine gateways. I resolved to create several, rotating between them and never using the same one twice in a row.

Gharlane had penetrated our fictional laptop presence in El Paso, so I feel no need to perpetuate that deception; thus, my new web of subverted routers can be anywhere. Furthermore, my 'laptop' presence will magically appear in random cities, displaying different physical MAC addresses, keeping anyone looking for us guessing. It took time to set it all up, and once done, I muttered to myself, "Trace THAT, Gharlane!"

Once my deeply hidden network cluster was set up and tested, I enabled the RedPhone and launched the call. Alex answered instantly.

"Hello Alex," I said without preamble, "Sorry to jump off abruptly yesterday. Something urgent needed attention. Any progress on unlocking his phone?" I decided against mentioning the change of venue.

"You nailed it. The passcode was 'BOSKONE' rendered numerically, just as you guessed. If you had not put us onto the Lensmen meme, we might have worked much harder and much longer to recover the data. We discovered a secure, encrypted texting application called "Bleep" he was using, and again the passcode to unlock it followed the Lensmen meme. That was the same app used by the gunman in Vegas."

I interrupted to add, "It was also the app used by the gunman who attacked us with Matt."

Alex acknowledged the datum and resumed his narrative, "He sent many texts using the name Helmuth; it appears he was a previously unknown player in the conspiracy. We're analyzing the messages to determine who he texted and what conspiratorial details we can unravel. I'm optimistic we can identify his cohorts."

"He's not Gharlane then. Too bad, as he seems to be the one after us. I had hoped to knock him out of the game and stop hiding. Clearly 'Helmuth' was talking to Gharlane and feeding him information. Be careful, Alex, don't assume this was Gharlane's only agent in your midst or that Nels is the only arm of Boskone."

"You have taught us a brutal, painful lesson, my friend. Before, I felt utterly confident in my people and my organization. But fortunately, I learned my lesson and won't be so arrogantly trusting in the future.

"We will continue studying Holm's phone and revisit evidence from the other cases. I will forward updates on our discoveries. I know now something of your tricks for stealthily reading your emails. Check your email; I will forward details and specifics via regular email."

"Use Public Key Encryption! Don't trust email to be secure. Gharlane might still read it if it's not encrypted."

"Right, will do. I've been complacent. Trust me; I've learned humility. But listen, pal, once this is all over, would you consent to teach us classes in your techniques? Perhaps even come to work for us as a subject-matter expert. I thought we had the best and brightest in our organization and in most measures, we do, but you showed us new ways to measure."

"We will talk about that another day. For now, we must break this conspiracy and return to my core mission of returning my friends to Planet Oz. I must also devise a strategy to kill the monsters on their world."

"Of course, we must take care of the Nekomata. But wait, before ringing off, somebody wants to say hello."

I froze — there's that word Nekomata again! What did Alex mean? The context implied the fur girls. And who else is there? Has Alex again placed us at risk? I hesitated and nearly hung up. Then, I shrugged. "Okay, put em on." I could hear him handing the phone to another, and a weak voice came on the line.

"Hello, Fitz." Jill! The limited quality of our network-mutilated voices made it hard to assess how she sounded, although she seemed weak and soft.

"Wow, hello Jill, it sure is good to hear your voice!" My girls perked up at the mention of her name and moved closer. "Alex says you had a close call!"

"Yeah, well, I am a Warrior! I gave as good as I got."

"That you did, so I hear. Good job! Just duck a bit faster next time! Hey, the girls want to say hello." The aliens were unfamiliar with a phone, though they had witnessed plenty in the last couple of weeks, and Stapleya had attempted to use the house phone at the hotel in Las Vegas. Stapleya didn't hesitate; she grabbed the phone before I could hand it over. She handled the unfamiliar device gingerly but quickly adapted, chatting freely. They traded the phone back and forth until I intervened and hit the speaker button, permitting us all to hear Jill. Alex had purposefully arranged his visit to Jill's hospital room to coincide with my anticipated call, to involve the convalescing agent.

They talked for another five minutes until I interrupted them with harsh reality. "Alex, it's wonderful to hear from Jill and terrific to hear the search is progressing, but Gharlane's still out there. Every second we're on this call, even with my extreme security measures, every second gives Gharlane another second to trace us. So, it's time to say goodbye; we will talk again tomorrow." With that, I disconnected. Stapleya and Wisceya gave me hang-dog drooping faces. They were justifiably disappointed, and I apologized profusely. Nonetheless, they understand, as well as I, the dire consequences of permitting Gharlane to find us.

Perfectly Petrified

With the covert channel disconnected and the phone securely packed away, I checked on my secondary communications methods. Launching the TOR Browser, I skimmed the Guardian postings. Perhaps another Personals advertisement might offer hope. I searched for anything with the word Boob or Petchy but found nothing. Someone pretending to be Petchy had used a message in the Guardian to inspire us to run from California. I believed that was Julie, inspired by her communications with the mysterious Arisia.

I wish I had pressed that question with her. But unfortunately, I have a knack for not getting answers from people, so I must work on my people skills. It's not precisely a failure to ask the questions; instead, it's more that I let them derail me when diverting with non-answers or incomplete answers.

That is the reason I am not a salesman. Machines are so much easier and more trustworthy. I know I'm often too much the nerd, but I have never had a computer intentionally lie to or deceive me.

I lack persuasiveness, miss what a salesman would call buying signals, and fail to "ask for the order." Instead, I stumble and mumble, get intimidated easily, and then accept non-answers when I should be pounding the table demanding information. I know I can learn better. I'm a good learner. I must grow a pair! Maybe the next time I see Alex, I'll punch him in the face merely to set the tone of our conversation. Yeah, I'm angry, mostly at myself.

My time on 'Planet Oz' improved my social bearing; I overcame my fears and anxieties in a crowd and learned to sing and tell stories to a receptive, adoring audience. But I melt and turn to putty when I meet opposition, especially with Alex, Teena, or Petchy. Teena, well, any male melts in her presence. Scratch the 'male' part. Her magic works on women too. Petchy is also pretty overpowering, although not for the same reasons. He's just pushy.

But Alex? Why? He's just a bureaucrat with some power. So why does he intimidate me so? He scares the living crap out of me, that's why. I am afraid of him in a deep-seated, visceral manner. By rabbiting when we did, I stood up to him. I will now take that to the next level, stand up to him face-to-face, and demand information. Maybe I won't punch him, but I can make him think I might.

We don't know if Arisia is merely another head of the "Eddore" hydra or if Arisia is their adversary, fighting them using similar techniques. I had a dark suspicion Arisia had been responsible for the betrayal that killed three of my friends and injured Jill. Unfortunately, I lack proof, though I have plenty of circumstantial evidence.

We have the menacingly evil Gharlane, Eddore, Helmuth, Boskone, and of course, Dr. Nels B. Holm. Does the 'B' stand for Bergen? Alex never answered that. I hope Alex has found him and is wringing answers out of him as we sleep.

Alex had previously used a similar ad to inspire me to call him, using the keyword 'Boob' to pique my curiosity. Would Petchy chance this simplistic approach to communicate? Maybe, though doubtful. I have no alternative idea how he might contact us on the run or how I might contact him.

On a whim, I again placed an ad:

Should Petch spot the ad, he might understand we are on the road. Maybe or maybe not, but the second line should tell him to post a message. Granted, it's a long shot. The downside is that our enemies are aware of this channel and could lure us out. I'm unsure whether a response might come from a friend or foe.

It had now been days since I checked my email. I did not expect communications from that quarter and had put it out of my mind. I quickly downloaded the accumulated junk and logged off. Skimming the digital detritus, I deleted the spam and phishing attempts, whittling away much of the inbox. Finally, one message stood out in the now much smaller pile remaining. It was from Matt.

"Fitz, we did not have a chance to talk. I'm serious about wanting to join you and provide support. Please call." The phone number that followed was his regular cell number, no RedPhone. I'm reluctant to again resort to a TORFone Gateway. Gharlane may have tricks I haven't fully understood, and he may be monitoring the gateway. I'm surely not going to place an open, unencrypted call that someone might trace. So, I decided not to call Matt.

There was no message from Alex. I hoped for new information, but it had been only a short while. So, it seems we have time to pass while we await reports on Alex's efforts at unraveling the web of conspiracy.

I'm confident this town has its unique charms, though I confess they're momentarily hiding from us. Spending our time amidst the dismal surroundings was not enticing.

We decided to explore the neighborhood and discover whether we might find a nearby establishment superior to the Jewel for our midday meal. I mean no disrespect to the Jewel, but it resides near the bottom of even our recently lowered scale. Unfortunately, we had aborted our intended upscale celebratory dinner in Roswell, and there seems no motive for a renewed celebration here. Even so, we wanted something more pleasant.

Walking a circuitous loop, passing the medical center, the local High School, through the down-trodden residential areas, and completing the circle back to the motel, we discovered only one nearby eatery was potentially a step up from the Jewel, the local Subway franchise. Although we missed Alien Pizza, the girls decided that the Meatball Pepperoni Melt constituted a marginally acceptable substitute.

Returning to the room while discussing our surroundings, I suggested spending one more night here, but tomorrow we should roll. Then, if we indeed had time to kill, perhaps we might play tourist and explore the state's natural wonders.

After a couple of hours of relaxation, I again checked our Guardian drop and my email inbox, with no results. So, we opted to stroll over to the Jewel for a light evening meal and spend an hour observing the diner's regular crowd while keeping a low profile.

The high point of the evening came when some of the regulars engaged in a high-spirited bout of arm wrestling. They didn't seem too organized; possibly a drop or two of alcohol factored into their ad hoc spirit. The main attraction was one local giant, taking all comers and winning every round. My ladies watched in fascination and kept whispering in my ear, affirming their confidence in my ability to take him and win the pot. Occasionally, he glanced my way as if to ask whether I cared to join the game. I smiled and shook my head, declining the invitation. It wouldn't be fair.

True, he was very muscular, with bulging biceps; we were well-matched, at least by appearances, and he had the experience edge. He seemed to make a regular practice of the contest. Although much more practiced at the game than I, he lacks the advantage of my fine-tuned genetics and aggressive off-world training regimen.

My ladies seemed intent on pushing me into the game. Perhaps they merely sought the amusement of seeing me humiliate him. I admit to feeling slightly shocked at the cruelty my friends displayed. I had seen flashes of similar aggressiveness on Planet Oz in the heat of the hunt but never in a social context. Of course, women play at dominance in their female ways, but they don't tend to square off in testosterone-fueled demonstrations of strength and power the way we of the lesser sex often do.

This could end badly.

Once my companions voiced their enthusiasm, the group of locals making up the audience became invested in persuading me to join in. I felt stuck, struggling to find a graceful exit — there wasn't one. What a lovely dilemma I'm riding the horns of; thanks, ladies. I had no wish to injure this fellow. He has done nothing to me other than extend an invitation to a friendly contest. But, on the other hand, I'm not particularly eager to lose.

Finally, shrugging, I agreed. We took our positions. I learned that his name was Big Jim. When Big Jim engaged, I merely matched his effort ounce for ounce. His muscles bulged, his tendons knotted, his face turned red. He could not move my arm, yet I did not move his. We sat there firmly locked in the competitive embrace for what must have seemed an eternity to him. I could have snapped his humerus, ulna, or radius, ruined his elbow or shoulder with a mere twitch. But, unlike the previous hot-blooded battle where the gunsel had drawn down on me with deadly arms, I felt no need to do so. My ego had discovered we could afford to lose gracefully.

I wasn't straining, not in the slightest, though I put on an act, grunting, huffing, and puffing as though I was in the fight of my life. But, for all his strength, I may as well face off against a five-year-old. As the clash dragged on, I sensed his exhaustion and muscle fading, and as his power slowly failed, I gradually yielded. Finally, I let him push my arm to the table, believing I had exhausted first, thus allowing him to win.

Massaging my 'overstressed' arm as though painful, I handed over the Hamilton of the bet. I wondered if he sensed the faintest hint of how narrowly he escaped a lifetime crippling injury for a meager amount of money that wouldn't even be the minimum hourly wage in most places.

My protagonist and his companions congratulated me on a worthy contest, advised me to continue working out, and invited me to try again the next time I came through town.

I had to join them for a celebratory round of drinks before I could excuse myself and escort my ladies back to our motel room.

Once we were alone, I gently rebuked the girls. "Why did you two goad me into that contest? Did you want me to injure that fellow? Or did you expect him to injure me?" My voice was gentle, but Wisceya dropped her eyes, sensing my anger. Stapleya seemed contrite but met my gaze. "He is the first earthman we have met who we thought might equal you. He seemed even bigger and stronger than you. We wanted to measure you against an equal."

"I see. You thought because that man was my size, he must have my strength. Did you expect him to beat me?" I asked.

Wisceya looked me in the eyes. "We have met few earth men. You are all much bigger and stronger than Nekomata men. We wanted to see a contest among equals. But, too late, we realize you are not equal. When we see you with Big Jim, we see he is not your equal."

They were tearful once they understood the enormity of what had transpired. While the ladies had known I possessed exceptional athletic prowess, they had not realized that I was so beyond the Earthly norm. They had not recognized the awkward, perverse position they had forced me into, thinking the contest would be innocent fun. I conceded I had worried excessively and over-reacted. I was hypersensitive after hurting and possibly killing our would-be assassin in Mesquite. Just because I am strong does not mean I should fear engaging in ordinary contests or that I risk losing control and hurting an innocent. If I remain calm, I can control any outcome. I don't need to uphold my ego.

I started at her using the term 'Nekomata' but held my silence for the moment, not wanting to derail the conversation. I must explore that, but first things first. We talked through the specifics of what they failed to understand and then hugged, and we all forgave each other for the near disaster. There was no harm, no foul, in the end, and we were only out a ten-spot in exchange for a valuable lesson — when you're hiding, don't put on a show!

Having resolved the conflict and absorbed the lessons learned, we retired for the evening, kissed, and made up several times. Then, when we were ready for pillow talk, I raised the deferred question. That was probably a mistake, pillow-talk is not the time for confrontation, but I was burning with curiosity. "Dear ladies, I would like you to explain something. First, Alex used a term I had never heard before. Then he used it a second time, and he seemed to be discussing you lovely ladies. Finally, you used it earlier this evening when talking about the men on your home planet. Sweethearts, what is Nekomata?"

Wisceya snickered. Stapleya laughed out loud. Then, seeing my puzzlement, she added, "Fitz, you're ignorant. We are Nekomata. You call us 'fur-girls' and our home 'Planet Oz,' but those are only the pet names you have given us. The Asherans call us Nekomata, or rather, our home planet is Nekomata, and we are of Nekomata because we are born there. We are the people of Nekomata."

My jaw sagged loosely, the gears in my head spun freely without engaging. Ignorant, huh. My brain engaged with a jerk! More like in the dark, as in that thing they constantly keep me in. No one ever told me the fur planet had an official name. I had jokingly called it 'Planet Oz,' and Petchy never said a word, never offered an alternative or correction. It was always just Planet Oz. Realizing that once again, my own nerdy failings entrapped me, I stared at the ceiling for several seconds, mulling over my dork-mastery. Once again, I accepted non-answers when I should have pushed for information. Stapleya is not Alex, "Then dispel my ignorance, dear lady, and who are the Asherans?"

"Petchy and Teena are Asheran. They are from the planet Ashera. So is Alex, I think," Stapleya said. "He has visited Nekomata with Teena and Petchy, so I think he is from the same planet."

I stared at her in stunned disbelief. "Oh, F**k," I said, a bit too loud. Then, I whisper-shouted, "What the ever-loving F**k are you talking about? Alex is an alien too?"

Both ladies nodded silently. Wisceya was wide-eyed, but Stapleya's face was calm, slightly smiling as though amused. I didn't recognize it then, but later I realized she still hadn't told all she knew.

I melted. I exploded. I cried. WTF? Saying this news affected my mellow, pillow-talk mood is an understatement. Decimated, I wanted to hit something. Or someone, preferably Alex. I jumped out of bed and started pacing. I was upset and not thinking clearly. Heck, I was so upset that I was barely aware of my surroundings — I paced right out the motel room door. Unfortunately, I didn't realize my mistake. Without knowing how I got there, I stood in the middle of the motel parking lot, naked, disoriented, and confused, unsure of which direction our room lay. I stared at the sky, on the verge of a total meltdown and collapse. I don't know how long I stood there. It was the middle of the night and very quiet. Then, a feeling of peace descended as though raining down from the sky. Holding out my hands, I stood there in naked bewilderment.

Then, Stapleya and Wisceya, now fully dressed, came running after me, wrapped me in a towel, and guided me back to our room. We passed by the night clerk's window; Stapleya whispered to the startled woman behind the glass, "Sleepwalking. He just had a nightmare, but everything is okay."

After some more talk, I recovered and forcibly reasserted my calm. We finally went back to bed, though sleep was another matter. My brain was still reeling.

Fitfully faux-sleeping, I finally arose and busied myself at the computer; I needed to "check out" for a bit, stop running, stop thinking about aliens and let my subconscious digest this new information. We needed a day away from our worries. I needed time to decompress and think things through. So, finally, I scouted out nearby tourist activities. The Petrified Forest National Park lies only an hour's drive from our roost.

There is a smaller Petrified Forest in California I have visited several times. I always hoped to see the National Park. But it took a few minutes to explain to my Nekomata (what a strange word) friends the nature of the attraction. Their waking hours are too occupied with the stone-aged struggle for survival to imagine vacations and recreational diversions. Nekomatans had not conceived the idea of a National Park or, for that matter, a 'Park' of any sort. Nekomata, Nekomatans. New words don't feel right. But in my new enlightenment, "Fur People" and "Fur-Girls" seem, I dunno, somehow inappropriate, as if suddenly politically incorrect. My head is still spinning.

Petrified trees presented another novel concept, as the girls seem unaware of similar phenomena in their world. I wouldn't doubt that perhaps some corner of "Planet Oz" displays identical phenomena, as I suspect is often the case in other things. However, the Nekomata daily struggles often preclude attention to factors unrelated to survival and the next meal.

Once I successfully communicated these concepts, the off-worlders became excited. Accordingly, our party checked out of the Jo-El early, rolled North on Highway 191 to pick up 180 at St. Johns, where we stopped for a pleasant breakfast at the Family Kitchen and by 9AM found ourselves at the turn-off to the Petrified Forest Road.

We spent nearly two hours touring the Rainbow Forest Museum, followed by a drive through the National Park at midday, stopping from time to time to absorb the breathtaking views. Unfortunately, we didn't have a camera, not counting my phone. I suppose I could have used it, but I was reluctant, given all the security concerns and questions. I insist it stays firmly off, except when being used for communications. However, we did buy some postcards with carefully staged professional pictures.

Presently, I forced myself to return to the reality that my friends and I aren't merely enjoying the luxury of a leisurely vacation. Evil people still chased us, and we urgently needed to find a safe harbor and check in with Alex. Pointedly, Alex has some 'splainin to do. Accordingly, a few hours later, we found ourselves ensconced in the glorious Wigwam motel, with our own private concrete and steel Teepee for a residence. Yeah, much as you might imagine. Still, it had a touch of charm and a museum, plus free WIFI. I felt like I was amid Radiator Springs, expecting to glance out and recognize talking, sentient, animated vehicles plying the street before our Teepee.

Once ensconced in our private Teepee, I again set up my networking misdirection, launched the RedPhone, apparently from Toledo this time, and called Alex. He answered on the first ring.

We gave superficial attention to the ritual pleasantries, and I knuckled right down to business, demanding a status update.

Alex said, "We found Dr. Holm or, more accurately, found his body. Unfortunately, he died in an automobile accident not 30 minutes after his hasty departure from this office. You were correct; HR reports his middle name as Bergen, consistent with the character in the Lensmen books. We're in the process of trying to unravel his true identity, although he had worked and lived here under that name for years. That alone hints the conspiracy is wide and deep."

"So, another actor dies unexpectedly! That is starting to be a habit. What was the cause of the accident?" I asked.

"That's the curious thing. The crash was a single-car accident, evidently driving too fast for a steep, curvy road and going through a guardrail and over a cliff. There is no evidence of foul play, and it doesn't appear to be a suicide. All indications are that he realized we had discovered his identity as the mole and ran to escape before his arrest and simply lost control. Yet is it too much coincidence to accept? We've been tearing apart his home, all his computers, bank accounts, literally his entire life."

I said, "I agree, too much coincidence. We don't know how but that doesn't mean Holm wasn't murdered. Any progress making sense of the messages?"

"Yes indeed. We have connected the assailants in Las Vegas and their 'handler' Gharlane to Dr. Holm, acting as 'Helmuth' and the mysterious Boskone, who seems to have been his boss. As a fan of Doc Smith, I assume you would not find it surprising that Boskone seems tied to massive drug operations. The Lensmen fascination doesn't seem to extend beyond Boskone. However, Boskone has tendrils reaching into every known significant illicit drug activity we have examined and many other unsavory endeavors such as prostitution and sex trafficking. It appears to be a massive, global crime syndicate that has operated below the radar of law enforcement for a long time."

I let out a low whistle. "We should have anticipated a drug connection as soon as we spotted the names 'Helmuth' and 'Boskone.' It's fascinating, but I fail to grasp how it ties into the girls and me. Why should they be desperate to kill us?"

"I'm unsure what threat you pose to them, although I have a wild theory. I suspect that there's an extraterrestrial connection via the portals your father introduced you to. If that's true, your ladies' presence on Earth jeopardizes that connection. I have uncovered one or two hints pointing that way, although as yet we have nothing conclusive. There were two distinct references to a place called Ploor, possibly an alien planet. Again, straight out of Doc Smith!"

I took a deep breath and let it out slowly, trying not to become sidetracked by Alex's acknowledgment of my biological connection to Petchy. He seemed to have finally read my book and now believes the tale as told. But, on the other hand, if he is an Asheran too, as Stapleya claimed, he knew it all along. I pushed that recognition aside as I considered the broader issue of 'Ploor.' I decided not to let Alex know what Stapleya had revealed. Not yet. I will hold him accountable, but not today. I need to lay my traps carefully.

I said, "If a far-flung interplanetary organization operated a massive criminal conspiracy, keeping that conspiracy hidden would be the motive to kill anyone endangering it, including their people. The possibility raises endless questions."

I paused again, gathering my thoughts, and after a moment, continued. "If indeed this idea holds water, where's the portal to Ploor, what's on Ploor and Earth, how freely can they move between the worlds? Are other planets involved? These questions and perhaps a hundred others come to mind."

Alex responded, "Yes, I have a carefully vetted team of strategists in the adjacent room working on the possibilities. We have no answers or very few, although we're compiling a list of questions. At the moment, I'm keeping my extraterrestrial theory under wraps. People won't believe it until they have their noses rubbed in it, and without overwhelming proof, it could derail the entire effort. So for the moment, 'Ploor' is just a circle with question marks on the connection diagram. As far as my strategists are aware, it is probably someplace in Mexico."

"I agree. We do not want anyone thinking about UFOs or Aliens; we want them thinking about criminals," I said. Then silently, I added, you don't want them thinking about aliens either, I bet. Then aloud, I asked, "How's Jill?"

"Jill has improved and is now well on the mend. Although she still has much healing to do, her doctor is sending her home, subject to visits by a nurse to check her progress, change bandages, and such. I was desperate to move Jill away from the hospital, lest she might still be a target. But no one else knows this; she's not recuperating at home. Instead, she's coming here to a secure ward where we can guard her and keep her safe. We also hope she can join my strategists, at least briefly each day, to guide them in making sense of the data we're uncovering."

"Alex, I beg you, use extreme measures. Never allow Jill to be guarded by less than three men and give her a weapon to protect herself. If I could be there and guard her myself, I would. And, unfortunately, I am by no means confident that you have no additional traitors."

"My friend, you've convinced me. I would have called you a raving paranoid two weeks ago, but I know better now. We are on total lockdown; no one leaves, no one uses a phone or a computer unsupervised. Personal phones are locked away, and use is only allowed with permission and supervision. Once they enter this domain, even my team strategists may not leave or communicate with anyone outside these walls while this conspiracy is extant. We scrutinize every phone for suspicious apps; every email crosses my desk."

I felt somewhat mollified, though darkly suspicious. I didn't want Boskone or whoever is behind this to get to Jill. I have seen enough friends die. "I beg you, think carefully about who you trust. Remember, Holm was among your most trusted people. No one can be above suspicion!"

With that, we exchanged closing regards, and I shut the phone down. I reviewed Alex's comments in my mind; something bothered me. Then I remembered the email from Matt. Alex had said every email crossed his desk. Might this be an exception? Should I mention Matt's email to him? Exceptions can be the death of security!

Going online again with the laptop, I sent Matt a reply and gave him my public key, then told him to send his public key.

WTF is going on with Matt? Is he an alien too?

A Vorpal Sword

Alex had undoubtedly given us material to ponder. But, as I grappled with the identities of inimical actors, I returned to that week-past small-hours strategy session, where we attempted to diagram what we knew, suspected, or imagined about the conspiracy. I needed to recapture our derailed train of thought.

We had that evening attempted to unravel a Gordian Knot of startlingly intractable threads. That we may have plucked loose a thread or two is meaningless, one cannot solve such a pertinacious problem by tugging at its edges. Instead, we must conduct a frontal assault on the heart of the mystery. Only the Sword of Knowledge may cleave the Gordian Knot. It is our task to forge that vorpal sword.

We had drawn a diagram. I wondered what became of it. If gathered up as evidence in the investigation, perhaps Alex now has it. I searched around for pencils and paper for doodling. Engineers need diagrams. Of course, I could undoubtedly draw something up on the computer, but I'm just trying to coalesce my jabberwocky thoughts into something less nonsensical, not creating a presentation. I longed for a whiteboard.

Poking around the desk drawer, I discovered paper and a pen and began scribbling. I drew a circle in the middle and labeled it '*Earth*' and within it wrote '*MiBs.*' Underneath, I wrote '*Matt,*' '*Alex,*' and '*Jill.*' I mused for a moment and added a tangential line from Matt and labeled it '*5th Column.*' I did the same to Jill; only I labeled hers '*6th Column.*' These lines suggested that Matt and Jill may have other interests or agendas. In addition to functioning as MiBs, are they playing different, more complex roles? Or is this all jubjub and Bandersnatch spawned by my frumious imagination?

I drew another circle to the left of the first, labeled it Arisia, and drew a line from the 5th Column designation of Matt to it. Next, I wrote '*Petchy,*' '*Teena,*' and '*Four Columns.*' Next, I added a question mark beside the label Arisia. Finally, I added question marks by Matt and the 5th Column, too, as I have no evidence for them.

Matt had pretended to represent the 5th Column at Alex's direction to draw me in, so I had concluded. Phil may have been the real deal, but he is dead now; I'm not even confident there is a 5th column movement. So I crossed out the 5th Column.

There is no proof Arisia is allied with Petchy and Teena. I began having dark suspicions it was not, even though Jill and Estelle had thought so. They worked for Arisia and believed they worked for the group we had otherwise referred to as the 'four columns.' Yet, somebody betrayed their location, and Arisia is the logical candidate. I prefer to believe Petchy's organization and supporters are not an inimical invading force. Instead, I trust them and think they're a benign, even friendly extraterrestrial agency working from the shadows to positively influence Earth without openly violating the spirit of what I like to imagine as the 'Prime Directive.'

As the fiction's greatest starship Captain said, "History has proven time and again that whenever mankind interferes with a less developed civilization, no matter how well-intentioned that interference may be, the results are invariably disastrous."

The quote and the directive itself stem from Science Fiction, but the phenomenon and the concerns it raises are undoubtedly realistic, as we observe from the history of Europeans encountering other cultures. If Earth's civilization becomes nakedly exposed to an advanced extraterrestrial civilization, there would be a tremendous culture and technology clash. Based on Jill and Estelle's comments, the MiBs understand this, or I think they do. They seem to be aware of the extraterrestrial influence and seemingly are working, with or without alien assistance, to keep it concealed below public awareness. Imperfections in their effort fuel the various UFO Conspiracy memes, providing grist for late-night radio.

Whereas the Fifth Column supporters, if any, place their primary loyalty with the extraterrestrials, the Sixth Columns place their loyalty squarely with Earth, differing from the MiBs only in their opposition to continued concealment, arguing instead for disclosure, and openly joining the interplanetary society.

Does that place me in the Fifth Column or the Sixth? After all, Petchy and Teena are my blood relations, even if I had no clue until that day on Nekomata. Of course, beyond our shared adventure, I have no cultural connection or familial loyalty. But nonetheless, I cannot believe they are enemies of Earth.

Continuing the Lensmen meme, all of these parties, Jill and the 6th Column, Matt, the 5th Column, and Alex and his MiBs, all would seem to be on the side of what Doc categorized as civilization. Whatever deceptions they are propagating, they all seem to have humanity's best interests at heart yet preserve vociferous disagreements about how best to serve that end.

The other collection of players seems to be somewhat the opposite. Those players consistently used names from the Doc Smith stories, whereas any such usage by Petchy or the 5th Column is unproven. In those tales, Arisia and Eddore were the adversaries, facing each other on the cosmic scale, with various segments of humanity as pawns in their conflict. The mysterious entity Arisia had communicated with Julie and Darla, the very use of that name and the betrayal which killed my friends, argues Arisia was loyal to Gharlane, not Petchy.

We have two known players in the conspiracy. Gharlane and Helmuth, the latter now dead. Helmuth also used the name Bergenholm, which was a character on the side of Arisia and Civilization in Doc's stories.

I had a sudden insight. I've been looking at this all wrong! The application of 'Eddore' to our adversary had been our invention, more specifically MY invention. All the signs suggest Arisia connects to Boskone, Helmuth, and Gharlane! That makes a twisted logic, just the kind of twist a scheming villain might employ.

My working hypothesis slowly coalesces. The mastermind behind this conspiracy leverages Doc's tales and employs names and memes from those stories as code names and subterfuge. Thus far, they have not used 'Eddore' as a villain's home. That was my invention, my failed hypothesis. I had invented that wholly from my imagination and my love of Doc Smith's Space Operas.

I belatedly recognize there is no reason to suppose both sides in this conspiracy would use the Lensmen meme. Instead, Doc's terminology seems to be a hallmark of the villains!

I drew a line through the label Arisia, leaving only the question mark. Whatever Petch might call his organization, I highly doubt it is Arisia!

Arisia, Helmuth, and Gharlane as actors, all having sent messages to operators hired anonymously via the "Bleep" app. Something called Boskone and a place called Ploor, which may equally be a town in Mexico as another planet for all we know, are behind what Alex believes is a massive criminal enterprise involving drugs and more. These people want to kill my ladies! Why?

Alex suggested their existence on Earth exposes interplanetary travel's reality, and Gharlane sought to eliminate them to conceal his off-world operation. Perhaps. If so, will they stop trying to kill us once we fully reveal the conspiracy?

They don't seem the type to give up easily. Me neither. I won't relax until my ladies are safely back on Planet Oz, preferably with Gharlane dead.

I stared at my doodles and strained to pull any additional insights from the events of recent days. The women watched me and listened as I bounced ideas off of them, sharing my thinking process. Stapleya seemed convinced Matt's wanting to join us hinted at possibilities we should explore. I believe she hopes he might be a part of Petchy's 5th Column, after all, a chance I highly doubt. But, on the other hand, perhaps she merely wants another male in our group for reasons unrelated to the conspiracy.

Wisceya wants Jill to join us again, but it will be days, if not weeks, before she will be well enough for that. Real-world bullet holes do not heal as fast as the movies suggest, nor do they always recover fully. Depending on the nature of her wounds, Jill may face years of therapy and recovery before she is wholly well, if ever.

The girls and I had spent the entire evening daydreaming, speculating about the threat we faced. It's difficult to quantify any gain from these cogitations beyond concluding Arisia must be our foe, not an ally. Perhaps that's enough.

After hours of thinking and doodling, we decided there might be a better way to spend our evening and thus retired to explore the possibility.

Sunrise in the high desert is no less spectacular than in the lower elevations, although it's less warm than our Roswell mornings. So, despite their natural insulation, my ladies found our morning ritual a trifle brisk. Conditioned to the much sultrier clime of Nekomata, they often find our Earthly environment bracing, though the local climate is hardly frigid.

Nonetheless, we greeted the dawn with steaming mugs of motel coffee, welcome, although falling considerably below my preferred Arabian Mocha-Java blend. Having smelled and tasted the local tap water, I had a good idea why. Water quality is everything to good coffee, and the municipal water is less than ideal. Finally, successfully having hoisted the sun aloft, we strolled over to the El Rancho to sample a Mexican breakfast.

Startlingly adequate, I concluded, considerably improved over our previous experience at the Jewel. The Steak and Eggs with Red Chili proved an excellent start to the day, and their coffee proved infinitely superior to our first sunrise mug from the Wigwam. I suspect the restaurant takes the trouble to use a good charcoal filter on their water supply. The girls sampled the spicy food with trepidation and, after a few cautious tastes, decided they liked it, undeterred by the searing, eye-watering spiciness.

After breakfast, we again embarked on a walking tour of the community, soon finding ourselves drawn into the Rainbow Rock Shop. We spent considerable time browsing the collections and potential souvenirs.

My friends wanted to buy a couple of souvenir pieces of petrified wood and other items, though they realized that they would not be able to carry them home when they returned through the portal. So I restrained myself, buying only a few picture postcards with professional photos.

I again considered digging out the phone and photographing my dear friends as they browsed. Nonetheless, I restrained myself due to the overruling security concerns. Even though I could disable WIFI and have removed the SIM card long ago, the risks of a careless mistake didn't suit my paranoid concerns. I had resolved it must stay firmly powered off, except when necessarily used in a carefully guarded manner to further our mission. I also worry the photos of the ladies might fall into the wrong hands, with unforeseen consequences. Perhaps I'm overly fearful, yet a careless mistake, such as allowing WIFI to connect accidentally to a local hotspot or even transmitting a beacon at the wrong moment, might be all Gharlane needs to locate us. My seeming paranoia had served us well, and I'm not ready to change course. The fewer our digital footprints, the less I worry.

We stopped at Joe and Aggie's Cafe to sample their Chili upon leaving the Rock Shop. I rated it five stars, or perhaps the rating should be five-alarm, and the girls agreed. Their sampling of Mexican spiciness at breakfast had prepared them for the extra flavorful Cafe Chili. Once again, I pondered the ways their Earth experiences might contaminate their pristine Stone-Age culture upon returning home.

Returning to our Teepee, I checked email and unsurprisingly found a message from Matt with what he claimed was his Public Key and an encrypted note attached. I opened it to discover he merely once again repeated his appeal to join us and stated he wanted to talk face-to-face.

Mystified, I speculated whether this was indeed Matt or a pretender seeking to deceive us and if indeed this is he, what's so important to talk about that requires we meet face-to-face?

After brief consideration, I prepared a terse response, asking whether Alex had cleared his emails. I can't decide how to address his rather odd request, uncertain whether I can trust Matt, assuming the emailer is positively Matt. I'm not feeling even slightly trustful at the moment.

Although still early for our regular afternoon call with Alex, I opted to initiate the session early and update him on yesterday evening's thoughts and conclusions. Alex answered on the third ring, and I got right to the issues at hand.

"Alex, I've been reviewing everything we know and no longer believe the messages from 'Arisia' were, in fact, from sympathetic '5th Column' entities. I believe instead, they originate with the same Doc Smith-inspired adversary that has been chasing us."

He responded slowly, as if thinking, "Yes, I suspect you're correct. However, no one left alive is known to be in touch with Arisia. Julie and her sister were the only contacts, insofar as we know. We will be on the alert for any reuse of the name."

"Anything new regarding Ploor or Gharlane?"

"No new messages or references to Gharlane have appeared since Dr. Holm's death. Forensics analysis of the various phones we've recovered leads us to Central Texas as a locus of origination for the messages. I'm skeptical. However, since I have been watching how easily you seem to evade our attempts at tracing your connections, I must consider Gharlane similarly capable."

I let the questions that statement raised bounce around the back of my noggin for now, although it didn't enhance my trust in Alex. Was he still trying to trace us? "So, you have nothing new on the Conspiracy?"

"I wouldn't say that! True, we have not yet unmasked the masterminds, but we have made immense progress in the lower echelons of their organization. I told you I had some of the brightest minds I could recruit working on this. They're not thrilled I have clamped down an iron dome of security, not permitting anyone to leave or communicate. They're rather frustrated with me, although they have produced results. Dr. Shepherd, our team leader, assures me we will have this wrapped up soon. We're mounting an enormous cooperative raid, all the military branches cooperating with the Mexican government. I have been working with the outside forces, organizing a massive international effort."

"Aren't you afraid somebody will spill the beans? You have your masterminds locked up, not allowing them to leave, yet you're mounting a massive mobilization for raids? That seems inconsistent!"

"Not at all. Almost no one outside my office knows it is real live-action. If you've seen the news the last couple of days, you may have seen all the publicity regarding a massive training exercise code-named 'Jade Helm.' Outside of the Generals in charge, only two people on the planet besides us two are aware this is no exercise! We're mounting the mightiest military operation since WWII in the guise of an innocuous unarmed training exercise! Except no one knows they won't be unarmed and won't be training. Even the troops in the field won't find out until the last minute. The actual strength of the forces involved will be several times larger than the news stories suggest. The news stories exist mainly to mollify the public regarding the military gear they notice moving through towns."

I mulled Alex's words. I had seen the news stories. The Twitterverse is shrieking madly over the states' impending 'Government Takeover' by the Military; Martial Law is about to descend. All a-twitter as it were! As I wrapped my noggin around all I had just heard, I realized this might be brilliant!

"I must hand it to you, Alex. At first blush, it seems nothing short of brilliant! Rather uncharacteristic of the government, isn't it?"

He laughed at that. "Thank you, I think. But honestly, I must credit much of the brilliance to my team of strategists. Shep, er, Dr. Shepherd, has been calling the shots and laying out the strategy, and I can fairly tell you he is one brilliant man."

"Interesting, I believe I need to meet this man. I respect brains; maybe we'll start a bromance."

That received a chuckle. "Fitz, I implore you, please come in and let us protect you here until we can pull this off. It will require almost five additional weeks of operations before we launch the offensive, and we don't know where Gharlane is or what he's up to. I want those beautiful furry ladies kept safe. Your ugly mug, too, for that matter."

"Maybe. You almost convince me. Let's wait a few days and watch how events unfold. Then, I'll think about it."

"Will you let me at least send an armed agent to watch and support you?"

"Who would you send, and don't you need every trusted agent there at your side?"

"I'll send Matt again if you'll allow it."

"The last we spoke, he wanted to come back," I said noncommittally. "I don't entirely agree, but I don't have a significant objection either. But, on the other hand, I'm not sure what he brings us in terms of protection, and his presence makes one additional person I must watch."

"He'll be armed. Surely, you'll agree to have an armed guard is beneficial."

I've been waiting for that opening for weeks. "Don't call me Shirley," I quipped, laughing. Alex gave a little cackle too.

I almost derailed the discussion at that point. I was aching to confront Alex about his Asheran secrets but now was not the time. I am not yet ready to tip my hand. Let him continue to think I am ignorant and in the dark. So yuk it up, Alex, I will soon have a surprise for you.

"Seriously," I continued, "I believe Matt will vouch that I'm rather capable without a weapon. I am a weapon, thanks to my off-world experiences. Remember, our assailant at Mesquite pulled a gun, and I wasn't armed, yet I took him, quite handily too. I don't believe that adding a firearm outweighs the additional risks and complications of adding another man to our group."

"He doesn't need to join your group. Instead, he can maintain a distance and monitor from a distant vantage point."

"I'll consider it. Tell Matt to set up a RedPhone and send me the number, and don't forget he must remove the SIM Card to prevent tracking. Then, I'll talk to him, and we'll decide."

I unceremoniously hung up the phone, not letting him debate further. I sat for a long time, mentally reciting a calming mantra. Inhale, hold, then exhale, telling myself, "I feel myself relaxing" on each intake. I had the shakes. I find confronting Alex immensely stressful.

The call had lasted longer than I intended, and I worried that it might have attracted attention. I scrutinized my remote router for hints of trouble. After several minutes I relaxed, satisfied our session went undetected. I wondered where Gharlane was, almost disappointed in an odd fashion that he wasn't on the job. Had my adversary given up and gone home to Ploor?

As I completed my call and shut down our complicated networking ensemble, my ladies demanded my attention for another matter. I think they understand how stressed these calls are. Sometime later, we realized the dinner hour had arrived; we girded our loins for polite society and headed down the street for Mr. Maestas's most excellent Mexican restaurant, a decent walk from our Teepee.

Show Down in Show Low

I received an email from Matt with his RedPhone number and his assertion that Alex knew of and blessed his contact with us. Being a naturally trusting soul, I confirmed this with Alex via a separate email. I was relieved. I had worried lest Matt might emerge as another mole. However, he reiterated he wanted to talk with me regarding something he could only discuss face-to-face.

I'm still feeling a degree of reluctance at allowing Matt to rejoin our party, although I'm powerless to say why. On the other hand, the girls were wholly in favor of the idea. Stapleya and I discussed the topic before I relented and reluctantly agreed to permit his joining us. Her motives were transparent; the Nekomata people are very open and free-spirited. What can I say?

I had no intention of telling him our location! Instead, I sent him a message instructing him to fly into the Show Low Regional Airport and check into the Showy River Hotel. That places him approximately an hour's drive from our Teepee and allows us ample time to look things over before making contact. I said I would meet him in the hotel lobby tomorrow afternoon. I lied.

In the regular afternoon status update with Alex, I broached the subject, confirmed Matt's meeting us in Show Low, and confirmed his flight time. There are few flights into and out of the regional airport, minimizing the opportunities for surprises.

We enjoyed the rest of the day playing tourist around Holbrook, retired early, packed, and departed our steel Teepee pre-dawn the following morning, heading south on Highway 77. We were much too early, by design. I intended to be in Show Low long before Matt arrived and scope it out. I do not want surprises.

We departed Holbrook without breakfast, so we stopped briefly in Taylor, AZ, for an infusion from Sonic's menu. I expressed surprise that the Sonic Drive-Thru opened so early, as I had not thought of them as a breakfast place. But they were open, and their brand of American Fast Food proved perfectly satisfactory as breakfast. That we were famished didn't detract from our pleasure one bit.

It was still early morning when we reached Show Low, hours before Matt's flight could arrive. We spent those hours looking over the town and the local airport, wary of any hint of surveillance or suspicious activity. I was nervous. My 'spidey-sense' had not sounded an alarm, but I was on edge. If Gharlane or an agent of his had figured out our rendezvous and lay in wait, they're thoroughly hidden.

I had told Matt to meet us in the lobby of the Showy River Hotel, although that instruction had been for Gharlane's benefit, a blatant misdirect. I had no such intent. I expected Matt to exit the airport, looking for a taxi, and I intended to intercept him and immediately leave town. Hanging around a hotel that someone might have overheard us mention was not in my plans.

I sent Wisceya to the terminal to watch for him while Stapleya and I stayed back and watched her and the crowd. I had gathered a few rocks to have handy if I felt a sudden urge to throw something. I believe I have mentioned I can throw things. We were as prepared and cautious as I could be. I harbored deep-seated fears of Gharlane's agents lurking behind every tree or corner. I worried that he or his agent might jump out, guns blazing at any instant.

At first, my fears seemingly proved groundless. Matt exited the terminal on cue, heading toward a waiting taxi; Wisceya approached him, greeted him with a hug, and diverted him toward the meeting spot I had selected just around a convenient corner away from our car. All seemed innocuous as they walked toward us.

They were halfway to the meet when suddenly my paranoia turned justified, my fears confirmed. Simultaneously, my 'spidey-sense' went into full-alarm mode and the taxi Matt had initially targeted accelerated and charged them. For an instant, my blood ran cold; my worst fears materialized as I spotted a gun in the hand of the driver, turning in their direction. I reacted with an adrenalin-fueled reflex! I unleashed a hard-thrown missile at the speeding car, hitting the driver's shoulder through the open driver-side window just as he aimed his handgun at my friends. That's gonna leave a bruise!

He dropped the gun and veered away as Matt similarly reacted, dodging back onto the sidewalk and drawing his weapon. Another of my missiles smashed the windshield, and a third rock again impacted the driver, this last, I believe, making direct contact with his temple. I seriously doubted he would cause further trouble. It was likely fatal if the blow had hit as hard as it appeared. Matt stood dumbfounded, weapon in hand.

Diving into our waiting vehicle, I gunned the car and pulled alongside the couple, shouting, "Jump in." They did, and we fairly tore out of there. We're NOT going to the Snowy River Hotel!

We raced out of town on Highway 260. I asked Matt to explain why they attacked, who had followed him, tracked him, and how. There must be another mole in the organization!

Uncertain what to do, I demanded he remove every article from his person, pen, wallet, watch, and hand everything to the ladies in the back seat. They could be examining everything for any hint of electronics.

A few miles out of town, I stopped the car and inspected everything myself, then demanded he resume stripping until we had examined everything, every aspect of his being, for any hint of how they might have tracked him. Fruitless, as it turned out. I allowed him to redress as, with a wry bit of internal humor, I recalled the night I had forced Jill and Estelle to undress in the face of my security paranoia. Matt, too was a good sport, although the fact we're exposed, out of doors in daylight was an inhibitor.

I did not find anything that might function as a tracker, not even his cell phone, which I confirmed he had turned off and removed the battery, so I started querying him. It seemed someone had known his destination but few specifics. How had he purchased his airline tickets? Had anyone made a motel reservation for him? Who outside the organization had known he was traveling? Who inside?

The only weak point was that he made his reservations under his own name. No travel agent or other intermediary was involved, but it seemed evident that Gharlane's agents were watching for unusual travel and had guessed he was coming to meet us. The assailant had not known what to look for, seemingly tasked with spotting Matt and killing him and whoever he met.

I would love to examine the driver's phone. I'm prepared to bet he had Bleep installed on it with messages that might help us unravel this thing. I told Matt we would ask Alex to investigate the case when we were again able to communicate.

Matt pulled out his phone and suggested using RedPhone to call. I shook my head. "Won't work," I explained. "Without a SIM Card, you need a WIFI hotspot, and whether using the SIM Card to access the Cellular Network or just using a local WIFI hotspot, they could trace a call to us much too easily. We need to stop somewhere and spend the time to set up my magic."

We kept on driving until we reached Overgaard, AZ, near the intersection with Highway 277. I decided we could call from here, with precautions, as even if they tracked us here, they would not know which direction we departed. I set up the laptop in the car and let Matt drive. We cruised around the town, looking for an open hotspot we could use. We found one near the Subway, which was perfect. We could address our communications needs and have lunch at the same time. Once connected to the WIFI, I re-established my magic network, and with my faux hotspot online, I enabled the RedPhone and called Alex.

Alex answered by asking, "Did Matt arrive without problems?"

I spoke rapidly, "He arrived but so did a gunman. They attacked us at the airport. I took him out, and we bolted before anyone could follow. He was driving a taxi, and I think I might have killed him. I'm confident I hit him squarely with a rock, and he lost interest. Such a blow could have been fatal. I suggest you intervene with the local cops, persuade them not to hunt us, and retrieve his cell phone for forensic analysis. We are busy making tracks away from there. Will call again when we settle somewhere."

With that, I dropped the connection and disengaged my remote router. Sandwiches in hand, we rolled west again, eating while moving. I had no reason to expect someone to trace my call any more than those before, but I knew better than to press my luck by sticking around. Besides, local cops might be looking for us for the contretemps back at the airport. That someone might have described our car seems likely.

We continued Highway 260 into Camp Verde, past the intersection with Interstate 17. I resisted the temptation to get on 17. In keeping with my continuing paranoia of highways and their growing network of traffic cameras, I opted instead to follow 260 to its intersection with 89A before turning North. Less than four hours after the Airport battle, we rolled into Sedona, home of mystical crystals and purported 'Energy Portals' and other 'New Age' balderdash. Although nothing suggested Sedona's claimed 'Portals' were related to the actual interplanetary portals, I reveled in the irony.

We settled into a quaint little place called the 'Cuddly Cactus,' and I set up our communications system again after a brief delay. I attached Matt's RedPhone to our clandestine WIFI, carefully explaining that he must never allow his phone to connect to a local WIFI lest it reveals our location. Those tracing us would be looking at the distant terminus of my faux connection, this time appearing in Cincinnati, Ohio. That should keep them guessing!

Alex answered on the first ring and didn't waste a moment on pleasantries. "Damnedest thing in Show Low! There's a wrecked taxi, the driver's missing, and no one saw anything, nor was there security video. The local police believe you attacked the taxi and kidnapped the driver."

I must say, I didn't expect that. I expected a search for a murderer, not a mysterious kidnapper with no clues left behind.

"Do they have a description of our car or us or anything?"

"Nothing, zilch, nada, a total blank. Almost as if a UFO swooped in and abducted him in the middle of the night!" I laughed inwardly at Alex's unintentional humor. Or is it? I'm never sure. MiBs aren't known for their jokes, although Alex had cracked a few subtle ones, especially the stale old 'Don't call me Shirley' knee slapper.

"So, to the best of your knowledge, they're not looking for us? Not the police in any case, not officially."

"Based on the surprise nature of the attack, someone's certainly after you. Not the police, though, not through official channels. Listen, Fitz, you've been fortunate twice. Please, I beg you, come in here and let me provide protection!"

He gave me the opening I needed to stand up to his dominating manner once again. I responded, "I want to differ with you slightly on the details. First, luck wasn't the operative factor; my training and skill, my innate abilities saved the day, not mere happenstance, not lady fortune. I fought back and succeeded against an armed attacker twice because of my skills and preparation. Second and more importantly, this attacker aimed squarely for Matt, not us, and he was surprised when I charged him. He was clueless about my presence. Third, I believe whoever hired him tracked Matt from California, although the why and how I will leave to you to investigate. Perhaps because he bought his plane ticket under his own name, that enabled them to spot and track him. Don't you think that's an egregious oversight? I'm also betting we would find "Bleep" on the attacker's phone."

I was winding up for a blow, and I could sense Alex's hesitation. I went on, "Of course, Matt and I share a similar height and build. Perhaps they mistook Matt for me, and the attacker's surprise came when he saw what he thought to be two of me. That opens the question of how they traced us and why they would make such a boneheaded mistake? Also, he didn't seem particularly interested in the girls. He would have waited until they were together instead of attacking Matt and Wisceya.

"Occam's razor dictates the simplest explanation: they were after Matt, not me, not the girls. Why? I have no clue. It also suggests that perhaps Matt was the attack's target in Mesquite and not the three of us. Twice Matt has gone into the field; twice he has been at the locus of a deadly attack. We're missing something."

Stapleya had been listening and silently mouthed the expression 'Occam's Razor' with questioning eyes. A novel phrase to her, no doubt. Perhaps she thought it involved shaving, which she seemed to find increasingly annoying.

Matt chimed in as we were on speaker, "Alex, Fitz is right. I rejected the idea at first, although he has since convinced me. That cab charged me, and when he pointed his gun, he pointed it at me! I have no idea why. If not for Fitz, he may have nailed me. He caught me by surprise. I stood there stunned, surprised, off guard, and didn't have my weapon out until too late."

Alex responded, "Understood. I will investigate, though at present no official law enforcement's searching for you, be careful nonetheless."

As we ended the call, Alex surprised me by injecting, "Shep sends his regards."

I have not met Shep, although I almost feel I know him from Alex's description. Why should he be sending his respects to a person he has never met? I shrugged, figuratively, chalked it up to Shep, as though likewise he feels as though he practically knows a stranger due to Alex's effusive commentary. I wondered what Alex had been saying about me.

I dismantled the connection, doubly wary of any possible detection, carefully checking the remote router for anything abnormal. Once offline and shut down, I turned my attention to my companions.

For the first time today, we're able to relax a trifle. I turned to Stapleya and addressed her question about Occam's razor. I reminded her of our discussion of science principles and the scientific method. I described the principle of Occam's Razor as an essential piece of the scientific process, the principle of fewest assumptions making for the likelier hypothesis. I promised a detailed explanation later and turned to Matt.

I asked him what he felt we needed to discuss so mysteriously face-to-face. I suppose I was hoping for some revelation that might yield a clue to the strange events of the last few days.

Matt sat at the room's desk and pulled out a large envelope with several sheets of paper. Thumbing the pages, he pulled out one and laid it on the desk. It was a part of a spreadsheet with a line of numbers. The words on the page technobabble, such as Haplogroup and STR-Markers. I studied it a moment and decided I was looking at a DNA analysis, specifically a 37-marker y-DNA analysis showing the first 37 common markers. I know little about DNA, and the numbers were meaningless. After a brief study, I glanced up from the page.

He said nothing, merely responded by pulling out another page and placing it on the desk beside the first. It appeared identical, except for the Kit number at the top of the page. I examined the STR Markers individually and confirmed a complete match. These two individuals are closely related. I knew just enough about DNA to know 37 markers is a minor DNA sample, hardly conclusive. Closely related, true, yet a longer string of data points would doubtless differentiate the two individuals. I also understand that y-DNA represents the male y-Chromosome, exclusive to males. We receive our y-Chromosomes exclusively from our fathers, and females don't possess y-Chromosomes; instead, inheriting two versions of the x-

Chromosome. Indeed, the DNA samples are unquestionably from males, and I am confident that the two men represented must have the same father or possibly grandfather.

Again, I questioned Matt with my eyes. He merely stated, "This one is mine," pointing at the first page, "and this one's yours! We're brothers."

I stared at him. I knew I had lots of genetic brothers out in the Universe. Petchy had stated that. In the program to develop a warrior to battle the singularity, he had spread his seed prolifically. So, meeting another of his progeny is inevitable, I suppose. But, on the other hand, I'm not entirely sure a bit of genetic data alone makes one a brother. Shouldn't the bond between brothers be deeper than merely some numbers on a page?

I extended my hand. "Welcome to the family, brother. Now what?"

Me and My Brother

It's a psychological mind-bender to recognize, understand, and acknowledge that I have anonymous siblings elsewhere in the universe. It's a total mindfuck to have one pop up and kick me in the balls with DNA evidence of our genetic connection!

Matt had been an orphan, raised by foster parents. Adopted by an older couple who are now deceased, he had no clue who his biological parents were or that he had siblings. However, Matt had noticed our physical similarities and used his MiB resources to compare his DNA with mine. But, of course, he did not ask my permission and procure my DNA legally. Even for a MiB, that's a grave violation of modern personal information laws. For example, in today's world of cybercrime and identity theft, a healthcare worker risks severe jail time for such a misuse of a patient's personal information under HIPPA laws. The Meta wars have firmly established formal ownership rules around one's personal, private identity data.

Nonetheless, that's how he discovered our link; abusing his power in the MiB. As a result, he risked his career and faced jail time.

Once aware of my tale, he desperately sought to uncover anything he could of his unknown mother and his otherworldly father. No doubt Petchy was his sire, as he admitted he had spread his chromosomes far and wide. Admitted! Hell, he boasted of it! As a prolific inseminator, Fitz has nothing on Petchy! At least I try to be discreet and confine such to those in need. To the best of my knowledge, I never have sired and abandoned progeny other than those on Nekomata, and there, 'abandoned' is hardly the right word. Gifted is a more appropriate term, as those babies were desperately wanted and would be cared for as though they were royalty. Which, I suppose, in a sense, they are.

I stressed that everything I knew I had put in the book and suggested that if we find Petchy, we should both ask him a multitude of very pointed questions, although, to be honest, I'm not sure I want to learn more.

I'm Fitz, a sovereign identity, a unique entity. My genome is not Fitz; it is merely one component, one building block of the complicated human being that is Fitz. Knowing more regarding the biological origins of my genome doesn't assist my coping with present-day life. I prefer not to dwell on the implications; thinking of myself as some form of alien seed is not comforting.

Yesterday's attack, the multitude of far more urgent unanswered questions it raises, my continued concerns about allowing Matt into our circle, and the danger that seems to be dogging him are issues that have me stressed, worried, and fearful. I need someone to support me, and the unfamiliar dynamic of coping with a new sibling does not help.

Matt and I traded stories until I pleaded information overload, suggesting we would talk again later. He seemed slightly miffed that I wasn't more eager to delve into the implications of our origins or more open to the level of detail he wanted to share. I'm just not comfortable going there right now. Besides, I have more immediate concerns. Finally, he took the hint and abandoned the topic. Though I felt terrible as I had hurt his feelings, I was relieved. Our connection seems more critical to Matt than to me, and I'm uncertain why.

Right now, I'm far more curious about the purported Sedona energy vortexes and the fantastic claims of otherworldly manifestations. I'm uncertain how to address the topic since I know interdimensional portals are actual. I have traversed a few of them personally. However, nothing I have seen hitherto presented the slightest hint that a portal such as I have experienced is, in any way, related to whatever it is that people are flocking to worship in this area.

Before my off-world travels, I would have laughed loudly and denounced the claims of 'Energy Vortexes' as the product of an overactive imagination coupled with inhalation of excessive quantities of Tetrahydrocannabinol, nor has that belief fundamentally changed since I learned about actual portals. However, I intend to leave no stone unturned in my search for an exit whereby we might transit to a safer world.

I picked the *Cuddly Cactus* for our home base because the Cathedral Rock Vortex is nearby. The Cathedral Rock Vortex is on every new-age vortex map and is reportedly one of, if not the most easily observed phenomena of its type in the area. Therefore, I intend to observe it, assuming it, in fact, exists.

I hoped we could spend a little time exploring. We had time this afternoon for a quick scouting trip. Thus, a twinkling later found us again in the car, headed down Highway 89A, headed for the junction with Highway 179. Following the directions published on the web, I turned left on the Upper Red Rock Loop Road and left on Chavez Ranch Road. Pulling into the surprisingly crowded Crescent Moon Park, I parked the car as near the creek as permitted, and then we walked toward the water, turning East along the creek toward Cathedral Rock.

The guidebooks stated that this is the best and most potent of Sedona's vortexes. Supposedly, a sensitive person can easily feel the energy upon approaching Cathedral Rock. I presume I'm not especially sensitive. Nor, apparently, is Matt. The guidebook states that Cathedral Rock is the only one of the four vortices in the area with so-called "feminine" energy. The energy of the vortex supposedly influences the feminine, although our ladies likewise sensed nothing. There were numerous other 'seekers' present, several of whom were oohing and aahing over their supposed perception of the energy, yet we felt nothing.

Let's rewind that. We utterly failed to sense anything that remotely resembled a portal as we grasped the idea or any energy vortex as we imagined such manifestations. We did, however, enjoy an intense mystical experience.

We experienced the exquisite pleasure of hiking in the beautiful terrain for a couple of hours as we climbed a 750-foot change in elevation in 1.5 miles. A nice hike for the physically able. We didn't find it challenging but understood how others might. We enjoyed exquisitely pleasant views of the Cathedral Rock Formation in the sinking afternoon sun. Then, just as we positioned ourselves for a proper view of the setting sun, it happened. The most spectacular sunset, the most spectacularly shifting colors imaginable. Simply breathtaking!

Portals may or may not occur here. I remain skeptical, tentatively attributing the claimed phenomena to clearly understood human psychological characteristics rather than ill-defined cosmic forces. Nevertheless, there is no doubt that cosmic forces are extant here, just perhaps not the ones the new-age acolytes would have us believe.

However, I'm not prepared to abandon the exploration after one attempt, although today's examinations must end with the day itself.

Picking our path cautiously back to the car in the failing light, the ladies chattered away about the spectacular celestial display. At the same time, Matt and I remained quiet, the search for a vortex forgotten in the aftermath of the overwhelming sunset.

Reclaiming our wheels, we followed the roads in the gathering gloom, headed back toward the Cuddly Cactus, picking up carry-out dinner at the nearby Crimson Chopstick for an informal meal under spectacular stars on the Cuddly Cactus patio, a perfect end to a long and stressful day.

We encountered minor stress over the sleeping arrangements. Matt, reluctant to share our communal sleeping arrangements, wanted privacy. That's not surprising. I had anticipated his unease and rented the detached condo instead of a more modest and less expensive single room. The condo had two separate bedrooms! So he could have his private space, although the girls were comfortable with sharing.

More than comfortable with sharing, Stapleya had specific designs on the new rooster, and I am certain Matt felt intimidated. Stapleya had become an unrelenting cougar in her sexual appetites during her time on Earth. Despite her mature years and great-grandmother-hood status, her sexual desire and competitiveness were evident.

Of course, the idea of a cougar is unknown in her culture; more than the term, the very concept, the distinction lost in the dearth of males, and the lack of fertility of adults much beyond puberty, Stapleya's remarkable though finally dissipated fecundity having been a rare exception.

Though I've asked, I have no idea how old Stapleya is nor how many children she has borne, but both numbers are high. Asheran high. Petchy and Teena are both positively ancient yet still young and vigorous. I suspect an Asheran was in some long-ago castle woodpile.

Home in her castle, an older, infertile woman would never usurp a fertile male's assignation with a fertile female due to the dire need for babies.

When I visited Castle Stapleya, her every effort went toward finding another potentially fertile womb for my bounty rather than draw my ministrations to herself. Conception always takes precedence over desire. She would flirt and tease, touch, and play but then direct my energies to someone better able to make productive use of the act.

In her time on Earth, Stapleya had responded to the radically different environment by freely competing with her daughter for my charms, and now it seems Matt had fallen into her sights. So, naturally, she is reveling in sexual opportunities. However, I shudder to think what might happen if she became unleashed on the unsuspecting male populace of Earth.

I fully understand how off-putting the free-swinging, hedonistic sleeping arrangements of the Nekomata can be to a person who is unaccustomed to such ways. So our first night together, Matt retreated to his space and eschewed Stapleya's company. She was hurt. "His loss," I told her, "I'm sure he'll come around. Don't take it personally. Earth's culture is very different; I'm sure he will quickly warm to the idea."

The following morning, we arose early and took in the dawn, again worshipping the rising sun. I'm falling in love with the desert. I never tire of the beautiful desert scenery, the spectacular sunrises, and sunsets. I'm rapidly convincing myself that I must settle in the desert once done with hopping from planet to planet, unraveling interstellar conspiracies, and slaying dinosaurs.

After a lavish breakfast, Matt wanted to call Alex. Alex and I had kept our regular calls to late afternoon, and it seemed a trifle early to call. However, after a brief discussion, I relented and set up my technological wizardry again. Matt watched my machinations with interest. I didn't offer to explain anything, and he asked no questions. I believed he lacked the technical expertise. Without the proper background, an observer would be unable to make sense of the maze of router menus and dialogs dancing to the tune my flying fingers played.

Having set up and dismantled this system several times, I had scripted the process such that every keystroke of my flying fingers became multiplied many times over. The complicated construction happens rapidly under the direction of my scripting. Without an opportunity to examine my scripts, my actions must seem almost mystical to anyone else.

I tend to guard my technical tricks closely, as they're my stock-in-trade. My tools and expertise are why people hire me. They say a magician never reveals his secrets, and I certainly understand the reasoning. Sadly, once a trick is exposed, it ceases to awe, and I sell awe as openly as any stage magician.

No matter the field, any businessman knows it's insufficient to be merely competent; you must dazzle the client. Image and presentation matter as much as the product, perhaps more. Excellent food in an unimpressive restaurant with a slovenly presentation will disappoint the customer. No matter how delicious the steak, the sizzle is what sells it, and I know how to provide that sizzle! My exquisite sizzle is what brings my customers back for more.

After a few minutes of digital legerdemain, I had our network cloaked and ready. Matt pulled out his phone and dialed, placing it on speaker so that we all could hear the conversation.

Alex was slow to answer, not expecting a call at this hour. So, it rang, one, two, three, rang again and again, until finally, on the sixth ring or maybe the seventh, Alex picked up.

"Hello, Boss," Matt said. "We're on the speaker; Fitz and the women are here too."

"Terrific," said Alex. "I have a ton of updates for you all."

Alex said he wanted to address several critical aspects of the fight he was preparing. But first, he updated us on Jill's condition; she's now settled into the facility, growing stronger by the hour and making significant contributions despite being on the disabled list.

After the update on Jill, I decided I must insert myself. It was time to push back and be the dominant one. "Alex," I said. "I want to talk with you before we get into the conspiracy status. You have lied to me, not once but several times, and I think it's time to lay our cards down face up."

Silence from the other end. After a dozen heartbeats, a soft, almost apologetic "Go ahead, Fitz" came forth.

"First, I will say that I'm not angry. Or maybe I am, but I understand, I think, enough to forgive. But this ends now! It's time to open the kimono and freely share. Are you willing to do that?"

"Fitz. I have to protect national security interests..."

"Balderdash," I thundered, slapping the table for emphasis. Then, more calmly, I said, "That's a cop-out, and you know it. We're not talking about national security. I have reason to believe that from the moment we first met in that hospital room, you knew about Nekomata and the battle on Ashera. Am I wrong?" I decided to drop the name Ashera intentionally. I wanted to hear his reaction.

There was a long silence from the other end. Then I heard an extended inhalation and a long sigh. Then finally, Alex responded. "Fitz, we need to have this conversation in absolute privacy." He didn't elaborate because I presumed, he did not wish to talk in front of Matt and the Nekomata. Of course, the women already know, but I assume Matt does not.

I gave him a long pause in response. I wanted him to think I was upset, and I wanted him to fear upsetting me, at least a little. But, of course, I was not, not really, but I am trying to play him as he has played me. But I realized that this is not my game, and I am not good at it. So then, finally, I said, "Okay, we will put a pin in it for now. But believe that we will have this conversation, and you'd better prepare to come clean."

"Fitz, I promise. Now back to the immediate situation. As I explained before, we clamped down an iron dome of security; no one can leave once they enter, no one may communicate outside except through myself or now Jill. But unfortunately, we can't continue this way. We must begin coordinating with other groups and do so with impenetrable security.

"Frankly, buddy, we desperately need your specialized expertise here. We're setting up remote command centers around the country, satellite offices staffed with our own trusted people to coordinate with other organizations. Not to detract from the meticulous work of extremely dedicated and outrageously competent people, but I need you in charge of the networking and communications. You're the most security-savvy network expert I know. The way you shuttle and obfuscate connections and block tracing and penetration is unlike anything I've ever seen. We need you doing that here; we cannot afford to allow a leak! This operation is the most extensive combined civilian and military maneuver ever, and I'm not exaggerating! We have queued up many severely evil people for some serious attention. We even have a lead on Gharlane himself, maybe."

He explained that the massive faux 'training exercise' commandeered multitudes of soldiers in the field and tens of thousands of vehicles, from MPRC to Aircraft carriers, from Helicopters to V-22 Osprey to F-22 Raptor, with armament to match. They have identified thousands of targets to attack, from Canada to Guatemala.

"Every civilian law enforcement organization and military unit in every allied country participates in this unprecedented international 'training exercise,' oblivious that the operation will morph into a live-fire action on the turn of a dime. Thousands of independent yet coordinated efforts, widely dispersed over some ten million square miles. A genuinely stupendous operation to take down a massive organization that had been out to kill us!

"Shep and his people have followed every thread, every intelligence lead, through layer after layer of obfuscation. But frankly, I can't understand how we could have done it without him. The man is a machine; he never stops, never slows down, practically never sleeps. I'm impressed that we still produce men of his caliber. I have been adding people to his team, and he has shown himself an astonishing leader. Not only have my own trusted experts come under him, but he has also pulled in people from academia. I haven't been able to vet all of them myself, but he has assured me we can trust them, and I trust him. But damn it, man, we need you too. We need every supernaturally competent person we can find!"

He called me supernaturally competent! Wow! I know he's sucking up, and yet I like it.

"We roll in a few weeks, and six months' worth of work is needed to launch. So, I desperately need you, Fitz."

Dumbfounded, I cannot respond to that. I need to think. I had been terrified of Alex. A few days ago, he was my sworn frenemy, wanted to capture me, now he wants my help. It's all too surreal!

Alex and Matt carried on the conversation for another five minutes, then terminated the call. Once done, I disconnected our secure network and shut everything down.

The girls were staring at me with blank expressions as if wondering what I was thinking. Then Matt turned to me and quietly said, "Well?"

I leaned back on the couch, put my hands over my ears, and closed my eyes, rocking slightly. Forcibly confronting Alex as I had was emotionally painful and draining. I needed the world to go away for a few minutes. The stress, the constant fear, running, and hiding have taken their toll. I can't process it. The pressure is overwhelming; I must step back and refocus before losing myself.

I sat that way for a long time, trying to untangle the situation, unravel where my loyalties lay, to comprehend how I had become involved in this untenable, impossible war. All I want to do is find Petchy, find a portal and go to Planet Oz. I want to kill dinosaurs and spend snuggle time with my dear Lolita. I want to raise my son and gift the furry ladies of Planet Oz with many more like him.

Jade Helm, massive international crime rings, drug wars, military exercises, it's all too much! Not my circus, not my monkeys! Not my wheelhouse!

After several minutes, Matt placed his hand on my shoulder. He had been talking, but I wasn't hearing. Finally, I opened my eyes.

"Fitz, we need to go back. Alex needs you, and he needs me. We're both much safer there than here."

I shook my head, unable to speak.

I glanced at Stapleya. She scooted over and held me as I snuggled against her luscious pelt. Wisceya joined us, and I just buried myself in their soft, sensual fur as if to retreat from an impossible storm. Several additional minutes elapsed. Finally, I stood, saying I needed air, and walked out the door.

When our gadgets fail to work correctly, sometimes the cure is to unplug them for a few minutes and then restart them. So yeah, I suppose I needed a few minutes unplugged.

I went for a run. A real run that pushed even my genetically enhanced heart rate into the target zone. I'm sure passersby spotted my hurtling form and stared in frank disbelief. I didn't care. I ran to Crescent Moon Park and jogged down thru the brush until I had a beautiful view of Cathedral Rock. I sat on the ground and stared at the magnificent twin buttes in the mid-morning sun. I'm uncertain how long I sat there, probably an hour, perhaps longer. I once read a book where the author stated his protagonist "took out his soul and examined it" when facing a crisis. I now know what he meant.

Eventually, I shook myself, took a deep breath, and started back toward our condo. This time I ran unhurriedly, belatedly acknowledging the need to maintain a low profile.

I arrived back at the condo, and Matt and the girls waited where I left them. I walked over to Stapleya and Wisceya and hugged them both dearly. Then, after a moment, I turned to Matt. "When do we leave?"

The Prodigal Son Reboots

It seems like a simple question; approximately four hours by commercial air or nearly a dozen by road. But there's one trivial matter to address, someone, possibly several someones, still want us dead, and they aren't shy about it.

Traveling by air implies serious complications. We noted what happened when Matt bought a ticket under his real name. I have no fake ID, and the girls don't have an ID at all, something unlikely to endear my ladies to the TSA, even without the complication of our real identities attracting bullets. Call me paranoid, but I have no doubts our enemies would crash an entire airliner to kill us. Somehow, commercial air travel doesn't seem attractive.

Another twelve-hour road trip was daunting. It meant a long time in a cramped car, and the villains are also still out to kill us. Nonetheless, it seemed the more practical option.

Matt called Alex again to advise him of our decision. Matt explained our transportation problem and asked for advice, and Alex had a ready answer. Time is critical. He wanted us to board a government plane and fly directly to the Bay Area, bypassing the TSA and other hurdles in much less time than driving. He told us to hang tight for a couple of hours, and he would arrange a secure flight. Then, all we would need to do is get to the airport and board the plane, leaving the TSA and, hopefully, all our enemies none the wiser.

The ladies admitted terror at the prospect of flying. It was beyond anything they imagined, although they had observed aircraft passing overhead. I reminded them that merely two weeks ago, they were as terrified of riding in an automobile and assured them that they would adapt to flying just as easily. They reluctantly agreed they trusted me and were game to fly if I reassured them and held their hands.

Alex told us to call him again in two hours and prepare to head for the airport. We opted to revisit Crescent Moon Park. Although the prospect of finding a vortex seemed unlikely, we could bask in the glorious landscape one final time.

We drove to the park, walked along the creek to a sweet viewing spot, and sat quietly on the ground, soaking in the magnificent scenery. Sadly, our time was limited, and we still needed to check out of our condo and throw our meager possessions in the car.

After less than an hour of soaking in the desert goodness, our little band bid goodbye to the beautiful landscape, and once again, Matt called Alex.

It seems Alex isn't as powerful as he thought. He intended to employ one of the Military Gulfstream G550 / C37B aircraft the DoD maintains for government officials and high-profile personages. Even for Alex, access to such a resource on a two-hour notice is a big ask. His problem was that although he could procure an aircraft, he couldn't do it in the timeframe he wanted. He couldn't bump a Senator, no matter how critical his need. Tomorrow was the earliest he could arrange air transportation. Driving should be faster, assuming no complications. After some discussion, we opted to drive. Stapleya and Wisceya seemed relieved that we were not to fly after all.

We packed, checked out, and hit the road. I opted to head up Highway 89A again, eschewing the slightly faster Interstate 17 for the first leg. My paranoia and mandate of avoiding the main roads still guide my choices. Unfortunately, that could not last, as there was soon no choice other than I-17, which ultimately connects with I-40 westbound outside of Flagstaff. There just aren't many alternatives to the Interstates.

Left to my own devices, I would have catered to my paranoia and continued north into Utah and eventually connected with US 50, the Lincoln Highway, a two-lane route much less exposed than Interstate 40. The problem is the time, as the meandering route would add hours to our trip, rendering Alex's secure flight the faster choice. In hindsight, perhaps waiting for Alex's flight might have been wiser.

Roughly twenty-four hours earlier, Alex had assured us that the police were not looking for us in connection with the events in Show Low. None of us knew that the taxi driver's body had turned up in the intervening time, and the police now have a description of our car and are seeking us in connection with the murder. Risks of driving increased markedly at that point, unknown to either Alex or us.

We had just passed the community of Ash Fork when my 'spidey-sense' jangled. I began looking around for the cause and noticed an Arizona State Trooper following us at a distance, a long way back but in view. My instincts were to avail ourselves of an exit, but there weren't any, not for miles and miles.

I tensed up and began scanning every direction. My subtle senses screamed in a full five-alarm alert. The only visible cause remained a single police car, but he made me decidedly uncomfortable.

I checked my speed, ensured I precisely toed the speed limit, and drove as smooth and steady as possible so as not to draw attention. It didn't help; my every nerve was on fire.

I spotted a second patrol car headed in the opposite direction and followed it in the rear-view mirror. As he passed the car following us, I noted that he suddenly slowed and crossed the median to join our pursuer. So now there are two on our tail.

I alerted Matt, pointed at the dash, and told him to grab his cell phone, put in the SIM card, and call Alex. Staying off-grid was less urgent than calling the cavalry!

Matt did so, and of course, there was no signal. Some days!

Our pursuers stayed behind us, content to follow at a distance. We were ascending a long grade. I hoped once crested, there would be a signal. I gripped the wheel and ground my teeth. I most definitely did not wish for a confrontation with cops.

With one car, even if there were two officers, I felt confident I could overpower them and not hurt anyone. Two vehicles and things become somewhat dicier. I don't want to kill anyone, especially cops. I'm squeamish, making me a poor hunter in a stone-age society. Still, if forced, I am capable, especially if my life or friends is in danger.

We climbed that grade for several long minutes, with Matt intently watching the signal indicator on his phone. Finally, we crested the apex, and as we did so, a signal appeared, and a few seconds later, the phone locked onto the network. Matt hit dial. Just in time, too.

Ahead of us, less than a half-mile lay a roadblock. A massive one, like something from a movie. My mind briefly flashed to the 1970s cult classic in which the cops chased the anti-hero cross-country and installed an enormous roadblock at the California border. There were ten or a dozen vehicles, although this roadblock lacked the fatal bulldozer blade of the movie. Small consolation. It appeared as if they had called out every government vehicle, marked and unmarked, sedan and dump truck they possessed. An overwhelming show of force.

Alex was slow to answer, and by the time he did, I had let the car coast to a slow creep as we approached the roadblock. Numerous weapons pointed in our direction; there was no question of fighting our way out of this one. Matt quickly explained the situation, asked for help, and then laid the phone on the dashboard, leaving the line open.

Putting the car in Park while carefully keeping our hands visible, we stopped and waited.

And waited!

Finally, three officers took positions around our car, weapons aimed, and told us to climb out of the car, drop to our knees and place our hands on our heads. We complied. I told the ladies to do likewise and not to speak or move.

I indicated the open phone on the dash and suggested the cop should take the call. He ignored me.

And we waited some more.

From the corner of my eye, I could see one of the officers on his phone, waving his fist and arguing vociferously. The argument continued.

Meanwhile, we were staring down the barrels of several weapons. Finally, after a few moments, one of the officers approached, frisked me for weapons, and zip-tied my hands. He had no idea how effortlessly I could break those; else, he would have used several.

He frisked Matt. Matt's weapon upset our host. Matt told him to check his pocket for his badge and ID. Removing Matt's weapon and extracting the badge, he glanced at it and took it over to the officer still arguing on the phone. The officer blinked at it and waved him away, still arguing.

I have no clue how long we sat there. The pavement ground into my knees, my back began to cramp. I'm sure the girls and even Matt was much less comfortable than I. Nonetheless, given the number of weapons pointed our way, we were powerless to do anything other than hold the position and submit to our fates.

If I were alone, I might fight even though the odds were overwhelming. I believe I've mentioned I'm rather quick and capable. I hoped they would be so startled by my strength and speed that I could prevail despite the odds. They had no idea what I could do, but I couldn't endanger my companions.

I was powerless, an ebullition of impotent rage. I'd rather face a hungry T-Rex! This situation precisely underscores why I wish to escort my girls back to Planet Oz and leave the MiBs and Gharlane and Helmuth and Boskone and all the rest behind. Please, leave me alone!

An eternity passed before the cop on the phone rang off and directed his men to lower their weapons. Then, finally, one came over and cut our zip-ties, though I felt tempted to snap my own rather than wait for him. I resisted the temptation.

As the situation began winding down, the roadblock was dismantled, and the multitude of vehicles dissipated until two patrol cars and four officers remained.

Finally released from the situation, they started trying to talk to us, apologies, questions, etc. Matt looked at me and slightly shook his head. Well, he didn't need to tell me! I wasn't going to say a single unnecessary word.

Returning his badge and gun, the cop tried to talk to Matt. Instead, Matt merely asked, "Are we free to go?" The officer stepped back and nodded.

Shaking with the adrenaline crash, I felt uncertain I could drive. Matt seemed less affected than I, undoubtedly more accustomed to dealing with Law Enforcement. I motioned to Matt to assume the driver's seat and settled into the shotgun position as I struggled for calm. If Alex had not come through and quashed whatever this had been, I shudder at how it might have ended.

I noticed the phone was still online, lying on the dash. So, wordlessly, I disconnected and powered it off. I didn't want to talk to anyone just then, not even Alex. Not. Especially. Alex.

One hundred miles passed uneventfully, and soon we found ourselves approaching Needles, CA. We stopped for food and fuel, and only then did I feel like talking about the events at Ash Fork. Well, not really!

I'm still a nervous wreck after our near-death experience, although I felt partially recovered upon reaching Needles. Thanks to our Ash Fork squid games, we had spent over five hours traveling from

Sedona to Needles. The sun still rode high, yet we all felt exquisitely exhausted. Perhaps I shouldn't speak for the others.

I felt thoroughly spent!

I doubted anyone would debate the point. However, we felt time pressure to move forward as the entire trip should have taken around 12 hours, and we have already blown almost half that on less than a quarter of the journey. We all needed food, refreshment, showers, and perhaps a nap. Especially a shower.

The drive from Sedona had taken a toll.

Scouting around Needles, Matt found us a cheap *No tell Motel* which would accept cash and not inquire into personal matters. Nearby was a 'Wagon Tongue' restaurant that drew our eyes. We checked into the motel and then darted across the parking lot to the kitschy western-themed eatery. Perhaps they weren't high-class, but the food was terrific, and we enjoyed a sumptuous dinner of classic American comfort food. Their Southern-Style biscuits and gravy rivaled my own. I seriously need to find a gym. I commented that Wisceya was getting fat.

Yeah, that's right. I am genuinely that stupid!

Our dinner was relaxing and pleasant, and we over-indulged. Our conversation was light and joking, purposefully avoiding the day's stressful events, seeking relief in a full belly, and a few giggles. I won't say I felt like singing "Clementine," but our spirits significantly improved by the time we had finished our meal.

After dinner, we returned to our rooms and made pleasurable use of the facilities, luxuriating in hot water and suds. Matt again insisted on a private room, not surprisingly, and an emboldened Stapleya voiced a desire to join him. He seemed reluctant, yet to my surprise, agreed after a moment's hesitation. She looked back at us, giving an evil grin and a wink as she took him by the arm and led him into the adjacent room. I gave her a discreet thumbs up and turned into my room, with Wisceya clinging to my arm.

We had agreed to a three-hour rest break. Suds, water, and a brief nap later, Wisceya and I arose briefly to watch the sunset from the balcony outside our room. It lacked the overpowering impact of the Sedona sunset but was nicely colorful. Unfortunately, Matt and Stapleya overslept, missing the show. After watching the solar display, we resumed our nap, as our three-hour clock reflected time remaining. A brief time later, Stapleya quietly knocked and asked to extend the stop another hour. Wisceya and I grinned at her and agreed.

Our three-hour rest break expanded yet again, and when added to our leisurely dinner, it was now nearly twelve hours after departing Sedona before we finally resumed our twice interrupted drive. So much for driving straight through and making faster time than waiting for an aircraft.

The 145 miles to Barstow drifted by smoothly and without incident. There was a brief stop for a burger and tank of gasoline, and then we were rolling again. We could finally abandon Interstate 40, although we were still traveling on a busy, closely monitored highway. That it was nighttime might work in our favor a little. CA-58 led us into Bakersfield without complications.

Matt intended to take Interstate 5 out of Bakersfield for the last 275-mile leg. However, I voiced my ill-content with traveling via the Interstate and argued for the slightly less-traveled Highway 99, known alternately as the 'Golden State Highway' through Fresno instead. The difference in mileage is insignificant, though the lower speed limit adds about 20 minutes to the trip.

We stopped again for fuel and a bite of food. Then, after another debate on the route choice, Matt yielded and headed up CA-99 toward Fresno. I can't prove whether there are fewer cameras and fewer opportunities for our enemies to find us. But my subtle sense was happier.

We stopped just north of Fresno briefly for an 'In-N-Out' break, emphasizing coffee for the driver and a quick restroom visit for the girls. In-N-Out is one California feature we missed on our Arizona, Utah, and New Mexico tour. Resistance was futile when the Nekomata spotted the giant red, white, and yellow sign from the freeway.

I retook the wheel as we left the burger joint, and we made rapid time into the Bay Area. Finally, we hit Modesto, where our route called for a turn west to pick up 580 through the Altamont Pass and into the Bay Area. Soon I pulled off the road and surrendered the wheel again to Matt since he knew the precise where of our destination and I did not.

Our destination, it turned out, was not the East Bay site where I had first met Matt but another even more thoroughly hidden and much larger secret facility in a canyon east of the Bay Area. Don't bother looking on a map; it does not exist.

Matt pulled into a parking lot and flashed his badge to the guard. A security guard came to greet us at the gate and escorted us inside and showed us to a pair of tiny but serviceable apartments where we could refresh ourselves. It was morning, the dawn just breaking as we arrived, and it would be soon time to begin work. The girls and I quickly refreshed ourselves and prepared for the job ahead.

My worries notwithstanding, the drive to the Bay Area proved successful, although, in the end, I wished we had just waited 24 hours for the plane. Instead, the hair-raising journey had required slightly over 20 hours.

The Lost Son Returns

I needed time for decoupling from the long drive, visiting the bathroom, taking a shower, and a few minutes just to lay on the bed and snuggle with Wisceya while steeling myself for the work to come. I presumed Matt and Stapleya similarly used the second apartment.

An hour later, I exited to find our security guard patiently lingering. I apologized for keeping him waiting; I hadn't realized he was standing by for our needs. Or to watch us. Creepy. "You're inside the belly of the beast, Fitz," I told myself. "Get used to someone watching your every move." I severely dislike this, though we're committed.

I had promised Alex I would take charge of building his network but emphasized how serious I was that he must make time for our private conversation once we were operational. I think he finally understood that I was on to him and intended to brook no further deception.

When Wisceya and I exited, the guard suggested she might wait in the room until I returned. I shook my head told him I expected to be working long hours, and perhaps she could lend a hand. I felt decidedly uncomfortable about letting her out of my sight. I inquired whether her mother waited in the adjacent apartment.

The guard knocked on the door, and Stapleya opened it. I asked if Matt was with her, and she shook her head. He had left a few minutes earlier and hadn't mentioned where he was going or when he might return. I suggested she accompany us rather than wait alone, to which she nodded eagerly.

The guard stared at the three of us for a moment, then shrugged and escorted us along a long hallway, a couple of turns, another shorter hallway, and finally to a sizeable double elevator. He escorted us into the car and pulled out a key as he did so, a rounded key of the type claimed to be pick proof, typically reserved for high-security applications. Glancing around, I noted an absence of buttons. Instead, a screen displayed an image of Psyche at Nature's Mirror. Innocence and purity? Odd choice, I mused. However, beneath the tablet resided a lock switch, apparently intended to receive the key held by our escort.

The guard inserted his key into the wall and turned. Psyche dissolved to reveal the image of a set of standard elevator buttons. He touched one, and a keypad appeared, into which he poked an eight-digit code. He poorly shielded his movements, and my baser nature took over. I saw the passcode he entered translated as "Gharlane." I found that most curious.

We went down. And down. I mused that I had finally encountered that classical Hollywood high-speed elevator descent into the bowels of the Earth.

The descent was rapid, and we stopped at a level bearing the label Operations Command. When the doors swooshed open, I gazed out upon a vast open-concept room with more gigantic computer/TV displays than I had ever seen in one place. The local Best Buy manager would be impressed. The room looked like a command center for a Science Fiction TV Show. A line of cubicles ringed the room, with giant display screens suspended above them. Smaller displays occupied the space beside the doorway of each booth, no unadorned wall space seeming permissible.

Interestingly, displays not actively displaying useful information were instead showing posters and imagery from Science Fiction, several of which I recognized as various images, book covers, and such from the works of Doc Smith. I smiled at that. Others displayed classical artwork from many sources. Some displayed more conventional graphics, a few movie posters, and various bands from the Grateful Dead to the Bobbleheads.

The center of the room captured the eye, the ceiling dominated by a gigantic display tree suspended from above, supporting numerous large-screen displays that are smaller than the wall-mounted ones but still large, high, and visible.

The middle also carried a massive donut-shaped circular console, broken into quadrants, the circular surface bisected by a curved, opaque divider. High-resolution desktop displays stood back-to-back, forming concentric rings, with their occupants placed elbow to elbow, facing their counterparts over the partitions and screens.

That's not correct, I realized after a moment. The offset concentric rings allowed operators to not look directly at one another. Instead, they gaze past each other to yet another display behind the head of their opposite. I noticed an absence of phones, but several technicians wore headphones with a small boom microphone. I speculated this doubled as telephone and entertainment. I idly wondered what tunes they listened to while working. I have always found the classical genre most conducive to creativity, Edvard Grieg presently my favorite, though tastes vary.

In the center of the circular console, underneath the display tree, resided an array of equipment racks holding a vast quantity of computer gear, routers, switches, and servers, clearly supporting infrastructure for the Ops consoles. Yet, the ever-present white noise of fans, hard drives, and air-conditioned airflow movement seemed strangely muted. I wouldn't call the place quiet, but the ambient noise level fell far below normal data room levels. Active noise suppression, I surmised.

Most Control Centers do not place the equipment and the humans in the same space partly because of noise. The room should roar like a wind tunnel, rendering speech problematic. Active Noise Reduction, such as that used in some aircraft and high-end automobiles, and careful airflow engineering must be the reason for the low decibel level. I further stipulated that Solid State Drives allow silent and speedy storage. I'd bet there is not a spinning disk platter in the rack. Even with all the equipment, the noise level was modest.

I have been in numerous Ops Centers, Control Rooms, and similar, enough to appreciate efficient design. This place is incredible! I'd love to meet the designer. Indeed, tons of work went into this. I glanced at my ladies, and they stared in open-mouthed wonder! I guess I was, too, although I hope I was slightly less obvious about it.

I wondered why so much of the support gear sat in the middle of the room and not sequestered in some closed-off annex as is usually the case. I mused that having the equipment at hand was convenient and possibly more secure, as someone could not sneak into the server room and muck about without being spotted. I wondered if there was another server room with additional storage, as expanding this array appeared challenging. I concluded there were probably supplemental servers sequestered elsewhere, but the live-action, real-time infrastructure all sat right here.

I stood there for long moments drinking in the spectacle, deducing how everything is interconnected, imagining the uses for the massive array of displays. Then, finally, one of the technicians detached himself from the group and came over to meet us. I recognized him instantly and didn't need the name tag to remember his name.

I first met Dale months ago when Alex held me captive. Dale was one of the techs brought to question me and verify my bona fides as a computer and networking expert. I had later joked that I would sue him for 'Physique Discrimination' since he and his fellows had assumed I was just a muscle-bound jock and could not possibly be one of their own. I won't claim we became drinking buddies after that incident, but we have encountered each other numerous times in professional circles and have maintained a strong familiarity.

Dale now runs this operation center and has been awaiting my appearance. He is pulling this center together, little is functional yet, but we are on a countdown clock to readiness. He had plenty of work laid out for me, work uniquely suited to my talents.

Dale seemed slightly disconcerted to meet the girls, although he greeted them warmly. It would be difficult for any warm-blooded human to do otherwise, especially a male. He raised his brows quizzically to ask, 'What are they doing here?' I ignored his wiggling unibrow and asked for an overview of the tasks on my plate.

Dale and I discussed the project before us, the timeframe to pull it all together, and what he hoped I could bring. Then he showed me to a workstation he had set up for my needs. Surprisingly, I recognized a couple of dear friends, my sweet little ultraportable from my home, and the laptop Estelle had purchased at my behest such a brief time ago. "We figured you would need your tools," he stated. "We touched nothing on either machine; we just wanted you to have them handy in case you needed them." Yeah, Okay. Would I be paranoid to wonder if that were strictly accurate?

Dale gave us a tour of the Ops Center and showed us the routine accommodations, such as the restroom and break room. The break room was much more than a break room. A virtual cafeteria suited for feeding the staff on duty, complete with a chef. One could obtain anything from a country breakfast to a full dinner. I noted with pleasure that my Arabian Mocha-Java blend was available, and I immediately grabbed onto an extra-large. I needed the caffeine infusion. The girls followed my lead and ordered a drink for themselves. I also noted provisions for naps, as several cubicles contained cots. A stressed worker could take a break and a short rest before resuming labor, suggesting anticipation of long hours at the console. No surprise there.

Chaos reigned. I learned we were building a massive SOC, a Security Operations Center within a Darknet. It would be the control center for a private Internet with private resources and communications channels linking hundreds of sites, remote operations centers, field command centers, and more but wholly disconnected from the Internet itself. No one could access anything on our network unless physically connected. We were building a complete, independent Internet from scratch.

Much of the work laid out was mundane and repetitive, although it did require highly specialized knowledge. A relatively unskilled technician could perform much of the actual work as long as strategic expertise oversaw the action.

There were hundreds of spanking new military-grade routers online, all running the factory-installed software and an extensive collection of military-grade servers to support the network applications. Of course, that is as one would expect, except for one detail. Typically, a team of bureaucrat-experts carefully certifies software releases deemed critical to the military. In regular times, disregarding the official versions and running any software image other than that officially blessed software could be a career-ending transgression, perhaps even prosecuted as treasonous.

The problem lies in the fact that the military approval process is ponderous, and as a result, the 'blessed' software often lags the state-of-the-art. Given the highly secretive nature of our mission, that's a weakness, as the officially blessed versions often harbor known security flaws. Anomalies that go by cryptic names such as FREAK, GHOST, Heartbleed, and Poodle have provided many opportunities for attacks against networks. Staying ahead of these is a never-ending game of whack-a-mole, as each vulnerability patched leads to the discovery of new ones. Unfortunately, the bureaucratic approval process is slow and cumbersome, making mitigation by exception routine, and even exceptions get deployed slowly and inconsistently, leaving vulnerable systems unprotected.

It would be easier if we genuinely built a pure Darknet with dedicated connections. Due to time and other constraints, we compromise, transporting large numbers of sessions across the Internet backbone via encrypted VPN tunnels. That means a risk of so-called 'man-in-the-middle' attacks, whereby an evil-doer could intercept an encryption key exchange, insert themselves into the encrypted tunnel and access the data. Commonly used software has weaknesses the bad guys can exploit. Software that cannot have keys intercepted or pre-computed is needed. Treason or not, we must do better than the officially sanctioned options.

My job required connecting to each router, verifying the existing software load and configuration, making notes of the potential vulnerabilities, and mitigating those vulnerabilities. That's a long, complicated, and highly repetitive task. Fortunately, I am a whiz with automation tools. Where necessary, I must install software suited to our needs, not only the systems software itself but the probes required to capture data for monitoring in real-time. This data stream will funnel into the "Threat Intelligence System" for real-time analysis. Given the size of the operation, it is a massive job.

Dale assigned one of his technicians to assist me, a young woman named Jessica. I asked if he thought one tech was enough. Shrugging, Dale said one was all he could spare, but more staff arrived daily. He hoped to have more techs soon.

Gathering the list of routers and purported software modules installed, I tasked Jessica with setting up a bastion host and creating an inventory YAML for each equipment class. Then I asked her to set up an Ansible playbook to query each server about its software and build a detailed table of what we have. Once we know what we have, we can parse that list, flagging anything that needs attention. Finally, I reserved a review of the latest releases, changelogs, and release data for myself. If our routers' officially blessed software contained vulnerabilities that have tested and proven solutions, I wanted to know it.

Stapleya and Wisceya occupied themselves watching Jessica and me at work. Then I noticed Wisceya hovering closely over Jessica as she was systematically connecting to each router and collecting the relevant data. Jessica proved to be extremely sharp on the job. An inexperienced newbie might have executed the same actions repeatedly, working through the long list. Instead, like a real pro, Jessica automated the process with Ansible playbooks and Bash scripts to ensure that the process required much less human interaction. Jessica soon reduced the job to merely pointing her shell script at each router, letting it run its course, ensuring it encountered no errors, and verifying the data. Slick and efficient, precisely the way I would have done it. I decided I liked this tech.

I looked over Jessica's shoulder briefly, verified she had the job under control, and left her to her own devices as I returned to my self-appointed task of reviewing our software options. It seems intuitively clear that we're headed for a disaster if the installation goes ahead as initially outlined.

It may have been three hours later when I emerged from my creative fog to check on Jessica. Stunned, I observed Stapleya, Wisceya, and Jessica seated at keyboards, banging away vigorously. Wisceya felt my eyes upon her and smiled coyly with a quick wink. She seemed pleased with helping; she and her mother aided in completing Jessica's assigned task list far faster than Jessica alone could have done.

I won't claim that my fur-girls progressed from stone-age inhabitants to computer geeks in hours. They remain entirely ignorant of the vast panoply of computer science. However, I have often remarked that they are brilliant and possess excellent memories and motor skills.

Jessica had built specialized scripts and taught the aliens how to execute them; the fundamental understanding required thus reduced to the minimum, thanks to Jessica's efforts. The job boiled down to pointing, clicking, observing, and recording, which required excellent memory and facile motor skills but little beyond that, plus knowing when to call for help if it doesn't work correctly.

They have nearly completed the long, arduous, and complicated task of cataloging the software in a small fraction of the time it would have required for one person alone.

I shook my head in mild disbelief and returned to my task. I must be ready for the next stage of our rollout when they're finished. We have work ahead.

The issues are multitudinous. First, the equipment had not shipped from the factory with the proper, 'government blessed' software installed; instead, a chaotic hodge-podge of different versions and options. That alone would have forced us to update all the equipment anyway. Second and worse, the official software was generations behind current best practice and contained at least three well-known, easily exploitable flaws. Thus, the official software was a leaking sieve of vulnerabilities, ripe for our enemies to exploit.

Looking over our options, I decided if I must buck the system and install unsanctioned software, I'm going all the way, ditching the 'blessed' software entirely for the latest in Transport Layer Security (TLS). There is a method to this madness; TLS has undergone massive revisions since its birth as SSL in the early days of the web. Numerous vulnerabilities have been discovered and fixed. However, even the latest version holds risks inherent in the original ancient origins of the net. Many stem from the need to support older, outdated browsers used in the general population, and some merely due to an original design lacking foresight.

We don't have those limits. Here in our own private little Darknet, we control the user's software and our own. Or, as my favorite TV classic put it: *"We will control the horizontal. We will control the vertical."*

We decide what security client resides on the servers, what security protocols the routers allow to pass, what security certificates the authentication servers will honor, and what browsers the clients use.

In short, we can build a virgin network without worrying about legacy browsers. As a result, I have a perfect greenfield in which to play.

I configured software loads with TLS enabled, SSL blocked, 4096-bit security keys, and extended validation certificates, and that was merely a start. Next, I turned on Ed25519 signatures and forced them to be mandatory for all sessions. Then, I blocked all older cryptographic hash functions and disallowed down-negotiation to lesser protocols on all servers. Next, I set up a private certificate authority to control encryption certificates. Finally, I created a DNS server with DNSSEC and forced all DNS services to use it. In short, I threw in every security wrinkle I knew, including the kitchen sink.

I finished my part of the job as Jessica, and the Nekomata completed theirs. I explained the next step to Jessica while Stapleya and Wisceya looked on in puzzlement and let them go to work on the project. I noted with pleasure that Jessica had already anticipated the next step and was fully prepared, with automation scripts ready. That gal was sharp and planned ahead. I wondered what she would look like in fur.

Jessica and the aliens tackled the next stage with enthusiasm. I watched them briefly and then returned to my next task, creating a new layer of obfuscation for anyone attempting to break into our network. I'm going to build a Honeypot network, my version of that kitchen sink.

A Honeypot is a trap designed to ensnare those who might attempt to access network resources inappropriately. In this case, I set traps that would ensnare those who might be trying to exploit known vulnerabilities that my updated protocols blocked. If someone tries an exploit, they will find themselves redirected to a "sandboxed" server that will respond in a manner that leads them to believe that they have succeeded, even though unknowingly triggered alarms and any data retrieved is meaningless.

We will know if someone attempts to intrude, and stand a decent chance of learning who, how, and where.

The work went on in this manner for hours. Finally, midnight approached when I noticed that I and my charges were starting to make stupid minor mistakes due to fatigue. We had traveled all night, had a brief respite, and then worked all day. Finally, I called a halt and decreed that sleep was in order. We were undoubtedly due.

My ladies' contribution to today's project impressed me and the various others involved. They had indeed earned their keep, despite lacking fundamental computer skills, and I told them so and, more importantly, promised I would let Alex know. Our guard appeared on cue and escorted us back to our rooms as we prepared to retire.

Matt had not returned to Stapleya's disappointment. She debated whether to return alone to their room or join us. Deciding that the prospect of sleeping alone was unattractive, Stapleya opted to join us. She instructed our guard that if Matt returned, he should wake her so that she might join him rather than let him sleep alone. He never appeared.

Death March

Our first day's work had been arduous and had followed a long overnight drive. We felt exhausted at the end of that day, though we would soon learn we lacked the first clue about what exhaustion meant. The days before us were much longer. Time pressure was upon us to complete this massive operations center and hemisphere-spanning network. Operation Jade Helm was near!

Mere sixteen-hour days are for wimps and slackers. Our people worked shifts of 24 and even 36 hours with only minor breaks and with only a ten-hour rest between them. Mortals cannot endure this brutal pace without chemical assistance.

Left to my own devices, I eschew chemical aids. Ordinarily, my use of pharmacology is limited to my daily Arabian Mocha-Java or, worst case, plain black coffee if my preferred aromatic blend of Mocha from Arabia and Estate Java is not available. Caffeine is quite seductive and addicting enough for everyday life. I have often stated I like my coffee hot and naked, just like my friends.

Coffee, black as the devil, hot as hell, pure as an angel, and steamy as love, can only carry one so far. Exceeding the limits of human endurance requires tools created in a lab, not brewed from a bean. Modafinil is the most effective and safest of the diverse stimulants crafted by modern pharmacology.

Caffeine, amphetamine, and modafinil similarly influence the brain's theta wave, promoting wakefulness. But modafinil alone increases alpha wave activity, raising alertness. Also, caffeine 'wears out' quickly, so another cup of coffee does little more to combat fatigue. A morning cup can do wonders to jump-start the day, but the benefits rapidly diminish beyond that.

I'm acquainted with modafinil. I've used it occasionally, although I prefer my natural wakefulness within a regular sleep cycle. However, modafinil can keep a person awake and working far longer, 36-hours or more being practical. Modafinil also improves working memory, digit span, and pattern recognition even in those not sleep deprived and is not wildly addictive, certainly no more than, if as much as caffeine. Thus, modafinil is very safe compared to other drugs.

Consequently, given the extreme time crunch we faced in this operation, the powers-that-be encourage modafinil. Indeed, management virtually mandates it. On our second day, I noticed a medical officer making the rounds, handing out tablets freely while recording the dosage and time of each recipient. She monitored the working time of everyone using the drug. She insisted that anyone who reached 40 hours of activity must take a ten-hour sleep break, even prescribing a sleeping aid if necessary, although discouraging the latter unless truly needed. The medic was also monitoring parameters such as our blood pressure, pulse, occasionally sticking fingers for a drop of blood for glucose checks, and who knows what else.

We were being pushed, carefully, to the limits of human endurance. My limits may be higher than others, but even my powers have their limits.

Realizing that my natural sleep/work cycle cannot hope to keep pace with this over-caffeinated, drug-enhanced crew, I surrendered to the inevitable and joined in. My ladies, desiring to help to the limits of their ability, likewise accepted our medical officer's ministrations.

The next few weeks flew by in a blur of 40-hour work cycles and 10-hour rests. I often napped on a cot in the Operations Center, snatching an odd wink before the next modafinil dose. We accomplished five days of work every two days, a brutal, gut-wrenching pace. Then suddenly, the day dawned, figuratively speaking — deep underground, we lost all awareness of the solar cycles — but the day came that, suddenly, it was complete! Finally, we had the network fully configured and operationally secure. The last Ops Console was up and online, the *Threat Intelligence System* maps were live, all the remote tactical centers were onscreen, and the battle plans were flowing. None too soon!

I had reached the limit of even my endurance. Deciding I had earned real sleep time, I gathered my ladies, and we repaired to the tiny apartment where we had spent our first evening. A luxurious ten-hour sleep, a shower, and a prodigious breakfast later, we toured the SOC to admire our handiwork.

I poked around a few minutes, checking various widgets. Finally, I noticed that my honeypots had trapped something. There were a rash of alarms and log entries, indicative that someone or something had indeed probed the network looking for vulnerabilities. I began pulling the log files for the affected honeypots, teasing out the particulars of the attempts at penetrating the system.

I was pondering this, speculating how to expose whoever had done so, when our familiar guard approached. He explained that Alex had asked us to join him in '*Strategic Command*.'

I asked Jessica to examine my Honeypots, the data I had pulled, and determine what she may. Leaving the task in good hands, I gathered the Nekomata and followed the guard to the elevator. I had no idea what or where 'Strategic Command' was, although I assumed it was analogous to our Security Operations Center, where the planners develop battle tactics and strategies. The brain to our brawn, as it were. I wasn't far off.

Our guard escorted us to another cavernous chamber. Alex greeted us at the elevator, with Jill at his side! Jill ran over and put her arms out for a massive bear hug. Then, she turned to the girls and embraced them enthusiastically.

Alex grabbed my hand in an effusive greeting. "Fitz, you are a sight for sore eyes! My Operations Manager says that you have performed miracles. I wish to thank you for your excellent work. You have made the impossible happen!"

"It is an impressive SOC! I have worked on some terrific systems, but what we have built here is exceptional. When you described building a system to coordinate the attacks against Boskone's organizations, I assumed it would be a rough, slap-dash, temporary affair, but this appears to be a permanent operations center, built to last."

"Indeed, Fitz, I have tremendous plans for what you have helped us build here."

In glowing terms, Alex described how he expected this complex to be the interplanetary Ops center coordinating all of Earth's interactions with humanity elsewhere in the universe. But, even now, Earth's best physicists were working on unraveling the secrets of the Portals in hopes of reaching out to other human-populated worlds.

Alex was excited to present the reality of extraterrestrial life and civilization to Earth's nations. He believed doing so would usher in a new era of peace and interplanetary commerce.

As we chatted, Jill and the girls disappeared toward the restrooms — to what end, I am reluctant to speculate. After talking for a while, Alex offered a tour of the facility, saying he wanted to introduce the team.

Strategic Command bore little resemblance to the facility I had built. Display screens and workstations abounded, but the environment was more subdued, low-key with softer colors, seemingly better focused on thinking and planning than executing. There was a central bullpen area with giant screens displaying *Threat Intelligence System* views, though not as large as the SOC, but instead of banks of cubicles surrounding the bullpen, there were walled offices. I recognized the desirability of being able to close a door and be inside solid, soundproof walls when discussing top-secret plans and strategies. Until someone creates the fictional 'Cone of Silence,' discussing top-secret matters in open cubicles is a bad idea. I judged this facility as thoroughly suited to its task as mine is to its responsibilities.

The walled offices were much larger than a typical office, indeed were mini-bullpens. Alex, saying he had someone special I needed to meet, knocked and entered one. As I followed him into the bustling room, a figure detached himself from the group and greeted us. I stopped, my jaw dropped, stunned into disbelief!

Alex smiled oddly and announced, "Fitz, I'd like you to meet possibly the only man to have done more to further this project than yourself, Dr. Shepherd. Shep, this is Fitz."

Shep smiled and gave a half-wink and a slight shake of his head to warn me. It was all I could manage to avoid showing my surprise, but somehow, I held my tongue! My brain locked up from the shock, which probably helped; otherwise, I may have blown the whole ballgame.

Extending his hand, he exclaimed, "Fitz, my boy, I have heard so much about you that I feel as if I know you! Indeed a pleasure to meet you. We should have dinner tonight and become acquainted! My apartment! Bring the alien ladies too; I want to meet them. You must meet my associate, Dr. Mathes, too! She is a great fan of your writing."

I stammered and mumbled before collecting my wits. "Of course," I finally blurted out. "Tonight, Dinner then? I can't wait to learn all you can share about what you have been building. I will let Stapleya and Wisceya know of the plans."

My heart pounded; I was barely able to speak. Who was Dr. Mathes? If Petchy is working here undercover as Shep, who could Dr. Mathes be? Dare I hope?

My brain spun, and my senses reeled as 'Dr. Shepherd' excused himself, pleading the urgent press of business, and returned to the group as Alex and I exited, closing the door. I wished Alex had left us alone so I could ask Petchy, err, Shep, several questions. Such as WTF? The promised dinner this evening must suffice.

Alex carried on with his tour of the center, and I noted with interest a large section devoted to 'Digital Warfare.' I met some of the 'D-Warriors' who were already in residence. Shortly Alex took my arm, and we ducked into a smaller office to speak privately. "Fitz," he started hesitatingly. "Jill has spoken of how much you distrust our organization, and I won't pretend it comes as a surprise. We operate in the black and, at times, weave our way through a minefield of shades of gray. There is real evil out there. I often share your concerns. We are not unaccountable, though that accountability is often as cloaked as our triumphs."

I stared blankly, not grasping his point or the direction of his words. I nearly interrupted him, but he continued before I could shape my thoughts.

"Trust what I say; we are the heroes. But unfortunately, there are incredibly evil people, not the least this current 'Boskone' organization. Evil people who leave a blood-soaked trail everywhere they surface. I wish it were unnecessary to do what we do. We stand for nothing less than civilization itself, standing against those who would enslave humanity for their benefit."

This time I did interrupt. "Alex, I agree there are nasty people on the other side, yet most people just wish to be left alone! Citizens shouldn't live in fear of criminals or their government. Unfortunately, I have tasted such fear of late, to my deep anger and frustration. If I could do it, I would leave the Earth entirely and live on Nekomata; the fur peoples' only fear is the dinosaurs, and a dinosaur's agenda is simple."

Alex nodded and continued, "Me too, my friend, me too. I would love to move to a pleasant 'Shangri La' and leave the fighting behind. Having met the ladies from Planet Oz, I can fairly say they are utterly charming people. Precisely the sorts of people my organization and I exist to protect."

That was the opening I was hoping for, so I held up my hand, took a deep breath, and began. "Alex," I said, "The time has come to settle accounts. You promised to come clean, and I am holding you to that promise."

He started to speak, but I again raised my hand to forestall his response. I wanted to get my licks in before he could engage. So I went on, "You knew about the interplanetary worlds of Ashera and Nekomata long before we met. Luckily for me, you betrayed that knowledge when you used the name Nekomata for 'Planet Oz.' I had never heard that name. That prompted me to quiz Stapleya. She is loyal, but she finally acknowledged that she knew her planet was called Nekomata and that Petchy and Teena came from a world they called Ashera, which I believe you know of also."

He nodded and grinned wanly. Then with a shrug, he said, "Go on, I suspect you have more."

"One more point and I will give you the floor to explain. Stapleya told me that YOU had visited Nekomata with Petchy and Teena! So, you not only know the Nekomata, but you are an Asheran too. Petchy and Teena are no strangers to you! So why the deception?" I let my voice grow stronger with the last, emphasizing my seriousness.

Alex was smiling as I finished. So far, the big confrontation I have been agonizing over has been no big whup. Easier than I expected, and I had not expected Alex to smile. That's unsettling. I had expected a more negative reaction.

Alex said, "Fitz, I admit I have been secretive and played things close to my vest, and that's an aspect of my job. Indeed, the first time I laid eyes on you, I knew you had come through a portal, but I did not know whether you were friend or foe. I had no idea who you were, and I put you through that interrogation because I feared you might be an off-worlder with bad intentions. I could not reach anyone in Dr. Shepherd's organization at that time. I did not know that he was injured or even that he was involved. I was in the dark as much as you."

I must have let my surprise show because he stopped and gave me an odd expression. So, I chimed in, "You're an Asheran and have been to Nekomata. How are you in the dark?"

He sighed. "Fitz, my friend, I am no more an Asheran than you. Pointedly, I am precisely as much Asheran as you; we share the same blood. You and I are practically brothers. Not that Shep is my father, but that my mother is Asheran. We are family by blood; we are very close, genetically speaking."

He paused as though this was painful for him. Finally, I asked, "You have been to Nekomata, right?"

He nodded. "Yes, I lived there for many years, took a wife, and raised children. I know the Nekomata well, but that was long ago. The last time I was there, Stapleya was a young child. I thought she wouldn't remember me. But understand, I was born on Earth, just like you. I am an Earthman as much as you, and my loyalties are with Earth, first and foremost."

I said, "I see. So, you were born and raised on Earth by an Asheran parent. Was your father a native Earthman?"

He nodded. "Yes, he was. After he died, my mother took me to Nekomata, where I stayed for a long time. But I eventually returned to Earth and entered the military. After my military career, I found a home in the Agency. I have worked my way up through the ranks over decades. I am not an infiltrator, not an alien pretender, or a double agent. Instead, I am an authentic Earth human and career civil servant. The fact that my mother is Asheran is no more remarkable than one whose mother was Greek or Scottish, or even Russian. I am a patriot as committed to my country as anyone of any background. That my mother happens to hail from another planet means nothing. You and I are very much alike in that respect; the difference is that I knew my mother was born elsewhere, whereas your father's origins were unknown."

I was speechless. Finally, I gathered my wits and asked, "When I talked and wrote about Petchy and Teena, did you not know who I meant?"

He shook his head. "I did not know either name. They invented those names for your mission. The man you called Petchy and discovered to be your father I last knew as Rufus. The woman you called Teena used Gwen the last time I saw her. More importantly, I had believed they were both killed when they chased an alien through a portal and never returned. I now believe that alien was one of Gharlane's men, as this latest war seems an outgrowth of the battles we were fighting then. That was more than a decade ago, and until recently, I had supposed them both dead."

I added, "Then Petchy is Shep now? But he is undercover, so no one is to know?"

Alex nodded. "Of course, he won't fool the Nekomata women; they know him well. But caution them not to spill the beans."

I sat in silence for a moment, digesting all I had heard. Then I asked, "Rufus, a.k.a. Petchy, is my biological father, making me one-half Asheran, the same as you, right?"

He nodded. I went on. "So, who is your mother?"

"I'm not sure I should tell you that."

Wrong answer! I bristled. "And I am triple damn sure you should! Damn it, Alex, you promised to come clean. I intend to hold you to that promise. When, on Nekomata, Teena confessed our relationship, she said they intended to keep me ignorant. Until now, they have succeeded. That ends now, here, today! I am totally, completely, overwhelmingly DONE with this 'close to the vest' BULLSHIT and am not letting you keep me in the dark. Now give!"

I guess I overemphasized my point. Alex shrank back from me, ever so slightly, and his eyes widened. At that moment, I realized Alex was as afraid of me, physically, as I am of him and the power he wields. Alex is a big, strong, and confident man used to being in control. He leaned back, placed his fingertips together, and said, "Fitz, my mother is here in this facility, working for me."

I shrugged. I could not think of a thing to say. I did not then realize I had again accepted an incomplete answer and allowed myself to be diverted from seeking the full truth. Damn smooth-talking aliens!

"Fitz, brother, I need you. Your skills, internal compass, and firm grasp of the moral boundaries we must skirt daily are precisely the qualities we need. Great leaders are extraordinarily rare. The power we wield is seductive and walking the fine line of justice is a constant challenge. Men have often lost their way in the warm, alluring glow of power and authority. Plus, your clandestine computer skills are the most amazing I have ever seen.

"Dr. Shepherd speaks highly of you and your talents, and his recommendation carries weight, quite aside from the Asheran connection! He is a rock star in his academic community, and when he endorses someone, it means something.

"Fitz, come to work here! You are the man I need to run my entire Digital Warfare group. I'm not certain that the group can even function without you."

Alex wants ME to be his D-Warrior! Not just his D-Warrior, to head up his entire team of D-Warriors!

I needed to sit down at that!

"Alex, I'm flattered. My priority at this point is to ensure my friends' safe return home. I'm not sure what my fate is beyond that. I suppose a father naturally holds a high opinion of his son.

"Officially, I never met the man before today and never heard of him before. I'm not a good liar. Deception does not come easily. Don't you and he worry that I might let the cat out of the bag?

"My head is reeling; I need time to process. I will talk with Shep at dinner tonight and seek his counsel."

Alex grinned. "I can't ask for more than that. But rest assured, I also want those ladies protected; they are as dear to me as they are to you. Especially Stapleya. So we'll return them to their home, I'm confident."

Just as we agreed to continue the discussion after tonight's dinner with Petch/Shep, Jill and the aliens reappeared. The girls seemed quietly excited, hanging onto Jill's arms. I asked what they had been doing. Stapleya merely stated that Jill had taken them for a tour and introduced them to some people.

Wisceya giggled slightly, grimaced, and said that Jill had shown them her scars. Both acknowledged their amazement that Jill had survived. I admitted that I had heard of what a close call it was and congratulated Jill on her rapid recovery. Although weeks have elapsed, she remains on limited duty and won't be back in the field for months.

The conversation carried on for several minutes. Then Jill excused herself, stating she had work awaiting her attention, though she promised we would visit soon and catch up on everything since the hotel shooting.

Once Jill departed, I told the girls that Dr. Shepherd and his associate Dr. Mathes were eager to meet them and had invited us to dinner. Not yet ready to pop the big reveal, I merely explained that I knew they would love to meet Shep and his associate. I hoped to find a more private time and place to discuss the dinner so they would know not to give away the show.

I noticed the girls were unsettled, which I attributed to seeing Jill and realizing how close to death she had come. They seemed to disagree on something but weren't talking.

Our visit concluded, we returned to the SOC to discover that Jessica had been studying our Honeypots. The assaults had come from multiple sources.

One of the sources was, oddly enough, me. I had used my TAILS laptop to attack some of the mitigated vulnerabilities to prove that the fixes installed had been effective. Undoubtedly, my fault. I had failed to clear the logs after testing due to fatigue near the end of the drug-fueled death march, an unfortunate oversight.

It would be of no consequence except for two aspects. First, my carelessness had caused Jessica to waste her precious time chasing down the anomaly, and second, I worried about how many other oversights I had permitted due to fatigue.

The other two remained unidentified. One originated at a workstation in the SOC. It had been no challenge to identify the workstation and the user account logged in at the time, though unfortunately, the individual responsible for that user account pleaded ignorance.

I told Jessica to retrieve the surveillance footage showing who was at the workstation. Of course, she had anticipated my request; unfortunately, the internal surveillance system was not yet operational as of the intrusion. Given the evolving 'under construction' status of the SOC, that is not surprising. I fear we have another potential mole, but we must wait until they try again. I suggested Jessica make sure the video system was functional for the next time and not create a security incident on the matter for now. Let's not raise unnecessary alarms.

The last one was especially puzzling. Jessica traced the source to Strategic Command, and the originating user account belonged to a technician in that group. So perhaps Strategic was merely looking over our shoulder, checking the effectiveness of my security.

Then again, perhaps there is a mole there too. I resolved to discuss it with Shep/Petchy tonight and not make an official case of it just yet. If we have a mole, creating an incident report might signal we are onto them. On the other hand, if it was innocent testing and verification, then there's no cause for a ticket anyway.

Soon, I could stand it no longer. I needed to talk to Jill alone. So I called her and asked if she could spare a few minutes for lunch and conversation. She agreed, and I again allowed the guard to provide escort. Meanwhile, my ladies were busy with Jessica, working on a strategy to entrap a mole if one exists, and I left them to their work.

Meeting Jill in the cafeteria, we grabbed a pair of trays and ducked into an empty office for privacy. The moment we were alone, she set her tray down and came into my embrace, not as a long-lost lover but as a dear friend long absent. I didn't read her actions as sexual, but then what do I know? When it comes to adult women's sexual cues, I am illiterate.

Jill started crying. "It was so horrible, Fitz. They just came in and killed them." She clung to my arm and sobbed, muttering indecipherable words of grief and bitterness into my chest. Minutes elapsed as she cried until finally, she collected herself. I dried her tears and comforted her. Finally, she composed herself, and we sat on the couch, collecting our trays from the low table.

"Jill, the ones we've lost will be best honored by eliminating these scum; we must ensure justice prevails. The upcoming battle will clean out their criminal co-conspirators, but we need to find the masterminds and deal directly and harshly with them."

We began eating our lunch and ate in silence for several seconds. Then Jill picked up the conversation. "That's the real problem. I believe the masterminds are not on Earth, and our actions will merely hand them a setback, perhaps not even a serious one. Unless we remain vigilant, they will regroup, rebuild, and return eviler than ever.

"I hoped I could contact off-world allies, Petchy and his people, the ones you called 'four columns,' for help. But, unfortunately, the upcoming Jade Helm will be for nothing unless we discover the means to carry the fight to 'Gharlane' or whoever is behind this."

She set her tray down and leaned into my arms again, another cathartic embrace. Once again, I felt confused, wondering whether this was as non-sexual as I first thought. For a moment or two, I almost expected her to embrace, to turn sexual, uncertain what to do. The signals I sensed were mixed. I waited for her to amplify her intent or need.

The moment again passed, and I struggled to comprehend what she wanted. Sex? If so, she seemed unable to indicate her desire—mere comforting in the aftermath of a horrific experience? Definitely! Yet somehow, this seemed more. With her mixed signals, I was not about to initiate sexuality.

Recognizing the depth of her relationship with Estelle, I never explored her interest in men, if any. Matt had indicated his belief that she was a committed lesbian, though I have no trust that he understands her, or women, any better than I. I'm an ignoramus.

I hugged and comforted her and waited.

I agonized over how much of what I knew I dared share. Finally, finishing our meal and collecting ourselves, I decided to drop a hint, just enough to give some hope.

"Jill, what became of the Sixth Column organization, and do you still hope to travel off-world to enlist the aid of allies?"

She nodded. "The link to the Sixth Column was severed after the shootings. I was hoping to reestablish communications, though perhaps the group's secretive nature suggests after Estelle's death, they have deemed our cell tainted and abandoned us to protect the organization."

I continued, "I have received communications from the 'Four Columns' and expect more soon. I'm hopeful that there will be an opportunity such as you have sought. Shall I then assume you are 'in' for whatever might develop?"

Her response was to throw herself again into my embrace. This time the signals were less ambiguous.

Dinner at Eight

Our dinner date with Drs. Shepherd and Mathes approached. The fur girls and I returned to our room to refresh and prepare. Finally, alone, away from the risk of being overheard, I told them about Shep's secret identity. Wisceya let out an excited exclamation and pointed at her mother, "I told you so; I knew that was her. I told you I didn't care that she had changed her hair and even her eyes; I knew that was her!"

Could it be that both Petchy and Teena are here undercover? I questioned the girls as to what they had seen. While Jill showed them around the center, they had glimpsed a familiar appearing woman through a doorway in another room. She had bobbed dark hair and dark eyes, quite unlike our crimson heroine. Though her height and form resembled Teena, she was much thinner, frailer, and older. Jill had told the girls that the people there were scientists working to study the data uncovered to date and formulate strategies for the upcoming missions. Unfortunately, the scientists seemed busy at that moment, and Jill had not interrupted to introduce the girls, promising to do so later.

Stapleya dismissed her daughter's belief that the strange woman she had seen at a distance, through a doorway, and in another room had been Teena. She also thought the woman seemed too elderly to be anyone they knew. It's trivial to alter hair length and color, difficult for other features, such as eye color, though age can also be deceptive. I'm not sure that's an obstacle to these people, given their genetic expertise. Petchy had appeared different, older, though I admit I had never seen him wearing academician attire and lab coat before.

Come to think of it, except for that brief time at our first interview; I had never seen him clothed. Teena either, for that matter. She had been entirely naked from the first moment I laid eyes on her. Other than travel packs and weapon belts, I had never seen her in any way dressed, so I'm less than confident I would recognize her clothed.

After considerable debate, the identification of the stranger remained inconclusive. Somehow, I had failed to ask Alex this crucial question when discussing Dr. Mathes. I think that was a subconscious protective instinct, as I feared learning Dr. Mathes was not Teena and that Teena was genuinely dead. We all agree on our wishes that Teena is alive and well and hope the mysterious stranger turns out to be her in disguise. However, we're not yet ready to take that leap of faith, although Wisceya held steadfastly and refused to be swayed. Nevertheless, we can barely contain our anticipation.

We had taken early leave from work, refreshed ourselves, and at the appointed hour, our guard escorted us to the apartment reserved for Dr. Shepherd.

The door opened quickly at my knock. "Welcome, Fitz! I see you have brought the charming alien ladies." His eyes twinkled as he greeted the girls as strangers, seemingly for the benefit of our guard. The girls were standing, staring at him, carefully holding their tongues. I was struggling to keep a straight face myself.

I turned to our escort and advised him that he could leave for a break; we would not be returning to our room for hours. As the guard stared blankly, seemingly reluctant to go, Dr. Shepherd nodded and told the guard he would call for an escort when his guests were ready to return to their rooms. Shep also asked the guard to please knock on Dr. Mathes' door to advise her that the guests had arrived and she should join us. Our guard formally saluted Dr. Shepherd with a smart "Yes, Sir!" and turned to depart. Clearly, Shep holds a higher rank around here than I.

Well, practically everyone does.

His apartment proved compact, although more luxurious than mine. As soon as the door closed, Dr. Shepherd dropped his academic persona and instantly transformed into our familiar Petchy! The girls unleashed their pent-up excitement and hugged him enthusiastically, babbling at him in Language. He greeted the girls enthusiastically babbled back at them for several seconds before turning his attention to me.

He surprised me by wrapping his arms around my bulk in an enthusiastic bear hug! "Fitz, my boy, wonderful to see you again! We have so much to catch up on; so much has happened!"

As Petchy pummeled away at my back in greeting, I felt the door open and close at my rear. I responded to Petch's enthusiastic welcome in-kind until I sensed a familiar presence. Psychic presence, pheromones, or merely keyed anticipation; whatever the mechanism, I instantly knew my love had arrived. I turned and found myself enveloped in a warm bundle of Amazonian femininity, passionately osculating as though to disrupt the very space-time continuum itself.

We embraced until the end of time, until the stars burned cold, until the twelfth of never.

I grew weak — something technical about the body requiring oxygen — finally releasing my too long absent Amazon, stepping back slightly to drink in her beauty, to inhale her intoxicating fragrance.

I did a double-take in shock and surprise! That this was Teena was unquestionable. Yet she appeared nothing like my Amazon Warrior! Tall, buxom, broad-shouldered, and athletic, tremendously sexual, all true, and yet also very much false.

She wore short black hair, her elegant but now profoundly aged features framed in a jet black, almost Asian appearing bob, her formerly iridescent green eyes a dark almond.

Her appearance could almost but not entirely pass for Asian, almost but not quite pass for Irish. In fact, she resembled Jill, except much larger in form and stature and much more, er, mature. And by mature, I mean elderly. Since I last saw her, she appeared to have aged several decades. Maybe a century or two. She no longer seemed to be my younger sister; she could almost pass as my mother. Hell, more like my great-grandmother!

I'm too kind. Teena looked unbelievably frail and elderly and wore Dr. Mathes' advanced years poorly. Shockingly so.

Petite is not a word one could apply to Teena. The apparent 'reading glasses' dangling from a cord around her neck perfectly complemented her academic wardrobe, yet she never donned them in my presence. Possibly they were merely an accessory to her academic costume. I supposed the newfound mature appearance was part of the disguise too. I could not detect makeup; she appeared entirely natural. More genetic engineering, I guess. Her radically aged appearance notwithstanding, she remains undoubtedly Teena.

We needed no words, embracing anew. I had wanted to ask them a million questions, but basking in Teena's overwhelming, feminine presence, I could not remember even one.

A discreet cough from Petchy intruded on our greeting. I stepped back slightly from Teena, and the girls from Planet Oz attacked, greeting her enthusiastically and nearly as passionately, with no less osculation. We're all eager to welcome Teena, young and vivacious or frail and elderly.

We eventually took our seats around the table, the fur-girls usurping Teena, landing either side of her. The table was cozy for five people, though laden with food. I wondered who had cooked. Petchy? The man is talented, can do nearly anything, yet somehow, I doubted he had done the cooking. He had never indicated ability or interest in food preparation in our months together. His focus always seemed to be on the consumption side of the equation. His cooking talents remain unknown, but he certainly knows how to eat, a skill I have seen demonstrated countless times.

I concluded he must have requested one of the cafeteria cooks provide our meal. We weren't particularly interested in the food, not that we didn't apply ourselves. Instead, we wanted to know where Petchy and Athena had been all these months and how they came to be here now.

"Fitz, my boy, I've told you I have lived on Earth for a long time. Dr. Shepherd is one of the multiple identities I maintain. Dr. Shepherd has been an academic presence in the Ivy League for several decades. However, he has often been 'on sabbatical' for months and months. When in residence, he has taught and lectured at every school in the Ivy League, plus a few that aren't.

"With some help from my friends, Dr. Shepherd has been a prolific writer, lecturer, and all-around academic superstar for decades. We, that is, my operatives and I, maintain a variety of personalities, ready for service. But unfortunately, the Dr. Shepherd persona is becoming aged. He must retire soon."

Sort of the way the 6th Column people had used Estelle. "Petch, I met other people that do something similar. A clandestine organization, they describe themselves as loyalists to Earth, desirous of disclosing the reality of an interplanetary presence. What do you know of them?"

He guffawed loudly! It seems he kept a substantial portfolio on them. He described our poor Jill being debriefed in her hospital bed, drawing a diagram she had attributed to me and discussing 5th columnists and 6th columnists and how we had imagined Alex's organization and Shep's organization. She showed them fitting into the puzzle and playing off one another.

Petchy admitted I had scored a hit with my speculations, though he balked at his people's portrayal as an invading force. "We have no interest in 'invading' anything other than destroying evil forces arrayed against humanity," he maintained. I felt relieved at that.

He continued, "I'm unsure what inspired them to employ the terminology and jargon from Doc Smith's classic space opera, although this Boskone organization is all too real. Someone read and took Doc's fiction to heart and used it as a game plan. Whether that entity is human remains uncertain. The true top, the true organizers, are not human; they are another species entirely. We know little about them, except they exploit humanity's baser instincts for their ends. We do not even clearly understand what those ends are."

That's the first I had heard of non-human alien intelligence. Before now, I had come to believe there wasn't sentient, non-human life in the Universe.

He sighed, whether to express frustration or something else. "Your 6th column friends, their secrecy fetish notwithstanding, host a few operatives of my own among their numbers. We have successfully exploited them on occasion in misdirection and subterfuge. They're an interesting bunch, committed to their mission. I like them, mostly."

I told him, "Jill was a member, I suppose you're aware, through her alliance with Dr. Rawls, and after Estelle's death, she is cut loose. However, she wants back in and to meet you or your boss to present a case for formal disclosure."

Petchy laughed lightly, "Did she say she wants Petchy to take her to his leader?" I wondered when the UFO and alien jokes would begin. I stifled a grin. Okay, it's a little humorous.

Only a little! Let's not have too much of that, please.

"Petch, I know that forces are arguing that a clandestine alien presence on Earth exists, and the government is covering it up. They champion full disclosure of this reality, opening the veil of secrecy. What is the reality? How much of an alien presence is there, and how is it kept secret?"

He paused at that. "Fitz, there are things I cannot fully reveal. Yes, many of our people are on Earth and are present in many high places.

However, the absolute numbers are not large, and we're not in control of your government or your world. We work more subtly than that, and yes, we aggressively maintain our secrecy, and the parties arguing for 'Disclosure' have noticed our actions on occasion. But the cover-up is ours, not the government. The government, the President, and chief executives worldwide do not know we exist. Perhaps there will be the disclosure you speak of one day, though probably not soon. Our only agenda is the preservation and betterment of humanity."

I stared at him blankly, digesting his words, deciding what level of belief I wished to assign. Although he may be my father biologically, that does not mean I trust him unreservedly. Although I don't know that he had ever overtly lied to me, I'm confident he has often omitted truths I would have preferred to hear.

"Does Matt know you are here? Is he one of your agents?"

Petch looked down, briefly, then, as if steeling himself, again met my gaze. "Fitz, Matt is not your brother. He's not my progeny. The DNA test he showed was fake. He is Boskone!"

That was unexpected! I sat there speechless, mouth hanging open. How could he be Boskone? He had been Alex's right-hand man!

I stammered out, "He was high in the organization and trusted by Alex. So how could he be Boskone?"

Petchy shrugged. "We're not certain whether he was truly Boskone or just a useful idiot seduced into carrying out a mission — serving as a mole in Alex's organization. When he abused his access to obtain your DNA record and fake a match to his, we began to suspect and investigate him. Also, you overstate his importance in Alex's organization. He was not exactly Alex's trusted right-hand man; a closer analogy would be an errand boy. He was a recent addition to Alex's organization, and, as a probie, he was provisional and not granted a high clearance. He had little access to classified information."

"Then who was trying to kill him?"

"We are. Or were!"

I must have appeared starkly incredulous! Petchy quickly walked back his comment. "We did not ourselves attempt to inflict violence on him, merely recruited one of Jill's 6th Column people to deflect him from the rendezvous at your hotel. When our investigation of his activities revealed him as a spy, I feared he might attempt to harm you or the girls, especially after the events in Las Vegas. We learned of his ties to our enemy the morning he flew to Show Low. The taxi driver became a desperate, last-minute recruit, the only asset I could raise on such short notice. Not even our asset. The 6th Column had planted him, and we simply sent him a text which he thought came from that organization."

I nodded understanding; I'm not sure I understood. Petchy continued, "The driver's instructions were to merely collect Matt and drive him away, causing him to miss the rendezvous at the hotel. But, unfortunately, the driver took the initiative when the simple taxi pickup and deflect failed, a hazard, I presume, of recruiting outside labor."

He sighed and paused a moment before continuing, "I doubt the taxi driver intended to harm or kill Matt, though his gun became a convenient tool for persuasion when Wisceya met and deflected Matt away from the taxi stand. You intervened at the sight of his gun, considerably complicating the subsequent events. The lesson here is that if one needs something delicate accomplished, hiring unskilled labor is not the best strategy."

I considered his words for a moment before responding. "That doesn't entirely hold water. Gharlane was, we thought, the one trying to kill us, and we thought he headed Boskone. So who is Matt working for? The attack in Mesquite, too, seemed aimed at Matt as much as us."

Petch shrugged. "Wheels within wheels, I believe. There seem to be two inimical organizations, both Boskone. One performs basic information gathering, spying, and espionage. They're responsible for the moles, the text messaging app, etc. They don't readily commit violence, mostly, as it would expose their cover. After the blow-up with the taxi deflection gambit and the crazy events in Ash Fork, we decided not to arrest Matt but to watch him closely and see who he contacted. With the knowledge recently gained, I no longer feared Matt would do you harm, although I did fear that at first. He is, however, a spy. After he returned, we almost immediately caught him attempting to crack into your SOC. Given the lockdown, we decided that he was not likely to reach out to his contacts soon and keeping a known spy in our midst was too dangerous, so we arrested him; he will not return."

I noticed the girls' faces drooped at that. They had liked Matt, especially Stapleya. I believe she was heartbroken he had not returned to her bed.

"And what of the incident in Mesquite?"

"The Mesquite incident wasn't us. Gharlane sent that one, I'm sure. Or, more accurately, the second group I was describing. The second Boskone group is deeply immersed in the criminal underground, especially the drug business, and is quick to attack anyone threatening their money stream. They're the primary targets of this Jade Helm operation. Their stock in trade is violence and intimidation. They will go to any lengths to protect their illicit enterprises."

He paused for a moment. I nodded, assimilating his words. "Are they alien too?" I asked.

He shook his head. "I suspect this group isn't truly Boskone, just lower-level functionaries in the organization and have no suspicion of the off-world organization that gives their orders. I suspect Earthly thuggery is mostly driving this group and their violence. Gharlane seems to use violence surgically and strategically. If necessary, he will assassinate someone, including crashing an airliner full of innocents to do so without batting an eye. But he prefers to use deception and subterfuge. These cretins seek violence as a first resort and execute it with enthusiasm and often in wholesale quantity."

I interjected, "You caught Matt attempting intrusion into the SOC. Appropriately, my honeypots logged attempts to do so from your offices, a topic I'd intended to address tonight. I presume that was he."

Petchy nodded in agreement. I added, "I'm surprised, as I hadn't thought he had any computer networking expertise."

Teena chimed in, "Perhaps he's sharper than you gave him credit for."

I cast my memory back to that afternoon in Sedona when he had watched over my shoulder with curiosity as I set up and tore down my stealth network. I had discounted his interest, not believing he could follow my actions. How much had he truly grokked of my methods? I shuddered at my carelessness.

Again, I have been a boob.

I had, ironically, thought of him as just another muscle-bound jock, not particularly technology-savvy — 'Physique Discrimination.' So, once again kicking myself for my stupidity, I vowed not to be so trusting!

I mused about Matt being trapped by Strategic Command and compared that to the traps sprung in Ops. "My Honeypots also logged an incident from Ops, attempting to gain unauthorized access. I fear we may have yet another mole in the house. We need to keep a solid lid on all communications until we trap and neuter them. I want to trap this one and use him to feed false information to the enemy if we can. With help from my ladies here, I have Jessica all set to spring a trap on the next attempt."

Teena's eyebrows raised slightly in surprise. "I wasn't aware that Stapleya and Wisceya were learning about technology."

I nodded at the fur girls and responded, "You'd be surprised at what they've learned. Perhaps these ladies are not ready to pursue a Ph.D. course in the subject just yet, but they're both quite cozy with a keyboard with a little supervision. They've installed much of the networking software Ops is using under the watchful oversight of Jessica. They are fast and efficient and rarely make mistakes. Their contribution to our effort deserves serious recognition."

She turned to the girls and began complimenting them and thanking them for their work, slipping into Language as she did so. But, of course, we are all fluent; Language seems much better suited for flowery praise and flattery, perhaps the way French serves romantic purposes more eloquently than English. And I might add, seduction, not that I had ever found the need to seduce anyone in Language.

Later, with dinner finished and fine liquor in hand, we had resumed using English. I put the proposition to Petchy as to our next steps. He thought about my question for a few moments. "Fitz, this massive Jade Helm is only a small piece, one battle of the war. It's what Alex knows of, certainly. It's aimed at rooting out much of the corruption and evil that has descended on Earth in recent decades, at least that special brand of evil that flows from Boskone."

Teena took up the thread, "If we had not been busy, so preoccupied with defeating the Artificial Intelligence of Ashera these last several decades, Earth culture today would be vastly different, more idyllic. Unfortunately, our inattention has allowed Gharlane's forces to flourish unopposed. Jade Helm constitutes a massive push to press them back until we can mount a full assault on their home world."

Petchy nodded. "We have limited control over Portals. However, we can block the majority of them and have done so. We purposely kept open only those that pose no danger and serve a beneficial purpose, such as one that opens on your lovely world." He nodded at the girls as he said this. "In light of recent events, perhaps we should have closed that one too; if we had, your poor child would still be alive." This last was squarely directed at Stapleya. "I'm so sorry, my dear."

"We have been totally unable to close three major portals used by Boskone to reach Earth. As a result, they infest not only Earth but other worlds too, via other still-open Portals. We must invade their world and close those portals!"

I stared at him with interest. Was he about to suggest?? I started, "We need to take these ladies to their home, and they need our help...."

Athena put her arms around me. "Fitz, my love. Will you rescue one more Princess in distress? Slay Talos in Cydonia one more time? Will you join me in another quest, save humanity one more time?"

To be continued...

If you liked Chromosome Conspiracy, please leave a review on the Amazon Chromosome Conspiracy Review page.

The Story Continues

The story of Jill's recovery and the ultimate battle with the evil Gharlane continues in Chromosome Warrior! Available on Amazon Kindle: https://www.amazon.com/dp/B01N984GDH

"Out of every one hundred fighters, ten shouldn't even be there, eighty are just targets, nine are the real fighters, and we are lucky to have them, for they make the battle. Ah, but the one, one is a ***warrior****, and that one will bring the others back." — Heraclitus of Ephesus.*

Call me Jill. It's not my name, though it has been my handle for years now. If I would tell the tale, you'd beg to understand where I was born, how lousy my childhood had been, what sort of monsters my parents were, that Dickensian sort of crap. F**k that! If you must know the simple truth, I'm an authentic ***Man in Black***, the real deal. That's all you need to know.

Years ago — never mind precisely how long — having little money and despite some 'spiritual' gifts, few obvious prospects due to my gender and stature, I decided to enlist in the service. I'm uncertain what I expected, a few adventures and travel the world, I suppose. Better than hooking — not that anything's wrong with that.

Petite, Chinese, and pretty; assets to a hooker, a hindrance to a warrior. I needed to kick someone in the teeth — several someones in fact — until they saw beyond my slender curves.

Discipline and training honed my natural strength and reflexes. Schooled in weaponry and marksmanship; I discovered I like weapons.

Chromosome Warrior completes the saga with the story of G.I. Jill, the lady "MiB" and her quest to defeat humanity's greatest enemies.

COMING IN SEPTEMBER 2022: A new series set in the ***Chromosome Adventures Universe***: Undercover Alien: The Hat, The Alien, and the Quantum War

Did you ever wish to be a superhero?

Rithwick Jahi Pringle, a.k.a. Ritz, has a keen imagination, vivid dreams, and unparalleled cyber skills, but his neurodivergent brain is out to get him!

Paralyzing anxieties, symmetry-demanding OCD, and unbridled geekiness hobble his superhero missions. He wears a White Hat for the Agency by day but dons the superhero cape on The Dark Web where he patrols the shadowy realm by night, dispensing Vigilante Justice to those beyond the Law's reach. When a new, otherworldly Director takes charge of The Agency's cyberwarriors, he is captivated, seduced, and drawn into a shadowy world beyond cybercrime, a deep underworld of dark alien villainy. They come not in spacecraft, and they fight not with particle beams and lasers. They seek not to kill, enslave, or even dominate humanity but to dismantle civilization and return humankind to the stone age. Allied with a friendly Alien faction and a budding young sidekick, his near-supernatural gift for cyber warfare is a powerful asset, but is it enough? Can the Hat turn the trick against humanity's would-be oppressors? *Join in this action-packed tale of Hackers and Spies; Aliens and Earthlings; Superheroes and Hats.*

Read ***Undercover Alien*** *today!* **There has never been a superhero like The Hat!**

About the Author

Your humble author admits to decades of experience in data networking, telecommunications, and Internet technologies. An accomplished motivator of technical and professional staff and an experienced technical team leader, he is a technology generalist with experience covering both hardware and software disciplines in many related fields. His present day-job is in Internet Security and Crypto, where he serves as CTO and Chief Scientist for a novel internet stealth startup company.

In his spare time, he satisfies his penchant for fantasizing about the future, technology, and societal forces by writing science fiction.

Follow Nathan on:

Thank you for reading Chromosome Conspiracy. Please visit the Chromosome Conspiracy Reviews Page and leave a review. Your honest review will help future readers decide if they want to take a chance on a new-to-them author. Mysterious algorithms determine which books pop up on things such as the "you might also enjoy this" suggestions. It takes a minimum number of reviews on some sites before a book is added to those "also bought" and "you might also like" lists. We Authors need your reviews.

The Writings of Nathan Gregory

Science Fiction

Chromosome Quest is the opening story in the Chromosome Adventures Series, introducing the protagonist 'Fitz,' the Mentor 'Petchy,' the Goddess 'Teena,' and the stone-age world he dubbed 'Planet Oz.' Their epic fight was to shut down the runaway AI on Teena and Petchy's home planet and retrieve the genetic database at the heart of the fertility plague.

Chromosome Conspiracy brings the stone-age 'Fur girls' to Earth looking for Fitz's help with a new problem. The adventure begins as he seeks to protect the fur-bearing alien women from the machinations of Alex Marco and the 'Men in Black,' that is until Fitz's girlfriend and several others are killed, and MiB Agent Jill Smith is badly wounded at the hands of a new super-villain. Facing a common foe, Fitz joins the Men in Black to fight the evil Gharlane.

Chromosome Warrior sees the fate of all human civilization hanging in the balance as Fitz, Jill, Petchy, Teena, Alex, and the Fur girls ally with a strange other-worldly energy-being against the evil Gharlane.

Non-Fiction

Nathan Gregory's non-fiction features a pair of documentaries that tell the untold origin backstory of today's commercial Internet. The creation and funding of the ARPANET and the technologies we use today are well-told, but there is another side to the story that academia has overlooked.

From its cold-war beginnings until its commercialization beginning in 1992, the Internet forbade any form of commerce. Yet, globe-spanning commercial networks existed for more than two decades before the Internet legitimized online eCommerce.

The story of the creation of the concept of remote computing we call 'Cloud Computing' today began in the 1960s, with the first globe-spanning commercial cloud coming online in 1972. From February 1972 until well beyond the end of 1992, these commercial networks carried the world's e-Commerce traffic while ARPANET and its cousins remained the private playground of academics and politicians.

The Tym Before... tells the story of creating these first commercial networks and the remote cloud services they powered.

Securing the Network tells the story of the subsequent commercialization of the Internet, beginning with the first commercial peering point, MAE-East, for which the initial order was placed on September 29, 1992. By mid-1993, the MAE was in place, and by 1994 it was carrying 90% of the world's commercial Internet traffic.

Kindle Vella Episodic Fiction

With the advent of Kindle Vella, I have begun some serials for publication in the episodic format.

A Walk in the Woods is a one-of-a-kind first-contact story is my first story in this format.

Tommie Powers and the Time Machine stands at four completed episodes. This story is a juvenile that is perhaps closer to a Tom Swift or Rick Brant story. Its fate depends on feedback from you, dear reader.

Made in the USA
Las Vegas, NV
29 October 2023

79901085R00177